Honeycomb Fire

Beverly T. Haaf

JERSEY PINES INK

A Pine Warbler Book

JERSEY PINES INK

For the original Queenie and Star

Honeycomb Fire

PROLOGUE

Somewhere Deep in the Yucatán

"THE GODDESS WILL COME." The white-haired High Priest lifted the sacred crown. His frail arms trembled from the weight of the soft, pure gold. "The goddess, like a queen bee returning to her hive, will come to guide us."

Torchlight blazed on the jeweled honeybee that ornamented the crown. The wings of the bee were gold filigree, its eyes were rubies and black jade. The body of the bee was a magnificent tear-shaped yellow diamond known as the Honeycomb Fire.

The old priest's gaze rose to a point above the heads of the kneeling men of the tribe who served as priests when he called them. He spoke again, his quavering voice echoing against the flaking walls of the temple chamber, its once-bright, heroic paintings now faded and leprous.

"From a far distant land, she will come to us. We will know her for she will safely travel the Path of Doom. The Three Stings will cause her no harm. She will solve the sacred riddle with ease. We will bow before her glory, her radiance will be unto us like the sun."

He began to shuffle in a slow circle, presenting the crown to the heavens and to the four corners of the earth.

Eduardo gave a sad, cynical smile. Leaning, he whispered quietly to

Luis, who knelt alongside him. "Let us hope her radiance will include the color of American money. We need a clinic and medical supplies."

The ceremonial language of the temple was the old Maya dialect, but Eduardo's irreverent whisper was in Spanish. He also knew English. He was a small man, stringy but agile despite a hunched shoulder that had been broken and poorly set when he was a child. Although he loved the simple village of his birth, he had spent time in the outside world and knew of its advantages.

Luis hissed for him to be silent, but Eduardo, third in command of the small village, whispered again. "If the goddess has connections with a pharmaceutical company *that* would answer our prayers." His gaze lifted to the crown's blazing jewel. It embittered him to see his people bound to an empty legend when there was a much more practical way to gain what they needed.

His circle completed, the High Priest faced the younger priests once again. Regardless of his disdain for the ancient prediction, Eduardo joined the others in repeating the final refrain: "The goddess who once walked among us will return to reclaim the great stone in her crown. She will come and lead us to greatness."

As the words of the refrain died away, Eduardo frowned. In the flickering light, the High Priest's eyes seemed to glow with unusual fervor, as if his earnest belief in the goddess was strengthened by some secret source. Unable to repress a shiver, Eduardo found himself wondering.

The ancient story might have some basis in truth. In some dim, forgotten century, perhaps some foreign woman had brought the diamond to them. But she hadn't been a goddess, he reminded himself, and she wasn't going to return. Despite the fact that the legend had endured among his people for many generations, it was worse than foolish.

Eduardo sighed. History would not repeat itself, he was sure of it.

CHAPTER ONE

MELISSA LIND LOOKED OUT the window of the tiny apartment bathroom and smiled at the people thronging the street. It was 1975 and the City of Philadelphia was humming with a Bicentennial buzz that would reach its peak on July 4, 1976—two hundred years after the signing of the Declaration of Independence and the establishment of the United States of America.

Melissa was excited even though she was no American history buff. It was the ancient Egyptians with their magnificent pyramids that captured her romantic imagination. They called to her as did the mysterious civilizations in what was once known as the New World. They also had their pyramids. Still, it was a thrill walking along Philadelphia lanes and boulevards where men like Benjamin Franklin, Thomas Jefferson, John Adams and the other framers of the Constitution had once walked.

Not that she had much time to think about it. She was always rushing here and there.

She took a breath, turned back to her mirror and slicked her honey-blonde hair to her nape and fastened it with a rubber band. "Idiot," she said, scolding herself as she scowled at her reflection. She was in a pickle with nobody but herself to blame. With her hair out of the way, she covered her face with white greasepaint. The white made the color of her eyes stand out, a startling clear blue, as blue as the sky on a spring morning, as her mother used to say. Mom, who had brought her up to count every penny.

The trouble had started with wanting a new apartment. Her old lease had been up and the new place wouldn't be ready until next month, but it was so perfect she had been willing to fork over security plus the first month's rent and a month in advance to reserve it. That also meant putting her furniture into storage and staying in a hotel for the duration, but she felt she could manage. Ha!

Then her car broke down. The horrendous garage bill had been paid for with plastic. She hated to do it, but money was tight and she needed the car for work. Then the irony of ironies, she lost her job. Almost immediately she found a better one, which was terrific, but it wouldn't start until fall, which was terrible.

It was now August and all she had until her first paycheck at the end of September was a savings account she refused to touch, a part-time job, and a maxed out credit card. It was enough to make her want to crawl into a hole and pull it over her head.

The final dilemma was her living situation. The hotel had been breaking her, so it had been wonderful when her girlfriend, Susie, whose husband's work took him away a lot, invited her to their place. Then, as Melissa learned, when the husband was home, she was supposed to turn invisible. When she told Susie she was returning to the hotel, Susie turned all weepy-weird. "I'm trying to help you, and now you're throwing it back in my face."

What a mess! Melissa couldn't win either way.

Sighing, she tugged on an orange wig and added a floppy black hat with a red flower that squirted. Her part-time job was playing a clown at children's birthday parties. Assignments were irregular and the pay was poor, but she loved working with little kids. Her degree was in primary education and her upcoming job was related—a toy company that would have her test-marketing products for young children. Her dream goal was to someday open her own preschool.

"If there ever is a someday," she muttered aloud.

Hearing her self-pitying tone, she grimaced. Okay, so she was in a jam, but it was time to stop whining and look on the bright side. She was young and healthy and usually had a good head on her shoulders. This bad patch would soon be history.

Impulsively, she squeezed the water bulb that fed the flower on her hat. A satisfying splash hit the mirror.

Feeling good again, Melissa picked up a towel and wiped the mirror clean.

RICK MALONE MOVED FROM the late afternoon sun on Philadelphia's South Street and into the comfortable gloom of his favorite bar. He was halfway down the long, narrow room, when a woman appeared as if from nowhere, bumping against him and losing her balance.

"Excuse me," she said with a feathery giggle as Rick placed a broad-palmed hand under her elbow to steady her. She was a redhead, with a full, pouty mouth and a low-cut, sparkling blouse. Tilting her head to look up to his height of six-foot-two, she batted her lashes. "Oooh, you saved me. I'll have to buy you a drink to say thanks."

Amused, Rick decided she hadn't bumped into him by accident. He liked her style, her red mouth and her dithery aggressiveness. He smiled down at her regretfully.

"I'm sorry," he said, "but I'm meeting someone." It wasn't true, he just wasn't in the mood. Too bad, because she looked as if she would be a lot of fun. Seeing her face fall, he arched a dark eyebrow. "Catch you another time, okay?"

His disarming manner had her smiling again. "Okay. I'll be looking for you." Fluttering her fingers, she was off somewhere else.

Les, the bartender, looked surprised as Rick took a seat on a stool. "You let that one get away?"

Rick gave a faint smile and a shrug of his lean, muscular shoulders. The woman was already forgotten; he had too much on his mind.

He had spent the morning in Maryland doubling his money on a thoroughbred two-year-old in training that he had picked up as a colt. His profession was buying horses at one stage and selling them later for a profit. *Pin hooking*, it was called, a Kentucky idiom he rarely used—to the uninitiated, it sounded either like an embroidery skill or something that should get him arrested. He had loved horses since he was a kid. With knowledge and skill and hunches he didn't bother to question, he had parlayed his love into a profitable career, but instead of being able to celebrate his latest success, he had come home to find bad news about his grandfather.

It disconcerted him that he'd had no inner warning, none of those half-awake, half-asleep doom-filled nightmares that always warned him when things might be slipping sideways. And if he now felt something, like a shiver from the grave, it was nothing but the after-effects of the bad news he already knew.

He was well into his drink when Les said, "Here comes your friend George."

Groaning, Rick peered into the mirror behind the bar, seeing beyond his dark-haired reflection to the chunky, red-cheeked face of George Keating. He and George were no longer close, not like they had been when growing up, living next door in twin-row houses and sharing everything. Time and different interests had drawn them apart, but they still ran into one another on occasion, the impetus usually from George. There was nothing the man liked better than tromping down memory lane. There were no new memories between them; the only things they now had in common were events that were old and tired.

Plunking himself on the vacant stool, George smoothed the off-white jacket of his leisure suit, worn with a yellow shirt printed with blue flowers, and ordered sparkling water with a twist of lemon. He threw down a fistful of newly minted Bicentennial half-dollar coins—all dated 1976 in advance. Rick frowned, thinking they were only available in proof sets. Trust George to be the first to get his hands on something ahead of the crowd.

"It's been a while, Ricky," George said with an inquisitive look. "What's with the hangdog expression? Love life gone sour?"

"I'm just sitting here having a drink, do you mind?"

"A drink that's running low, I see."

George signaled for Les to take care of it, the gesture shooting out the cuff of his shirt, revealing an elaborate cufflink of ivory and gold.

"So, Ricky, if we don't talk about women, how's work? Buy any bum horses lately?" He laughed, and then seeing Rick's tightly closed expression, he shrugged. "Okay, two down, let's try for a third. How's your grandfather?"

Rick winced. "You don't give up, do you?"

"I can tell there's something wrong. It shows on every line of your face."

Wryly, Rick lifted his refilled drink in a mock toast. "To George Keating, the society photographer. The man who thinks he knows faces."

"Who *knows* he knows faces," George corrected. He paused to blow his nose. His summer allergies were in full force and his nose was red, his eyes watery. Putting his handkerchief away, he took a sip of his drink, his expression becoming reminiscent. "Remember the old days? Remember your grandfather's visits? He didn't come often, but he sure made an impression, handing out ten spots and spinning his adventure tales."

"Uh-huh," Rick murmured, sure of what would come next. "And now you'll remind me of the hours we spent planning to treasure hunt for a diamond that never existed."

"Only it did," George protested, looking wounded. "We researched old books, remember? It was brought to the New World by one of your ancestors. A later ancestor failed to reclaim it and then your grandfather failed too, so we were going to—"

Rick cut him off. "The story exists. It's not the same thing."

The truth of the yarn didn't matter. It was the magic the old man had woven around them, the way he had made Rick believe he could grow up to do anything, and be anything. God, how he had looked up to his grandfather, how hungry he had been for his approval. It wasn't until he started planning his future that he learned how conditional that approval had been.

To the old man, the only acceptable careers for Rick were white-collar ones, with regular hours and his nose to the grindstone. Anything to keep him from becoming an aimless alcoholic like his father. Working with horses was out of the question. That was especially frustrating to Rick because it had been on his grandfather's ranch that he learned to love them. Horses, what was wrong with that? Rebelling, he followed his own path and eventually found success, believing that his grandfather would see that what he had done was the best for him. He hadn't reckoned on the old man's stubbornness. He should have known. For Stanton Malone, the only right way was his way.

Abruptly, Rick realized there was no sense in thinking he could drown the subject of his grandfather. George was the one person he could share the bad news with. He took a breath. "I got a letter about him today. He's had a heart attack."

"My God!" George leaned forward. "How bad is he?"

"Bad enough. He's home from the hospital, but it's still touch-and-go."

"What are you doing here? Why aren't you in Florida with him?"

Rick gave a grim shake of his head. "Because the ranch is off-limit unless I knuckle under to his demands, which I won't do. He didn't even want me to know about his attack. It was Xavier who wrote to me."

"The cook at the ranch?"

Rick arched an eyebrow. "How many Xaviers have you ever heard me talk about?"

"Okay, okay, but I still don't get it. I know you and your grandfather had a falling out and he came up with a crazy ultimatum, but that was three years ago. You've never said much. I assumed you had smoothed over your argument."

Rick grimaced. "It's not the kind of argument you can smooth over."

"Are you nuts? He threatened to cut you out of his will. You're his only heir—if you don't get his millions, who will? I would smooth things out if I had to stand on my head."

"Not me, buddy," came Rick's terse reply.

"Do the two of you at least talk?"

"I've called a few times, but when he hears I won't come crawling, the conversation is done."

"Ricky, Ricky, be practical for once. What is he asking? Settle down with a good woman by the age of thirty, that's all he wants. You're twenty-nine and your birthday is at the end of September. Don't you see how time is running out?"

Rick shrugged. "When I blow out my candles, my inheritance blows out too."

George looked sick. "I can't believe you're joking about it. Even if you can ignore the rest of his bundle, what about the ranch? You always said it was the only thing you cared about."

"True." Rick stared into space. Growing up, he had spent weeks at the ranch each summer, far from his squabbling parents and safe with someone he had believed really cared. Even more than the ranch itself was what it symbolized—all the good years that he had known with his grandfather. When the old man said he would deny that to him too, Rick knew his grandfather was willing to erase everything between them. It had been almost more than Rick could bear, but he had come to terms with it. Now, Xavier's letter had churned it up fresh. All at once, he realized that the ranch no longer mattered. He sat up stiffly, stunned by this revelation. What did matter was his relationship with his grandfather.

George was still rattling on, his tone peevish. "All that hush-hush stuff about the place. You would go off for weeks at a time and I wouldn't know where you were."

Rick couldn't help laughing. "How could an eccentric old Midas maintain his hideaway if he published the address? It's the only boyhood secret I ever kept from you, buddy."

His smile fading, he pushed away his unfinished drink. "If we could only set aside our difference and sit down and talk like we used to. He's s made that impossible. And I can't bust in, not on a heart attack victim."

"Then do what you should have done ages ago. Waltz down with some woman. 'Hello, meet my darling wife.'"

Rick looked disgusted. "He's old and sick but not stupid. He's got to approve of her first."

"Okay. 'Meet my darling fiancée.' Get wise, Ricky. From everything you say it's the only way he will open his door. After that, you can make your peace or start another fight, but you'll never have a chance to do anything if you sit brooding in Philadelphia."

Rick hesitated as he thought about it, then he shook his head. "Showing up with a woman would only make things worse. In addition to everything else, we don't agree on females." *Flashy and frivolous* was how his grandfather had once summed up his taste. The image of the redhead came to mind and he saw the old man's thumb turning down. "He's a guy who had one great love in his life. He could never understand that's not my style."

"Then find someone he will approve of. Hey—wait a minute!" George snapped his fingers. "Ricky, have I got a woman for you!" A calculating grin split his face. "A woman your grandfather will find impossible to refuse."

CHAPTER TWO

IT WAS A FRIDAY EVENING, the last weekend in August, the sky aglow with fading streaks of sunset. Melissa Lind stepped off the crowded bus and started walking. Waiting to cross at Walnut Street, she stood watching traffic rush up from Independence Square, feeling nervous and excited at the same time.

George Keating—yes, *that* George Keating—had invited her to a bash at his home.

It had floored her when he called. They had met in upscale Bucks County where she had been playing a clown for a children's birthday party. She and a hired magician kept the children entertained while George, a photographer best known for his portraits on the covers of magazines like *Vogue*, had taken pictures. When he had gotten in touch days later, she popped out with what seemed a logical question.

"You mean you want to hire me as a clown?"

"No, no." He had chuckled. "I'm throwing a party for friends. I enjoyed meeting you and would like to see you again."

She had accepted—who wouldn't?—but it puzzled her. Chatting at the birthday party had been pleasant, but there had been no sparks, and she hadn't said anything to make him think she could run with his affluent crowd. If anything, she had said the opposite.

Reaching his multistory address, she paused to look up at the building. Maybe George liked to balance his parties out with a few strays. She grinned. Or did she underestimate her incredible sex appeal? In high spirits, she sailed into the foyer, the high heels of her sandals tapping against the marble tiles. Whatever was going on, she was bound to get an interesting evening out of it. And best of all, she had a reason to go out that evening instead of hiding in Susie's guest bedroom to give Susie and her husband time alone.

UPSTAIRS, STANDING AT THE window of George's penthouse, Rick Malone gazed up to the lighted statue of William Penn that stood atop City Hall, the tallest allowed structure on the Philadelphia skyline. No building taller than Billy Penn's hat was the gentleman's agreement, but developers were always trying to buck the rule.

"Yo, Billy," Rick said, lifting his champagne in a toast to the statue, "So far, so good, but never take anything for granted."

Turning from the window, he surveyed the spacious living room. George's parties were always a kick, with live music, great food and a theme, this time, Pompeii before Vesuvius, as depicted in a gold-framed oil painting displayed on one wall. Buffet tables sat heaped high with tasty platters and draped with laurel garlands and roses—silk roses to protect George's sensitive nose. Rick remembered one time in school when kids brought in small pets: dogs, cats, two parakeets and a parrot. George had started sneezing, his nose running all over his face, which had gone scarlet.

Rick's smile faded. Tonight, George was set on introducing him to some woman who would solve all his problems. Fat chance. Still, he was curious to see what his old friend had come up with. He had been so blasted cagey, only saying she'd handled kids for him at a birthday party. Rick knew the kind of women George liked. It had him imagining a show-off intellectual who might think kids' bedtime stories were written by Pynchon or Oates. Didn't sound like fun.

Brooding, he took a sip of champagne. He didn't much like the idea but he would have to find somebody himself because he had decided George was right about one thing. If his grandfather's notion of happiness was seeing him drag a ball and chain, he should play along. Suppose the old man had another heart attack? Rick recoiled from the thought, but not the conclusion: if he wanted a chance at reconciliation, he'd better not waste any more time.

His gaze came to rest at the foot of a wide staircase. There stood George in the midst of a crowd, a blonde woman at his side. Was she the one? Rick narrowed his eyes. She was slender, with pale hair pulled away from her face, the curling ends brushing her shoulders. Not the snooty lady of his imagination but still nothing to make his pulse gallop. Why had George been so eager for him to meet her?

Shrugging, he deposited his champagne flute on the tray of a toga-clad waitress, straightened his tux jacket, and started off through the crowd. Might as well see how she looked at close range.

He was nearly there when a parting of the crowd showed her again, her head tilted as she spoke to George, presenting her face in a three-quarter view. Rick came to an abrupt stop. If the painted Vesuvius had uncorked for real, he would have remained unable to tear his gaze from her face. In that instant, he knew exactly why George found her perfect. She had reminded him of the portrait that had once hung in Rick's childhood home—an oil painting of Sonja Andersson Malone— his grandmother at age twenty-eight. Although she had died only a few years later, she remained the only woman to have held his grandfather's heart.

Staring, Rick re-assessed the blonde, her straight nose, firm chin, and abundant pale hair. She wasn't a look-alike, yet she projected the same gentle aura that he remembered from the painting. It was in the sweet curve of her mouth, in the soft parting of her lips. Her eyes held that same tender, expectant shine as if she believed only good things could happen.

Rick's thoughts tumbled. If this woman would agree to go with him to Florida, there was no doubt they would be welcomed with open arms.

His grandfather couldn't help but approve of her. Rick would pay her for her trouble, of course. No one would be harmed and he would have the opportunity to sit down with his grandfather once again before it was too late.

The crowd closed in again. Getting a grip on himself, Rick walked around a cluster of party guests and made his way to George and the blonde.

"Ricky!" George spoke expansively. "Just the person I was hoping to see." He showed a sly grin as he guided his companion forward. "Melissa, this is my friend, Rick Malone. Rick, meet Melissa Lind."

Melissa smiled. "Hi, glad to meet you." *Rick Malone.* She had read about him in a recent Sunday Magazine. He did something with horses and there had been a picture of him looking amazingly cheerful for a man who had sold a horse that was now winning races for somebody else.

Rick took in Melissa's appealingly quirky smile and greeted her with his easy charm and a smile of his own, saying with appreciation, "Hello, Melissa!" She was tall, he liked that. But, despite how terrific her green silk dress looked with her coloring, there was no glitter, no pizzazz. She wasn't his type. Perfect. His grandfather couldn't stand the type of woman who appealed to him.

"You've shown up at just the right time, Ricky." George beckoned. "I'm giving Melissa a tour of my treasures. Come on, there're new items upstairs in the gallery that you've never seen."

Rick slipped a hand under Melissa's elbow. "Prepare to be impressed," he murmured sotto voce.

She rewarded him with a megawatt smile, eyes sparkling. Okay, he decided, so she was vivacious. But there was also a naive air of oh-isn't-this-exciting! He winced inwardly. Naive women were as boring as a race with no odds.

On the second floor, George put on his one-man show, leading them from one room to another with flourishing gestures, presenting a Ming vase from Singapore, a jewel-handled sacrificial blade from an ancient temple in India, a rare Persian prayer rug he had tracked down in the Mideast.

"Rick's grandfather was my inspiration," George said to Melissa. "A fascinating old gentleman, he traveled all over the world. The stories he told us, the way he kept us enthralled." He slid a glance Rick's way. "You'll have to ask Rick to tell you all about him."

"Oh?" Melissa gave Rick an anticipatory look.

Instead of picking up on George's lead, Rick deliberately switched the subject. He would find his own way of introducing his grandfather, thank you, and he would do it in his own sweet time.

Downstairs again, George excused himself to greet newly arrived guests. Rick steered Melissa toward the buffet, relieved to be free of his old buddy and his bragging. How could two guys from the same poor neighborhood come out so different? Acquiring the rare and priceless was a passion with George. Rick liked nice things too, but only enough to be comfortable.

Their plates filled, he gazed around for a place for them to sit. There were empty tables in the reception room, but the music, which would normally have captured him, now struck him as too loud. After signaling a waiter, who also wore a toga, to bring along the plates and beverages, he led Melissa through the great room and toward the rooftop terrace.

As they walked, he reflected that he had never before attempted to deceive his grandfather. Ironically, the old man might have approved of him more if he had tried. In amassing his fortunes, Stanton Malone had employed both shrewdness and craft, skills he admired in others. A grandson with a touch of the chameleon would have made sense to him, but Rick had been cut from a different bolt of cloth. Social fabrications, like graceful lies to pretty women, were easy enough, but when he felt strongly, he had no patience with games. This is me, was his stance, like it or lump it.

"Oh, so pretty," Melissa said as they entered the walled terrace.

Preoccupied as he was, Rick probably wouldn't have noticed if she hadn't said anything, but she was right. Misty twilight shone over the candle-lit, glass-topped tables and rattan chairs casually positioned among shadowy arrangements of potted plants.

She gestured to the view across the South end of the city.

"So lovely," she said. "There's the Delaware River and Penn's Landing and, look, that square-rigger restaurant ship, the Moshulu."

Rick murmured something appropriate, his gaze by-passing the view she spoke of and sweeping along the river, which lay dark and brooding under the twinkling lights of the Ben Franklin Bridge. He led the way past other guests and to a private corner where graceful vines climbed a lattice.

As the water placed their plates and beverages on the ledge of the terrace, Rick slipped him a folded bill.

"This is nice," Melissa said cautiously, glancing around and not wanting to sound as if she was complaining, "But . . . where will we sit?"

That's when Rick noticed there were no chairs where they were. People had probably dragged them away so they could sit closer to the view.

"We'll sit right here," he said as he overturned two large earthenware pots, dusted them with a flourish, and spread his napkin over one of them for her. He grinned. "How's this?"

She laughed and sat. "It's like we're having a picnic!" Cheerfully, she arranged her napkin and plate on her lap.

Picnic? She sat like a lady, her ankles crossed, and her movements dainty. Her comment had sounded so wholesome, so . . . he couldn't find the right word and settled for *sunny*. Again, not to his taste, but her manner would no doubt hit his grandfather exactly right.

MELISSA TOOK A BITE OF a shrimp-filled pastry. To die for. She glanced at Rick. He was to die for, as well. He seemed awfully nice and she'd noticed when he'd tipped the waiter. She didn't know much about wealthy folks, but she thought they just ignored people who waited on them. George certainly had behaved that way at the upscale Bucks County house. Rick obviously wasn't like that, which was good. She also liked his longish, narrow face, with its strong lines and stubborn chin. A lock of his wavy black hair dipped over his forehead and she had to fight off the temptation to reach up and smooth it back into place. A faint, bluish cast of beard growth showed along his jaw. He was a man who would have to shave a second time to be smooth for a late evening. She smiled to herself, admitting she was a sucker for dark-haired men,

Rick cleared his throat. "George said he met you at a kid's party."

"Yes." She was alerted by a change in his voice. His tone has become businesslike.

"He told me you're temporarily out of regular work. I might have a job for you."

"Oh?" Disappointment washed over her. Now she knew why she had been invited—George had known Rick might want to hire her. Drat. Rick was the most interesting man she had met in ages. She had assumed he was unattached, not some married guy after a party clown for his kids. Then again, she could use the work, couldn't she?

Taking a breath, she smiled and quipped, "Have nose will travel."

"Huh?" Rick stared.

She stared back. "Didn't you want to hire me to dress up as a clown? That's what I was doing when George and I met."

"Not exactly." A clown? No wonder George hadn't gone into explanations. "But it is a masquerade of sorts," he said as he leaned forward. "Let me tell you about my grandfather"

CHAPTER THREE

At EIGHT O'CLOCK THE following Monday morning, Rick opened his duffel bag on his bed and started packing. He had originally planned to pick Melissa up in a taxi, but George, who had just arrived, insisted on driving.

"I told you," George said, sitting down, "I feel involved. I knew it would work. Once your grandfather heard you wanted to introduce him to some woman, out rolled the red carpet. But how did you persuade her to go?" Settling back in his chair, he tented his fingers. "But then, why do I bother to ask? You always could work magic with the ladies."

Rick scowled. Sleep had eluded him the night before and he was in no mood to chew over the time spent with Melissa as if she had been a hot date. The night after George's party, he had taken her to a club where they could talk further. He had been aware of eyes turning when they were shown to their table. She looked good, sure, but that only mattered in connection with his plan.

Over the phone, his grandfather had sounded awful. He had claimed he had just awakened from a nap with a frog in his throat. Rick figured his pride had him disguising his weakness. He tried to cheer himself as he visualized the delight that would cross the man's face when he saw Melissa.

"Exactly what I'd hoped for you," he would say, able to rest easy at last because he knew his grandson was settled. Which would be true, only he didn't need to know that Rick had secured his future on his own. And it had nothing to do with finding a honey-vanilla blonde.

George gave him a sidelong glance. "Bet it helped that Melissa's down on her luck."

"Like what?"

"Didn't she tell you she was hoarding pennies until her new job started?"

"She talked about what she would do at her new job, that's all." She'd said she'd be working with kids using toys the company made, things for the beach and the sandbox, which he guessed explained her happy-face outlook. He rolled his extra socks and stuffed them into the boots already in his bag. "I wanted to pay her something. She said an all-expenses-paid trip to Florida sounded good enough."

He remembered her reaction when she learned how sick his grandfather was—as if she really cared, which was sappy when she didn't even know him. The idea of helping somebody was clearly the main draw, although there had been a sticky moment when she had asked, "Why me? You certainly know other women." Braced for a hard time, he had answered, "I had just learned how ill he was and then we met. Call it fate. My grandfather has always had a soft spot for blue-eyed blondes. You just seemed right." She had swallowed it hook, line and sinker. Good thing he wasn't out to really scam her. She was too damned trusting, too gullible. A sugar cookie.

"She talked plenty to me about her money jam," George said in a faintly acid tone. "I got treated like a pal. You, she was trying to impress."

Rick shook his head distractedly. If one of his women friends had spent herself into a hole, he wouldn't have been surprised, but Melissa had seemed classier than that. He liked being generous and was always bailing somebody out, but the bottom line was that he didn't respect irresponsibility—not when he remembered his parents drinking up money that should have put food on the table. Then he caught the tail end of what George had just added: "Maybe she's holding out for the real action when your inheritance makes you lord and master of the Western World."

Rick tried not to bristle, but damn it, George made it sound like he should be eager for his grandfather's death.

"That subject of an inheritance never came into our conversation," Rick said shortly. "All we discussed was me seeing my grandfather again." Actually, he had talked quite a lot. Funny how easy she'd been to talk with.

George made a satisfied sound. "Do this right and you'll end up with the ranch plus a whole lot more."

Bristling, Rick opened his mouth to repeat how he really felt, and then he closed it. Explanations were useless. As long as he knew he was acting for the right reason, that was enough.

George sneezed. "You haven't gotten a parakeet or something, have you?" His voice held the whiny tone that had made him the butt of countless jokes when he had been a kid.

Rick gave him a long-suffering look. "Take one of your allergy tablets, George."

A few minutes later, Rick slung the straps of his duffel bag and carry-on over one shoulder and picked up his guitar case.

Standing, George asked, "That goes too?"

"When I go to the ranch, so does my guitar."

George showed sly approval. "Yes, tug your grandfather's heartstrings, remind him of the days when he was your personal Santa. Smart move."

"Yeah, that's me, one smart move after the other." The guitar, a long-ago gift from his grandfather, represented a lot more than that, but there was no use trying to explain. He felt strongly about being loyal to old friends, but a little of George went a long way.

They picked Melissa up at her friend's apartment and reached the airport in time for Rick to arrange for a rented car to be waiting in Orlando. The clerk was cute, with a perky ponytail.

"Now, Sir," she chirped, "as to car preference—" She smiled coquettishly. "Sports model? Convertible?"

"Sounds good."

"Any special color?"

"Sure, red." He smiled back at her. She had eye-shadow with gold flecks and dangling earrings. He liked the look.

A few minutes later in the waiting room by the departure gate, George said in a quiet aside, "Ricky, you asked for a red car? If you want a new image, shouldn't you go for something more conservative?"

Rick didn't bother to answer but he was thinking that the old Rick Malone was just fine. As a rebellious kid, he had never backed down from a confrontation even when knowing he wouldn't win. Now, from a more mature vantage point, he suspected that if he had bent to the dictates of the "right" school and the "right" degree, his grandfather would have winked at whatever career he might have chosen afterward. He shook his head. That was the kind of game-playing that had always driven him up a wall. He prayed that this time, for once, he and his grandfather would be able to get along, because if they couldn't, what was the point?

FAR IN THE DISTANT jungle, where parrots and hummingbirds flew from one hardwood tree to another, a brown-skinned youngster sat at the feet of the old High Priest. It was a good day for the aged man—his thoughts clear, his bones free from pain. The child's face wrinkled in concentration as he puffed air into a handmade flute. The resulting noise was a weak, watery trill.

"Like this," the priest corrected, gently taking the instrument from the child. He blew against the flute softly. A clear and haunting sound emerged.

"Me try again," the child said.

The priest returned the flute.

This time the child produced a clear note. The priest murmured in appreciation. Jumping to his feet, the boy ran to his grandmother, a woman named Ynez. Looking up from preparing flat cornmeal cakes to bake in the stone and clay oven, the woman pretended to be annoyed.

"What? You want another flute? There's not enough work in this village that you two can sit around all day making music?"

Not cowed in the least, the child repeated his request.

Grumbling, Ynez wiped her hands on a cloth. She went into her hut and returned with a second handmade flute and followed outside to see what would happen. She expected nothing much.

Age and youth worked, first the priest, then the boy. The boy finally managed a familiar little tune from start to finish.

"We will now play it at the same time," the High Priest said. He looked at Ynez. "At your signal, we perform. Clap your hands."

With a sigh, Ynez clapped her hands.

Together, the two musicians performed the tune well enough to squeeze a smile from Ynez. The final notes still trembled in the air when a bird trilling from the bushes joined in almost perfect synchronization.

The child laughed in delight.

The aged man nodded wisely. "It is wonderful and strange how different things can fit together."

"Birds and flutes," said the child.

"All things," the old man answered. "All things work together in a foreordained pattern." As he spoke, he touched the symbol of his priesthood, a bee-inscribed gold pendant on a chain about his neck.

CHAPTER FOUR

THE FLIGHT FROM PHILADELPHIA to Orlando soared upward. Melissa and Rick sat in the front row, first-class seats, with plenty of open space for Rick to stretch out his long legs. Ahead, on to one side, was a rest room marked for first-class passengers only. She had only flown once and *not* in first-class. Rick had generously given her the window seat. Unexpectedly, she shivered.

"You okay?" He glanced over. "If you're cold, I have a jacket in my carry-on."

"No, I'm fine. Thanks."

Despite her words, she wasn't sure if she was fine or not. Things had happened so swiftly that she hadn't allowed herself much time to think. Now that they were actually on their way panic crept in. Was she nuts? Even if it eased an elderly man's final days, wasn't there something basically wrong in pretending to be someone's fiancée? Then she reminded herself of the look in Rick's eyes when he talked about his grandfather. There had been a sincere concern, a deeply-felt caring. Besides, he was well known and respected, a person with influential friends. Even though she didn't know him well, he was someone she should be able to trust.

She relaxed, her natural exuberance returning. If Rick was certain this pretense would ensure his grandfather's happiness, she was comfortable in going along. And the timing was perfect, giving her a way to get out of Susie's hair for a few days without offending her. Maybe it was stupid, but that was one reason why she had refused to accept payment from Rick. His showing up had been an answer to a prayer. No sense in being greedy. The other reason was that he was a stranger. No matter how respectable he was, she didn't like the idea of it. *Don't take money from strangers.* Her mother would be proud.

After the plane leveled and the seat belts could be undone, a stewardess ran through the drill about oxygen masks and exits and life vests. Melissa watched, hoping she would never need the information. Rick paid no attention. She guessed he had flown a lot. When the stewardess was done, Melissa gazed out the window, watching landmarks dwindle and blur to nothing. Finally, there were only clouds.

Rick shifted. She glanced around, seeing him bend and take something from the small carry-on he had stowed behind his feet.

"Here," he said, opening a small blue velvet box and handing her a ring. She gasped at the wide yellow gold band set with a sparkling, pure white solitaire. He smiled at her reaction.

Dazzled, she slipped it on. In wonder, she moved her hand, seeing the stone catch the light. If they were going to pretend to be engaged, she guessed it only made sense that she show up with a ring.

"It's breathtaking," she said.

"Not too plain?"

"Are you kidding? How could a diamond ring be too plain?"

"Okay." He nodded. "I didn't think anything too flashy would be your style."

It made her feel funny, him analyzing what he thought of as her style. *Plain?* Was that how he saw her? Mentally, she played back his words and found reassurance. He had said he didn't see her as flashy which was a different thing. What she was, she thought, the right kind of woman to show off to his grandfather. Did that also mean she was the right kind of woman for him?

No, she was getting ahead of herself, but the idea of being his type of woman gave her a thrill. Of course, he wasn't ready to settle down—

that's what this trip was all about. Rick's grandfather wanted him settled, but he was busy making the most of his freedom. She recalled his playful responses to the flirting of the rental car girl and to the airport restaurant waitress when he'd stopped to buy cold drinks. At twenty-six, Melissa wasn't ready to settle down yet either.

She suppressed a smile. Her high school reunion was coming up. She hadn't thought about an escort, but suppose she asked him? Boy, imagine the response from her old gang if she walked in on the arm of a man like Rick Malone.

"Here," he said, handing her a folded slip of paper. "Put it into your purse and then I'll explain what it is."

Puzzled, she did as he asked, then said, "So what is it?"

He grinned, but his eyes were serious. "Maybe I made this sound like a trip to someplace like a resort, but it's not like that. It's a weird situation and I can't thank you enough for helping me out. It will probably be more like a nursing home visit than a vacation."

She nodded. "I understood that. The man is ill. What's the paper?"

"It's the sales slip for the ring. The ring is yours." He put his hand up to stop her before she could say a word. "There's nothing to discuss. The jeweler where I bought it knows me and I've already made arrangements. Once we're back home, you can keep the ring, or exchange it for something else, or turn it in for the money. Anything you want to do with it, go right ahead."

"But—"

"No buts." He shook his head. "Discussion closed. Don't even say thank you. I'm the one who's thanking you."

She sagged back in her seat. The ring had to be worth a lot. *A lot.* He had given it to her and it wasn't open for discussion. She found she couldn't think straight. After a few minutes, she murmured that she was going to the rest room. Rick was busy with a pencil, working figures in the margin of the magazine, which was something about horses. "Sure," he said absently, not glancing up.

She didn't need the rest room, she wanted privacy. She was glad she only needed to walk a few steps because her knees felt wobbly.

Inside the small enclosure, she locked the door then opened her purse and took out the sales slip. She gasped aloud. There was only one place in the room to sit, so down she went, her knees feeling weaker than ever. She couldn't stop staring at the sales slip. The ring cost $6,400 dollars.

Six thousand, four hundred dollars! If she exchanged it, that would mean no more money worries between now and the first paycheck of her new job. And the way Rick had refused any discussion meant he wanted her to have it. Another thought struck. When her visit with Rick's grandfather was done, she could find an inexpensive place to stay in Florida and escape Susie's awkward hospitality. If she absolutely needed additional funds, she could now afford to tap her savings account and replace whatever she'd withdrawn later. When the time came, she could fly home to her new job and her new apartment.

Hold on, she thought. What happened to those high standards about taking money from strangers? She should do some thinking. Giving the ring back was an option, regardless of what he wanted. But for now, it was hers. Standing, she examined her reflection in the tiny wall mirror. She was pale, but her eyes were bright. And why not? Melissa Lind with six grand on her finger. *All right!*

AFTER LANDING IN ORLANDO, they waited in the sprawling baggage room to collect their luggage. Rick's duffel bag and Melissa's suitcase came down on the belt of the baggage carousel together. He swung them off and set them on the floor. Then, looking up the ramp, he frowned.

Melissa knew he was searching for his guitar case, but there was no sign of it yet. "It will be along," she said in a soothing tone, trying to ignore a headache caused by the dryness of the plane's air conditioning. She had taken aspirin and wished it would hurry and start working.

Rick looked tense, she thought, the muscles of his lean jaw rigid. Although he had been relaxed during most of the flight, toward the tail end, he became edgy. She figured she understood why. As they drew closer to their destination, his concern about his grandfather had ramped up. He'd said the man had sounded awfully weak over the telephone. He was probably dreading finding even greater weakness when they arrived.

Off to one side, a young woman with a mane of black hair that was so glossy it had to be a wig struggled to pull a bulging suitcase off the moving belt.

"Allow me," Rick said, stepping over to heft the woman's suitcase from the belt with ease.

"Hey, gosh," she said as she grinned up at him. She wore a strapless top and her low-cut tiger-striped culotte skirt showed a trim midriff. "Thanks a million."

He grinned back at her. "My pleasure." He kept grinning as he watched her walk off, her hips swaying.

Melissa couldn't restrain a flare of jealously. Immediately, she scolded herself. She had no claim. He could smile at anyone he liked, and now the smile he'd shown the wig-woman had turned into a scowl as he looked back at the empty moving belt.

He turned to Melissa. "It hasn't shown up yet?" he demanded as if she had missed it.

A sarcastic answer jumped into her head: *Maybe it* went *by while you were busy playing Sir Raleigh.* She got a grip on herself.

"Not yet," she said, trying not to sound short. She understood his concern. Luggage could go astray, but with her headache, darn it, she wasn't in the mood to be glowered at.

HUNCHING HIS SHOULDERS, RICK jammed his hands into pockets of his dark blue flared slacks, worn with a wide belt with a brass buckle stamped with a horse's head. Shortly before landing, he had dozed briefly and suffered an anxiety dream about being stuck in a cold, dark place, like being frozen in stone. He had awakened in a sweat and started thinking of all the ways the trip could backfire. Superstitious or not, now that they had landed, he found himself looking for omens.

If something bad happened to his guitar, it would be a clear message that the trip was ill-fated.

He gave Melissa a sideways glance and saw her massage her temple. He was about to ask if she was okay, when she said, "There's your guitar."

Yes, there it was! He felt he'd gotten a reprieve. He grabbed it. Kneeling, he opened the case and ran his fingers over the strings, making sure that everything was really okay.

As he closed the case and stood, Melissa said in a determinedly cheerful tone, "I'm looking forward to hearing what you do with that. George said you played a marvelous flamenco guitar."

Rick's relief over finding his guitar unharmed turned to annoyance. "Chatty George," he muttered. George had always been something of a pain, but ever since introducing him to Melissa, he had acted too damned involved. "What else did he tell you?"

Glaring, Melissa snapped, "That you were good-looking and sweet-tempered. Now I suppose I'm going to hear that you don't play guitar, either."

Startled, Rick gave her a look. He had been acting a total bore and she'd called him on it. Chuckling, he observed her with new interest. "You've got your moments, Melissa Lind, you know that? Here I was thinking you were the type who never lost her temper."

She tossed her head. "I don't have a temper. I don't get mad, I get even."

He burst into laughter. "Ah, come on." He could tell from the way she stiffened that his laughter had put her back up even further.

"It's the truth." Her expression was defiant.

"Okay, here's a test." He was trying not to let loose with another laugh. She looked so cute standing with her arms folded and her eyes shooting sparks. "If I handed you a lemon, what would you do?"

"I'd make lemonade."

"Ha! I knew it."

"Then I'd dump it straight down the front of your pants."

"*Okay!*" He chuckled in appreciation. Although her fairytale princess look hadn't won him over, it hadn't mattered. What did matter was her resemblance to the portrait. Now, he gave her a closer look, noticing that her eyes were an extraordinary shade of blue. Although her navy and white outfit was reserved, she looked good—and when she wasn't glaring like a hangman—this image nearly made him lose it again, she had that quirky little smile he had liked from the start. Maybe she had possibilities after all. How would she be if she ever cut loose?

Dampening any remaining traces of laughter, he cleared his throat and said in a faintly formal manner, "Now that we have our luggage, let's go collect our rental car."

"Fine," she said flatly.

WHAT SHE'D TOLD RICK about getting even was true—if the cause was important enough, only it never had been. The closest she'd come to it had been in the summer before her senior year in college.

Her job had been with a temp secretarial agency that sent her to work for a man who couldn't keep his hands to himself. The other women in the office knew what he was and said he was also cheating on his wife, and that the redhead he took on three-hour business luncheons was really for funny business. Their advice to Melissa in dealing with him was to laugh it off and keep out of his way. Complaining would only give her a black mark with the employment agency.

She took their advice, but it wasn't easy. Then one afternoon the boss's wife, who seemed awfully nice, came in and found his office empty. She said it was important for her to find him. That was Melissa's chance. He was with his redhead at a nearby hotel. Melissa knew because she'd made his lunch reservations. But did she rat him out and let the wife find him in a compromising situation? No, she couldn't make herself do it. She didn't want to be the one to reveal trouble to the nice wife. Besides, it was none of her business.

But boy, if there was ever anything that was *really* her business, Melissa vowed she'd wind up her nerve and let the chips fall.

IN THE AIRPORT, AS Rick walked along with Melissa and their luggage, he silently chuckled over her lemonade threat. She had more spunk than he'd thought and it amused him, but when he'd settled up with the car rental agency, the sight of his vehicle made him forget everything else. The car was exactly what he'd ordered, a snappy red convertible that looked even better than he'd imagined.

Encouraged, Rick held the door so Melissa could settle in the front passenger seat. He then stowed their luggage and pulled out of the lot.

Feeling good, he thought ahead to the route.

Even in his prime, his grandfather had kept a low profile; no name emblazoned on buildings, no celebrity photos in the gossip sheets. Still, his power had been known. On occasion, Rick had been approached by reporters trying to track down rumors of a hidden ranch retreat. Rick had always pulled a long face and told them his grandfather was as good as a stranger, that all he knew about him was from the news. Pretending helpfulness, he would say he had read about an apartment in Paris or was it in Switzerland? Or it seemed he had heard about a big property in Australia. Maybe that's where his ranch was.

Now, with the old man long retired, Rick figured the world had lost interest. Still, he protected the secret. Although he doubted that the name Stanton Malone would mean anything to Melissa, by habit he had referred to him only as "my grandfather." After the visit, she would of course know who he was, but Rick foresaw a problem only if she mentioned it to the wrong person by chance. An unlikely scenario, but to keep on the safe side, he would take a circuitous route to his destination. That way if anyone did ask her where the ranch was, she wouldn't really know.

They had been on the road for several minutes, passing through the suburbs, when his glance into the rearview mirror revealed a gray car behind them. Was it the one that had pulled from the curb when they left the rental lot? He frowned, and then dismissed it as coincidental.

"I never thought about us having a convertible," Melissa said. She opened her tote bag. "I love an open car, but I had better put on a sun lotion."

Rick glanced her way, seeing that for all the attention she was paying to the road, he needn't be concerned about their route. He murmured something noncommittal, thinking that she had just enough tan to make her skin glow. Did she glow like that all over? He envisioned bikini lines, then mentally brushed in intriguing details that were shaded rose and gold.

Another look into the rearview mirror showed the continued presence of the gray car. On impulse, Rick turned a corner and entered a development. He took another turn, going down a quiet street. Slowing, he checked the rear mirror.

MELISSA'S ATTENTION WAS ON a mirror too—her compact mirror, which she had propped against her bag. The car made a turn and she readjusted the mirror. She combed her hair back and tied it with a scarf, but the lotion she'd applied had dissolved her makeup. Better put on more. She wanted to look her best when they arrived. And be on her best behavior, too.

She couldn't get over how stupidly she had acted at the airport, the way she'd lost her temper. Thank God, her headache was finally gone. Rick hadn't been in the best mood either. Neither of them had been, so she had provocation. But still, she shouldn't have lost her temper.

Her thoughts jumped ahead to what Rick had told her about the ranch. She hadn't known there were ranches in Florida, but it was apparently a big business in the state's interior. Not that his grandfather was much involved. Rick had explained he was retired from the cattle business but there still were a few horses.

She finished with blusher and lipstick. Her cosmetics case slid a bit when they made another turn, but she got it straight and reached in for eye makeup, her thoughts still on Rick's grandfather. The sick old man apparently lived alone except for a few servants. Despite what Rick had said earlier, she hadn't expected to see anything like a resort, but rather a big old rambling house—comfortable enough, but shabby around the edges. If there was ever a swimming pool, probably nobody used it anymore. Rick's eyes glowed when he talked about the place, but she figured he was still seeing it through the impressionable eyes of the boy he had once been.

The car swerved sharply.

Startled, Melissa jerked her head up, expecting to witness some traffic emergency, but the road ahead was clear. Turning, she stared at Rick. She'd been applying mascara. Lucky she hadn't poked out an eye. "What's going on?"

"There's a car following us."

"What?" She glanced over her shoulder at the road behind. "There's nobody there."

"I just turned a corner. Dammit, it wasn't following that close."

Melissa stared. "Are you kidding?"

"I couldn't believe it myself at first. Then, I tried some tricks and the car kept on our tail."

"Tricks?"

"Yeah, I took some turns— there! There he is."

"That delivery truck?"

"Behind it. A gray car. It came around the corner, then the truck pulled out from a side road at the same time and gave him cover."

As he spoke, he slowed and the truck pulled out to pass them.

"There's nothing behind the truck," Melissa said. "If there was a car, it was going someplace else, not following us."

Rick was silent a moment, then he said, "I think there's an orange grove off to the right, or at least there was the last time I was around here. I'll pull in and wait and see."

"Sure," she said, rolling her eyes.

Accelerating, he took another turn and spun into an orange grove, taking a grassy trail that went down between rows of trees. Slowing, he angled the convertible off the trail and parked so it was hidden.

"Now we'll know for sure." He got out and stepped to a view of the road. After a hesitation, Melissa followed. The long grass tickled her ankles, making her worry about snakes. This was so dumb.

Standing beside him, she looked up the trail toward the road. The empty road.

"Well?" she said.

"Shhh."

"Oh, sure, like the driver's going to hear us."

After another few minutes passed with no vehicles in sight, Rick's tense shoulders relaxed. Straightening, he turned. Dappled light filtering through the leaves of the orange trees showed his bewildered expression.

"I took some crazy turns," he said. "It seemed the driver always showed up again, but at a distance, as if playing clever." He rubbed a hand through his hair. "Maybe I let my imagination run wild." He looked at her. "You must think I'm a fruitcake."

"It's the strain of the trip," she said, giving him an excuse. The fact that he could see how badly he had overreacted made her feel better, but still, why would he think they were followed in the first place?

"You've got eye stuff on your cheek," he said. "Did my jockeying the car around make you do that? Sorry. Wait—" He stayed her hand as she automatically reached toward her face. "Let me. You'll only smear it worse." With his handkerchief, he gently dabbed at her cheek.

"There," he said as he tucked his handkerchief away. "Perfect."

She thought his voice sounded husky and sort of far-away. He gazed into her eyes, his expression softening.

She stared back, unable to move. It was warm in the grove, the sun beating down like a pulse, the air scented with drying grass and citrus. The heat made her feel dizzy or was the lightheaded sensation caused by Rick's nearness and the expression in his eyes? In the plane, there had been a couple of times when their shoulders had brushed, and when they left the plane, the crowd had pressed them together, flooding her with physical awareness. Her sensual feelings had ebbed but now they were back again a hundredfold. He stood so close. The only sound was the buzz of insects and she felt the beat of her heart. He was going to kiss her, she thought, feeling she could barely breathe.

He bent his head and his lips touched hers. Sensation washed over her. She never would have guessed that this man who could be so impatient would so gently caress her lips. Trembling in helpless response, her mouth softened under his. She pressed closer, sliding her palms up against the lean muscles of his chest to his shoulders.

Rick felt fireworks building inside of him. He hadn't planned this, hadn't intended it, but now that it was happening, he couldn't think of a sweeter scene than being off in the middle of nowhere with a woman so warm and willing in his arms.

Just how willing was she? His kisses were gentle and disarming as he stroked her hair and then his hand slid down softly to the small of her back, then lower, the pressure firm, insistent. She seemed to melt into him. The orange grove was secluded, the grass thick and soft. His imagination soared. Worse things could happen than showing up at his grandfather's with her all dazed and starry-eyed. She would look good in love, he thought. The image rose in his mind, the tenderness he would see in her expression, the glow . . . .

Confusion swept through him. He wanted—hell, he didn't know what he wanted, except that when he got to his grandfather's, he needed a clear head. The sudden welter of thoughts cooled his blood and he broke their embrace.

He thought Melissa looked startled when he'd so abruptly withdrawn. Then she said, "Next time, why not just say we've run out of gas."

He blinked, caught once again by that quirky lift of her lips. Slowly, he smiled. "I strive for the unique approach."

"You certainly achieved that."

"For encores," he said lightly, stroking her cheek with his knuckles, "I do the chase with bullets whizzing by." But despite his show of aplomb, his melodrama over being followed made him feel like a jerk. Ever since leaving Philadelphia, he had been on edge. And then, holding Melissa, kissing her . . . .

The memory of his quick rising passion gave him a jolt. He chased it from his mind. What the hell, it had only been a kiss.

CHAPTER FIVE

ABOUT THIRTY MILES FROM the ranch, Rick's anxieties about his grandfather started growing again. Xavier's letter had held few details about the heart attack. Since the letter was written in secret, he couldn't ask his grandfather about his recovery when they spoke on the phone. He'd sounded so weak. Rick imagined him bedfast and hooked up to oxygen. He wished he knew for sure what he would find when he got there, but there was nothing to do but wait. God, he hated situations where there was no action he could take.

Melissa spoke up. He welcomed the distraction.

"I've got to know something." There was determination in her tone as if she expected an argument. "You cut me off at the airport, but shouldn't I know about your interest in music?"

"My music?" He didn't know what she meant.

"About your guitar. I know things about you that a fiancée should know like you have no brothers or sisters and that you put yourself through college on a sports scholarship and that you buy and sell horses for a living. Since you've brought your guitar along, it must mean something, only you've never said anything to me about music. A fiancée would know."

"You're right." He nodded. "I didn't think of it." He told her that his playing wasn't professional, but he sometimes sat in at a South Street club with some musicians he knew. He expanded on the subject. "My grandfather gave me the guitar when I was a kid. At the ranch, you'll meet the man who taught me to play. You should know about him, too. He's the cook and his name is Xavier."

"Sounds like an Italian saint."

Rick chuckled. "You should tell him that. He's from Cuba, mixed-race, a big guy." He didn't know exactly why he enjoyed talking with her except that it was somehow entertaining. "He was an eye surgeon, in his homeland. Then he made the mistake of speaking out against the government. One dark night, he got his hands smashed. Good-bye career."

Melissa gasped. "It was done on purpose?"

"Yeah, on purpose." Little girl, he thought, no tough experiences; knew nothing about life. "It wrecked his ability to manipulate the delicate instruments used in eye surgery and he turned his back on medicine. His father owned a restaurant so he had some experience there. When he escaped to this country, he became a cook."

"Couldn't he have become another kind of doctor?"

"Not according to him." She seemed so sympathetic. It should come across as drippy, only somehow it didn't. "He says politics and medicine are too mixed in his mind. He wanted a simpler life, and being a cook was it. I can't say that I'm sorry and you won't be either. Not when you taste one of his meals."

She was silent for a while and then said, "What about *your* accident? After college, I know you played pro football, but that ended when you injured your ankle. Did it happen in a game?"

"No. It was a road accident." This was more stuff she must have gotten from George because he hadn't mentioned football to her nor his injury. He sighed. No sense in being annoyed with George for filling her in. The man had wanted to give her some background and it was nothing to be ashamed of. Football had been his way to an education without his grandfather pulling the strings. Afterward, the chance to go pro had been a way to bankroll his future. His injury had ended that. He still managed to reach independence in work he liked but it had taken longer. He didn't like talking about his accident, but she was right. As a fiancée, she would know.

"I was driving an open Jeep, jouncing along a rough trail just for the hell of it," he said. "A fox darted out. I swerved and missed the fox, but the Jeep flipped." It had happened seven years ago, but at times when he was drifting off to sleep, he would have flashbacks of helplessness, of being lifted up and then falling, unable to do anything about it. "When I landed, one side of the Jeep landed on my ankle. The bone shattered."

She winced. "Did it take long to recover?"

"A while." Months actually. The doctor had said it looked like a piece of china hit with a sledgehammer. It had been his left ankle. It had been a long time before he could easily move around again.

"You weren't wearing a seat belt?"

He caught the censure in her tone. Miss Prim and Proper. "My Jeep didn't have roll bars. If a Jeep has roll bars, you wear a seat belt and the bars protect the driver if the Jeep flips. Without roll bars, a seat belt pins the driver in place. If it flips, the Jeep lands with its weight on the trapped driver. It's better to fly out and take your chances. I took my chances and only got a bum ankle, okay?"

"I see," she said.

He could tell she wasn't convinced. He stared ahead at the road. Did she think following the rules was a guarantee? Maybe he had been too judgmental about her debts. Dancing along, never thinking about having a piper to pay . . . must be how she got in over her head.

They reached the ranch around four o'clock.

Rick drank in the view. The style of the house was rustic, of natural wood with cedar shingles. It was massive, two stories high, with a one-story wing set at an angle that had glass along a corridor in the front. The corridor led from the great room to the library and opened to the greenhouse. As usual, everything looked flawless, not a single detail left unattended.

Melissa gasped. "It's marvelous."

He grinned. "I told you about it. What did you expect?"

"Something like a ranch from a cowboy movie, with the land all dry and dusty. But there's a green lawn, palm trees and flowers. It's wonderful."

He couldn't help enjoying her enthusiasm. The place *was* wonderful. His gaze moved from the sprawl of the main structure to the fence and the beginning of the grazing land. None of the horses were in view, but he could picture them. The ranch had never looked better. It was home, he thought, feeling an unbidden tug of emotion. More home to him than anywhere else in the world.

At the door, Herman, a much older man who Rick had known forever, greeted him exuberantly. "Rick! Good to see you!" The two men gave shared a rough embrace and then Rick introduced Melissa.

"My lady," Herman said with a little bow, and then he said to Rick, "Your grandfather will be napping until five o'clock. "I'll show you to your rooms and then bring up your luggage."

"We'll fetch it together." Rick gave a nod to Melissa and then he went with Herman to the car. As he did so, he thought: Three years of not seeing one another and my grandfather is taking a nap. What does that mean? Was he too weak to even get up?

Rick chatted with Herman as the man took Melissa's suitcase and he carried his own duffle bag as they went upstairs. Melissa had the guest room with a view out the front. The three of them paused at the door.

Herman said, "When you two are ready, "you will find refreshments waiting on the terrace."

After Herman left, Rick said to Melissa, "I'm going to my room and I'll come back for you in about a half-hour. We'll go downstairs ahead of my grandfather."

She nodded, still looking bedazzled by the elegance of the house.

Rick's room, at the head of the stairs, was the one he e always had. It overlooked the terrace at the rear of the house and gave a long side view of the wing and was down the hall from Melissa's.

After unpacking, he went into his bathroom and skimmed his razor over his jaw, wanting to look his best. Being at the ranch again took him back to the time when he had believed the sun rose and set on his grandfather's opinions. Irritated by his sense of regression, he left his room. He would find Xavier and learn the prognosis for his grandfather.

But then, outside in the corridor, which, after a turn by the steps opened to a balcony overlooking the great room, Rick came to a stop, stunned to hear the old man's voice floating up.

Recovering, he hurried to Melissa's room and knocked. She smiled as she opened the door. "Rick, in my room I have a vase of—"

"Later." He cut off her words, keeping his own voice low. "Come on, we're meeting my grandfather."

"Now? But, my shoes—" She still wore her outfit from the plane but was barelegged and barefoot.

"Get them." It crossed his mind to wonder if Sonja ever went around barefoot. Back then, weren't people more formal? Irritated, he shook the thought away. Melissa would look great. But would his grandfather agree? He tried to imagine seeing his grandfather again—at least he wasn't bedfast, not if he was in the great room but he was probably in a wheelchair.

Melissa stepped from her room wearing stockings and sandals with neat little heels. Feminine. Ladylike. Exactly right. He took her arm and led her down the steps. At the landing, he saw his grandfather.

Forgetting about everything else, Rick could only stare. Although there was no wheelchair, the man's gnarled hand gripped a cane. He was painfully thin, his once-broad shoulders stooped. His grizzled hair had gone completely gray but his eyebrows were still mostly black. Over the years, Rick's references to his grandfather as an "old man" had reflected various moods: fondness and respect for his wisdom, or irritation because of his dictatorial ways, but now, for the first time, he saw the man as truly old. His heart twisted in a way he hadn't known was possible.

"Grandfather—" His voice sounded tight. "It's good to see you."

Stanton Malone acknowledged his greeting with a faint smile, then with a surprisingly crisp motion, he dismissed Herman, who had been at his side. He gazed back at Rick in his familiar way, as if measuring him, eyes hooded under his heavy eyebrows. "I decided I couldn't wait until five, Grandson. It's been a while."

"Yes." Rick cleared his throat. The man looked frail, but far from ready for that final ride in a big black limousine. The lines of his hollow-cheeked face showed a stern, implacable pride and his eyes glowed with fervor.

"Hair's gone a bit grayer," Rick observed, feeling he should say something about the changes. "But you look good."

Damned good for somebody teetering on the edge after a near-fatal heart attack, he thought, but then again, the man had always known how to put his best foot forward. Despite the infirmities, Rick saw that the courage and force that was his grandfather still burned bright. He felt a momentary urge to rush forward, to embrace, and to be embraced. He steeled himself, holding back.

In control again, he moved forward with Melissa. "Grandfather, I would like you to meet Melissa Lind, my fiancée."

Melissa gave the formidable, gray-haired man a tentative smile, her visions of sitting at the bedside of a sweetly vague old darling going up in smoke.

Stanton inclined his head in a bow. "Miss Lind, Melissa, welcome. I trust you will enjoy your stay here."

"Thank you. I'm sure I will." She had a moment of anxiety, wondering if she could pull off her act, then sensing that the man's formality was reserve rather than coldness, she rushed ahead. "Mr. Malone, the orchids in my room are spectacular." Having caught a glimpse of a greenhouse as they drove in, she took a chance and said, "Did you raise them?"

He chuckled, clearly delighted. "As a matter of fact, I did. Perhaps later, I'll take you on a tour and you can see for yourself."

"I would love that, thank you." She glanced toward Rick, seeing his smile and knew he was pleased with his grandfather's response to her.

"Come, along, both of you," Stanton said, directing the way across the great room, with its cathedral ceiling and skylights, and on toward two double glass doors that opened to a terrace with a swimming pool to the far right.

"I believe Xavier has refreshments waiting," Stanton said.

As they stepped outside, Melissa saw a huge man with a swarthy complexion. He looked to be somewhere in his fifties, his short-sleeved shirt and dark trousers covering a body that looked magnificently fit and strong. Seeing Rick, he let out a whoop. Rick went to him and was enfolded in large, muscular arms and drawn up against a massive chest and his feet off the floor. She watched in fascination. Stanton gave a dry chuckle. "Xavier is impressive, is he not?"

She nodded. So that was Xavier, former eye surgeon, guitar player, and working cook, but give him a turban and metal armbands and he would be her idea of the genie with Aladdin's magic lamp.

Rick brought the man over and performed introductions.

"Rick's lovely lady," Xavier approved, his smile showing a gold tooth that only added to Melissa's picture of a benevolent genie.

She smiled. "Rick's talked about you a lot. You'll be glad to know he's brought his guitar along."

"Excellent." Xavier beamed. As he released her from his gentle handclasp, she was aware of the damage Rick had mentioned, the scarred and twisted fingers.

With a bow, Xavier withdrew.

Rick escorted Melissa toward chairs arranged near the pool. They went slowly, keeping pace with Stanton's more measured steps. Measured, but firm. *He seems in awfully good shape*, Rick had said in a low voice to Xavier after their greeting. Xavier had replied, "Your homecoming has made him rally," which was about what Rick had thought. He hoped the old man didn't push himself and overdo it. One good thing, he seemed to like Melissa.

As they took their seats, Rick narrowed his eyes, taking a new look at her. He wasn't sure how she managed to appear serene and animated at the same time, but she pulled it off. She sat on a cushioned wicker patio chair with her back straight, feet together and tucked back a little to one side. Reserved, yet winsome, her lips curved. He thought of Sonja's expression in the portrait and wondered if the old man was even dimly aware of why he responded to her so readily. Not that it mattered. What mattered was that it was working.

Aloud, Rick said to his grandfather, "It's great to see Xavier again. By the way, George Keating says hello. You remember George, right?"

"Indeed." Stanton's gaze was piercing. "Do you still run interference for him, still smooth his way?"

Rick shook his head. George with his plumpness and allergies had been the butt of other kids' jokes. "Shows you haven't been up North recently. George is in the big time now. He needs nothing from me."

Resting back in his chair, seeming to be at ease in the warm air and refreshing breeze, Stanton asked Rick what he had been doing. Rick gave a cautious but truthful reply, not sure how far the conversation should go.

"Horses . . ." Stanton said. "It was here that you became fascinated with them."

Rick nodded and made a vague gesture. It struck him that maybe, just maybe, his grandfather wasn't trying to criticize but sincerely wanted to know about his work. Wouldn't that be a switch? Rick felt tempted to add nothing more out of fear of saying the wrong thing but then decided that was being a coward. The subject had been brought up and he would answer.

Resting one ankle on the opposite knee, projecting a comfortable air he couldn't entirely feel, he said, "Of course, back then I had no idea of what my work would entail, the record keeping . . . tracing bloodlines, finding the right buyers, the right sellers."

He emphasized the management angle, which he knew his grandfather would relate to. Encouraged by a nod, he launched into a tale of a recent meeting in San Francisco, one that lent itself to the reciting of facts and figures.

Stanton made a few comments and asked more questions, none

with the bristling censure Rick remembered from the past. The man turned his attention to Melissa. "Tell me, young lady, how did you and my grandson meet?"

Rick held his breath at first, and then was admiring her skill with the story they had agreed on, which glossed over how recently George had introduced them.

"Ah," Stanton spoke as if a mystery had been solved. "George introduced you. You're a fashion model."

She blushed prettily, looking flattered by his assumption. "Because George is a fashion photographer, you mean? No, I'm trained to teach kindergarten but when I couldn't find a full-time position, I worked with a school supply company and did some odd jobs. I'll soon start something new, research and development in children's toys."

Stanton Malone's eyebrows had zoomed skyward.

Melissa explained a little more, and then glanced over at Rick with an eager smile, as if seeking his approval.

He couldn't restrain a grin. There was no question she was bowling the old man over. Are you a model? No, I'm a kindergarten teacher. A priceless exchange. No flashy showgirl this time, no would-be psychedelic rock singer. A kindergarten teacher. His grandfather had nearly swallowed his teeth.

The right kind of woman—you won't have to worry about me anymore, Rick thought, warmth stealing over him as he reflected that for the first time in years, he and his grandfather had a conversation and the old man had truly listened. Thank God for Melissa. Now that he had pleased his grandfather in one area, perhaps the man would relax a bit in others.

The satisfaction Rick felt outweighed his sense of guilt. It had taken a white lie to do it, but it seemed a small price to pay to repair a broken relationship.

He glanced over at Melissa. The sun was lowering, but the wind had stopped and the air had become more sultry. Herman came in to murmur something to Stanton about dinner. In the lull, Melissa angled her head and lifted the heavy, honeyed mass of her hair from the nape of her neck. The gesture was unconsciously graceful. No wonder his grandfather was smitten, he thought. Even though she was nowhere near his type, he had to admit she was easy on the eyes.

AFTER DINNER, PLEASED WITH how her visit was going, Melissa thought that Rick hadn't been kidding about Xavier's delicious meal. After dinner, Xavier rose to clear the table and Rick's grandfather said they would have coffee and drinks on the terrace.

She and Rick followed his grandfather to the terrace, Rick close to him so he could take an arm if needed, but the old man stubbornly, if slowly, made the way on his own way by using his cane.

Xavier came out to serve them and then left. The night was warm and the starlit sky was clear and beautiful. Since his grandfather had said he wanted music after dinner, Rick had his guitar ready.

The song Rick played was *Fire and Rain*.

Melissa closed her eyes to listen. She remembered the first time she heard James Taylor singing the song, the lyrics a unique combination of sorrow and hope. She thought of Xavier's ruined medical career, of Rick's hope of truly reuniting with his grandfather while there was still time. She prayed that's what was happening.

As he played, Rick was thinking of the past with his grandfather and of how much joy there had been in his life back then. When he was younger he had ridden the horse his grandfather had given him, pretending to be a Comanche warrior riding over the plains with only a knotted leather cord for a bit and bridle. He effortlessly rode bareback, his young strong legs and thighs keeping him secure as they raced, the wind stinging his eyes and whipping his hair back from his face. He'd thought he'd be a jockey and experience that wonderful speed with a bold responsive animal time and time again.

An old wrangler who worked at the ranch told him he'd grow too large to be a jockey, but if he learned enough he could become a trainer. He would have a stable filled with horses, some of them his. Owners and jockeys would trust what he said and did. Now, it was the buying and selling and traveling, all of which he enjoyed. Not until he retired would he become a trainer.

Skillfully he fingered the tune into the notes of *For the Good Times*. It was a song about lost love. He thought of his grandfather's undying love for his Sonja and doubted there would ever be a woman he would care for that much. He was regretful when he thought of his lost time with his grandfather and his hope that with Melissa's help, there could be good times with the old man once again.

IN THE NIGHT, MELISSA awoke. She groped for her watch on the bed table and read the luminous dial. It was two in the morning.

She thought about why she was in Florida. Rick's grandfather had accepted the sham engagement without question, but he had plenty of other questions, and answers, too. His business acumen was impressive. When she mentioned her goal of someday starting a preschool, he had brought up points that the experts she had previously consulted hadn't considered, like future franchise possibilities.

The elderly man's shrewdness made it easy to forget his illness and he looked much better than she'd expected. Rick had been pleased to find him doing so well, too. Whenever she'd glanced his way, she had found him smiling.

A thump came from outside in the corridor.

Startled, Melissa peered toward her closed door. Her first thought was that Rick's grandfather had been stricken and had come seeking his grandson's help. Then she reasoned that the infirm man couldn't have gotten up to the second floor. Besides, he had servants to call. But then what had she heard? Deciding she wouldn't go back to sleep without checking it out, she slipped into her robe and slippers and went to the door. It opened quietly on well-oiled hinges. A glance down the corridor showed the stairway end of the corridor dimly illuminated by a moonlit skylight.

"Lissa!" came a whisper. She whirled to look in the other direction. There, only a few feet away stood a dark figure.

Startled, she gasped and backed into her room, but then a voice said, "Shhh . . . it's okay, it's me."

Rick. He moved toward her.

She stayed in her doorway, staring up into his shadowy face. "I got up because I thought I heard something," she said.

"Sorry." He spoke in a whisper. "I didn't mean to wake you. I went down the rear steps for a snack. I'm heading back to my room."

There was a silence, and then he touched her shoulders. "Lissa . . ."

For a moment it seemed to her that he would take her into his arms. She remembered their kiss in the orange grove and a warm yearning swept through her. But then he said softly, "Go back to sleep."

He gave her a gentle little push that made her step further back into her room. "I'll see you in the morning," he said and closed her door between them.

Standing where he had left her, she smiled. *Lissa.* The name had slipped smoothly from his tongue, his half-whisper making the soft word sound additionally sensual. *Lissa.* Was that how he would whisper her name when they made love?

Abruptly, she reminded herself that their relationship had never been personal—except for that kiss in the orchard.

Remembering, the corners of her lips turned up further. From the start, even though Rick's main concern had been his grandfather, there were times when he gave her an approving smile as if she had struck a deep chord within him. As for her own feelings, she didn't know where to begin. Aside from his good looks, he was warm and caring and just plain special. There was no way of knowing about the future but considering the chemistry between them, well . . . smiling, she touched the ring. Maybe someday she would wear his ring for real!

On impulse, she peeked out her door, expecting to see him entering his own room. Instead, he was moving quietly down the main staircase,

She watched as he disappeared from view. He'd said he was returning to bed. What was really going on? She waited a moment and then padded to the top of the stair. Her view was of the huge pillars that separated the entry from the great room, illuminated faintly by the skylights. Below, somewhere to her right was the dining room, which she couldn't see.

Where was Rick?

She was straining her eyes in the dimness when a grating sound drew her attention. She caught sight of Rick's shadowy form and realized he must have bumped against a piece of furniture, causing it to scrape on the tiled floor. She thought she heard another sound, very faint and off in a different direction. Rick must have heard it too, for he stood still for a long, listening moment, then he moved on between the pillars, stealthily heading toward the entry. She leaned forward. What was he up to?

Puzzled, she watched him slip outside. From her vantage point, she could see through a first-floor window He stood in the protective shadow of a group of plantings. His attention seemed directed toward the wing of the house. Stanton had taken her down that way before dinner, leading her from the great room to a windowed corridor and passing by what he'd said was the library. They'd ended up in the greenhouse, where he had dazzled her with his orchids.

Not really thinking about what she was doing or why, she crept down the stairway. On the first floor, she took several cautious steps and looked toward the entry, but all was in shadows. She felt like she was lost in a creepy house, like in the movie *The Haunting*. She'd seen it in her early teens. She and a girlfriend had clutched each other's hands throughout the scary parts, which was really the whole movie.

Tentatively, she reached out, not wanting to run into anything. She touched what she realized was the high carved back of one of the dining room chairs. She suddenly understood that she'd gotten turned around. The stairs flared out at the bottom. She'd noticed the graceful curve when she'd gone upstairs earlier. Now instead of the steps taking her forward, her slippered feet had followed the curve and she had stepped down facing the dining room. To her right was the glass door that led out to the rear yard of the house

She moved to the door and could make out the expanse of the wide terrace in the moonlight. She touched the door handle. It felt loose and she found it unlocked. Frowning, thinking that everything should have been locked for the night, she pushed the door open and took a half step outside. To her right was the shining expanse of the swimming pool and to her left was the wing that ended with the greenhouse.

Amused that she had intended to go toward the front of the house and ended up at the back, she thought it was good she wasn't an ancient explorer. Send her to guide the Norsemen out to sea and they never would have found the New World.

Her self-amusement faded as she caught a glimmer of light from the area that came before the greenhouse. The library. It had tall windows and through one of them, she saw the movement of a small light, the kind a prowler might use.

She pressed a hand to her lips. Rick's cloak and dagger actions suddenly made sense. He had become alerted to something suspicious, like somebody coming in through the door where she now stood and sneaking through the house. Rick had gone to investigate. First, going down what he'd termed as the rear steps and then coming back upstairs and heading for the main staircase. That's when he'd unintentionally wakened her. Now, he was heading toward the library from the outside. He was alone and could be in danger.

Still standing in the terrace doorway, her heart pounding, she knew she had to find Xavier and tell him what was going on. When he'd brought in their meals, he'd come to the dining room from a corridor that must lead to the kitchen. His quarters were probably behind that. She would make her way to the corridor and Xavier.

Before she could put thought into action, she heard a sound behind her. Was Rick back inside? She turned her head around to look but before she could do more than that, something slung around her waist and yanked her from the open doorway and a voice grated in her ear, "Scream and I'll break your neck."

CHAPTER SIX

IGNORING THE COMMAND, MELISSA jerked her head up and took a breath to scream. A hard, bony hand clamped across her face, closing her mouth and pinching her nose. The only breath she had was her inhalation for the scream that never happened. She kicked and squirmed and scratched, frantic to free herself as she was helplessly dragged across the dining room carpet, friction pulling off her slippers. The dragging continued. The heels of her bare feet made no sound as she felt tiles beneath her heels. She tried to tear the hand away from her face but her captor was too strong. Head swimming from lack of oxygen, she threw out an arm to grab on to something. Her fingers slid uselessly along a corridor wall.

She was barely conscious when her shoulder struck a doorjamb. The hand that stifled her breathing left her face and she was thrown forward to the floor.

Landing hard, she lay on a rug gulping in huge draughts of air. The man's foot gave her body a shove forward and she heard the sound of the door closing. He shoved her with his foot once again. Head still reeling, she finally lifted herself to an elbow and saw the yellow glow she had earlier seen glimmering from the library's tall window. A small flashlight sat upended on a bookcase shelf, illuminating the displeased expression of the man who stood beside it. A man with a chunky face.

George Keating.

Her first thought was one of trembling relief. She was in trouble and a friend had miraculously appeared. Then she realized how wrong the scene was. George's angry hiss confirmed it as he spoke to the man who had captured her.

"Vince! You were to see if we had been heard, not to return with a witness."

"George?" Melissa's voice was a frightened croak. "What are you doing here?"

"Finding this treasure map, my dear." As he spoke he slipped an ancient-looking rectangle of paper into a protective envelope. "Rick never said which book it was in, but I succeeded as I always do." He chuckled nastily. "So romantic, pressed between the pages of an old journal about Merida City."

Vince said, "If you've got the map, let's clear out."

George made a theatrical sound of dismay. "Oh! I forgot the introductions, didn't I, my dear? Vince is the gentleman who bugged that snazzy red car so you could be followed to the ranch."

Melissa turned her head to look up at Vince, a tall, raw-boned man. She realized that George didn't know she wasn't the only one up and about. Rick was on the prowl. He'd surely get here soon. She had to keep the conversation going. Best to ask about the treasure map. George would want to brag. She'd stall and give Rick time enough to arrive and take charge.

"Come on, let's go," said Vince. "What do we do about her?'

"Let me think."

"We could take her with us."

"I said, let me think." George sneezed, pulled out a handkerchief, sneezed again and blew his nose. "Dusty old books," he muttered.

"We could use her as a hostage."

"Will you shut your mouth!" George jammed his handkerchief back into his pocket. "Kill her," he decided. "Your skill with the terrace door left no signs of a break-in. Make it look like an accident. No one will ever know we were here."

"No!" she said. "Please, you can't—" She saw the expression on George's face. Without hesitation, she cried out as loud as she could.

Vince's hand clamped over her mouth again. Squirming, she tried to bite his hand. His other arm came down like a crowbar and knocked her to the floor. With one hand still covering her mouth, he twisted her arm behind her back and shoved it upward, the pain excruciating. She stopped struggling. The pain eased. She looked up at George

He said, "When I set up this scheme, I had no wish to see you harmed, but as the old cliché goes, you now know too much." He gestured toward an empty plant stand shaped like a brass elephant, its rounded back about a foot and half off the floor. "Vince, smash her head against that brass piece. Strike it hard, but only once. We want it to look as if she was wandering around, came in here and tripped and fell."

She made a final attempt to escape. Vince yanked her arm higher. Paralyzed by agony, the fight went out of her.

"Careful," George warned. "We don't want signs of a struggle."

Releasing her arm, Vince grabbed her hair and yanked her to her knees.

For Melissa, time seemed to slow down. The elephant, directly before her, loomed in horrid detail. Beyond terror, she could only imagine her head driving forward, her skull cracking . . . .

CRASH!

"NO!"

Melissa had never imagined death to be so noisy, so filled with yells and shouts. Vince was gone and she lay with her elbow pressed on something brittle that cracked under the pressure. If this was the next world, it seemed awfully physical.

"Melissa!"

That was no spirit guide calling, it was Rick! Still on the floor, her eyes straining in the poor light, Melissa saw Rick tackle George. Grunting with effort, they grappled together, their feet crunching on the scattered glass that had come from the French door when Rick had burst through.

With a shout, Vince moved to go to George's aid. From her place on the floor, Melissa grabbed his leg. He sprawled face first. She hoped he hit the elephant on his way down. She rolled away and staggered to her feet. Screaming for help, she went toward the door, found the light switch and flipped it on.

Blinking in the sudden glare, she saw Rick pounding George with his fists, driving him backward. George sagged against a bookcase.

Rick stared. "George?" It was obvious he hadn't realized until that moment that the man he's been pummeling was his old friend.

Melissa looked down at Vince, who lay moaning. She grabbed a heavy onyx vase from a low stand and was ready to knock him down again if he tried getting up.

Rick's shocked question showed his disbelief. "George, what the hell are you doing here?"

Groaning, George put a hand to his stomach and struggled to straighten up. "Don't be dim, Ricky. It's about the map to the Honeycomb Fire. It's about Georgie-Porgie Keating, the red-nosed fat boy finally winning out over you."

Speechless, Rick's jaw sagged.

George, his florid face twisted in a sneer, laughed harshly. "You had it all Ricky: the looks, the charm, the rich grandfather. Self-indulgent fool. You thought the only plan was using the girl to deceive your grandfather, but I always have my own agenda. Even now—"

Yanking a pistol from under his jacket, George fired without warning. Melissa screamed as Rick stumbled backward. George pulled another shot as Rick fell, and then turned the gun toward her. With a yelp, she threw the vase in his general direction and then did the only other thing she could think of. She flipped the light switch again and dropped to the floor. A shot exploded harmlessly as darkness fell.

"Hold it!" A man's voice. The door slammed back against the wall. There was more gunfire, then shouts of panic and a scurry of motion. Melissa saw dark figures crowd out through the broken window.

The light came on again. George and Vince had escaped and Rick lay motionless. "Rick!" At the panic in her voice, Xavier turned from his pursuit of the culprits.

"Rick's been shot!" she cried. Unmindful of the broken glass, she crawled to his side. In horror, she saw blood on his left temple, soaking his hair and the carpet. "Oh, God! He's been hit in the head."

Stanton Malone, who had turned the light back on again, thumped his way into the room, looking like an Old Testament patriarch with his gray hair flying, his long night robe dragging around his legs.

"Xavier! My grandson. . . . ." Leaning on his cane, he labored to catch his breath. "Attend to my grandson."

Standing, Melissa searched frantically for a phone. "We have to call for an ambulance."

"Wait." Still breathing hard, Stanton moved to touch her arm. "Let Xavier examine him first."

Melissa stared at the elderly man. Why wait for even a second? Rick had saved her life and now his own life might be hanging in the balance. Excitedly, she cried, "We need help now."

"Please . . . ." Gaining control over his breathing, he said, "Before we do anything, we must know how he is." With difficulty, the old man lowered himself to his knees beside Rick. "Xavier?" His voice quavered. "There is so much blood."

Xavier's tone was reassuring. "Head wounds bleed, but it seems to be little more than a graze. There is also blood on the floor." Xavier looked toward the broken shards of glass around the full-length window that Rick had careened through and then down to Rick's feet shod in slip-on shoes that had protected the soles of his feet, but not the top and ankle of his left foot where it had been sliced by a glass shard. The shotgun Xavier had been holding now lay on the rug beside him as his scarred hands moved expertly over Rick. "His pulse is good, his breathing steady. He has been knocked unconscious, but I doubt it's serious."

"He's still been shot," Melissa argued, wondering if they had all gone crazy. Wildly she looked around the room. Where was the telephone?

Herman came in through the broken French door. He also carried a gun. "I chased after them but they got away," he said, and then he saw Rick and gasped in horror.

"Don't worry," Xavier assured. "He's regaining consciousness."

Stanton Malone uttered a thankful prayer and sank weakly back on his heels.

Rick groaned.

Hardly daring to breathe, Melissa knelt next to Rick, and said, "Rick, can you hear me?"

His eyelids fluttered open. He stared up at her without comprehension.

She clasped his hand. "Please . . . please say you're all right."

His eyes focused. He grinned weakly. "Heaven."

"What?"

"I'm seeing an angel."

She laughed weakly, relief washing through her. This man, this wonderful, wonderful man was all right.

"Hey," he said with swift concern, wincing as he moved his head. He struggled to lift himself to an elbow. "You okay?"

"I thought you were dead." She tightened her grip on his hand. "I thought George killed you."

"Who?" Stanton Malone interrupted, his tone sharp.

Rick's face twisted in a combination of disgust and fury. "George Keating." He looked around the room. "Where is he?" He started to get up then stiffened, sucking air in through his clenched teeth. "My ankle." He cursed. "When I busted in I came down hard on my bum ankle."

"George Keating was here?" Stanton demanded. "Why? And how would he know where to come?"

Rick made an angry sound. "It's my fault. He took us to catch our plane and stayed with us when I arranged to have a car waiting for us. He knew which agency and what car I was getting and where I was picking it up. He must have taken a later plane but had arranged for us to be followed from the airport. There was this gray car—"

"He had Vince, the other man, bug our car," Melissa interrupted as she rubbed her sore shoulder. "Like in a spy movie. That's how we were followed even after we thought we weren't."

"I trusted him. I don't know how I could have been so stupid." Rick cursed again. "George came here because he wants the map to the Honeycomb Fire."

"George said he found an old map," Melissa said, feeling more alarmed by the minute. George was a thief, a potential murderer. Why wasn't anybody calling the police? And how come the servants had guns?

Trying not to tremble, she kept her eyes focused on Rick. "George boasted he'd found the map in an old book . . . ." She hugged her arms about herself, feeling deathly cold. "He told Vince—"

Breaking off with a shudder, she stared at the brass elephant, remembering how George had ordered Vince to strike her head against it. If it hadn't been for Rick, her head would have been smashed like a peanut. The image suddenly struck her funny. She giggled. She knew she was probably hysterical but it was still funny.

Aloud, she said, "Vince was supposed to hit my head against the brass elephant, smash it like a peanut." She looked expectantly at Rick and his grandfather, waiting for them to start laughing too. "Elephant. Peanut. Get it? If only I'd had on my clown suit it would have been perfect!" Only they didn't seem to see the humor and that struck her as funny too.

She started laughing so hard she couldn't stop, and then all at once, she was sobbing instead.

CHAPTER SEVEN

THE LIBRARY WAS STATELY, lined with tall wooden cases filled with books, Rick's grandfather took charge, smoothing Melissa's hair and murmuring comforting words.

"The police," she sobbed. "Why don't you want the police?"

Rick, still sitting on the floor, started to speak. Stanton silenced him sharply, but when he addressed Melissa again his tone was soft.

"Think of me as a silly old hermit. The danger is passed, my grandson is safe and the thieves have fled. All I wish now is to be spared the disturbance of additional strangers tromping about."

"But—"

"Shhh," he soothed. "Believe me, it is for the best."

A cup of hot tea appeared as if by magic. Melissa, still bewildered sat in a chair, gratefully sipping the hot brew as Herman swept up broken glass. He had earlier brought towels, some for Xavier for staunching blood and others to use for cleaning up spilled blood after he finished clearing away the glass. Xavier now had medical supplies. He had determined that in addition to the head wound, Rick's injured ankle had been strained as it had swollen slightly, but the worst was the open wound from the glass cut.

"This wound is narrow, but it needs stitches," Xavier said.

"Stitches?" Melissa echoed. *Now* they would get a doctor.

"Xavier is quite capable," Stanton said.

The big man bent down to Rick. "Put your arm about my neck." He slipped one of his own arms around Rick's back, the other under his bent knees, and lifted Rick bodily from the floor.

When Rick was settled on a couch with his left leg up, Xavier started working. When the ministrations to the head wound finished with a bandage, he moved to deal with the cut. Melissa closed her eyes, hearing Xavier's soothing voice and Rick sucking his breath in sharply more than once. She didn't open her eyes again until Rick called to her and said, "I'm all fixed up. Are you all right?"

"Of course I am," she said, a stubborn note in her voice.

"Good," he said, and then, shaking his head with admiration for her spunk, he muttered to himself, "Geez, a clown suit!"

Melissa took another sip of the tea and straightened her spine. After the way she had broken down, she desperately needed the feeling of being in control again. Taking a breath, she looked at Stanton Malone and managed a brave smile.

Stanton started to return her smile, and then he stiffened. He stared hard, and then shifted his gaze to Rick. Expressionless now, he stared into space for a moment, sent another glance at Melissa, and then spoke in a low voice to Herman who had finished putting the room to rights. Nodding, Herman left the room.

"Mr. Malone, are you all right?" Melissa asked, concerned.

Hearing her question, Rick's head snapped around. "Grandfather? All this excitement can't be good for you. I'm sorry, I—"

Stanton cut him off, his tone flat. "I'm quite fine, thank you."

Melissa wasn't convinced. Something was wrong, only what?

An uncomfortable silence fell.

Herman returned with a large flat package wrapped in brown paper.

From his position in a leather-backed chair, Stanton crisply dismissed both Xavier and Herman. Alone with Rick and Melissa, he leaned back, tenting his fingers. Although his knuckles were swollen with arthritis, the distortion strangely increased their impression of power. He fixed Rick with a formidable gaze.

"Grandson, explain further. How did George know where to hunt for the map?"

Seated on a couch with his leg and bad ankle propped on the ottoman, Rick realized that anything he wanted to say would only sound like excuses. He had been an idiot. All these years George's continued interest in his grandfather had nothing to do with the old man's welfare. All he had wanted was the address. And the map. George's oozing sympathy, his eagerness to lend a helping hand . . .it had all been a slick manipulation and he'd never questioned it.

"I'm waiting, Grandson."

Rick gritted his teeth. "When we were kids, I told him the map was hidden in the library. I didn't say which book and he didn't know where the ranch was, so I didn't think it mattered. It was a mistake."

"An understatement. Even with all his clinging, there was always an unsavory streak in George, a sly envy. Didn't I warn you against him, even back then?"

"Yeah, you warned me." And he hadn't listened because George had been his friend. Or at least, that's what he'd thought.

Stanton Malone sighed heavily. "Grandson, you cannot begin to appreciate how delighted I was to hear that you were at last settling down. Now, everything is a question in my mind." He paused for a moment, and then took a breath. Fixing Rick with an arrow-sharp gaze, he demanded, "Can you honestly tell me that you didn't cook up this scheme?"

Rick stared. "George coming here? My God, no! There was never—"

"Not robbing me," Stanton corrected impatiently. "He used you. His attack tells the truth about that. I meant your engagement." He cast a glance at the ring on Melissa's hand. "An elegantly understated piece of jewelry. Certainly not to your taste Grandson. Is it to Miss Lind's?"

His eyes lifted questioningly to hers, then returned to Rick. "Or was it a choice made to please me? I find it suspect that it was George who introduced you. How long ago, really, did it happen? When did you buy the ring? If I inspected your financial records, would I find the ring conveniently purchased in time for this trip?"

When Rick maintained a stony silence, Stanton spoke again. "Grandson, dragging the details from you piecemeal would no doubt prove tedious. To save time, let me say it's become clear that you and Miss Lind hoped to use her imagined resemblance to my Sonja to your advantage."

With a gasp, Melissa opened her mouth to speak. Stanton fixed her with a warning glare. "Miss Lind, don't try my patience."

"She wasn't in on this," Rick said, wondering what his grandfather meant by *imagined*. Although there was no way to justify his actions, he could make sure that Melissa was in the clear. "Don't blame her. She—" He'd surged forward, which made his head thump and his bandaged angle twist painfully. Biting back a groan, he said, "She had no part in it. She didn't know what was going on."

Stanton grunted. "Your attempts to protect the lady are chivalrous, but in vain." He reached for the package Herman had left beside his chair and slid it around so it rested against his knees. Leaning down, he tore off the wrappings.

Rick, who had been about to speak further in Melissa's defense, fell silent as the portrait of his grandmother was unveiled. It was an oil portrait showing an oval-faced beauty, with long-lashed blue eyes and perfectly contoured cheeks colored a soft rose. Her soft yellow hair was waved in the style of the Twenties. She looked exactly as Rick had remembered.

Looking at Melissa, who also stared at the portrait, Stanton said, "Can you see this and still deny hatching a plot with my grandson?"

Eyes wide, she moistened her lips. "The picture—"

"Yes?"

She stared at the old man in horror. She'd never seen the painting before but he thought she had. He believed she and Rick had hatched up this scheme, but they hadn't! She shrank from his gaze, knowing he demanded an answer.

In a weak voice, she said, "Her coloring is like mine, I guess. If you didn't know me, you might think, you might think . . . you might think it looked like me."

"Indeed. And more than that," Stanton said. "This woman, as you are already aware, is Rick's grandmother. She has been dead for many years. Rick's only knowledge of her appearance came from this portrait, which explains his error. Although you resemble this particular picture, you do not, except in the most general sense, resemble the living Sonja."

"Hold on," Rick protested, feeling as if he'd gone over a fence without his horse. "If the portrait doesn't look like Sonja, how come it hung in the house when I was a kid?"

Stanton pursed his lips. "Your mother fancied the idea of an in-law as glamorous as a film star. This portrait is one she had made from a photo of Sonja. It fit into her fantasy. To me, it showed a stranger. After your parents' untimely deaths, this came back to me. I simply locked it away. His severe gaze landed on Melissa's white face. "A clever scheme," he approved with reluctance. "And even though you don't really look like my Sonja, I admit I was quite taken by you. But as things are now, my dear, your plan is doomed. There is no way your appearance will help Rick regain his inheritance."

Inheritance. The word echoed in Melissa's head as her shocked gaze flew to Rick. His attention was on his grandfather. "I'm telling you," Rick said, "keep her out of it. She had nothing to do with it. She wasn't involved."

Stanton lifted his brow. "Under the circumstances, I find that difficult to believe."

"Well it's true," Rick insisted. "It's true, so believe it."

Watching them, Melissa's thoughts reeled in sick dismay. Rick hadn't brought her to the ranch out of a deep concern for his grandfather. He had brought her to con the elderly man out of his money. It had all been a trick, a lousy trick. Humiliation washed over her. What a fool she'd been. She had believed she was helping him to do something nice. She had also believed he liked her. Instead, what he'd liked was her resemblance to the woman in the portrait. To him, she was nothing but a pawn in his rotten money-grubbing scheme. And now Stanton Malone believed she was as much a two-bit crook as his lousy grandson.

She glared at Rick. All her life she had tried to look on the bright side. Except for a few times when things turned sour, she would grump for a while and then it was, chin up and forge on. But nobody had ever conned her like this, leading her on with a smile while laughing out of the other side of his mouth. Rick had to have known she was falling for him. He had probably laughed over that too, thinking how it made their faked engagement look all the more authentic. Well, he'd outsmarted himself this time. She had told him she liked to get even, but this wasn't like that silly man with roaming hands. This was personal! And it hurt, really hurt. This time, Melissa Lind was out for blood.

Still arguing with his grandfather, Rick said, "She didn't know about the portrait or anything else. Blame me, but don't—"

"Oh, dry up," Melissa snapped.

"What? Who, me?" Rick stared at her. "I'm only trying to —"

"Give it up, Malone." To think she had thought he was special. He was special all right, a special brand of garbage.

She lifted her chin. "We've been found out, so stop whining."

Rick looked to his grandfather, who watched them both with a curious expression. "I don't know why she's saying this stuff," Rick said, sounding bewildered. "She was an innocent, completely in the dark." He made a helpless gesture. "I figured—"

"Right," Melissa interrupted, "you figured." She still couldn't believe the fool she had been. Threatening tears stung her eyes, but she blinked them back. Rick was already in hot water—she would make sure his goose was cooked. "You figured this and you figured that, thinking you could waltz down here and bamboozle the old geezer on his deathbed. You made it sound simple—snatch the bank books, grab the antiques and jewelry and we'd be on easy street." She glared. "I was an innocent all right. Too dumb not to see you weren't as smart as you pretended."

Rick was in shock. Had she gone bonkers? He had never called his grandfather an old geezer, and banks weren't where the man kept his money. Nor did he collect antiques and whatever else she was babbling about. And damned if she wasn't still talking, doing even more damage.

"Okay." She met the older man's eyes defiantly. "You've got us dead to rights. I bet you'll be calling the coppers this time."

Rick cringed. She sounded like a filmmaker's idea of a Roaring Twenties gun moll. If his grandfather had a low opinion of his past lady friends, he must be thinking he'd really scraped bottom with this one.

Stanton studied Melissa for what seemed a long time, then to Rick's surprise, he smiled. "I haven't changed my mind about the police, Miss Lind." His voice was almost gentle. "What I want to do is make a deal with you and my grandson." His tone hardened as he turned back to Rick. "You want your inheritance, is that correct?"

Rick stiffened. After all that had happened, saying that his real aim had been to reestablish their relationship was going to sound as phony as a tin horseshoe. He met the old man's eyes. "The ranch," he asserted boldly. "You promised it to me. That's what I want. That's *all* I want."

"Point taken," Stanton said, and Rick saw a glimmer of grudging respect. At the same time he had never felt so frustrated. He had been deceptive, yes, but he had never held the attitude he was being accused of. Melissa and her loony comments—what had gotten into her?

Stanton rested back in his chair. "Although you have failed to meet my original conditions which were to settle down and prove yourself responsible before your thirtieth birthday, I've decided to give you a second chance. I shall set you to a task. Complete the task, and the inheritance you desire is yours."

Rick gave his grandfather a suspicious look. "What's the task?"

"Beat George to the Honeycomb Fire—" Stanton paused. "And bring it back."

"What?" Forgetting about his injuries, Rick jerked himself upright. Wincing, he eased himself back into place. "You can't be serious. That big yellow diamond is nothing but a story."

"Is it? You have a bullet crease to remind you how seriously George takes the story."

Rick realized that George did believe it. Believed it enough to kill for it. As a kid he'd believed it too, but once he was grown it was like Santa Claus and the Tooth Fairy, adventure yarns that his grandfather had enjoyed spinning as much he'd thrilled to hear them. Still not sure what his grandfather was expecting, he said slowly.

"I'm to go after George." He imagined the satisfaction of catching up with his ex-pal. "And I'm to see if I can find the diamond." He started to laugh. Hell! Maybe the story about the diamond was true. There were books that told of it, family history and legends. Sure, maybe it was true. And if it was, better him than George to find it. "And is the deadline still my birthday? That only gives me three weeks."

Stanton shrugged. "As Miss Lind so diplomatically put it, I'm an old geezer. Who knows how long I can last. Yes, Grandson, the deadline is still your birthday." He paused, and, then said, "One more thing."

His tone made Rick tense. "Yes?"

"Miss Lind goes with you."

"What?" Judging from the recent run of conversation, Melissa was the last person he'd trust at his back. "You're kidding, right?"

"Wrong. The two of you got into this predicament by scheming together. Let's see how successfully you can scheme to bring back the diamond." He gave Melissa another long look and then turned back to Rick. "Grandson, you've heard my terms. What is your pleasure?"

Melissa interrupted. "You mean the deal is off if I refuse to go? If I don't cooperate, he can't get the inheritance he wants?"

Stanton shifted his hooded gaze to her. "Yes, but there's an incentive for your cooperation. If you and Rick bring back the diamond, it's yours. You can either keep it or sell it to me for the sum of two hundred thousand dollars—the amount coming off my grandson's future inheritance, of course."

She sucked her breath in sharply. "You, you'll guarantee the money?"

"I'll put it in writing."

"And to get it, I have to go somewhere—" She pointed a scornful thumb. "With him?"

"That is correct," Stanton said.

She thought of what she could do with the money in regard to the preschool. No messing with bank loans. Not struggling to hold down a job while she tried to establish a business in her free time. She could start off with a truly professional set-up, the best facility, the best location . . . and best of all, it would be paid for by the man who had used her for a chump.

She narrowed her eyes. "Double it! Make it four hundred thousand and you've got a deal."

Rick couldn't believe Melissa's nerve. Nobody, but nobody, bargained with the old man like that. Holding his breath, he waited for his grandfather's angry outburst.

"Done," Stanton Malone said. "Four hundred thousand it is." He pulled himself to his feet. "I see it's still dark outside. Rick, I will send Xavier to assist you to your bed. With what lies ahead of you, you'll need your rest." He bowed to them both. "I will see you in the morning when you can start making your travel plans."

"Hold on." Sacked by the swift turn of events, Rick gave his head a groggy shake. "This is nuts. We can't go after that diamond. Are you forgetting? George ran off with the map."

Stanton paused in the doorway and regarded his grandson with a pitying smile. "Are you forgetting who you're dealing with? I may be old, but I don't live in the Stone Age. I have copies."

Mouth agape, Rick watched his grandfather leave the room. As the door closed, he turned on Melissa, taking his confusion and frustration out on her. "What's up with you? You've got him convinced you were in on this up to your neck."

She widened her eyes innocently. "Gee, do I?"

"Yes, damn it. The truth was bad enough, but you made us out like Bonnie and Clyde. What's the idea?"

She smiled vindictively. "The idea, mister, was to make you look bad. The worse I look, the worse you look. I get even, remember?"

Rick squirmed. "You didn't seem like this before."

"*Before* is the operative word. Before George wanted to smash my head, before I found out that instead of helping you do something nice to help your grandfather, I was being used to bilk him out of his money."

"It wasn't like that."

She laughed without humor. "You're going to try telling me your inheritance had nothing to do with coming here?"

He said nothing. Why waste his breath? She wasn't in the mood to listen.

"Defrauding a sick old man," she muttered, shaking her head in disgust.

This annoyed him enough to come back with something he wouldn't have ordinarily said. "You did get a ring out of it."

Her eyes flashed. "Thank you for reminding me." Jumping to her feet, she yanked off the ring and disdainfully tossed it toward him. "This time, I'm holding out for a rock that's worth the effort."

Catching the ring, he stared at her. She looked and sounded tough, but he saw a haunted expression flicker across her face. She knew she was remembering how George wanted to smash her head. Her lips trembled. He thought she was going to lose it again but then she flipped back that gorgeous hair and stood tall.

Damned if she didn't look magnificent.

SOUTH OF THE TROPIC of Cancer, the nighttime jungle retained the scorching heat of the day, but inside the sacred temple, the air held the coolness of ancient stone. Eduardo, who had been too restless to settle for the night, had arisen and left the sleeping village, telling no one except Luis that his destination was the temple.

Now, deep in the belly of the earth, he oiled the gears of the trap called the Great Sting. Although he couldn't identify what troubled him, he sensed danger. The only thing of value that the village possessed was the diamond that embellished the crown of the goddess. The only thing he could do to protect it was to make sure the traps were in good working order. Passing under the zigzag carvings, he climbed back up through the maze of passages. At the exit, he adjusted the concealing veil of growth and then moved on to the thick jungle where the narrow Path of Doom led from the world outside the village and the secret it held. Any interlopers having heard of the diamond would eventually come to this path, thinking it would lead to the temple yet it led only to their death.

The thick jungle growth pressed on Eduardo from both sides as he placed the plank that allowed him to safely cross the trap of the Fire Stings. He walked on, the jungle still pressing inward as he moved to check the trap called Many Stings.

That done, he would normally have returned the way he had come, but on this night, uneasiness sent him further along the carefully maintained path that kept the jungle growth from overwhelming it— the growth that kept interlopers on the path the People of the Goddess desired to lead them.

Emerging from the impenetrable jungle, Eduardo gazed around in the glow cast by the half-moon. Perhaps no trouble brewed. Perhaps it had all been his imagination.

Still looking around, he had gone only a few more steps when without warning, something careened out as if from nowhere and smashed down upon his crippled shoulder. Stunned, he fell to the ground. Before he could reach his weapon, his assailant was upon him, using the butt of his rifle as a club.

Dazed, Eduardo looked up. The man looming above him was Diaz, one of the men who traveled with Benito Carranza, a pilot who flew in supplies to the far side of the village. They used a small airfield hacked from the jungle back when the flying machine had first become known.

"You dog." Eduardo spat. He had never trusted Carranza and his three companions and he now knew the source of his unrest. "You hope to steal the Honeycomb Fire."

"True." Diaz's broken teeth had a dull gleam in the starlight. "Tonight, Carranza and the others have come to terrorize your village. With guns at your children's heads, someone can be persuaded to lead us to the crown of the goddess."

Eduardo now heard distant sounds of gunfire and shouting.

Anxious for his people, he stared at Diaz. "If Carranza fights there, why are you here?"

Diaz chuckled. "I came on foot from the airfield and circled around. I alone saw you creep from the village but I lost you. I waited here for you to lead me to the place where I can claim the diamond for myself."

Eduardo glared. "Never would I betray my people's treasure."

"No?" Diaz's booted foot slammed into Eduardo's side. "Stand. Lead me the safe way."

Diaz prepared to deliver yet another blow, but Eduardo, clutching his pain-wracked ribs, moaned, "Don't keep hurting me. Please don't!" Groaning, he struggled to his feet. "I'll do it, but to save us both, you must stay the length of two arms behind me."

Diaz smirked. "Now I know there is a delay in the timing of the traps. To keep safe, I must tread directly upon your heels."

Eduardo flashed him a glance that mingled hatred with despair and did as he was instructed. He began the trek back, his gait slow and painful, Diaz urging him on until they came to the place where the Path of Doom began.

Diaz made a sound of pleasure at the path faintly visible through the overhanging treetops thanks to the brightness of the sky.

"So easy," Diaz chuckled.

Only as they neared the trap of Many Stings did a sly smile touch Eduardo's lips. He felt the rifle barrel press against one shoulder blade. Diaz, holding the gun awkwardly, followed so closely they could have been matching spoons.

They stepped on together until all at once there was a grating sound from under their feet. Eduardo spun to face Diaz, tearing the rifle from the startled man's hands as the ground beneath them disappeared.

Both men dropped. Eduardo's descent was jolted to a stop when the rifle, which he held crossways above his head, caught on either edge of the pit's rim. Diaz plummeted to the stone floor below.

Gritting his teeth against the pain of his crippled shoulder, Eduardo levered himself upward and scrambled to his feet. From below, he heard Diaz cry out sharply. This was followed by sharp slapping sounds and more outcries of pain and confusion. A light suddenly showed from the pit as Diaz switched on his flashlight and cried out in terror.

Eduardo knelt and peered into the pit. By the glow of the fallen flashlight, he saw Diaz dancing a mad jig. Stinging scorpions, too many to count, covered his body. As his thrashing grew more violent, the vibrations drew more scorpions from the walls.

Eduardo waited until the mechanism of the trap door began its movement. With a grinding, the stone restored itself to its former concealed position. What a comfort to hear Diaz's screams muffled. A comfort also to know the cries would soon stop altogether.

Scrambling to his feet, Eduardo hurried along the path and safely over the First Stings, pausing only to lift up and return the plank to its customary place. He then raced toward the village, where the sounds of fighting had ceased.

Luis, who had been coming to get him, met him on the outskirts.

"We have men wounded but we have all survived," Luis said."

"What of Carranza and the two who were with him?"

"They are dead, but Carranza escaped. He was injured. We shall hear of him no more."

"So I hope," Eduardo said doubtfully.

As wicked as Diaz had proved to be, Carranza, the ringleader, was sure to be worse. And having lost this fight, Eduardo was certain the evil man would return, even more determined to succeed.

Inside the village, Eduardo found women and children weeping and the High Priest stunned by a blow. Fortunately, the most serious injuries to the People of the Goddess were several men with flesh wounds and one with a shattered wrist.

"This will not heal well," Eduardo observed. Anger gripped him. "Modern things are what we need, yet we wrap ourselves in old tales that make us victim to thieves."

As if stirred by Eduardo's heretical words, the High Priest seemed to rally. He leaned forward, his expression suddenly frantic. "Tell me," he said urgently. "Is the crown safe? Does it still lie unharmed?"

"It is safe," Eduardo answered, gentling his tone out of mingled pity and respect. "There is no need to concern yourself. The thieves did not even come close to it."

The High Priest muttered a thankful prayer.

Eduardo merely shook his head.

CHAPTER EIGHT

IN THE MORNING, RICK had just returned from hobbling to the bathroom, wincing as he did so when there was a knock on his door and Xavier came in.

"Let's have a look," the big man said. After examining it, he said, "Still puffy, but the cut is already starting to heal. Be careful with it today and tomorrow and we shall see."

"Yeah, sure," Rick grumbled. The ideal plan would have been for him and Miss Get-Even to follow on George's heels, but it was nuts to leave if he wasn't at his best. All the same, he argued. "Come on," he said as Xavier put a lighter-weight bandage on the head wound. "I've played entire games with my ankle puffed up."

"And then I imagine you couldn't walk when the game was done," Xavier said. "Also, that was before your accident and the damage. Give yourself time to heal. Where you will go, you want your ankle to be dependable."

Rick grimaced. "Guess you've heard about the treasure hunt."

"Yes, your grandfather says there will be rough walking." Xavier straightened. "He waits for you on the terrace. Do you still like your eggs turned over easy?"

Remembering Melissa's attitude, he said, "Make them sunny side up. I need to see something to brighten my day."

His boots gave his ankle needed support and the walking stick Xavier had given him with orders to "use it," helped as well. Rick set off for breakfast, contemplating anew George's betrayal and his willingness to murder to get what he wanted. It was clear he had never understood his old friend. How could he have been so blind?

On the terrace, he leaned his walking stick against a chair and gave his grandfather a reserved greeting. Taking his seat, he glanced around. "Melissa not up yet?"

Stanton smiled. "Your partner is tougher than you think. She's already on her way to town to make purchases for her part of the journey. Considering your condition, she will do your shopping, too. I've given her a list. When does Xavier think you'll be ready to travel?"

"Two days, maybe three." He didn't like turning over his arrangements to Melissa. He also didn't understand his grandfather's surprisingly placid mood. Pouring himself a cup of coffee, he thought about it. With all the power the old man had once wielded, the infirmities of age must be difficult to bear. The circumstances of last night had put him in a position to give orders again. Rick smiled to himself. With the way it was affecting the old man, maybe it was worth it. Then he thought about George and his expression turned grim. "I can't wait to see my old buddy again."

Reading the emotion behind Rick's words, Stanton showed disapproval. "Violence isn't the way. I'm having inquiries made into his affairs."

"What's that going to accomplish? You can't nail him for breaking and entering without jeopardizing your privacy."

"My inquiries will be discreet. Not only has George invaded my home, he's a thief and a potential killer. Given his character, I'm confident there will be a multitude of shady avenues worth exploring. By the way, Herman examined your car and found this—" He held up a small electronic instrument. "I believe this is the 'bug' that allowed George to be led here."

Rick narrowed his eyes. The next time he felt there was somebody on his tail, he would trust it.

"Already I have learned interesting things about George," Stanton continued. "He won't escape punishment, that I can promise."

"I don't like old friends taking shots at me." Rick took a burning swallow of his coffee. "After I catch up with him, there may not be much left to punish."

Stanton's eyes twinkled. "Don't count too much on your paths crossing. Your delay because of your injuries won't be the disaster you fear. I told you many stories about the Honeycomb Fire, but one thing I never revealed was that the existing map contains deceptions. At the starting place, the city of Merida, George will immediately be sent in the wrong direction."

Rick stared at his grandfather. "And you never told me?"

Stanton uttered a rude sound. "You can thank your lucky stars. What would you have done with the information except share it with your childhood friend? Now, however, the time has come for you to know." Leaning forward, he explained.

LATER, RICK WENT OUT to see the horses. There were three of them: old Queenie, a grey who was now mostly white and old Star, now a faded brown but still with that bright star design on her nose. And his own horse. A beautiful chestnut Arabian that was young when his grandfather gave it to him for his twelfth birthday.

"You'll grow together," his grandfather had said. "His name is Buster, the same as my first horse."

At the time Rick had been honored to think his horse had a name important to his grandfather, but later it had occurred to him that if it was his horse, he should have had the privilege of naming it. Just one more example of how firm his grandfather's hand had been on everything.

Xavier came out and helped Rick saddle Buster, and brought over a mounting block for Rick to step up on and mount without bending his ankle and threatening the stitches.

As Rick rode Buster, he remembered Clem, who came to the ranch when he was a kid. Clem was a squeaky-voiced wrangler who knew everything there was to know about horses, including riding and training and what to expect from any horse you were dealing with. He taught it all to Rick, who was eager to drink it up. It was Clem who gave him the knowledge he couldn't have learned in any of the fancy schools his grandfather had wanted to send him to—the knowledge that led him into the career where he could be his own man.

After his ride, Rick spent the rest of his day in his grandfather's library researching routes and making travel plans. Melissa kept out of his sight after her shopping but that night at dinner, he spoke to her.

"Things are falling into place. By the time we leave Friday morning, all our travel arrangements will be set."

Instead of acknowledging his words, Melissa directed her attention to Stanton. "We'll be leaving Friday morning," she informed him as if she hadn't just heard it from Rick.

Rick took a testy breath. Since the night before, she had been giving him the cold shoulder. He couldn't blame her and he was determined to keep it from getting under his skin. He helped himself to Xavier's excellent spicy chicken. "When I've had to make explanations about my travel arrangements, I've been saying I'm a writer for a travel magazine."

Stanton chuckled. "Yes, you can hardly admit you're following a treasure map."

Rick started eating as if he had nothing more on his mind than food but now that he was more used to the idea, he found himself looking forward to the journey. It would eventually take him and Melissa deep into the wilds of Quintana Roo, one of three Mexican states on the Yucatán Peninsula. Bounded on the East by the Caribbean, the coastline of Quintana Roo was increasingly becoming a vacationer's paradise. In the interior, however, there were sections where isolated groups of Maya Indians still made their homes, people whose ancestors had built the ancient cities that now lay as intriguing mounds of rubble. Old ruins, wild jungles, natives speaking ancient tongues . . . and best, was the hope that trip would help heal the harm he had done to the already strained relationship with his grandfather.

Melissa spoke. "The treasure map is old. There must have been hundreds of changes in the country since then, thousands."

"I'm considering possible changes when I—" Rick began, and then he saw that Melissa was still directing her comments to his grandfather.

She said, "The ancestor who drew the map—"

"Don Miguel," Rick supplied.

"Yes," she said, as if it had been Stanton who had spoken. "The map shows the diamond in an old temple. How come Don Miguel never went back for it?"

"The records show he intended to, but he apparently died before that could happen," Stanton said. "We only know that his map has been passed down through the family. In more recent years, there have been two attempts to go after the stone. In the 1800s, Richard Malone, that's my grandfather, started off only to be forced back, and in the 1920s I myself made an attempt. An unsuccessful one, unfortunately."

"We suspect a family jinx," Rick said lightly, trying to hide his chagrin over being shut out. "As to the changes, they haven't touched the country we'll be going through near the end of our journey. What we'll see there will be roughly the same as what Don Miguel saw in the sixteen hundreds."

Continuing as if deaf to him, Melissa addressed Stanton. "I looked at a modern map and there don't seem to be many good roads in the direction we're headed."

"If there were roads, the wife of some damned highway engineer would be wearing the diamond," Rick interjected with a growl.

How long was she going to keep on treating him like a pariah? He had tried to apologize, but there seemed no graceful way to say that yes, he had used her, but not to the extent he had been accused of. Instead of an apology, it came out as an excuse. He didn't blame her for being mad, but the way she acted, as if he had ceased to exist, was like a stone in his shoe. The more he tried to walk away from it, the more it annoyed him.

EARLY FRIDAY MORNING, XAVIER and Stanton stood watching from the ranch house veranda as Rick and Melissa took off down the road. As soon as they were too far away to look back, Stanton, who had been standing erect, sagged heavily into a chair.

Xavier gave him a swift look of concern. Seeing that the aged man seemed to be at ease, he cast another glance after the disappearing car and smiled. "Rick is eager to begin the journey. He tried to hide his emotions, but I read them clearly."

Stanton chuckled. "I read them too, my friend." After a thoughtful pause, he said, "I have recently found life losing its savor, but this venture has renewed me. I've told him that if he is successful, he can take immediate possession of the ranch."

Xavier showed surprise. "You would give up your retreat?"

Stanton ran his gnarled fingers over the ebony head of his cane. "There are other retreats. I've decided I would like to see what he makes of this place. I have never doubted his abilities. Could it be that I haven't placed sufficient value on his interests? Let him have the ranch while I'm still around. Let me see what he will do. It intrigues me." His eyes twinkled. "The woman also intrigues me. She's far different from the others he has known."

His smile faded abruptly. "Xavier . . ." His tone showed a rare uncertainty. "This journey . . . do I make a mistake in sending them off alone?"

The other man stiffened. "Didn't you tell me that Rick and the devil who tried to take his life would travel in opposite directions?"

"Yes. I'm depending on the misdirections of the map to keep them apart."

"You're now saying that might not be enough?"

"I'm not certain," Stanton answered slowly, meeting Xavier's eyes. "George Keating is a dangerous man and far from stupid. Perhaps I should hedge my bets."

CHAPTER NINE

THE RED CONVERTIBLE THAT RICK had rented at the airport would be returned to the local rental agency by Herman He was now driving a 1968 Toyota Corona that had been his grandfather's—also red, which amused Rick. Flashy old guy, he thought to himself, more power to him.

They were a few miles down the road when Melissa said, "How long do you think this entire trip will take?"

"What's this?" he questioned. "A voice that speaks directly to me?"

His tone was light, but Melissa knew her chilliness during the past seventy-two hours had put his patience to the test. He really had a most expressive face, she thought sourly, remembering he had been almost touchingly earnest when trying to explain and apologize. As if anything he said could diminish her anger. Okay, so maybe he wasn't such a rip-off artist in regard to his grandfather; the point was he had *used* her. He hadn't even thought she had redeeming features. If his grandmother had looked like King Kong, he would have searched for a date at the zoo. He had made a fool of her and she was never going to forgive him. *Never*. And now she was stuck going off with him to who knew where or what.

She thought of how she'd thrilled to the stories from ancient history and the magnificent Egyptian pyramids as well as the pyramids of Mexico and South America. But was that where she was going? No. Stanton had given her a picture of an area that had ruins, yes, but without the grandeur that had once captured her romantic imagination.

If it hadn't been for a cross-country hiking trip one college summer, the shopping list from Stanton would have scared her from the journey. But now it was all packed in the car: clothes for roughing it; sleeping bags; and other such gear.

The funds came from Rick's future inheritance—if he earned it—Stanton had said, which suited her just fine. And then there was George. Thank God for the inaccuracy in the map, which Stanton had assured her would send George miles off in the wrong direction. Wonderful! It was one thing to lie safely in bed and think of ways to get even with Rick, but another thing to face the reality of George popping up like a jack-in-the-box, gun in hand.

Out of the blue, Rick said, "Are you sure everything you bought was for this trip and not a bunch of luxuries you had shipped to your home address? Your double-the-money deal with my grandfather showed a streak of greed, you know."

She sniffed and said nothing, refusing to dignify his remark by replying.

He shot her a sideways glance. He regretted how deeply he had involved her in his family drama although she sure seemed to be bearing up. The promise of big bucks that she could use for her preschool plans had been the winning ticket for her.

He took in the trim fit of her fawn-colored slacks and sleeveless blouse and the shine of her hair in the bright morning sunlight. Maybe a woman didn't always have to glitter. On her feet were western-style boots, stylish, yet practical. He wore his boots too. They would need them where they were going.

"You know what I can't figure out?" he said abruptly. "What you and my grandfather kept finding to talk about." Maybe she wasn't worldly-wise, but she was no dummy. In the past, his grandfather had scorned every woman he had found attractive, yet there was Melissa, passing herself off as a failed con artist and she had him eating out of her hand.

"Every time I looked," he said, "you two had your heads together."

"We talked about lots of things, including his adventures when he was young—retracing Hannibal's route across the Alps and his stay with the gypsies in Granada."

She had found Stanton to be a fabulously interesting man. Now that he had accumulated a vast fortune, he had turned his interests to behind-the-scenes charity work. She truly admired him. How would *he* feel about attending her reunion?

"And of course," she added, "we talked about the journey he started but never finished—his search for the Honeycomb Fire."

Rick remembered his awe when listening to those same tales as a child. "Yeah, but when that oil well he'd invested in came through, he quit having fun. From then on, he concentrated on business."

"Even though he didn't succeed, he had fun with that too," she said. "You can tell when he talks about it." Her time with Stanton had also given her a crash course in entrepreneurship. Considering her past bad luck, it was hard to believe that her dream of a preschool might soon be within her grasp. It was also hard to believe that she hoped to achieve her goal by following a treasure map. Was that wacky or what? When she had listened to Stanton's exciting tales, anything had seemed possible, but now that the adventure had begun, she wondered if she needed her head examined.

FROM ORLANDO, THEY FLEW into Miami, where they switched planes. As soon as Rick took his seat aboard the craft that would take them to the Yucatán, it hit him hard: he was really doing it. After all these years, he was truly going after the Honeycomb Fire.

He felt the purpose of his mission change. Despite his enthusiasm over family history and the fact that records pointed to the diamond still lying hidden in the ancient temple marked on the map, he had viewed the journey as a formality to save his grandfather's pride; one that would allow the man to accept him back as the properly humbled Prodigal Son. But now for the first time, he found himself committed to the quest itself.

An almost forgotten memory rose to the surface of his mind. He saw himself as a wide-eyed boy on the day his grandfather had first shown him the map. "Someday, Grandson," he had said, "you will succeed where others have failed."

He had believed it then. And now, after so many years of thinking of it as simply an adventure yarn to delight a kid, he found himself believing it again. Emotion gripped him. He would succeed, he vowed. His forebears had failed, but he would not. He would find the great yellow diamond and triumphantly bring it home.

Shaken by the force of his commitment, he fastened his seat belt and rested his head back and sent his thoughts ahead to their arrangements after reaching Merida. There, they would take a small, private plane to a logger's landing strip near the ruins of Mayapan. If the reference points on the map kept checking out, they would soon be ready for the final leg of the journey, which would entail going through the jungle on foot. It looked so smooth and easy on paper, but despite his new resolution, he wasn't blind to the possible difficulties.

He closed his eyes for a moment, and then opened them again, hearing the sound signifying that the seat belt sign had flashed off. Taking a breath, he became aware of the world around him once again. A glance toward the window showed nothing but blue. He assumed they were already over the waters of the Gulf, but from his aisle seat, there was no way he could be sure.

Seeing that Melissa had her nose stuck in her shiny new Yucatán guidebook, he said, "If you're not going to look out the window, how about if we switch seats?" He saw no reason for her not to comply, but she gave him a look and said far too sweetly, "Thanks, but I find the natural light better for reading."

"Right." Pity the poor jerk who tried messing with her before this mood blew over. He became aware of the faint ache of his ankle. Not wanting to dwell on it, he pulled a small, leather-bound journal from his carry-on. It had come from his grandfather's library and was entitled *Ways and Byways of the Ancients, the Account of a Traveler from Merida.* First published in the middle eighteen-hundreds, the journal was the book from which George had stolen the map: a crucial book, only George hadn't known it.

Rick opened the journal, studying again the print on the yellowed pages, but soon he found himself sneaking a glance over at Melissa. Involved in her reading, she looked cool and composed. The old man had clued her into the realities, hadn't he? Spiders the size of dinner plates, snakes with venom that could send a man into a screaming fit in two minutes and dead in fifteen. He wished he knew if she was truly prepared. Stubbornness made him clamp his jaw. After her deep freeze act, he wasn't going to have her think he was hungry for conversation.

Turning a page in her guidebook, Melissa read that despite the heavy rainfall of the Yucatán, dryness was a persistent problem because the water drained quickly through the porous limestone under the skimpy soil. Still, as Rick said, there was enough water to support jungles. A photo of a woman in a native costume showed a background of impenetrable green.

Impenetrable. The paragraph on flora and fauna spoke of parrots, butterflies, and hummingbirds, plus lizards and "swamps where civilization has not yet intruded." Great, save us from civilization. Who needs paved roads, telephones, and toilet paper? She did, that's who. She sent a furtive glance in Rick's direction, envying his ability to take the trip in stride. She would have liked to talk with him, a little at least, but she didn't want to risk revealing her fears.

The plane landed smoothly in Merida. Followed by Rick, she saw there was no fancy walkway, just down the steps from the plane to the tarmac. The sweltering heat wrapped around her as close as the air in a cloakroom filled with children's wet coats. According to the charts in the guidebook, August in Yucatán was hot and humid. It was worse than she had imagined. Yuck. She hated to sweat.

Inside the terminal, which wasn't all that much cooler than outside, she waited with Rick for the pilot of the private plane that would fly them to Mayapan where there was a nearby cenote. The guidebook had told her a cenote was a water-filled sinkhole caused by the collapse of the limestone surface. If the exposed cenote walls had serpent carvings, it was the one marked on the map. A map, which Stanton had said was deliberately confusing. If the Mayapan cenote didn't have carvings, the one that did would be at Chichen Itza. In that case, they would return to Mayapan and the same pilot would fly them to the town of Piste, which was near Chichen Itza.

Looking around the airport, Melissa surveyed the crowd of tourists, colorfully garbed natives and suited businessmen, their speech an animated jabber of tongues. She tapped her foot.

"I thought the pilot was supposed to meet us," she said. "You told me you paid in advance. He should be ready and waiting." She wanted to get moving before she chickened out.

"He'll show up," Rick assured, impressed by her eagerness. By this time, he had feared she would start having second thoughts. "The travel agent I spoke with claimed he was extremely reliable."

"Mr. Malone?" A small-boned man dressed in jeans and a white native shirt with pleats down the front stopped before them. "I am Teo. You are waiting for my plane?" He shook hands with Rick and gave Melissa a polite nod. "I am sorry but there is a repair that must be made. My cousin, he has gone to get a new part."

Rick frowned. "How long will this take?"

"Maybe three hours."

Rick figured that probably meant five hours at the very least. "What time will you have us landed at Mayapan?"

"It will be today, I absolutely guarantee," Teo said.

Rick's frown deepened. "If we arrive late, it will be too dark to visit the cenote I want to see."

"Perhaps, but if it is too late, José, he is another cousin, he will give you a place to sleep for the night. In the morning he will show you the way to the cenote."

"Isn't there another plane?" Melissa said.

"No, I am sorry," Teo murmured regretfully. He brightened. "But while you are waiting for the repairs to be done, Alvero, he is another cousin, he will take you to a nice hotel where he works. You can refresh yourselves there. No charge. When the plane is ready, he will bring you back here. This is a good idea, you agree?"

Melissa dragged Rick aside. "Ask for your money back. There must be another plane."

"Maybe, but this is the only one I could find available today."

"We're at an airport, aren't we?" There had been a time when she would have been more patient, but not with a man who would run her over without a second thought. She waved an imperious arm. "Find another plane."

"Look." He drew a ragged breath. He liked a show of spirit, but there were limits. "We're in this together. Shouldn't we at least *try* to get along?"

"What's that supposed to mean?"

"That I'm doing the best I can. Our arrangements are complicated. Teo's probably got relatives involved in this deal all the way down the line. If we get somebody new, we'd lose more time in the long run."

The way she clamped her lips and said nothing told him his logic left her with no choice but to agree but her silence showed how little she liked it.

Cousin Alvero turned out to be a short, plump fellow who wheezed when he put their luggage into his car and wheezed even more when he took it out after parking in the back of what he said was a hotel.

"This way," he said, shuffling ahead to unlock a service door. Melissa sent a questioning look at Rick, who merely shrugged.

Inside a hotel corridor, Alvero unlocked another door and directed them into a pleasant-looking room with a king-sized bed.

Puffing, he set down their bags. "This is yours until I come to return you to the airport. You will have several hours." He cast a sly look at the bed.

Ignoring Rick's grin at Alvero's obvious suggestion, Melissa said, "We'll go out and find something to eat."

"Then you will find the hotel restaurant most agreeable." Alvero handed Rick the room key and then added sheepishly, "If you visit the restaurant, may I please ask you to use the service door where we entered and walk around and come in from the street? It will also be necessary to prop the service door open so when you return you will be able to get back inside."

After Alvero left, Melissa exploded. "We're not supposed to be here! He sneaked us into a room that he knew was empty."

"Now we understand why there was no cost," Rick said. At least she wasn't blaming *this* on him. "Lighten up. We're not hurting anybody. Teo wanted to make sure we were comfortable since he wasn't ready when he thought he would be."

Sitting on the side of the bed, he pulled off his boot and examined his ankle. Not being able to move around during the plane ride had caused it to swell but the cut was nearly healed.

"I like your idea of getting some food," he said as he adjusted the bandage which hid a copy of the map wrapped in plastic. A second copy of the map was in his pack. "Let's wash up and go out. You want to use the bathroom first?"

As they left the hotel, Melissa was still unable to understand how Rick could feel so comfortable with their "borrowed" accommodations. She watched uneasily as he jammed a folded paper into the hinge of the service door to keep it from locking.

"Suppose somebody shuts it while we're gone?" she said.

Her question amused him. "Then we go in the front and the heck with Alvero. Quit fussing."

Once on the main street, Melissa felt the desire to put space between herself and Rick. "It's too early for lunch," she said at the street entrance to the hotel restaurant. She gestured toward a row of shops across the street. "I'll look around. I'll meet you behind the hotel in an hour."

Not waiting for his response, she walked off, unable to stop thinking of how she had sat on the hotel bed before leaving, and heard Rick running water into the sink in the adjoining bathroom.

It had struck her just how close they would be during their journey and how awkward the situation could become. To think she had ever found him appealing. How could she have been such a dunce?

An hour later when they were back in the room again, she shook out the head scarf she had bought.

He gave it a look. "Big-time spree on Fifth Avenue?"

"I thought," she said archly, "we were going to try and get along. I bought this for a reason. The men here stare as if they've never seen a blonde. I started feeling self-conscious."

"Next time, don't go out on the street alone," Rick said, realizing he didn't like the idea of other men looking at her. She was his responsibility, whether she liked it or not. Miss Priss with a mean streak. He grinned. She was something all right. Made life interesting.

Ignoring him, she sniffed in a way that indicated she would do as she pleased. "Let me see that old book you had on the plane. Is it the one where George found the map?"

"Yep." Still grinning, he pulled out the journal.

She read its title. "That's what I thought. They had tons of these in the gift shop across the street."

He stared at her. "You're kidding."

"Why would I? It's probably a popular curiosity. The man who wrote it lived right here in Merida in the 1800s. He was a European who got hooked on exploring the ruins."

Rick frowned. "I assumed I had one of the few copies left in the world."

"You may have an original, but there's a pile of reprints."

Rick's frown look smoothed over. It didn't matter how many copies existed; what mattered was that George didn't know he needed one. With that thought, he remembered Clem, the horse wrangler, who once gave him advice about wagering on horses.

"My old Pappy was a wise one, boy, not that I was smart enough to take his advice, but Pappy told me, 'don't ever make a bet unless it's a sure thing.' And you know what, boy? Nothing in life is ever a sure thing."

Rick shook his head over the memory and with that, a knock sounded on their door

Melissa looked up, startled. "Who could that be?"

Rick chuckled. "Who do you expect, the hotel room police? It's our ride. The plane must be ready early."

CHAPTER TEN

THE MAN STANDING OUTSIDE the motel door was wiry and mustached and definitely not Alvero.

"My name is Pedro," he said with a heavy accent. "Your pilot, his plane, she is still broken. He has found another plane for your journey I have come to carry you to the airfield."

Melissa shot Rick a hesitant glance. He nodded reassuringly and gathered their bags, glad she was no longer trying to play boss. When they were settled in the rear seat of Pedro's rattletrap car, Rick was further amused when Melissa, still sounding uncertain, asked, "Are you another cousin?"

"No, I am not." He laughed as if she had made an excellent joke. "I am an uncle."

Explaining that the plane was on an airfield at a farm, Pedro took them on a route that led from the city and into fields of spiky henequen. "Five years it must grow before the first harvest," he explained and began a detailed lecture about the plant, from the first planting of seedlings to the many useful products made from the fibers, such as rope and twine

Pedro's chatter was informative at first, but as the trip wore on, Rick's attention shifted to the increasingly poor road conditions and the fact that there were only occasional huts along the way. Suppose Pedro wasn't on the up and up? The man's knowledge of Teo and the plane had made him appear legitimate, but he might have accidentally come by his information and decided to take advantage. Rick remembered his disregard of Melissa's caution but suppose she had been right? God, if he had gotten them into some mess . . . .

"We are here!" Pedro announced. He brought the car to a halt in front of a thatched-roof hut.

Rick narrowed his eyes. As far as he could see in any direction there was nothing but endless henequen. "Where's the airfield?"

"It sits down the road." Pedro quickly slipped across the front seat and got out on the passenger side. He opened Melissa's door. "The pilot, he soon comes to take you the rest of the way. Señorita, it is much cooler to wait inside the hut, in the shade."

His alarm bells ringing, Rick was about to tell Melissa to stay put when Pedro's arm snaked forward. He grabbed her wrist and yanked her out of the car.

Taking no time to think, Rick swung his legs up and scooted across the seat after her, going out feet first, keeping the door open with his boot as Pedro tried to shove it shut. Rick's heels slammed into the dust. Too focused to even wince as his ankle absorbed the strain, he barreled straight for Pedro, who was struggling with Melissa, who was screaming like a banshee and beating his head with her purse.

Rick slammed against Pedro in a bone-cracking body block. The car keys, which the man had been holding in one hand, sailed high. With a leap that would have had fans cheering, Rick snatched the keys from the air.

"Into the car," he shouted to Melissa. That's when a man who had been inside the hut stormed out with a club.

The next thing Rick knew, he was flat on his belly in gritty dust with his assailant astride his back. Before he could make a move, a rope looped about his neck and pulled tight and a harsh voice grated in his ear, "Lay still or the woman dies."

A second blow from the club turned everything black.

When Rick opened his eyes, he felt that a short time had passed, yet dim light indicated that darkness had fallen. He lay face down on a dirt floor. There was another earth-like scent in the air that he failed to identify. He tried to move and choked. A careful assessment told him that the rope about his throat was also looped around his hands and feet. Attempts to free himself put dangerous pressure on his tethered neck.

Still dazed, he lay quiet, trying to regain his bearings. It wasn't night, he realized. He was inside the hut. It was windowless, but glints of sunlight showed through the chinks. Outside, Pedro and the other man argued. Rick's thoughts went to Melissa. His heart started to thud. Where was she? What had they done with her?

"Rick?" Her voice was a frightened whisper.

Painfully, he turned his head toward the sound. Through the hazy gloom, he saw her, sitting on the floor not five feet away, her hands apparently tied behind her back.

"Are you all right?" he demanded anxiously.

"I'm fine."

He thought she sounded shaky. "You're not hurt? They didn't—"

"No, I'm fine, really, except that they got all our stuff. My purse, your wallet, our luggage—Rick, they've got everything."

The journal, the copy of the map in his bag, Rick thought, outrage shaking through him even as he realized that was the least of their troubles.

The tremor in Melissa's voice made it clear she was fighting tears. "What . . . what do they plan to do?"

"Shhh," Rick ordered. The disagreement between the two men outside had caught his attention. He wanted to listen.

Melissa heard Rick's shocked intake of breath. "What is it?" she asked. The men spoke in Spanish—she hadn't understood a word. She hadn't realized that Rick knew the language.

"George." Rick cursed bitterly. "George is in Merida. He's hired those creeps to take us out of the game."

Melissa gasped. "But George is supposed to be off in another direction."

"They talked about a red-faced gringo who hired them," Rick whispered harshly. "Who else could it be? George must have figured out the map was leading him wrong and returned to Merida to start all over again. Somehow he spotted us. Shhh—I want to listen."

Distraught, Melissa wondered what the men were arguing about. After taking the time to tie them up, they surely weren't going to hurt them, were they? Robbery and dumping them in the hut was bad enough. But then, as she heard the voices outside grow louder her certainty wavered. Suppose they planned to finish them off but couldn't agree on the method?

A car door slammed. Another door did the same. The engine started and the car roared off.

"Rick . . . ." She hardly dared hope. "Do you think they left?"

"Sounded like it."

"Both of them?"

"Sounded like that, too." He attempted to laugh, only it ended in a choke. Recovering, he said, "I couldn't catch everything they said, but Pedro kept yelling about his horoscope and his pregnant wife. I think he's superstitious, scared that doing anything to harm us might mark the baby."

"Thank God." Weak with relief, Melissa let out a long breath.

"Don't sound so thankful," he said bitterly. "We've been left in this godforsaken place to rot." And it was his fault, damn it. Rick Malone, in a jam because of being too trusting. If only he hadn't dragged Melissa into trouble as well. The next time she sounded paranoid, he would pay attention.

"I'll bet nobody much comes this way, do they?" she said. "If we call for help there's nobody to hear."

"That's the picture," he said, surprised by her relative calm. His grandfather had been right. She was tougher than he would have thought. Being left trapped and without water—she had to realize it was the same thing as killing them. It just wouldn't be fast.

Melissa muttered an unladylike phrase. "If they expect to come back and find us a couple of corpses, they've got another think coming."

Her feisty attitude would have made Rick laugh if he hadn't already learned that laughing was a mistake. Angling his head, he used the corded muscles of his neck to keep the rope's pressure off his windpipe. Damn George, damn him to hell.

Through the gloom, he saw Melissa wriggling around on the dirt floor. What did she think she was doing? His gaze slid along the wall behind her. There was only a table, a barrel and other objects he couldn't identify in the poor light. It didn't look like a place where anyone lived. His attention returned to Melissa. It appeared she was trying to go backward, only she was getting nowhere.

"You're against a table," he said.

"I know. The rope that's tying my hands is looped around a table leg. If I can tip the table, I can slip free. My wrists will still be tied, but I'll be able to move around."

"What good . . . oh, I get it. Your fingers will still work. You can untie me."

"Yes." He saw that the table proved too heavy for her. "I'll help," he said and tried to squirm over, but his ropes pulled tight, sending him into another choking fit.

"It's okay," she said, "I've got another idea. The floor is dirt and I found what feels like a piece of broken pottery. I think I can use it to scrape away dirt from under the table leg and then slip the rope out from underneath."

As she worked, all was silent except for her strained breathing and the scraping of the pottery shard in the earth. "You're doing great," Rick encouraged, hoping he was right.

"Ouch," she muttered. "There's a loose stone that keeps getting in my way."

"It's okay," he said. "You can manage. You can do it." Scraping dirt away by the spoonful and with her hands at such an awkward angle . . . her bound wrists must be killing her, he thought. His were killing him and he wasn't even moving. He turned his energies inward, trying to find a position that would ease his tight muscles. One good charlie horse and he would end up strangling himself.

It seemed like eons had passed, but at last, he heard her say, "I did it! I'm still tied, but I'm free of the table."

"Terrific! I knew you could do it!"

"Thanks. I think there's enough slack between my wrists so I can work the rope under my bottom and pull my legs through. It will be a lot easier to untie you with my hands in front." She rested a moment and then started to work her bound hands under her rear end. She uttered a sound of discomfort. "This dratted stone again. I almost sat on it."

In the dim light, Rick watched her struggle and hoped she wouldn't get stuck halfway.

"Houdini did maneuvers like this underwater," she said, trying to bolster herself. "Wait, let me get my boots off," she said, talking more to herself than him. "There! My boots are too big to slip under the rope." With a sound of triumph, she slipped the heel of first one foot and then the other through the loop made by her bound hands. "Did it!"

"Melissa Houdini," Rick said with a cheer.

She laughed in relief. "If those jerks had tied my feet, too, I never could have made it." Dizzy from the exertion, she collapsed, and then abruptly sat up again.

Hearing her gasp, Rick asked, "What's the matter?" He thought she had hurt herself, but when she spoke, it was with a tone of wonder.

"What's been bothering me isn't a stone, it's a statue. It was half buried in the dirt. It looks like a primitive figure. The kind in museums."

Rick drew an impatient breath. "If you don't do something quick, I'm going to be a museum piece myself."

"Right." She laid the statue down and scooted over to start work on his ropes.

It seemed to Rick that another eon passed, but at last, he felt his ropes go slack. Groaning in relief, he slipped free.

"Pedro's marvelous henequen," he said with a curse, twisting his wrists to restore the circulation before he could cast the tangle of rope aside. He felt a welcome pain as he laboriously straightened his legs, unkinked his back, rubbed his arms and aching throat. There was a comic strip with a Middle Ages setting that had always cracked him up—one that showed straggle-haired prisoners chained in a dungeon and making wise comments. He didn't think he would ever smile at the cartoon again.

"Now me." Kneeling before him, Melissa held out her bound hands.

Because she had put so much strain on her ropes, the knot was super tight. "Wait a minute," he said. "Let's get outside where I can see better." Holding to the wall of the hut for support, he dragged himself to his feet, every joint and muscle screaming.

On stocking feet, Melissa went on ahead. She pushed open the unlocked door and sunlight flooded in.

Moving painfully to the doorway, Rick stood blinking. The full realization of just how narrow their escape had been caught up with him. The way he had been hog-tied, Melissa could have died right there beside him and he would have been totally helpless. The emergency over, his legs were as weak as water. Closing his eyes, he leaned back against the door frame.

Standing with her bound hands extended, Melissa glanced up into his face. "Are you all right?"

He forced his eyes open. "I'm fine." Drawing a breath, he got himself under control. He finally worked her rope free and let it drop.

"That's wonderful, thanks." Massaging life back into her wrists, Melissa gave him a vague, lopsided smile. Now that she was loose, she seemed stunned, as if she had never trusted it would really happen. "The map." She seemed to grope for words. "The map, do we still have the other copy, the one under your bandage?"

"Yep." He had already checked.

"Great." She forced a laugh, but when she spoke again, her voice was unsteady. "I guess . . . I guess no harm was done after all."

He realized she was going through the same thing he had experienced a moment ago. "Lissa, it's okay now, the danger's over." He reached to comfort her, but she turned away.

"The statue. I'm curious." She lifted it from the floor and brought it to the light. The pottery figure was about five inches tall, a seated man wearing a necklace of tiny skulls.

"Rick, look—" Awe had come into her voice. "It really looks old, doesn't it?"

"I don't know about that sort of thing," he said, unreasonably annoyed that his attempt to comfort her had been pushed aside. But, she was right, the statue did look ancient.

"Maybe a farmer found it and gave it a toss," she speculated, her eyes wide. "Maybe he never thought of it as an artifact or didn't care. I wonder what a museum curator would have to say."

"Oh-oh," Rick said.

"What?" she asked.

Facing the inside of the hut, he merely gestured. Light poured over the table that had been in deep shadow before. Lined up on the counter like soldiers were a dozen statues identical to the one in Melissa's hands, some of them already fired, others still wet. Along the wall sat several molds and the barrel held supplies.

"Pedro and company are in business," he said, realizing that what he smelled earlier had been wet clay. "This is a pottery works."

Melissa stared at the no-longer unique figure in her hands. "They made this?"

"That's how it looks. Their kiln is probably outside."

"Phony artifacts." She sounded sick.

"Or reproductions," he suggested, thinking that sounded better than phony.

She gave the statue a dirty look and dropped it to the ground. "I knew it wasn't really anything."

"You did not." Her statement was so ridiculous that he had to laugh.

She glared at him "I was just trying to take my mind off being robbed and tied up and left to die, okay? When Pedro's not busy mugging people, he's pedaling junk like that to unsuspecting tourists."

Despite her indignity, she sounded ready to cry. Rick understood. With the frightening experience over, she had gone flat. If the statue had been valuable, it would have pumped her up again, but now that she knew it was worthless she had crashed.

"It will be okay," he soothed, wanting to see her smile. "We're going to get even, remember?"

She only shook her head.

"Hey—" Again he reached toward her. "If it hadn't been for you, I'd still be tied up like a rodeo calf."

For a second time she turned away. "Let me get my boots. We've got to get out of here before those clods change their minds and come back."

"You're right," he admitted, trying not to feel rebuffed a second time. "The guy with the pregnant wife is liable to start thinking that leaving us to die is bad luck too."

"There's only one road back to town, isn't there?" She had her boots on her feet again. Although it must have been ninety in the shade, she stood with her arms hugged about herself as if chilled. "Suppose we meet them along the way?"

Hating the trapped look that had come into her eyes, Rick gave a confident shrug. "We would hear them coming." He made a motion toward the thickly planted henequen. "We can walk along the side of the road. If we hear anything, we jump into the field and hide. They won't know where to hunt. We'll be okay. Come on, let's go."

Hoping his plan was as smart as it sounded, he moved toward the road and then realized Melissa wasn't with him. Turning, he was puzzled to see her searching in a patch of weeds.

"What are you after?"

"This is where Pedro dumped my purse. I thought I saw something sparkle." She stood upright again. Opening her palm, she revealed a tiny bottle of perfume and a bright copper penny. "This is it. All we've got left. All this and where am I? Flat broke all over again."

He spread his hands. "It could be worse."

"Sure. We've still got our health."

Not knowing what to say, Rick cleared his throat. "Okay, let's make tracks. We've got a long hike to get back to the city." He wasn't going to say it aloud, but if George was in Merida, it was probably the worst place to go, only they had no choice. At least George wouldn't be looking for them. As far as he knew, they had been put on ice for keeps.

He now saw that Melissa was carrying something else.

"You didn't pick up that statue again, did you?"

"I'm taking it with me." She gave him a pointed look. "It's my reminder that even when something looks really great, there's probably a trick."

CHAPTER ELEVEN

TRUDGING ALONG ON THE poor excuse for a road, Melissa thought back to the moment when she had shrugged off Rick's attempts at an embrace. Maybe she should have taken the time to enjoy his little show of gratitude. There *was* something attractive about him. Why couldn't she be a user too? Sure, get what she wanted, then toss him aside like a flattened toothpaste tube.

She frowned as she thought how mean-tempered she felt. What had happened to her chin up and move on attitude?

"So tell, me," she said. "What's this about George thinking he could understand the map if he returned to Merida?"

"It's this way," Rick answered cautiously, wondering how she would react. "There's a problem with the map."

"In addition to the misdirection?"

"Yes, you can't go by the map alone. You also need that old journal from my grandfather's library."

"The one you brought along?"

"Yes."

"Why am I only hearing about this now? I thought the map was just tricky." It was hardly a typical map, she remembered. There was no outline of the peninsula and no geographical reference points. Instead, it had sketches of clues to look for along the way: a water hole, a picture of a stylized serpent, a cave, and then the diamond, placed like an offering on the altar of a stone temple with zigzag carving. Faded text running down the left side provided directions, with only one known location stated: *Start at the city of Merida.*

"You seemed to know about the misdirection, so I assumed you knew about the journal too." Rick lied, knowing darned well that if she had known about it, she would have shown a different kind of interest when she had seen all the copies in the shop. It had been nice to know his grandfather had left *something* for him to tell.

"Nobody breathed a word to me." She swatted a fly away from her arm. Lord, it was hot. "Suppose you fill me in."

He supposed he should. "Okay. I could show you better if we had time to look over the map, but the main point is that when the directions say to go southwest from Merida to an ancient ruin, you're really supposed to go southeast."

"The journal says that?"

"In a roundabout way." As he talked, he squinted up at the hazy glare of the sky. The breeze blowing through the henequen fields felt like a blast from a furnace. "There's a number on the map that appears to be a unit of measurement but it's actually a page number in the journal. On that page is an ancient native poem about the sun rising in the west and setting in the east."

"So you're supposed to reverse east and west?"

"Head of the class, Teach. My grandfather didn't catch on until he started after the Honeycomb Fire himself. When he couldn't find ruins where the map said they should be, it dawned on him that the number might refer to the journal where Richard had kept the map. Fortunately, he'd brought the journal along."

Melissa groaned. "And George didn't but he can find a copy in any tourist shop."

"Sure, but how's he going to know he needs it?"

"He'll catch on fast enough if Pedro's job includes turning over what he swiped from us," she said, her tone disgusted. "George is going to recognize it as the book where he found the map. Since you brought it he'll figure it's important. One good thing, we can get a copy if we need it—if only those creeps hadn't swiped all our money."

"Yeah," Rick said. "The map might have more tricks. We can't be sure. We're the first to try and follow it all the way." He saw that she had fashioned a sling from her scarf to carry the worthless statue. Why didn't she just pitch the damn thing? Shrugging, he continued. "Once my grandfather realized he was supposed to go southeast instead of southwest, he decided the ruins were most likely those of Mayapan, where the map marks a cenote. A cenote is—"

"I know what it is, I did my homework." She repeated what she had read in the guidebook. "Despite abundant rainfall, much of the Yucatán is dry, with its streams and rivers *under* the ground. When the limestone crust *breaks* through over a water source, the resulting sinkhole is called a cenote. It's a deep, natural well."

Rick grinned. "It sure is swell traveling with an educator. The problem is, Mayapan might be a misdirection, too. There's another number on the map by the sketch of the cenote. It could be a reference to a journal page where the author mentions the cenote at Chichen Itza."

"That's the famous one," Melissa said, referring again to what she had read. "That's a sacred well. Valuables and maybe human sacrifices were thrown in it to appease the rain god." In the back of her mind, she thought there was a big pyramid there, the kind she'd always wanted to see.

She said, "If you think we should go to Chichen Itza instead of Mayapan, why not go directly there?"

"Because I'm not sure. Suppose the number on the map doesn't mean what I think? We need to check out the cenote at Mayapan. If there's a carving or a serpent, we'll know we're on track. In any case, I want to buy another copy of the journal."

"Uh-huh, maybe get it with your charm?" She was being mean again, but so what?

"Something will come up," he said, not sure he was as confident as he sounded. "We'll get another copy at that shop near the hotel, find Alvero and go back to the airport. Everything will work out."

They hiked on in silence, Rick wondering where George was now. He wished they could set a faster pace, but he knew his ankle wouldn't stand up to it. He slid a glance at Melissa, taking in her bare arms, the tender flesh of her throat exposed by the open collar of her blouse. He had seen her apply sun lotion before they left the motel. It seemed a million years ago. He hoped she wasn't getting too much sun. Her skin was gold-kissed peaches and cream. He imagined its texture, imagined warm silk beneath his fingertips.

Abruptly she spoke, sounding troubled. "This business about the map and the journal working together can't be right. Your grandfather said that Don Miguel brought the Honeycomb Fire to Mexico during the time of Cortez. His map can't possibly contain references to a journal that wasn't written until the eighteen hundreds."

Rick made a face. "Don't you trust anything? The map we have is a copy of Don Miguel's original." Rick remembered loving the idea of having a Spanish adventurer as a forebear. "He came to the new world with an English wife and a big yellow diamond—both of them won in a gambling game."

"Trading a woman like property?" Melissa was momentarily sidetracked. "That's disgusting."

Rick's eyes glinted with amusement. "At least when he ran into trouble with the natives, he kept the wife and gave up the diamond."

"Shows he had some sense."

Yeah, sure, Rick thought to himself. He said, "The story is that he stumbled into a village that worshiped the god of bees. The villagers took one look at the honey-colored diamond and wanted it as a tribute to their god. They sealed the stone in the temple altar wall and that's where Don Miguel had to leave it."

"And that's where it still is today?"

"That's what we're banking on. Don Miguel intended to return and reclaim the stone only that never happened. Apparently, nobody looked at the map again until the eighteen hundreds. In the time of Don Miguel, the New World was a mystery, but by the time Richard came along, the ruins of Mexico had caught the public's imagination.

Richard thought the original map had become too obvious, so he made it more of a puzzle. He recopied it, adding clues that worked together with the journal. Understand now?"

She gave him a withering look. "I would have understood a lot sooner if someone had bothered to explain. What happened to Richard?"

"His luck with the natives was as jinxed as Don Miguel's. He ended up getting chased clean out of the territory."

Melissa rolled her eyes. "Poor Richard. And here I am, hooked up with his namesake."

"My luck will be better."

She sniffed. "So far, I'm not impressed."

Rick focused on a crossroad that showed up ahead. His instinct told him a right turn would lead back toward the city. He had just opened his mouth to say so when he heard an approaching vehicle.

Hearing it too, Melissa blanched. "Pedro . . . he's coming back."

Remembering their plan, Rick grabbed her arm and hauled her into the field of spiky, saw-toothed henequen. They flung themselves as flat as they could between the rows. Seeing Melissa's frightened face, Rick placed a reassuring hand on her shoulder. "Keep down. It's like I told you, nobody will look this way." He prayed he was right.

The rumble of an engine grew louder.

Cautiously, Rick lifted his head. "That sounds more like a truck. I don't think it's coming toward us. I think it's traveling along the crossroad."

Melissa's eyes widened with hope. "If it's somebody else, maybe we can hitch a ride."

"I'll check it out." Leaving her, Rick wormed back the way they had come. At the edge of the road, but still hidden in the field, he peered through the henequen and caught a glimpse of blue. Pedro's car had been a dull green.

"It's not them!" Jumping to his feet, he beckoned wildly to Melissa. "Come on." Shouting in Spanish, he staggered out to the roadway as a battered blue pickup truck started across the lonely intersection.

Melissa dashed past Rick. Waving her arms, her hair flying, she headed toward the truck, which was a broken-down pickup with no fenders, no doors.

Seeing her, the driver screeched to a stop. He stared in open-mouthed astonishment as she ran up to him.

"Please," she cried, gasping for breath. "Help us."

Still staring, the man slipped off his hat and clasped it soulfully to his chest. He was in his middle years, squat and homely. "Señorita?"

Before she could speak again, Rick caught up and addressed the driver in Spanish. After a brief conversation, the man nodded. Giving Melissa another awed look, he spoke again to Rick, then beckoned for them to get in.

"We're in luck," Rick said. "He's going our way and he'll drop us off near the hotel. By the way, good move with the damsel in distress act."

"It wasn't an act, and he's an angel."

"Yeah, well he says you're like a princess in an American picture book." At her expression of pleasure, he snapped, "Let's get this mutual admiration society on the move."

The ride in the blue truck was a memorable experience, Rick gripping a rope tied around the windshield to keep from falling out; Melissa, sitting in the middle with the freshly baked idol on her lap, jounced first against one man and then the other. She still considered the driver an angel, although at close range he didn't smell like her idea of a heavenly body. Not that she was in a position to criticize. It hadn't been a day when her top priority was wondering if her deodorant was working.

The driver stopped at their hotel. Climbing down stiffly, Rick and Melissa thanked him. On impulse, she fished the perfume from her blouse pocket.

"Give this to him," she said to Rick. "It's not much, but he may have a wife or daughter who might like it."

"You do the honors. It will mean more. Tell him this." Rick spoke words in Spanish which she repeated as she handed the perfume to the man.

To her surprise, the truck driver's swarthy complexion reddened as he shyly accepted the token. Looking flattered but embarrassed, he stammered his thanks then he gunned his engine and drove away.

Melissa frowned. "What did you have me say?"

"You told him, 'For one of your many sweethearts.'" He cocked an eyebrow. "Too flowery?"

"I guess not." She couldn't help laughing. "How did you learn Spanish? From Xavier?"

"Right. He'd learned to temper the Cuban accent when he went into medical practice." He glanced around, alert for danger. The streets seemed to be deserted, but he kept his eyes sharp. He had been fooled before. He wasn't about to have it happen again.

They crossed the street to the tourist shop that had copies of the journal, only to read a notice that it was closed until evening.

"Taking a long siesta," Rick said. He automatically looked for his watch, but it was gone. Pedro had swiped it, of course.

Melissa frowned. "I saw a shop at the airport. Maybe they have the books. If not, we'll have to come back here." She made a face. "How we're going to pay for it is still beyond me."

"I already told you," Rick said, annoyed. "I'll think of something. Actually, he had no idea what, which is what annoyed him. After another glance around, he steered Melissa into the front entrance of the hotel.

The lobby, with its potted palms, paneled walls of dark oak and faded oriental carpets, gave off an air of shabby respectability. Rick slid his gaze across the only occupant, an elderly woman sitting at a small table playing a game of solitaire. Reassured, he led Melissa to the main desk where he asked for Alvero.

"He's still on duty," Rick said to Melissa after a brief conversation with the clerk, "but the clerk's not sure where to find him."

"The plane must be ready. Maybe he's looking for us."

"I thought of that," Rick said. "He might keep checking the room he gave us to see if we've returned."

The idea of leading Melissa down the long carpeted corridor where the room was located rattled him. George could be anywhere. Suppose he was in the hotel? He sent a narrow-eyed glance around the lobby. If they ran into trouble, their odds would be best in the most public area.

He said to Melissa, "I'll see if I can find Alvero. You find a corner to wait in, okay? I'll be back in a flash."

CHAPTER TWELVE

AS HE STRODE OFF, Melissa saw the grime on the back of his shirt and his trousers. She realized she probably looked no better. A downward glance confirmed her guess—she was as filthy as if she had been on the road for weeks. The scarf had fallen away from the fake statue in her lap. If she rewrapped the statue and tied a stick to the bundle, her hobo costume would be complete.

"Excuse me." A fastidious male voice.

She turned to see a well-groomed older man wearing a crisp plaid shirt and well-pressed shorts. A camera on a strap hanging around his neck identified him as a tourist.

He gave her a purse-lipped, condescending smile. "Miss, do you by any chance speak English?"

Melissa took in his superior expression. A princess one minute, a pauper the next. Sure kept a girl from getting a swelled head. "Yes, I speak English. May I help you?"

"Perhaps." His eyes, pale and colorless behind expensive, yellow-toned sunglasses, had a shifty look that put her on her guard. "I couldn't help noticing the statue you're carrying. Might I see it?"

With a guilty start, she tightened her hold on the pottery, thinking he had recognized it as Pedro's work. If so, would it lead to trouble? Just as quickly she realized she was probably being ridiculous.

"Sure," she said, folding back the cloth so that he had a full view of the pottery figure.

He touched it with a reverent fingertip, his eyes glimmering avidly as he examined the same details that had so impressed her when she had first seen it herself. He gave her a sidelong glance. "May I ask how you came by this?"

She replied with a half-truth. "I found it in the middle of a henequen field."

When Rick returned ten minutes later, he found her where he left her. She started to say something, her expression eager, but he overrode her. "I found Alvero and wait until you hear this," he said, disgusted. "Shortly after he parked us here, George and Vince showed up and talked with him."

"With Alvero? Are you sure?"

"I'm sure. George told Alvero he had seen him driving with two friends of his from the United States and he described us. Alvero, trying to be helpful, explained we were waiting here for our plane to be repaired."

"And that's when George dreamed up his trick with Pedro," She made a sound of exasperation. "How soon can Alvero get us to the airport? If we can't find the journal there, we're going to have to come back and wait around until evening. I hate the idea of being in the city with George here, too."

"Agreed, but Alvero's still at work and can't leave the hotel for another hour." Rick wanted to be on the move. "Maybe we can hitch—" His eyes went wide. "What's that you're drinking?"

"Soda." She held up the bottle she bought from a hotel vendor. "Sorry, I forgot, I got one for you, too." She handed it over.

"Lady, you're a life saver." Gratefully, he unscrewed the cap and gulped the cool drink and then stared at her again. "Where did you get money for soda?"

Eyes sparkling, she lifted her hands with a flourish and fanned a row of tens and twenties. "For once, Malone, I'm loaded. We can catch a cab to the airport.

In the cab, Melissa explained how she came by her windfall.

"A man approached me and asked about the statue. There was something sneaky about him. She repeated the half-truth she'd told him.

Rick stared at her, not sure where the story was going except that it must be good if she had gotten money out of it. "You didn't mention that the statue was one of many?"

"He didn't give me a chance. He immediately turned official and asked to see the registration that authorized me to conduct an archaeological dig. I told him I didn't have one."

"That's sure the truth."

"Right. He then said it was against the law to remove artifacts from the country. I said I doubted it was an artifact. I told him I had originally planned to take it to a museum, except that the person who had been with me when I found it thought it was probably a reproduction."

"That's true, too," Rick agreed, fascinated. "I suppose this convinced him all the more that the statue was genuine?"

"He never said. What he *did* say was that if I turned it over to a museum, I would still get into trouble because the Mexican government is cracking down hard on archaeological theft. I would probably be put in jail."

"What?"

"For seventy-two hours without being charged, that's what the authorities can do here. He assured me I would probably be released as soon as I convinced them I'd intended no crime, but that the experience would be extremely unpleasant."

"What a shyster. Did he have a solution to your problem?"

Melissa smiled. "How did you guess? He explained *he* was connected with a museum. If *he* turned in the statue, there would be no unpleasantness, so I would be doing myself a favor to hand it over to him."

"Which you refused to do."

"I told him I would go to the museum with him and I wanted to go immediately."

Rick laughed. "Bet that thrilled him."

"Not exactly. He said it wasn't convenient for him to go to the museum today but he had another solution."

Rick burst into delighted laughter. "Why am I not surprised?"

"I have no idea. He said he felt sorry for me and really wanted to help. To save me from having to wait around until he could go to the museum, he would give me ten dollars for the statue. I said I was willing to wait. The price just kept going up, and well . . ." She gave him another smug smile. "As they say, the rest is history."

"History indeed." He realized he was having fun. Not so surprising, actually. From the first, there had been something about her company he enjoyed. Maybe the range of women he could find appealing wasn't as limited as he'd thought.

At the airport, the taxi dropped them off near the area for private aircraft. They found Teo inside the plane with the door open. Seeing their bedraggled appearance, his eyes widened. "What happened to you?

Rick shrugged. Before leaving the hotel he and Melissa had washed and cleaned up as best they could in the rest room, but with none of the shops open, they could do nothing about their ruined clothing.

"A small problem. It caused a delay."

Teo gave their appearance another look. "I left a message at the hotel to tell you the part for the plane arrived late. Where is Alvero?"

"We came on our own. Say, remember me telling you I'm a writer working on a magazine story? Well, it turns out there are a couple of men with a rival magazine who want to get the story ahead of me."

"Ah!" Teo's eyes brightened as if this story somehow explained the way they looked. "You are trying be first with the scoop?" He pronounced it "ess-co-op." It took Rick a few seconds to catch the meaning.

"Exactly. Earlier, you told us there wasn't another small plane available, but maybe these guys found one. Would you know if they did?"

"You think I make story so you will fly with me, no? I told you the truth. All other pilots had other jobs today. If your rivals want another plane, they must wait until daybreak."

"I hope they're waiting in a hotel full of roaches," Melissa said vindictively.

"Amen," Rick echoed to her and then turned back to Teo. "You said the part arrived late. Is the plane ready?"

"There's one more thing to adjust and check." Teo reached with his free hand for a wrench that lay near the open doorway.

"I'll help." Rick grabbed the wrench and climbed aboard the plane.

Melissa called up. "I'm going inside the terminal to check out that shop."

"Wait for me. I'll go with you."

"Don't bother. Help Teo and pray the shop has the journal so we don't have to run back to town." And risk running into George, she thought, suppressing a shudder. Seeing that Rick was about to argue with her, she waved a hand. "I'll be careful. Don't worry. I'll be right back."

The shop was further inside the terminal than she had remembered. A group of tourists traveling together stopped between her and her destination. She had to detour around them and couldn't see the shop clearly until she was almost upon it. Her heart leaped into her throat. Vince stood beside a magazine rack outside the shop's open door, lost in an X-rated tabloid. Three pieces of luggage sat unattended on the floor behind him. Melissa's eyes were drawn like a magnet to the corner of the book poking from the zippered side of a canvas bag. *The journal.* Not a new reprint. The one stolen from Rick. Then she saw George standing inside the shop at the cash register line, his back to her.

Her heart hammering painfully, she paused for only a second before making her decision. Slipping the journal out of the bag might not be as easy as it looked. She would snatch the whole bag.

Not even glancing to see if she might be observed, she glided smoothly forward, and passed behind Vince, slowing only enough to dip down and grasp the bag's handle. Booty in hand, she circled to go back the way she had come. Fighting the urge to run, she kept expecting at any moment to hear the dreaded cry, *Stop, thief!*

Not until after she was outside the terminal did she dare glance over her shoulder. There was nothing behind her except harmless travelers. She broke into a run, the bag bumping against her thigh as she reached the tarmac and dashed to where Rick and Teo stood beside the plane.

"Get in!" she yelled, praying the plane was ready. "Start the engine."

The two men stared at her stupidly.

"George is after us!" she cried, a statement she feared was all too close to the truth.

Taking action, Rick shouted to Teo, who responded by hurrying aboard the craft. Melissa flung the canvas bag inside ahead of her and scrambled in after it. Rick followed on her heels.

As Teo's small plane moved down the runway, Rick, not sure what was going on, said, "You're saying George was at the airport?"

"Yes. Look! This canvas bag is his. I stole it! I got your book back!"

Rick's mouth fell open. "I'll be damned."

With the plane still moving slowly, she looked out the side window and saw George standing outside the terminal, his fury-distorted face as red and congested as a man in the throes of a stroke.

"Poor George,'" she said with a laugh. "I would have loved seeing his face when he found his bag missing."

Rick spoke with a growl that hid his concern. "Yeah, and if he had realized a second sooner, you would have been caught. He and Vince must have been right on your tail."

She shrugged. "A miss is as good as a mile."

"God." Rick closed his eyes as he thought of what might have happened. Didn't she realize her close call?

Melissa realized indeed, but it was having the opposite effect from what Rick might have guessed. After all she'd been through and the resulting victories, she felt ready for anything. The Honeycomb Fire was as good as hers. She could practically feel the weight of the diamond in her hand. Sorting through George's bag further lifted her spirits.

"Look, his antihistamines—you said he pops them like candy. And here are water purification tablets, a flashlight and other camp and medical stuff. And, wow!" Her hand emerged from exploring a side pocket. "*Cash!* Enough for another plane ride."

Finally able to relax, Rick shook his head. "You've sure topped yourself this time, lady."

He laughed and told her about that time in grade school when George had such a difficult time when kids all brought the pets to school. He said, "I can imagine him now, hightailing it from shop to shop, trying to replace what you've relieved him of so neatly. He's going to have a fit if he can't get his usual brand of tablets."

With a satisfied sigh, he settled back. The quest for the Honeycomb Fire was turning out to be even more exciting than he had dreamed of as a kid. Of course, as a kid, he'd never imagined a partner like Melissa.

THE HIGH PRIEST PEERED up into the haze of the afternoon sky. As usual, he had accompanied the other men to work in the fields even though his legs tired easily and he needed assistance. All morning he kept to his task of guarding the water jugs. What danger might befall the jugs without his vigilance was anyone's guess but they all agreed it was good for a man to feel useful.

Lunch was now over and the men rested in the shade after hoeing the crops since sun-up. It was the hour when the priest usually fell into a nodding doze but today for some reason, he remained wakeful and alert.

Eduardo lighted a cigar and rested back in the long grass, idly listening to the conversation between the aged man and his son, Balam.

"The stone in the crown calls to her," the High Priest said.

"I am sure," Balam responded patiently as he assisted his father to his feet. "Come from the sun and into the shade. I will find you a comfortable place for your afternoon nap."

As the voices of the two men faded, Eduardo watched the smoke from his cigar lift and curl in the humid air. He wondered what

Balam thought of his father's gibberish. He also wondered how much money the diamond might bring to the village. Eduardo rubbed his bad shoulder. Balam was faithful to the old ways but how much more practical to exchange the sacred relic for cash. If it were sold, there would be no need to continue maintaining the traps and worrying about thieves like Benito Carranza.

When Eduardo thought of Carranza, bad feelings soured his stomach. Had he died in the jungle, which would only be fitting for such an animal, or had he survived? Apprehension gave Eduardo's stomach a cruel twist. If Carranza lived, there was trouble ahead. He would surely make another attempt to steal the diamond.

CHAPTER THIRTEEN

MELISSA'S AND RICK'S FLIGHT was uneventful except for the bouncing caused by a thunderstorm that came and went in fifteen minutes. Their landing on a tiny washboard of an airfield hacked from the surrounding rain forest rattled their teeth like loose seeds in a gourd but their feet were soon on firm ground.

Teo introduced them to his cousin, José, who had been waiting for them. The man's smooth golden complexion and characteristic hawk-nosed profile marked him as the possessor of Maya blood. After parting from Teo, José drove them in his Jeep to his home, where his wife invited them to share a supper cooked outside over a smoky fire that helped ward off the mosquitoes. Having gone without lunch, Melissa found herself ravenous. While the others kept up a lively conversation in Spanish, she devoured tortillas and a spicy stew of beans and goat meat.

After the meal, José and Rick went outside together. José's wife cheerfully waved Melissa away from helping with kitchen work. Pointing to Melissa's hair, which she had tied up when she'd washed before supper, José's wife had handed over a comb and directed her to a pleasant adjoining sitting room.

Rick returned alone and sat in an opposite chair. He started to say something to her when José's three-year-old daughter, Ofelia, skipped into the room. After giving Melissa a suspicious look, she went to Rick and reached up. He lifted her to his lap. Melissa frowned. Children usually went straight for her. What was Rick's big attraction? He grinned and raised his brows at the child. She giggled charmingly. Melissa got it. The child was a flirt. Rick's kind of gal.

Containing to smooth her hair, Melissa watched. Although the conversation was in Spanish she could follow along because the words and actions were self-explanatory.

In a teasing tone, Rick asked the child a question. She pointed to her chest and said, "Ofelia!"

Rick laughed and covered his eyes. "Where's Ofelia?"

"No, no!" the girl protested, laughing and trying to pull Rick's hands away from his face.

Rick then pinched her nose lightly and poked his thumb from between the fingers of his clenched hand as if he had her nose.

"No, no!" Ofelia giggled, grabbing his fist.

Melissa watched in fascination, seeing a side of Rick she hadn't expected. What she *had* expected was that he'd be annoyed at the child's interruption.

She saw him in a new light. Yes, Rick wanted the ranch, but he also had sincerely loved his grandfather. She also saw how high-handed Stanton had been in trying to run his grandson's life. Rick had refused to allow it. Two stubborn men, caring for one another, but neither one willing to take the first step. And then Rick had shown up with a fake fiancée, one he thought resembled his beloved grandmother. From then on there was nothing but trouble, and her worst trouble had been her false belief that Rick cared for her personally.

Now, they were partners in a race to find the yellow diamond—if it still existed. She trusted the bargain Stanton had made with her and yes, she would take money from a stranger if it meant her preschool. As for Rick, his mission was finding the diamond. Did he really want her along? Well, tough luck. She was sticking. They just had to stop snipping at each other.

Withdrawing from her thoughts, Melissa saw that Ofelia was

running a hand along Rick's cheek and chin. He laughed and removed the child's hands from his face. She put them back. His face showed a blue cast and the intrigued child kept running her plump fingertips over the roughness and giggling.

Ofelia's mother called. The child scrambled down and ran off.

"Found a new admirer, I see," Melissa said, but without the sourness she would have used earlier.

Rick laughed. "Yeah, that kid is really something." He turned serious as he leaned toward her. "We can borrow José's Jeep so we can go see the cenote."

"Now? It's getting on toward sunset." The events of the day had caught up and all she could think of was sleep.

"From what he said, we can be there and back by dark." He frowned. "He also said there are no ancient carvings."

"Then why are we going?"

"I need to see for myself. I explained that our magazine readers are hikers who like visiting sites with archaeological interest. If there are no carvings or statues we'll push on."

"It still sounds like a wasted trip. That temple on the map looks as if it has zigzag carvings. Does José know of any ruins with that sort of design?"

"No, but he says there could be anything in the wilds of Quintana Roo—including unfriendly natives determined to keep to the old ways."

"Let me guess," Melissa said. "They're descendants of the same groups who chased Richard."

"You've got it," Rick said. "The Chan Santa Cruz natives who were out to kill or enslave any non-Maya who stepped into their territory."

Melissa's hair now hung smooth about her shoulders. She continued to groom it, the comb gliding through the golden strands in easy, graceful movements that Rick found hypnotic. He had to blink twice before going on with what he had started to say. "My grandfather hammed up the story about Richard and the natives for all it was worth. He used to have me sitting on the edge of my chair."

Melissa smiled, imagining him as an eager little boy.

"Richard managed to escape," he said. "I could see him scrambling through the brush and swinging from vines like Tarzan. Somewhere after going through the cave, he found the zigzag ruin. What a thrill that must have been. And even more important, the altar was still intact. Before he could break into it, a different group of natives appeared. He had to leave the prize and run. He hid in the cave, scared to death that the guys from one side or the other were going to find him. Malaria fever caught up with him and with his last torch burned out, he was alone with no company except maybe bats."

As he told it, Rick remembered how the drama had gripped him. "He had no food and the only water was what dripped down the walls. Half dead, he eventually took a chance on making a break for it and he finally got back home. He intended to make a second try for the diamond, but he died before he could." He shook his head, thinking of the bitter disappointment.

"You're talking about going through the cave," Melissa said. "I thought it was simply a landmark that we'd pass on by."

Hell, he thought, taken down a peg. He had assumed his dramatic retelling of Richard's adventure had caught her under its spell, but she was fussing about the cave. "We go through it," he said.

"I don't suppose it's like a Bat Cave in Batman and Robin."

"No, it's a cave where winged mammals hang from the ceiling. What's the trouble?"

"I'm afraid of bats. When I was a kid, one of them flew into our house. It got into my hair." She saw his skeptical look. "They say it doesn't happen, but it does. I was fourteen, old enough to know what happened."

"Okay," he said slowly, still skeptical. "What happened?"

"I was upstairs in my bedroom, hanging my head upside down and brushing my hair and feeling sorry for myself."

"Run out of allowance, huh?"

She gave him an arch look. "No, I felt I was too tall and that I everybody was making fun of me behind my back. When I stood up, my frizzed hair must have added six inches to my height. I wished I had the nerve to wear it that way to school. The other kids thought I was too tall? I would show them *tall*."

He chuckled. "At fourteen I was convinced life was over if I didn't beef up. I pumped iron till I dropped."

He wore a short-sleeved shirt and she eyed his biceps, beautifully lean and strong, but what she said was, "Wasted effort, I see."

"Uh-huh." He chuckled. "So when does this monster bat come into the story?"

"When I heard a commotion from downstairs. It was my mother running around with a dish towel, trying to shoo a bat outside. I didn't know what was going on. I went to the head of the stairs. That's when the frantic bat sailed up and flew into my electrified hairdo. I went nuts. Yelled and screamed and tried to tear the bat loose as I ran into my bedroom. All of a sudden, the bat worked free. My window was open with no screen and it flew out." She shuddered. "The experience was *horrible*. I kept shampooing my hair. I even thought about cutting it all off."

He winced. "Please say you didn't."

She smiled. "Nobody would have noticed if I had."

"I would have." Unable to help himself, he leaned forward and reached to finger a honey-colored strand. "If I had gone to your school, I would have noticed."

"You wouldn't have looked twice," she retorted and moved her head, pulling her hair from his touch, yet all the same she was pleased. "Anyway, the point is, I definitely do not care for bats."

His fingers tingled and it seemed he could still feel the softness of her hair. "What I still don't understand is why you didn't know about the cave. It's marked as plain as day, a dotted line going in on one side and coming out the other. Didn't you study the map?"

"Apparently not enough. I hope you're wrong about bats. Going out tonight is enough to think of right now."

He got to his feet. "Stay here if you want."

"Nice try, Malone." Standing, she quickly braided her hair. "Any place you go, I'm sticking like glue."

He stared at her. "Are you saying I might cut out and leave you behind?" Is that what she thought about him?

Melissa narrowed her eyes. Did she really believe he might leave her stranded? No, she guessed not. In all they had been through, he had always acted . . . well, protective.

She stood and tucked her arm in his. "Off we go," she said sweetly, thinking that Rick was a carbon copy of his grandfather, always thinking he was right. Look at the times he'd assured her of his rightness whenever she put up a protest against something he wanted to do. Sometimes he *was* right, but that fake trip to the airplane in the henequen field had darned near killed them. But her keeping that statue that earned them money and then swiping George's canvas treasure trove were huge points on her side of the ledger—if she was keeping score. Which, she decided, she was.

CHAPTER FOURTEEN

THE ROAD TO THE CENOTE wound through trees, a logging route kept in fairly good repair. Rick stopped the Jeep by the roadside marker that José had told him to look for and climbed out. Melissa joined him, staring uneasily at a pile of stones topped with a beribboned metal cross. Did it mean somebody had died there? She decided it was better if she didn't know.

"Here's the path," Rick said. "Looks well used. José told me the cenote provides water for area families."

The thick trees sheltering the path made it seem as if night had fallen, but at the clearing where the cenote was located, the sunset sky overhead was still bright. The limestone sinkhole was about thirty feet across. The sheer sides dropped twenty feet to the water.

"They drink this water?" Melissa said, gazing dubiously into the algae-hazed surface, glad that her beverage that evening had been well-boiled coffee.

"José told me it's fresh water fed by an underground network of streams." On one side stood a wooden contraption and several ropes.

"Those ropes must be what they use when they lower their buckets down to where the water is fresh," Melissa said. "Or they could use those steps."

Rick, who had stopped to stand quietly in the hopes of gaining a sense of the place, frowned, distracted by her words. "What steps?"

"The ones leading down to that ledge." She pointed.

Limestone projections along one side of the cenote reflected the waning light. Rick, who hadn't noticed the projections until she pointed them out, shrugged. "Looks more like natural outcroppings."

"And that makes a difference?" Typical male behavior. If he didn't discover something, it might as well not exist.

Resuming his silence, he closed his eyes for a long moment and then opened them. The cenote was all wrong; he was suddenly positive. A bird called out a shrill, parrot-like screech. A rain forest was far from silent, he realized, becoming aware of a persistent background hum from living creatures: frogs, insects, lord knew what else, but to him, it was as if they were all saying, *wrong, wrong, wrong.* He circled the cenote and came back to his starting place. "There's nothing. You were right. The cave we want is south of Chichen Itza."

"Then we can save some time," she said. "New roads follow old trails, so the road from Chichen Itza to Quintana Roo is probably the same route that Don Miguel took when he first drew the map. We don't have to hunt for a cenote at Chichen Itza because we already know it exists. We can go south from that point without actually visiting the cenote."

Rick shook his head. "I'm following the map. If it says, go to a cenote, that's what we're going to do."

She was about to give him an argument, then a thought came to her. "Wait a minute, what about the steps?"

He gave her a questioning look.

"They may be natural outcroppings, but they still go up and down. If you would bother to look, you would see that they end where there might be a niche. Suppose the serpent carving is there?" As she spoke, she swatted away mosquitoes. Thanks to George's insect repellent they weren't actually biting, but they were still a nuisance. "I can't wait to get out of here but it does seem stupid to leave without making sure."

Rick sent a thoughtful look toward the shadows in the wall far below. "You could be right."

"Golly-gosh, do you really think so?"

He ignored her sarcasm. "I'll take a look."

The way down was easy except for a scare when a piece of limestone loosened from under his foot and fell. Feeling the strain in his bad ankle, he righted himself and looked down as the dislodged chunk splashed into the water. The disturbed surface of the pool rippled, and then calmed, reflecting a sky of purple-edged clouds. It made him feel disoriented as if he couldn't be sure which direction was up. He was glad when he reached the sturdy ledge.

Slipping George's flashlight from his pocket he found there was nothing more than a shadowy crevice behind the ledge. He poked his head in and shined the light around. There was no carving, no statue, no indication that the space had ever been used for anything.

After rubbing his ankle for a moment, he was preparing to retrace his steps when he saw Melissa starting down. "There's nothing to see," he called.

"Somebody's coming," she said in a hushed voice. Surprisingly surefooted in the waning light, she joined him. "I heard voices."

"Did you hear a vehicle?" Rick asked

"No, people walking."

"It's only somebody after water.'" He jostled aside to make room for her on the ledge, stepping partly into the crevice.

"I thought of that," she whispered, "only who would come so late? I suddenly started thinking, suppose it's George?"

"To track us here? That's impossible"

"Maybe, but so far this has been a trip where more things have gone wrong than right. We shouldn't take chances standing out in the open."

Rick suddenly heard voices too but he still didn't think the newcomers could have anything to do with George.

"We have to get out of sight," Melissa said in a panic, crowding against him.

"Okay," he said, figuring that teetering on a ledge over a cenote wasn't the best place for an argument. He backed into the crevice, pulling her in with him. There wasn't much room, but they were in deep shadow and fairly well concealed. He sat on a rocky shelf with Melissa between his knees, facing away from him and sitting back on her heels.

She tried to tell herself to calm down, but the approaching darkness seemed to magnify the possibilities of danger.

"There's only one roadway here," she whispered, turning her head toward Rick so the sound stayed within the enclosure. "If it's George and he sees the Jeep, he'll suspect it's us."

Figuring it was useless to reason with her, Rick shifted his position as much as he could in the tight space. His ankle ached and the wall behind him was chilly and rough. The small enclosure smelled of mold. Melissa had spooked herself but she was right about George being a problem. They couldn't keep on looking over their shoulders. He would have to find a way to put his ex-buddy out of commission for good.

He shifted again, discovering that by angling his head, his cheek rested against her hair. His one hand was clasped about her rib cage and he became aware of the soft weight of her breast resting just above his hand. There were worse places to be, he decided, beginning to appreciate the sweet pressure of her body snuggled between his thighs.

"They're coming closer," she said in a tight whisper, drawing back against the warmth of Rick's body. Thoughts of George filled her mind. Was any treasure in the world worth this kind of hassle? She would eventually have the preschool on her own. It might take years, but at least she would be alive to enjoy it. Her fingers touched something slimy-soft on the rock. Lizard, she thought, recoiling. But then, as she rubbed her fingers together, she realized what she had touched had only been moss clinging to a gritty niche. Still, it was disgusting. This place was horrible. If it wasn't for Rick's comforting presence, she wouldn't last another minute.

She tensed as the voices grew louder. Although she couldn't make out the words, she gradually realized that the cadence didn't sound like English. She started to think more logically. Even if George had managed to somehow fly to the jungle airstrip after them, he would need a vehicle to get to the cenote and there'd been no sound of that.

A masculine voice drifted down from somewhere overhead. Then a feminine laugh. She leaned forward to listen. Rick frowned at the chill he felt when Melissa's movement put a space between them.

The words sounded like the Maya language. "You were right," she whispered to Rick. "It's people coming after water."

"Yeah, but . . . ." He pulled her back against him, blissfully enjoying her soft warmth. From nowhere, he was inspired to whisper, "It may be a bandit."

Startled, Melissa gasped. "What?"

"Bandits bring their women along," he said, gratified that her surprise had her snuggling closer. By some miracle, her breast had settled gloriously in his palm. "Don't move," he murmured. "We've got to stay just as we are. The forest may be full of them."

Confused, Melissa heard a feminine laugh from above. Before she could say anything more, Rick dipped his head so that his lips touched the incredibly soft flesh behind her ear.

Another laugh drifted down to them, the tone seductive. An answering murmur came from the man. The voices seemed to be moving away.

"We can't take anything for granted," Rick cautioned, moving his other hand in a gentle caress. "We've got to stay put until we're sure."

"It's lovers," Melissa hissed. Where had he gotten this stuff about bandits? "Lovers," she repeated. "That's what they are."

From the shadowy distance, a faint, feminine exclamation of pleasure was echoed by a triumphant male chuckle, all of it lost in the chattering as the birds called to one another.

"Wow," Rick said, his breath soft against her ear. "I guess you're right." He nuzzled her cheek. "This is embarrassing. We can't just jump out on them."

"No, we—" Melissa suddenly became aware of Rick's lips moving against her skin, became aware of the warm position of his hand. She realized also how good it felt, both the kiss and the caress. Damn him. He had been teasing, taking advantage. Bandits. How could she have fallen for such a line? He was impossible. The situation was so ridiculous she couldn't even be mad, but she knew what she could do.

"Rick . . ." She made her voice a sigh. "What should we do? Just stay here?"

"I guess." He spoke against her hair. "I guess we'll have to." He grinned. What punishment, cruel and unusual. No telling how long they would be trapped there together.

To his delight, she started angling herself around to face him, moving cautiously on her knees so that no sound could be heard above. As if anybody up there was listening. His pulses jumped as Melissa drew even closer.

"Rick . . ." She lifted her hands to his shoulders. "When I thought it was George, I was so frightened."

At least that's what he thought she said. He wasn't really listening. She felt so good in his arms. He drew kisses along her jaw, kissed her ear, her eyes. "It's okay now," he murmured. "It's okay."

"It's okay because I'm with you."

His heart gave a leap as a sense of pride and power surged through him. There were no longer any thoughts about whether she was his type or not. She depended on him, she needed him.

"Lissa . . . ." There was something important he wanted her to know. "Lissa, what you said earlier about me leaving you? I never would. I'm not after your share; you've got to believe it."

"It doesn't matter," she murmured, thinking only of the lesson she was about to teach him. Her arms went around his shoulders, one hand tangled in his hair. The strands, thick and soft, tangled vibrantly around her fingers. She bent forward, her lips finding his.

He was thrilled to have her act as the aggressor.

"You're wonderful," she whispered, her voice a breath of sound.

She moved against him in the most fabulous way. Desire became a pulsing ache as he gathered her close. He felt her other hand move to join the first as she nestled closer. Shuddering, he closed his eyes. What she was doing now . . . he could barely breathe.

Her lips sought his again as her fingers toyed gently with his shirt collar, easing it from the nape of his neck, caressing, teasing. She seemed to be doing something with his shirt only he didn't care what as long as she kept kissing him, whispering so softly, pressing her body so sensuously against his.

Then he felt it and gave a jerk. Sliding down under his shirt and over his skin was something cold and damp and decidedly unpleasant.

"Shhh," Melissa whispered, firmly gripping his one shoulder as she smothered her laughter. "We don't want to disturb the lovers, do we?" She unfolded her clenched fist completely, dumping the rest of a handful of slimy moss and grit down his back.

CHAPTER FIFTEEN

MUCH LATER THAT EVENING, Melissa lay in an incredibly comfortable Yucatán hammock hung outside of José's hut. A welcome breeze cooled the summer night. Her thoughts were on Rick, who slept in his own hammock not five feet away. The taste of his kisses lingered on her lips, her body still tingled from his caresses.

She couldn't be on the verge of falling for him all over again, could she? She knew firsthand the kind of woman who truly caught his eye: the flirty car rental girl and the woman with the tiger-striped coulotte. That seemed so long ago, but nothing had changed. If he was acting differently now it was only because she was handy. As for her response to him? Her gaze lifted to the sky where southern stars formed in unfamiliar constellations. Everything was so different here, with Rick the only known entity. That's all it was.

In his own hammock, Rick lay with a blissful smile on his face.

After Melissa's lousy trick, which he knew he deserved—although it had been worth it—she had turned away and given him the silent treatment. It hadn't been an angry silence, however. Everything in her manner had spelled satisfaction. *Fixed him*, that's what she'd been thinking. He saw as clearly as if he could read her mind. *Fixed him good.*

Figuring it best not to get himself in any deeper, he'd kept quiet until he was pretty sure the lovers must have left. Then he had cautiously suggested they leave. Let her think her silence had cowed him, he'd thought, amused. Making their way by starlight, they had gone up the way they had come down. Without further incident, they left the cenote, Melissa still refusing to favor him with a direct word. Oh yeah, he thought, his smile broadening, she was quite the character. Hard to remember he had ever had a lukewarm reaction. Definitely not lukewarm now, better believe it, he thought, shifting uncomfortably. He burned for her, damned if he didn't.

He forced his mind to the conversation he had with Teo before they had landed. If this cenote wasn't the correct one, José would return them to the airstrip to meet Teo who would fly them to Piste, a town near the ruins of Chichen Itza. Rick had explained he wanted to avoid the risk of running into his "magazine rival." Actually, Rick's real hope was to find someone in Piste with whom he could make a deal to solve the problem of his back-stabbing buddy, George.

Unbidden, his thoughts returned to Melissa, lying so close, yet so far away. The way he was starting to feel about her . . . .

Damn, the last thing he needed was more complications. He frowned up at the stars wheeling overhead, feeling as if he were the one doing the spinning. His relationship with women had always been so simple. Mutual lust, a few laughs, and then goodbye without regrets. It would be different with Melissa. She was the serious type, the kind he always had the sense to steer clear of, and yet, he couldn't deny he was drawn to her. No answers, no solutions. Staring at the unfathomable stars, Rick continued to spin and burn until sleep finally took him.

IN THE MORNING, HE told Melissa about the arrangement he had made with Teo the day before. "The airport is in a town called Piste. That's right near Chichen Itza. We couldn't ask for anything better."

She looked up from refolding clothes that had been in George's pack. There had been a T-shirt that fit Rick and she'd taken a khaki shirt. It hung off her shoulders, but at least it was clean. As for the rest, she was trading for items with José's wife. "Nothing better except skipping the ruins entirely," she said.

He brushed off her comment. "Teo knows someone in the town who might rent us a car, and he told me where to find him. By this time tomorrow, we should be well into Quintana Roo." There was another matter to take care of in Piste, but he wasn't going to talk about it until he knew it would work out.

After breakfast, José returned them to the airstrip and Teo. They took off, Rick in the co-pilot's seat, barraging Teo with questions as they passed over miles of flat, tree-covered landscape.

Sitting behind the pilot's seat, Melissa had a view of Rick's profile—the proud line of his nose, his firm chin. He needed a shave. One thing that hadn't been in George's pack was a razor. At breakfast little Ofelia had shied away from him, apparently having decided he had become too strange. He had been put out by the child's rejection, which made Melissa laugh. When he wasn't being infuriating, she found him a thoroughly entertaining man. She still had to smile over the way she'd outsmarted him the night before. He had his good points but she was keeping her wits about her, especially when it came to anything personal. Despite the times he had put her welfare ahead of his own, she couldn't forget how he had used her. She wasn't letting down her guard.

When Rick helped her down from the plane in Piste, she couldn't help smiling at his expression when he saw she had covered her hair with a black shawl she had gotten from Jose's wife. She'd bartered for it with items in George's pack.

He raised an eyebrow. "In mourning?"

"Trying to avoid it. When George comes along, he'll ask questions. We're tall and foreign but at least my hair color won't stand out." With an air of satisfaction, she added, "That's also why Ofelia was shy with me, the color of my hair."

"Nah, she just liked me better."

"Until this morning."

"Ummm." He rubbed his jaw. "I've got to do something, don't I? You like your men smooth?"

She looked bored. "What I like or don't like in that department can't possibly be any concern of yours."

"Uh-huh," he said, telling her he knew better.

"Uh-huh," she said, reconfirming her original statement and telling him he was wrong. It was then that she noticed a trio of unsavory-looking characters lolling near a shed. One of them, a man with bull-like shoulders and a fat stomach straining the seams of a soiled shirt, had an especially menacing stare.

"Let's see about renting the car," she said, wanting to be on their way as quickly as possible.

Eyes narrowing, Rick followed her gaze and spotted a mean-looking customer giving her the once-over. Damn, that had to be the guy Teo had said might help solve his George-problem. And best to keep Melissa out of the way.

"This is a town where men make the deals," he told her. "You had better wait in the snack shop." He gestured to a lean-to with an open counter that looked out on the airport buildings. "Teo said if we needed any help we could ask her. She's okay, she's Teo's sister-in-law.

Melissa's eyes widened. "Is there anywhere that man doesn't have relatives?"

"Beats me." Rick chuckled as he led her to the shop.

RICK'S MEN-ONLY DEAL took longer than Melissa had anticipated. Wandering a bit from the snack shop she found a place to buy underwear and toiletries and a long-sleeved shirt, and then she returned to where Rick had left her. It was well over an hour before she saw him appearing from behind a gaggle of tourists. Bidding Teo's sister-in-law a hasty goodbye, she hurried to meet him.

"Where have you been? I was—" She broke off, sniffing the air. "You've been drinking?" She could hardly believe it. There she had been, pacing the floor and gnawing her nails to the quick, and he had been off swilling alcohol.

"A few beers to be sociable," he said. It was the middle of the morning and hardly his drinking time, but he'd had good reasons. "You were worried about me?" The idea clearly intrigued him.

"Yes, but don't puff yourself up." His lack of consideration had wounded her, not that she intended to admit it. "We're in this together, you know."

He grinned. "You were worried about me. Come on, fess up."

She lifted her chin. "We have a deadline. To think you've been wallowing away our time in some bar. It's appalling."

Smiling, he reflected on the time when he had been convinced she lacked spunk. It was true he had been in a bar but he hadn't been wallowing. Still, because she had accused him of it, he decided to let her stew a bit before he explained. Flourishing a hand, he directed her attention to a car that had been hidden by the crowd of tourists who had now moved on.

"Lady, your carriage awaits."

Melissa looked and saw a relic of the Fifties, with raised tail fins and colored turquoise and white. She tightened her lips. If this ancient wreck was supposed to justify his long absence, she wasn't impressed.

"They stopped making those ages ago," she said "Does it even run?"

"Like a top." He had never driven a car like it before and was going to enjoy the experience. "We're to deliver it to the same town in Quintana Roo that we're heading for. And we only have to pay for the gas."

She missed the charm entirely. "What's this boat get, four miles to the gallon? We'll end up broke all over again."

"We'll do fine," he said, offended, by her criticism. Where did she get off finding fault with every decision he made?

She folded her arms. "Easy for you to say. It's money I got us that you're burning."

He felt his hackles rise. "What are you saying? I'm not pulling my share of the load?"

"What I'm saying is you snipe about me and money, like accusing me of buying luxuries and shipping them home." She was in earnest, her cheeks pink. "I've always been careful and I resent you acting as if I'm some kind of a spendthrift."

He blinked at the turn of their argument. His teasing about luxuries had been so long ago he'd forgotten about it. Before he could respond, she said loftily, "It's true that when we met I was in debt, but—"

"Okay," he said. He hadn't meant to get her really upset.

"Okay, *what*?" she asked suspiciously. "My being in debt certainly wasn't a familiar condition, and I'm sick and tired of—"

"Okay, I'm swearing off. No more cracks about money as long as you leave the subject alone too." Before she could say anything else, he said, "Do we use this car, or not?"

"Yes, of course," she snapped. Getting him to agree hadn't been as satisfying as she had anticipated. After all, *some people* didn't worry about money because they were counting on a big inheritance. So there.

The ride to Chichen Itza was as smooth as Rick had promised, but instead of enjoying it Melissa worked on her second annoyance—why did he insist on visiting the cenote? He *knew* it was the one on the map. Taking the time to go there was dumb. Bet your bottom dollar George Keating wasn't wasting *his* time on foolishness.

Upon arriving, they paid for their tickets to tour the ruins, which consisted of acres of mown grass studded with reconstructed buildings. They were magnificent. This was exactly what Melissa had always dreamed of seeing, but she couldn't enjoy it. After all, she muttered to herself, this wasn't a sightseeing trip.

In a far different frame of mind, Rick enthusiastically gazed around as they followed the signs to the cenote. "Imagine, when Don Miguel breezed through here in the sixteen hundreds this place was still alive."

"Which is the way I would like to keep us," Melissa said shortly, looking around but only to make sure no danger lurked nearby. After all that had happened, keeping a weather eye out had become second nature.

Rick remained unperturbed by her lack of enthusiasm. "I wonder how it felt to be one of the conquistadors."

Not answering, Melissa supposed he fit the romanticized image of a conquistador himself, lean and bronzed, his dark eyes alight with adventure. He was still one of the best-looking men she had ever spent time with but super illogical. She gave another guarded glance around, making sure the other tourists were as innocent as they appeared.

She suddenly grabbed Rick's arm, bringing him to a halt.

"Look." Excited, she pointed toward an open-roofed colonnade called the Temple of the Warriors. Behind a central statue were huge twin columns in the shape of serpents. "Those columns. Couldn't either one of them be the serpent that's drawn on the map?"

Rick stared, and then laughed aloud. "Damn, you've got a good eye." On the map, the serpent was sketched as if it rested on its belly, but the column had the huge jaws of the serpent on the ground with its tail in the air. "I was looking for it the other way around. I would have missed it."

"Well, then, we've found our clue." Melissa sighed in relief. "We know for sure this is the right place. Now we can move on."

"Not without seeing the cenote first," Rick said. "We're too close not to take a look."

Melissa threw up her hands in disgust. "You complain about how stubborn your grandfather is. You're about the same."

"Me?" Walking on, he felt oddly pleased to be compared with the old man, even in the negative. "How about you? Who are you like? How come money is such a touchy subject? That heredity, too?"

She made a face at him. "My father took off and mother was left alone to raise me. There wasn't anything extra, but we managed. And," she interjected pointedly, "we *always* paid our bills on time."

He ignored the jab. "Where's your mother now?"

"She died before I started college."

"I'm sorry."

"Thanks. Can't we walk any faster?"

"Sure." He grabbed her hand and quickened his step, relieved that his ankle was feeling good again.

The trail to the sacred well was a grassy path leading through the trees. The scent of the water came to meet them in advance, a faint algae odor mixed in with the fragrance of a red-flowered shrub that tangled along the walkway. They reached the end of the trail and found they had the place to themselves.

Having seen one cenote, Melissa figured she had seen them all, but as she stared at the immense sinkhole, she was unable to restrain a gasp. "This is huge! Two or more of José's cenotes could drop in here with room to spare."

Rick was equally amazed. The guide sheet had said eighty feet deep, but he still hadn't been prepared for the immensity.

Mesmerized, Melissa stared into the greenish water lying so far below. How would it have been to have lived here centuries ago when sacred ceremonies were still performed?

Somehow she and Rick had continued to hold hands. He tightened his grip. Wincing, she glanced up and saw his faraway expression. "They were here," he said softly. "I can feel it. They were here. That's what was missing at the other place."

Startled, Melissa wasn't sure what to think. "Don Miguel and Richard?" she questioned, staring at him. "You think you can sense their presence?"

"Something like that." He gave her a look that dared her to make something of it. "This place feels right. The other place didn't, okay?"

She frowned. Malone was an Irish name and the superstitions from the ancient Druids and Celts may have included a penchant for second sight. Who would have guessed she would hear this sort of talk from this blunt-talking man of action.

CHAPTER SIXTEEN

IT WAS LATE AFTERNOON. The men were home after completing their day's work in the fields. Seated in the lean-to which contained the village's old short wave radio, Eduardo finally made contact with a hospital on the Caribbean coast where Kan, who had been injured in the skirmish with Carranza's henchmen, had been taken for surgery. With much relief, Eduardo learned that Kan would regain the full function of his hand.

Eduardo thanked the operator, shut down the radio and carefully covered it with a plastic tarp that protected it from the weather. He then started the short walk to the hut he shared with his wife and daughter. The slanting sun showed the fading colors on the massive blocks of stone that ran along the dusty path. Simple huts now stood where once there had been a great city. Finding it painful to think of the grandeur his people had known in ancient times, Eduardo quickened his step. Coming to the front of his thatch-roofed home, he found his young daughter and her friends sitting outside dipping threads into liquid dyes.

Eduardo's wife looked up from the hearth where she cooked dinner. "Have you heard? The High Priest asked us to prepare for a celebration. I will make a fruit sauce with honey to serve over small cakes."

Eduardo gave her a blank stare. As third in command, he should have been consulted if there was to be a special event.

His daughter held up a colorful length of cloth. "Look, Papa. My friends and I are decorating our capes for the celebration. We're dyeing thread to embroider new designs."

Eduardo smiled in brief acknowledgment of his daughter's work, then turned back to his wife. "Kan will be able to use his hand again, which is reason to make merry but the High Priest can't be talking about that because I haven't yet told him."

"I don't know his reasons," Eduardo's wife said. "He didn't explain. Perhaps we are to prepare for the return of the goddess. Has he not been saying that the stone in the crown calls to her?"

Eduardo snorted. "How does Balam respond to this notion?"

Although the High Priest was chief and most revered, his son Balam was the true head of the village. Childish as it was, Eduardo suddenly found himself wishing that the stories of the goddess were true. If only she *would* come to reclaim her treasure. If the diamond in the crown couldn't be used to aid the village, it was nothing but a curse. So let her claim it and at long last free the People of the Goddess from the threat of ruthless thieves.

"Balam says we should heed the wishes of his father," Eduardo's wife replied. "How many more celebrations can the old one enjoy? We should humor him. Besides, the good news about Kan makes sense of it." Her eyes showed a sudden sparkle. "The village has been unsettled since the attack. With Kan recovering, is it not time to rejoice in our deliverance?"

"Yes, you are right." In the face of his wife's enthusiasm, Eduardo forced a smile but the attack on the village was vivid in his mind. He could only wonder how much more blood would be spilled for the sake of the Honeycomb Fire.

RIDING IN THE FANCY old car, Melissa sighed and relaxed against seat cushions that had only a few rips mended with black electrical tape. She said, "I know George can't catch up so fast, but I'm glad we're on the move again."

Rick figured it was time to tell her. "I took care of him."

"Who, George? What do you mean?"

"Teo told me of a man that could help. He's going to watch out for George and Vince. That's why I was gone so long."

She frowned. "What do you mean, *watch out*? How's that supposed to help?"

"He's going to hold them for us."

"You mean, like prisoners? Who would go for a scheme like that?"

"This guy. Benito Carranza. He didn't even blink."

"Is he *another* one of Teo's relatives?"

"No, Teo doesn't even like him." Rick hadn't much liked him either, even after three beers, but he figured he didn't have to. "He's tough. He's a pilot and he's been a bounty hunter tracking escaped convicts through the jungle. Work has been slow and he's hungry to make a few bucks. You should have seen his smile when he heard my magazine will pay a reward for keeping my rival off my trail."

"More lies about your mythical magazine."

"Yeah, well, everybody can't have your scruples and it's a damn good thing. Carranza has friends throughout the area. They'll make sure George and Vince don't slip through their net. He has a place where he can hold them, not hurt them or anything, just hold them. When we come back this way, we'll hand over his reward. By that time we'll have the diamond, so my grandfather won't balk at wiring us the money. I'll pay him back later."

She gave him a surprised look. "You'll pay him back?"

He looked puzzled. "What else do you do with a loan?"

She said, "I thought the whole idea of this trip was getting your inheritance. Why not just take it out of that?"

"This trip is about my grandfather and me."

He'd said that before and now she guessed she believed it. She said, "After what George hired Pedro to do to us, it seems fitting to make him a prisoner. When this is all over, what's going to happen to George?"

"The police, I guess. Do we care?"

"Maybe we don't."

Atta girl, he thought with an inward smile. Mean Melissa.

"I'm glad we're staying in a town, tonight," she said in a change of subject. "It will be wonderful to have a hot bath and the chance to wash out a few things." It was also wonderful not to have to worry about George. "Maybe we can find a pretty hotel."

"Okay," he said slowly. "I'll see what I can do." *Pretty hotel? Wash out a few things*? Was this a vacation? His inward smile turned tender. She was a damned good sport. Why shouldn't she have the best?

A signpost at the start of the southbound highway marked their destination, *Felipe Carrillo Puerto*.

"The town used to be called Chan Santa Cruz," Rick said, turning the car onto the highway. "Named after the Indians in my grandfather's stories about Richard."

"The ones who chased him into the cave?"

"Right. He arrived shortly after the Maya rebellion against the Spanish, and—"

"The Caste War," Melissa interrupted, having seen the term in her guidebook.

"Right on, Teach. You also know about the flying ant?"

"The flying what?"

"Guess not." Rick looked smug. "The Maya had almost won the war to take back their land, but on the brink of victory, they saw the flying ant. Its appearance was a sign of the rains and the time for the planting season. The Spanish couldn't believe it but the Indians simply laid down their weapons and returned home to their villages to plant corn."

"That makes me like them. What good does it do to win the battle if the families back home starve?"

"Nice sentiment, but no way to win a fight. Their departure gave the non-Maya settlers time to get help. Soldiers poured in and the slaughter began. Indians were killed left and right. Some of them escaped to the jungles where they banded together and revived the cult of the Talking Cross."

"*Revived*? You don't mean that. They didn't have the cross until the Spanish introduced Catholicism. The cross is a Christian symbol."

"Not necessarily." She thought she had all the answers, did she? "The Maya had a pre-Columbian cross that represented the gods of the four cardinal directions. They later tied this in with the Christian symbol for what my grandfather called the 'double whammy.' The scheme was put together by a trio of revolutionaries who holed up in Quintana Roo—a priest, a spy and a ventriloquist. Growing up, I suspected the old man of telling tall tales but records showed it to be true. Through the ventriloquist, the cross 'spoke,' giving the rebels the courage and inspiration to keep up the resistance. They called themselves *Chan Santa Cruz*, 'people of the holy cross.' They held control of Quintana Roo for years. They were a rough lot and it was a place where they made their own rules."

"*Back then*," Melissa emphasized. "Now it's a state."

"Sure, but the jungle is still the jungle—bad water, mosquitoes, poisonous snakes." Talking about it made him appreciate the difference between himself as a kid and as an adult. Back then he could only see the adventure now, although he was still raring to go, he could also see the risks.

They reached town and stopped at the nicest hotel, the lobby featuring the Moorish tiles that spoke of the Spanish Colonial period.

While Rick spoke to the woman at the desk, Melissa started having second thoughts about such nice accommodations. How much money did they have left? They each had a share of George's money and Rick had taken care of their flight expenses from Mayapan, and then he went off on his own at the airport, presumably spending more. She had lost track of their finances. Maybe the hotel was too much of a splurge. Before he could sign the register, she drew him away from the desk.

"Do we have enough to pay for this?"

He lifted an eyebrow. "Right, we're economizing. We ought to save by bunking in together."

"Come on. If we really can't afford this hotel—"

"It's okay, honest." Ironic how he had chosen to razz her about

137

money. Their upbringing had given them such different views. Because of her hard times, she had learned to hold on tight while he had learned to relax and enjoy when he could.

The bellboy insisted on carrying her "luggage," which consisted of a string bag containing items that Melissa had bartered from José's wife. Rick's luggage was George's canvas bag.

Her room was at the end of a hallway near a secluded courtyard. Rick dismissed the boy with a tip. "Tonight we'll find a good place for dinner. Something more special than the hotel dining room." Smiling down at her, he was thinking that the evening would be as much fun as he could make it. He liked imagining the pleasure he would see on her face. "You take a nap, rest up for a big evening. I'll get the supplies we'll need, deliver the car, then take a rest myself."

Something in his manner made her suspect he was up to something. She lifted her chin. "We'll visit the market together. And I'll ride along when you return the car."

"Sure, but I figured you were tired."

"I am, only—" Wondering why she bothered to pussy-foot around, she blurted, "Maybe you wouldn't leave me stranded, but that still doesn't mean you might not take the car and go off on your own."

"Go off where?" Her words made no sense to him.

She stiffened her spine. "Finding the Honeycomb Fire was your boyhood dream. Suppose you've started thinking you don't want to share the thrill of finding it? You and your jungle horror stories."

"You thought I was trying to scare you?"

"Maybe. If you've got any such ideas, I'm putting you on notice. I've more than earned the right to find the diamond along with you, and it's a right I'm willing to fight for."

"For crying out loud! I was trying to show some consideration. The only thing I was scheming was showing you a nice evening. Hell, you see nothing but plots against you."

She flushed, knowing why she was raising a fuss. She had fanaticized he was interested in her once and she'd been wrong. Now she was on the verge of letting her guard down again. Was she making a mistake?

She had to be sure. "It wouldn't be the first time you cooked up a plot involving me. You *used* me. I haven't forgotten."

"Well, I have." It seemed so long ago as if they weren't even the same people that they had been then. Her doubts wounded him. "We're supposed to be partners, lady, and one of us at least is taking it seriously. Here—" He tore his bag open to show what was in it, then tossed it inside her room. "Take all the stuff, take the journal. Where am I going to go without that?"

"Rick, wait, I—"

Ignoring her words, he propped a hand against the corridor wall to steady himself as he ripped the map from beneath his ankle bandage. He thrust it into her hands. "Now you've got that too, and here—" He yanked a roll of bills from his trousers pocket and shoved that at her.

"Rick." She didn't know what to say, what to do.

He turned his empty pockets inside out. "There, are you satisfied?" His face was flushed with emotion. "All I've got left are the keys and if I fail to deliver the car on schedule, every guy in this town will be out for my blood. We just got rid of George. You think I want a new posse on our trail?"

Overwhelmed, she tried to explain. "I only thought—"

"I know what you thought."

"Come on, this is ridiculous."

"Damned right but it wasn't my idea."

"I know and I apologize." Guessing she had better demonstrate her good faith, she handed back the roll of bills. "Here, if you want to do the shopping by yourself, go ahead."

He accepted the money, but he still wasn't mollified. What kind of skunk did she think he was? It was important what she thought of him. He hadn't realized until now just how important.

He took a deep breath, trying to calm down. "Maybe you're justified in feeling a little bit suspicious, but damn it, I thought I already made myself clear. I'm not after your share."

A *little bit suspicious*? His choice of words set her off again. She tossed her head. "I never accused you of wanting to take the diamond away from me. The way your grandfather set it up, I knew I was protected."

His face darkened with indignation. "And you think that's what rules me? I'll tell you the real reason. It's because that's not our deal, that's why. I care about finding the diamond, yes, but I don't care two pins about owning it. I did some things that were wrong and I admit it, but even if I cared about being rich, which I don't, you've got no idea how wealthy my grandfather is. What he's willing to pay you for the diamond is a drop in the bucket."

"You seemed shocked enough when you heard me ask for it."

"Only because he was allowing you to bargain. Usually, once he makes up his mind, that's it."

She had no trouble believing that. "Okay, so you weren't trying to grab my share but that's not what had me worried."

"Then what in the devil did?"

"I told you. I thought you wanted to find the diamond all by yourself."

"Damn it, I never thought any such thing. Sure, finding it was my dream but cheating you out of being there too? Jeez." He ran a hand through his hair. "Where did you get such an idea?"

"I'm just saying what I thought."

"A dumb thought."

"Maybe it was." She gave him a weak smile.

He gave a gruff nod. "What we both need is some rest. I'll call for you around seven and we'll do the town, okay?"

From now on, he thought as he left, he would make sure he was one hundred percent straight with her. There wouldn't be a single thing he said or did, that would give her cause for doubt.

Inside her room, Melissa stood blankly for a moment, replaying her quarrel with Rick and remembering how her suspicions had appalled him. Loyalty rated high on his scale. That's what had upset him most about George, wasn't it? He had believed they were friends, only George had betrayed him. Thinking it over, she decided that Rick was now applying the same high standards of loyalty in his relationship with her. They had an agreement to get the diamond together and welshing on a deal simply wasn't part of his character. He was someone she could trust after all.

Feeling better about him than she had felt at any time since the trip had begun, she examined her room, which had tiled walls and a decorated ceiling from which a fan spun slowly over the double bed. There was also—hoorah!—an air conditioner. She turned it up to high and stood blissfully in front of the chilly blast as she stripped. Gathering her soiled clothes she scrubbed them in the bathroom sink, then draped them over a chair in front of the air conditioner to dry.

The bathroom had no shower stall and no curtain, just a spray fixture in the corner of the tiled room and a drain in the floor. Weird, but it looked like it would work fine. As insurance, she left her towel hanging on the outside of the door where it should stay dry.

She took a shower and washed her hair, wanting to look as nice as possible for the evening ahead. Lately, all she had been was grubby. How had Rick been able to stand looking at her?

Naked and clean, she slipped into bed for a nap, realizing how tired she was. What a day. She had been awakened at dawn by a crowing rooster and had been on the go ever since. *So close*, she thought, thinking of the Honeycomb Fire. Thank God she no longer had to worry about George. That was another thing she had to thank Rick for.

They were honestly partners, she thought. Closing her eyes, contentment coursed through her and followed her into sleep.

WHEN RICK'S KNOCK SOUNDED, the sun was lowering in the sky. Melissa was ready to go except for her shoes. She opened the door, seeing his tall frame silhouetted against the light slanting across the open courtyard behind him. He moved and she could see him more clearly. There was something rugged and tough in the hewn lines of his freshly shaven face, something arrogant in the tilt of his head. His slight smile quickened her pulse and made her wonder if he were ready for something other than simply the nice dinner he'd spoken of. He wore a new shirt. It was a pale blue guayabera, the native style garment with pleats down the front.

"Nice shirt," she said.

He grinned. "Didn't cost a cent. You bartered for your new outfit, I wagered for mine."

"Oh?" She tilted her head. "Like how?"

"I'll explain later." Appreciatively, he took in the picture she made in the *huipil* she had gotten from Juan's wife. It was a native sack dress of white cotton, sort of like a fancy pillowcase, with embroidered flowers on the square neckline and the hem. It was a style worn by every Maria, Rosa and Inez all through the Yucatán, but he'd never seen one look so good.

Made self-conscious by his stare, Melissa fluttered a hand. "This was the only dressy thing I have to wear."

"I like it." The garment, made for a much shorter Maya woman, was well above Melissa's knees, revealing her long, slender legs. He watched as she slipped her slim, high-arched feet into a pair of sandals. She turned to pick up her black shawl.

"Forget that," he said brusquely. She had combed her hair up at the temples but left the rest of the luxurious mass free to tumble about her shoulders in rich and glowing curls. He couldn't believe she would think of covering it up. Fingers brushing hers, he took the shawl from her hands and dropped it on a table. His eyes darkened. "George is yesterday's news and as far as attracting attention from other men, don't worry, you're with me."

She hesitated, not sure how she felt about his authoritative manner, then she gave in. There was an undeniable charm to his protectiveness and his assumption about the interest of other men made her smile. Once out on the street, she said, "So, what do you mean, you *wagered* for your shirt?"

"I won it on a bet. I went to the market after siesta and found some guys laying odds on squirrels playing in the trees. They had tails so long they looked like monkeys."

She sniffed. "The squirrels or the men?"

"The squirrels," he explained with exaggerated patience. He might have known she wouldn't care for gambling. "I wagered that a particular squirrel could make a certain jump. The other guys thought it couldn't." He took her arm as they crossed a street. "I won enough for this shirt and to pay for an even more special evening, and some extra besides." All the money they had before was what she had managed to get, but there was nothing like having cash of his own.

"Suppose you lost?"

"Never happen." He steered their path around a man with a curb-side jewelry display. "I only bet on sure things."

"On a *squirrel*."

"I won, didn't I?"

She shook her head. "You're impossible. I don't know why I bother to try and hold a sensible conversation."

"While I was in the market, I bought some personal stuff, like soap and a razor." He touched his jaw as he spoke. "And also a machete for cutting through vegetation. I knew we couldn't expect much of a trail to the cave, and I met an old-timer who confirmed it. He remembers hearing about the cave as a kid. A family story about an old relative, a Santa Cruz holdout who lived there as a hermit for years. His great-great-grandparents took him food until he died. Nobody goes there now. It's all grown over. We'll have to cut our own path."

There was a strained note in his voice that he tried to hide. For the second time that day, he had suddenly been gripped by an unexplainable concern for Melissa's safety. It left him shaken.

The first time had happened in the market when he had shopped for the machete. He had bypassed knives bearing gloomy inscriptions in Spanish, one of them reading, "All roads lead to the tomb."

Ordinarily, the sayings would have amused him, but this time it struck a sour note. The machete he selected was serviceable and plain. The knife sharpener had just finished putting an edge to the blade when a strange foreboding had raked its claws down his spine.

Danger. He knew it was danger for Melissa.

His concern for her had been so powerful that he had rushed back through the streets to the hotel, but by the time he reached her door, he found that the irrational fear had fled as mysteriously as it had come. Stupidly, he had stared at her closed door. What was wrong with him? He had been on the verge of bursting into her room and there now seemed no reason for it. Feeling confused, he had withdrawn to the adjoining courtyard where he paced, still keeping an eye on Melissa's door as his adrenaline level sank back to normal. The swing of his emotions baffled him. As close as he was to victory and with the threat of George removed, it seemed he should have no concerns at all.

Yet now, the same premonition had returned.

As if through a fog, he heard her say, "You said the cave entrance was hidden by overgrowth. The jungle will have had even more years to grow and keep us from finding the temple."

His surroundings faded as the premonition gained strength, filling him with horror as a phantom message formed clearly in his mind: *If she goes into the temple, she will die.*

CHAPTER SEVENTEEN

RICK'S PREMONITION RAISED GOOSEFLESH. He'd had bad feelings in the past, but nothing ever like this. Never so specific. *Death at the temple, death for Melissa.*

Was he going nuts or what?

"So much for the wilds of Quintana Roo," he heard her say as they passed by a laughing crowd. "Look at the sunburn and fancy T-shirts. Half the people in town are tourists."

"Vacationers from Cancun and Cozumel, driving in from the ruins on the coasts," he said absently.

"From the way you talked earlier today, I'm surprised that the state has roads at all."

He struggled to shake off his bad feelings. "Things have changed since the government discovered the tourist dollar. At least you won't see many outsiders at the restaurant I heard about this afternoon. It's a local spot, with good regional food."

She looked interested. "Like what?"

"We'll soon find out, it's not far." The effect of the weird premonition was finally fading, thank God. He focused on where they were going. He'd heard talk that the restaurant that sounded interesting, served venison and other wild game. He wasn't saying that to Melissa. She'd start thinking the menu included bats.

"I found transportation for us tomorrow," he said.

She raised her eyebrows. "Another squirrel bet?"

He laughed. "Not exactly. He's a farmer with produce he's taking to a place near the cave opening. He'll stop in the morning to pick us up."

"Are you sure it's the right place? I thought the cave was a secret unless you had a map,"

"The fact that the cave leads to the temple is the secret. The cave itself isn't. The place is grown over, ignored for ages."

"Your grandfather didn't ignore it."

"Yeah, he did. He thought he could find the temple from the air but that didn't work out." Rick shrugged. "He didn't have much to say about his failures."

They turned a corner and started down a sidewalk that ran along a stucco wall. They were halfway down the block when startling growls and shrieks came from overhead. Rick glanced up and got a quick impression of something dark and ponderous streaking down upon them. Grabbing Melissa about the waist, he yanked her hard against him as he stumbled backward, pulling them both up against the wall. A concrete flower pot crashed to the spot where Melissa had stood but an instant before.

Rick stared at the smashed mess, shards of busted pottery and crimson petals scattered like drops of blood across the pavement. But for luck and the love of God, Melissa could have been lying there too, broken and bloodied. Sounds issued from overhead. Rick lifted a dazed stare to a balcony where there were sounds from a snarling cat and a growling dog. The cat clambered to the balcony ledge where a pot similar to the one that had fallen must have been placed. Yowling, the cat leaped to an adjacent balcony and disappeared. The dog barked twice in apparent satisfaction and all was quiet

In the abrupt silence, Rick shifted an anxious gaze to Melissa. "You all right?"

"Yes." She stated it firmly as if made of stern stuff indeed, but her face was pale. She shuddered when she glanced at the broken pot.

Rick gathered her close, his fingers tangling in the silk of her hair. Was this the cause for his premonition? Here he had been in a lather about doom-filled threats and it was an idiot pot of flowers that could have finished her off. It would have made him laugh if he wasn't still so rattled. The streets around them remained silent. The barking dog and crashing pot had attracted no attention. If Melissa had been by herself, she could have been struck down with nobody to see it, nobody to help.

His pulse throbbed as he became acutely aware of her warmth within the circle of his arms, the scent of her hair, the manner in which the curve of her body placed sweet pressure against the juncture of his thighs. Desire licked its flame through him, igniting a crazed urge to scoop her up and carry her off to some hideaway that would be theirs alone. He would cover her body with his, make love to her and keep her safe. Nothing would ever dare harm her again.

Her fingers tightened on his arm. She gestured upward. Her face, so pale before, now showed a flush. "I think we've got an audience."

Disconcerted, he looked and saw a little girl peering over the balcony railing. A woman joined the child and called down an anxious question in Maya. Another woman appeared on the balcony where the cat had fled.

"We're all right," Melissa called up, making a guess as to what the woman had asked. "We're okay, no one was hurt."

"Come, on," Rick said, taking Melissa's hand. Nobody around when it could have mattered, but let him wish for a bit of privacy and the place was jumping. "Let's clear out before we're news at eleven."

The sound of music and laughter and the smell of food reached them as they turned the corner. The restaurant sat on the opposite side, a low building with a large outdoor eating area shaded by a vine-covered trellis.

Rick guided Melissa across the street, his hand lightly touching the small of her back. Even that slight contact made his fingers tingle and his sense of anticipation increase.

Envisioning a secluded table for two, he paused at the flower-covered archway that formed the entrance to the bustling dining area. He saw couples dancing, a white-garbed trio providing the music. The long tables were picnic-style, with benches.

There was none of the intimate atmosphere he'd had in mind.

A masculine voice rang out from behind, the greeting spoken in Spanish. It was Hadwin, one of the men Rick had met in the market that afternoon. Hadwin introduced his girlfriend. Forcing a smile, Rick introduced Melissa. The last thing he wanted was a double date, thank you, but that was what Hadwin had in mind.

"You will sit with us, yes?" Without waiting for an answer, he herded Rick and Melissa inside and to a crowded table where introductions flew. Pitchers of sangria, bottles of beer and bowls of spicy snacks were passed down the table for the newcomers.

Still on his feet, Rick prevented Melissa from sitting. "I think we'll dance first," he said, sending Hadwin a wink. The man nodded and returned a knowing grin.

The dance area was a square of earth, hard-packed by countless feet stepping in time to the music. Reaching it, Rick turned Melissa to him and drew her into his arms.

Their bodies collided gently and her senses swirled. He smelled of shaving soap and a warm good scent that was simply him. She closed her eyes and rested her head on his shoulder. His breath fanned the feathery curls at her temple, a dizzying, butterfly touch that threatened her equilibrium.

"This is more like it," he murmured against her ear. "One dance, then we'll find someplace else to eat. Someplace where it's just us."

Melissa was all for it, but he sounded so certain she would agree that she couldn't resist teasing. "I don't know if we should. What are your friends going to think?"

"What friends?" He was amused that she was giving him a hard time. Her lips were saying one thing, but the message her body sent was entirely different. Did she think he couldn't tell? He spun her around, liking the way it took her off her balance and made her cling.

"Hadwin and the others at the table," she answered breathlessly, feeling the weight of her hair settle about her shoulders as their steps slowed. The vines twining across the top of the trellis screened out the sunset, but suspended lanterns cast a downward glow that emphasized the hollows under Rick's cheekbones and sharply cut the angle of his jaw. He looked tough, she thought, tough and dangerously attractive. Her conquistador.

A rapid pulse beat low in her throat, but she managed to keep a cool tone. "In town only a few hours and you've already got buddies and plans for the evening."

"Not with them." He lifted her arms and gently looped them about his neck, drawing her closer, aligning her body more perfectly with his.

The upward slant of her arms left her feeling exposed and vulnerable. She resisted for a moment and then surrendered, lacing her fingers together at the back of his neck. "Spanish eyes," she said on impulse as she gazed into their depths. "Spanish blood and an Irish name."

"Black Irish." He smoothed his palms slowly along her rib cage, grazing the sides of her breasts. "Know what Black Irish means? It goes back to the Spanish Armada."

She shivered at his touch. "No, I don't know."

He smiled, his eyes heavy-lidded. "Oh, the things I've got to teach you, Teach."

She touched her lip with her tongue. "About being Black Irish?"

He chuckled. "That too." His hands slipped lower to encircle her narrow waist. His thumbs moved in little circles, unhinging her, making her go warm and soft, making her melt against him.

"Tell me," she said, barely recognizing her voice. "Tell me about being Black Irish."

"My grandfather said—"

"More of his stories."

"True ones." He nuzzled her hair as he talked, kissed her temple. "The Armada sank when it was close enough to Ireland for sailors to swim to shore. Some of them stayed on to marry and raise families. Don Miguel's son was one of them." His hands lowered to cradle her hips, welding her to him. "He took a redheaded colleen to wife. They had a daughter born with his coloring."

His hands were on the move again and he heard Melissa gasp softly. No longer dancing, they simply swayed in time with the music. "The daughter married a countryman named Malone and it became the family name. From then on, each generation has had a son with Spanish dark hair and eyes."

"And you're the bid for this generation?" She wondered if she still made sense. It was hard to keep her thoughts together, hard even to speak.

He touched her hair. "Up for grabs to any blonde or redhead who wins my heart."

"A weakness for fair-haired women."

"A family weakness." His voice had gone husky. "Don Miguel Senior's English wife was blonde. And Sonja too, you saw her portrait."

"Mmmm." She loved how it felt when he stroked her hair. "Sounds about time for another redhead."

"Think so?" He twined a honey-colored curl about his fingers.

"Without a doubt." She felt as if she floated, weightless and free. What had they been talking about? Oh, yes. "Has there been another redhead since the Irish colleen?"

"Richard's wife."

"Richard?" For the moment, she couldn't remember who that was.

He smiled. "You know, Richard, my namesake, who went through the cave, who changed the map."

She laughed softly, feeling giddy. ". . . who milked the cow that tossed the dog . . . ."

"Who kissed the maiden all forlorn." He lowered his head and his lips met hers. Lightly, exquisitely.

"Not forlorn," she whispered, warmth curling low in her stomach. *Wild*, she thought to herself, that's how he made her feel, wild and reckless as if there were no rules. Emotion pulsed, spinning her senses and weakening her knees. She lifted suddenly trembling fingers to his cleanly shaven cheek.

"Yes," she said.

He raised his brow in question.

"Yes," she whispered, remembering what he'd asked once before. "I like my men smooth."

He gave her a long, intense look, then swept her close. A dark, breathless sweetness seized her as his mouth once again blended with hers. Her blood sang, fire rushed through her veins. All caution gone, she clung to him, deepening the kiss.

The only thing she remembered about leaving the restaurant was the moment when they passed under the flowered arch and he plucked a blossom to twine in her hair. The evening air had seemed effervescent and as bright as a rainbow. Halfway to the hotel they found a marimba player who performed just for them. They danced in the street, kissed without caution. Rick threw coins in the musician's hat, then laughing, they continued on. The hotel entry enfolded them in a haven of purple shadows. They embraced there, then embraced again in the courtyard outside their rooms, sharing long drugging kisses that left her dazed and wanting more. One arm about her, he opened his door, led her inside and locked the door behind them.

For a long moment he simply held her close, torrid warmth seeping through both their bodies. Their lips clung. With an increasing sense of wonder he felt her yielding, surrendering, her body softening against the hardness of his. On the bed with the fragrance of crushed flowers swirling around them, he sought her mouth again. He could go on kissing her forever, he thought, but then she moved against him and kisses were no longer enough to assuage his leaping hunger.

Her fingers were nimble as she helped him draw off the *huipil* and cast it aside. A sunset glow filtered in through the closed shutters and suffused the bed in a rosy haze. Rick caught his breath. He had known she would be beautiful, but he had never dreamed she would be so exquisite. His lungs constricted with a pleasure that was almost pain. She was like music, he thought, like those rare times when his fingers had touched the strings of his guitar and found a mystical sequence that sang on the air, a perfection that had no equal.

She reached for him, her hands feverish. His clothing was gone, then she was in his arms again, flesh against flesh, fire and ice.

He had always taken pride in his skill as a lover, had always stood at an analytical distance even in passion, but with Melissa, he was swept away. Lost and drowning. With her there was no need for coolness, for calculation. It was as if they were two halves of one person, each knowing exactly where to touch, how to move. Pleasure soared. He groaned, shuddering on the edge of control, trying to hold back. Too fast, he thought, too fast.

"Lissa . . . ." He wanted to say they had all night, that there was no need to rush, but she whispered his name and arched her back, her thighs silken steel about his hips. The thought came to him in a shattering burst that no single night with her could ever be long enough. One night, a thousand, could never be enough to satisfy him. With a shuddering gasp he sank into her fire and softness and was lost and could think no more.

It seemed a long time later that Melissa stirred and opened her eyes. Starlight filtered in through the shutters, bathing the room in an ethereal haze. Beside her Rick lay sleeping, one arm resting limp and heavy across her waist, his legs warmly entwined with hers.

Drifting in a drowsy afterglow, she listened to the rhythm of his breathing, slow and deep, and remembered all they had shared. Now that they had finally come together, it seemed inevitable. Once she had learned to trust him, there could be no turning back. Even so, it was with a sense of wonder that she remembered her heedless abandon. He had freed something within her, sparked emotions and desires she had never known before.

Gradually, she became aware of his changed breathing. The cadence was quickening, becoming harsh. He uttered some wordless sound. His arm jerked spasmodically.

Dreaming, she thought, fascinated, *he's dreaming.*

She shifted to free herself from the weight of his arm and was surprised at the tension she found there. She trailed her fingers down the muscled arm and found his fist clenched. Intrigued, she levered herself to one elbow and gazed down upon his shadowed face. His eyes were squeezed tight. He grimaced, the expression fierce, his face as clenched as his hand.

Tenderly, she touched his forehead in an attempt to soothe the knot of his brow. His arm jumped as if he dreamed of striking a blow. What nightmare beast was he confronting, what battle did he fight?

Abruptly he sat bolt upright, catching her unawares. His eyes were open, their expression wild and frantic.

"Lissa?" He focused on her, but still seemed caught in his nightmare world. He gripped her upper arm with fingers as chilled as stone.

Alarmed, she called his name. He released her arm but only so he could clasp her close. "Thank God." His words burst out in a strangled gasp. "Thank God, you got away."

"*Rick*." She wasn't sure what to do. She took one of his hands and chaffed it between hers. "Wake up," she pleaded. She touched his face. "Rick, wake up. You've been dreaming."

He blinked. She could almost feel his struggle to make sense of her words. He shook his head as if to clear it. "The temple . . . we . . . ."

"We're at the hotel in Carrillo Puerto." She touched his face again. "It's night. We're still at the hotel. We don't leave for the temple until tomorrow."

His eyes sharpened as reason returned. "A dream?" Slowly, his shoulders sagged and he buried his face in his hands. When he looked up again, his expression was haunted. "I dreamed we were at the temple, and we . . . ." He shuddered.

"It's all right now." She embraced him. "It was only a dream. It's all right."

He lay back in the bed, taking her with him to rest against the matted curls in the center of his bare chest. His heartbeat thudded under her ear, sounding as if he had been running for his life.

"You frightened me," she said in a quiet voice.

"Yeah, you and me both."

She lifted her head to look at him. "Are you okay now? You want to talk about it?"

"I guess." He drew her to rest on his chest again. His voice darkened as he started to relate the dream. It was still so real to him, so vivid. "We had gone through the jungle, no problem. And through the cave too. Simply whooshed through it."

"Whooshed?" she questioned, hoping to lighten his mood. She was rewarded with his chuckle.

"Whooshed through on the wings of many bats," he teased and kissed the top of her head. "It was like magic, you know how dreams are. All at once, we were at the temple."

"How did it look?"

"I don't really know." He sounded calmer, Melissa thought, and his heartbeat had slowed. "We were just there. Other people were there too. They knew you."

"You're kidding. Who were they?"

"Natives, maybe, I'm not sure. It didn't make sense." The circle of his arms tightened. "I was afraid for you."

"Really? Afraid for me?" The thought endeared him to her. "How come?"

"I just was, that's all." He was remembering more of the dream now. It tied in with his earlier premonitions, he could see that. Danger for Melissa at the temple, sure, it all hung together. The eerie foreboding had stayed in his mind and had created the nightmare. The explanation should have made him feel better, but somehow it didn't. He guessed he was still too close to it.

"Then what happened?" she said.

"The scene changed, switched to a dungeon." He frowned, remembering having a dungeon dream back in Philadelphia, only this time it had more details. "Vincent Price stuff, Edgar Allen Poe. Chains in the walls, red-hot pokers, the Inquisition all over again."

"You mean you were in a torture chamber? Oh, God . . . what happened?" No wonder he had awakened in such a state.

"Nothing much happened," he said, thinking quickly. "The dream changed to something else. It seems silly, now."

"I'm sure it wasn't silly at the time," she soothed.

Rick murmured in agreement, glad he had followed his instinct to lie. She must have forgotten she had been in the dream too, forgotten that if he had been in a torture chamber, she had been along with him. Jagged metal, the raw, cold scent of fear. Thank God her question had stopped him before he had said what really happened next. He shouldn't have talked about it in the first place. Dwelling on a bad dream could only make it worse.

Inspiration struck. "Going to bed on an empty stomach, that's what brought it on." It was as good an explanation as any, and maybe it was even right. "I'm starving. I wonder what restaurants are open. We never had dinner, you know."

She realized he was right. "How could we have forgotten?" Her tone was mischievous. "How did we let dinner slip by?"

"Yeah, how did we?" Stroking her back, he became aware of her slight weight pressing down upon him in all the right places. "I think I'm starting to remember."

"I can tell," she said with a laugh, lifting herself away. "I thought we were talking about getting something to eat."

"You're right." He swung his legs over the side of the bed. Too much of the nightmare still lingered in the room. "Let's ride out of this corral for a while. We need a change of scene."

When they were dressed and in the courtyard, he listened a moment then said, "I don't hear a sound from the street." He looked at the new watch he'd bought when purchasing backpacks and supplies. "Two-forty-five," he said.

They found the lobby, lights turned low. The desk clerk was asleep on a couch. Backing away so as not to disturb the clerk, Rick said, "Everything in town has been long shut down."

"But it's a Friday night," Melissa argued feeling unreasonably insulted. Now that she was up and about, she was ravenous. She thought of the central city nightlife back home. "At this hour in Philadelphia, there are places still open."

Rick chuckled. "We're not in Philadelphia, Toto."

She made a sound of frustration. "We could go out and make sure."

"Trust me. Philadelphia is miles away."

She gave him a dirty look. "I mean, go out and see if any restaurants are still open." Even as she said it, she knew she was being ridiculous. This tiny town . . . of course, nothing was open this time of night.

"Come on," he said.

"Hey," she said, having to skip to keep up. "Where are we going?"

"You'll see." He led her through the empty dining room and through a swinging door to the deserted kitchen. He found the light switch.

"What now?" she asked, uncomfortable with being where she wasn't supposed to be.

He made a quick check of the rear corridor to be sure there was nobody to be disturbed by the light, then said, "We raid the refrigerator." He took bills from his pocket and placed them on the chopping block. "There," he said. "That makes us honest." He turned to the refrigerator as confidently as if he owned it.

Melissa didn't budge. He was acting even bolder than when they were sneaking in and out at the hotel in Merida. Where did he get his nerve?

"Chicken," he said.

She thought he meant her, and then she realized he meant the plate of cold chicken he pulled from one of the shelves. She stared at the plate. The chicken did look awfully good. Her gaze moved to the bills on the chopping block. How much had he put there? Knowing him, it was bound to be more than enough.

Resolve took form, helped along by the gnaw of hunger. If their dinner was paid for, she should at least check out the menu. She rummaged in a box of fresh fruit and brought grapes and a pineapple to the table. Her mouth watered and she realized that any doubts she'd had were gone. Rick stood frowning in thoughtful concentration over the chicken and a bowl of cooked rice. Curious, she asked, "What are you going to do with that?"

"I'm still thinking."

"Whatever, we're having pineapple with it." She hoisted a knife. With a flourish, she dispatched the crown.

"Take no prisoners," Rick said, watching with fascination. It had taken her a moment to get into the spirit, but once she did there were no holds barred. With a flash of remembered pleasure, it occurred to him that she followed similar principles in other areas as well. She was a special woman, no question. He had never known anyone like her.

They ate like greedy children, laughing and remarking on how delicious everything was—the cold chicken and rice mixture was an outstanding creation and no fruit had ever tasted so sweet or had been so expertly prepared.

Finished, they cleared away the mess. On impulse, Rick added another bill to those already on the chopping block.

"For the waiter," he said. He met Melissa's eyes, wondering if she were about to object. It was going to spoil it for him if she did. He didn't like explaining himself, still, he gave it a try.

"The guys around here live close to the bone. We've got all we need. You'll know that when you feel the weight of your backpack in the morning." He finished with a shrug, convinced she wasn't going to understand. But then she surprised him.

"We enjoyed ourselves, didn't we?" She glanced around the kitchen, then looked again at the money and smiled up at him. "We've got plenty. Why not?"

He laughed aloud as if feeling a warm rush of sunshine. She *did* understand. "Yes," he said, "that's it exactly. Spread the wealth around."

Melissa picked up the last piece of pineapple and took a bite. "Whoops." Juice ran down her chin. She was about to wipe it away, but Rick leaned his head close to hers.

"Ummm," he said he brushed her lips with his.

She laughed. "What's the idea?"

"Neatening up all that sticky juice . . . ." He kissed her chin, then her throat, following the downward trail the juice had made.

"Goodness," she said.

"You must have taken a bath in this stuff." His expression was comically stern. "It seems to have all run down under the front of your dress."

She looked contrite. "We can't have that."

"No, not at all." He led her to the doorway, switching off the kitchen light as they went. "We'll have to do something about it."

Shortly, back in his room, she whispered, "There too? It's hard to believe."

His chuckle was soft in the darkness. "Pineapple is treacherous stuff."

"But I wouldn't think . . . oh, my. Oh . . . ."

Much later, when the last soft murmur of their lovemaking had faded away, Melissa lay in the quiet darkness, sated and glowing, remembering all that they had shared. Partners, she thought, and for the first time since the trip had begun, she wondered if she wanted the word to mean more than simply being partners in finding the diamond.

CHAPTER EIGHTEEN

THE SUN WAS UP AND Melissa was dripping wet, her hair streaming. She'd just turned off the shower when Rick joined her. She felt the rush of cooler air, then warmth as he took her into his arms.

"Morning, lady," he said, his voice soft and slightly husky.

"Morning, yourself." Lifting her face to his, she found it impossible to believe she had once harbored doubts about him. Even though their situation together was only temporary, he had shown warmth and caring and integrity. She remembered his nightmare fears on her behalf. As primitive as it sounded, he was a man who would defend her to the death. He wouldn't even think about it, he would do it because it was right. It spoke of the basic bond between the sexes, time-tested and true, caring and protecting and surviving—and doing it together. When it was all over they would go their separate ways, but for right now, she couldn't imagine herself with any other man.

She drew back a fraction, teasing him with her water-beaded flesh, breasts and belly and thighs, just grazing his. Softly, she said, "I thought you would be bringing me my towel."

"In a minute," he answered, closing his eyes and moving lightly against her, prolonging the delicious sensations until, with a shuddering sigh, he could bear it no more. Drawing her close to his body, he reached out an arm to the shower control and the water fell around them like a curtain.

As their lips met he found it impossible to remember a time when he could ignore how beautiful she was. Impossible also to remember a time when he had believed a woman should be a momentary whim, one who was quickly forgotten. None of that applied to Melissa. She was unforgettable.

A sound gradually reached them through the rushing water.

Cursing under his breath, Rick realized that what he was hearing was someone pounding on the outside door. "It must be the farmer I told you about," he muttered, reluctantly releasing Melissa as he stepped back.

By the time she dressed and had brought her packed things from the room that had been hers, Rick, also dressed and ready, said, "The farmer's waiting." Thinking of the interruption in the shower, he added, "This watch is better than nothing but back home, first thing, I'm getting one like Pedro swiped. It will have an alarm, keeping us on track."

"I thought Mexico was a place where everything got done *mañana.*"

"Don't believe everything you hear." Reluctantly he turned from the picture she made, her hair still damp, and her face bright and glowing. As they walked outside, Rick cast his thoughts ahead. By late afternoon of the next day, they should be standing before the altar of the zigzag temple. Anticipation rippled through him. The Honeycomb Fire was almost theirs. He saw himself placing the stone in Melissa's hands, seeing the stars in her eyes. Damn. It would be the moment of his life.

THREE HOURS LATER THEY were deep in the jungle and he was starting to wonder if this adventure was all it was cracked up to be. The farmer had let them off near a mule trail. All had gone well until the trail ran out on the far side of a small settlement, leaving them facing a tangled wall of green. Rick had rechecked the compass he'd bought, then started chopping, with Melissa behind him. He used a technique one of the men in town had advised—a diagonal slash of the big jungle knife to the left, another cut to the right, then a high slash to remove growth dangling down in the middle.

Overhead there were constant sounds from birds, maybe monkeys, and the sounds of other creatures moving through the trees, all making them constantly aware that this world was unfamiliar in all its ways.

Pausing to rest his machete across his knee, Rick slapped at bugs, then adjusted the sodden rag tied around his forehead that kept sweat from his eyes. *Slap!* More bugs. All too immune to repellent. Melissa was doing the same. Crawlers and buzzers and biters, plus tiny transparent ones that flew up before their faces in clouds. They got going again and after a time, the tangle thinned and there was a path again. They followed it until another compass check with the map showed they were veering off. Now Rick was back to slapping mosquitoes with one hand and chopping with the other.

Slash. Cut. Slash.

Would there be any daylight left by the time they reached the cave? From what the old-timer had said, the cave opening lay in the midst of a rocky clearing. That would be an advantage for setting up camp, but it would be a pain working by flashlight. Scowling, he envisioned groping around to find a place to hang the hammock and fumbling for dry wood to start their supper fire.

Recognizing the defeating drift of his thoughts, he pulled himself up sharp. Hell, if a man couldn't tell the difference between a race for the Triple Crown or a ride in Central Park, what was the point? He had dreamed about this journey since he was a kid and never once imagined it as easy. This was the stuff that created legends. He should relish every minute—he owed himself nothing less.

His head on straight again, he returned to work with renewed zest.

Melissa, garbed in her slacks and the long-sleeved shirt from George's pack, climbed over patches of weedy growth. Her legs were long but Rick's were longer. He strode easily over brush that she had to struggle through.

Lift. Step. Lift.

Hope your boot doesn't land on anything that moves. Or bites.

After a while she took a turn cutting a path herself, thinking she could do better. Mistake. The machete weighed a ton, the vines were like thick wire cables. Every time she lifted her arm the straps of her heavy pack painfully chafed her shoulders.

"It's hard going," Rick confirmed in a soothing tone when he accepted the machete back.

She stood on tiptoe and kissed his bristly cheek.

"What's that for?" He looked baffled but pleased.

"For not going all-male superiority. For not being smug."

He grinned. "I'll remember that."

"Please do."

Slash. Cut. Slash. Lift. Step. Lift.

The character of the jungle floor changed and the growth thinned once again. Encouraged by the spell of easier going, they slung off their packs and broke for lunch. Seated on a fallen log, they shared fruit, tortillas and cheese. High in the trees over their heads, birds squabbled in the branches. Beneath their swinging boot heels, a line of ants marched to and fro. Her mood of relaxation ebbed slightly as she found herself looking beyond the trip. Adventures had a way of coming to an end. Once she and Rick turned the diamond over to his grandfather, what then? Abruptly, she asked, "What did you and your grandfather fight about in the first place?"

He swallowed a bite of cheese, then said, "It goes way back."

"Tell me."

He studied his long-fingered hands, flexing them as if considering sign language instead of speech. "He has strong opinions; I don't have to tell you that. My father was supposed to make his own fortune, the same as him, only it didn't work out. After some lousy breaks, Dad fell in love with the bottle. Mom screamed at him a lot, but she liked the sauce too."

His face twisted as he remembered. Melissa moved close and her touch steadied him.

"The only time I ever saw them laugh together was over too many drinks," he continued, his gaze distant. "My grandfather claimed they made a rotten combination. That with a different woman, my father would have been a different man. My mother died when I was ten, my father when I was in high school."

He fell silent. Melissa slapped away a winged speck that had its own ideas about lunch, becoming aware again of the muggy press of heat and the persistent odor of decay. Everywhere she looked was green except for a parasitic plant nestled high in a net of vines, spilling cascades of white dabbed with pink and the palest blue, like a bridal veil caught up with colored ribbons.

Gently, she asked, "So you went to the ranch to live with your grandfather?"

"Yeah." He shifted his position, not actually facing her, but not looking away, either. "As a kid, I always spent happy relaxed summers there but I guess my dad's death made him decide I was his last chance to prove he could raise somebody right. He and I had always gotten along great, but all of a sudden there was nothing but rules, only not the same rules as there had been for my father. I wasn't supposed to make a fortune. The old man had already done that. What I was supposed to do was keep regular hours, end up with a regular job and be a regular bore. And he was going to tell me how to do it every step of the way."

"So you rebelled."

"I raised pure hell." He balled up the last scrap of tortilla between his fingers and flicked it to the ants. "If something matters to me, I go after it. Tell me I can't get something my way and I'd rather have nothing at all."

"Sounds like rebellion to me."

His expression lightened and he met her eyes. "More a case of cutting off my nose to spite my face, but given the same circumstances I'd probably do it all over again."

She smiled. "Such a proud nose. Don't do anything to harm it, please." She kissed his nose, nuzzled his rough cheek, then his jaw. She heard his soft chuckle, their breaths mingling as he allowed her to keep her touch light. There was so much passion in him, she thought, yet so much tenderness too. His self-involved parents, his iron-willed grandfather . . . had any of them cared about the person he really was?

Rick rechecked his compass. "I hope we're not veering off. No sign of the trail and the map is too keyed to landmarks to be much help."

Melissa frowned thoughtfully. "Should we backtrack?"

"Not yet. Let's keep going this way for a while longer."

With that, they fastened on their packs and started off again.

Melissa tripped on an exposed root and grabbed a vine for support. Hearing her cry out, Rick spun around.

"Get it off!" Her voice was shrill.

He saw her writhe, saw her wild gestures. *Snakebite*, he thought, rushing to her. The anti-venom kit. Was it in his pack, or hers . . . .?

"Spider web! It's sticking all over me! Oh, God . . . ."

"Are you bitten?" he demanded, heart pounding. A spider's bite could be as dangerous as that of a snake.

"No, I only ran into the web. It's got all dead bugs in it. Get it off!"

Relieved, he laughed. "It's okay now. As long as you weren't bitten, it's okay."

"I saw the spider." She shuddered as he brushed the last of the web away. "It was all horrible, like a fungus with legs. I hate spiders. And their webs."

"I thought it was bats you hated."

She tried to give him an icy stare, but couldn't maintain the expression. "I'm a baby, I know," she admitted, leaning against him. His shirt was damp, he smelled of bug repellent. So much for romance, but leaning against him felt wonderful, regardless. "I never dreamed this would be so hard. I wish we were already there."

He gave her a light caress. "I'm chopping as fast as I can, said Lizzie Borden."

Smiling, she pulled away. "A comedian yet."

He turned serious. "You doing all right?"

The concern in his eyes lifted her. "Yes, I'm doing all right."

They started off again.

Slash. Lift. Slash. Step. Cut. Lift.

Another spider web. That's what Rick thought when he heard Melissa's muffled shriek, but when he wheeled about he saw her standing as rigid as a goal post, staring into the brush. What was it? Some animal?

Then he saw it too.

A child. Two arms lengths away from Melissa, peering through the leaves. A little boy, maybe six or seven years old. Staring at them unblinkingly. As quick as a magician's rabbit, he disappeared. There was a fading rustle of leaves, then silence.

"Did you see him?" Melissa looked stunned.

"A Maya kid." Rick shook his head, as stunned as she. "There must be a village nearby."

She frowned. "If there's a village, that means—"

"A trail." He grinned as he finished the sentence for her. "Come on, let's see where he went."

The bushes the boy had vanished into were thick, but soft and willowy. Rick sheathed his machete. Tucking Melissa behind him, he plowed through, making swimming motions with his hands.

They soon emerged on the other side. There was no sign of the boy, but there was indeed a trail.

Delighted, Melissa laughed. "And who says there's no answer to prayers. I wonder where the boy—"

She heard Rick suck in a surprised breath.

Warning shrilled in Melissa's head like a fire drill alarm. There on the path, not three yards from them, the boy had reappeared. He wasn't alone. With him was a Maya man with a machete in one hand and a maniacal grin on his face.

Time seemed to stop. Melissa was acutely aware of Rick standing frozen beside her, his own machete sheathed uselessly at his side. The native's eyes bored into them. Now that the first shock was over, Melissa saw that the stranger wasn't smiling at all. His mad grin was formed by a scar that pulled one corner of his mouth upwards. By his side was a hawk-nosed woman.

He addressed Rick in Spanish. Rick answered in a gruff tone. Looking sly, the man nodded and made a show of putting his machete away. He was strong-looking, but scruffy, with shoulder-length hair that looked untouched by a comb. Looking beyond his disfiguration, Melissa saw a resemblance between him and the boy. Father and son, and maybe the mother, she reasoned.

Speaking again, he waved for them to precede him down the path.

Without taking his eyes from the man, Rick spoke guardedly to Melissa. "His Spanish is worse than mine, but I think he said his home is nearby. I think we've been invited to dinner."

Melissa made a joke of her fear. "If we're on the menu, let's decline."

"I doubt we've got a choice. Not the way we're outnumbered."

Melissa didn't know what he meant, then sounds from the other side of the trail made her look. She saw another native man with a knife in hand and a woman, both unkempt and rawboned. Melissa cringed. The man, woman and boy to the left, the couple to their right, sinister bookends to a story she doubted she'd enjoy.

The knife man studied Melissa, then spoke to the scar-faced man. They exchanged a few rapid words in the Mayan tongue. Glaring suspiciously at Melissa, the woman tried to interrupt, but her man waved her off. Breaking into a grin, his eyes roved across Melissa again before he addressed Rick in Spanish.

"He says his name is Jakes," Rick translated brusquely. "He's just seconded the invite."

"Lucky us. The event of the season." Melissa had drawn closer to Rick. "You can bet the woman isn't in on it. Did you see how she looked at me?"

It was how Jakes had looked at her that bothered Rick. As if she was up for grabs. *Just try*, came his murderous thought.

The father barked a command and gave the boy a shove. He scampered to Melissa and held out a hand as if to escort her.

The expression on his little face was angelic. Despite the unsavory adults around him, he was only a child, Melissa thought, innocent and appealing. Charmed, she reached out. With a whoop, he grabbed her hand and yanked her forward. Caught by surprise, it wasn't until he dragged her past his father and the woman with him that she realized how neatly she had been separated from Rick.

The boy's father barked an order and they all started walking. Melissa cast an anxious backward look. The slight movement of Rick's head seemed a message to play along for the moment.

Shaken, she plodded along beside the boy ahead of his father and the hawk-nosed woman. Rick was behind them, followed by the scar-faced man and his woman. Clearly, she and Rick were prisoners. Only why? From behind, she heard Jakes' woman berate him sharply in the Mayan tongue. He seemed to be trying to placate her. Perhaps the woman wanted to let them go. Melissa could only hope.

They emerged at a clearing where a small yellow dog yapped a frenetic welcome. The settlement consisted of three crude thatched huts with chickens scratching in the dust. Two Maya women and two native men, one heavy-jawed, the other narrow-faced, stood to observe their arrival. One of the women held a crying baby. A naked toddler played nearby.

At the sight of two more men, Rick grimaced. The odds had gotten worse. And worse yet, one of the men held a shotgun. He didn't know who the natives were, but he had a feeling that if he didn't come up with something fast, he and Melissa might end up as Quintana Roo plant food.

The boy's father, who seemed to be the head honcho, his scarred face winning him extra points in the intimidation department, snapped out orders that galvanized the two standing women into action. One dashed to swat the dog into silence, the other one swept her crying baby into a hut. Then, without warning, Jakes and Scarface plowed into Rick and he went down.

Laughing, they dragged him up by his arms. One of the other men joined in. Next thing, his pack and machete were gone. That's when the hawk-nosed woman dived toward him, grabbing at the arm one of the men held in a vice grip. Yelling something Rick couldn't understand, she dragged her ragged fingernails down to his wrist. With a demented magpie screech of triumph, the woman whirled away with her shiny prize. Rick stared down at his gouged arm. Damn it all to hell! His better-than-nothing watch was gone.

Melissa saw what was happening to Rick and started forward, having lost track of Jakes' woman. Her name seemed to be Cissy— either that or Jakes had only been saying "yes, yes," to her in Spanish in answer to her nagging. She felt hands grasp at her backpack, pulling her backward.

She jerked away and spun around to see Cissy, who had come up from behind. Jabbering in Mayan, the woman signaled for Melissa to unfasten the pack. Shaking her head, Melissa backed off a step. The woman's brown face contorted in an expression of raw hatred. Just that fast, she sprang forward, clawing Melissa's face, yanking her hair.

Although Cissy was a head and a half shorter, she was stocky and work-toughened and Melissa had never been in a physical fight. More by instinct than design, she kicked. Her booted foot struck Cissy's knee. She felt a flash of victory until Cissy grabbed her leg. Overbalanced by the pack, Melissa toppled backward and landed hard. Her head jerked and she saw stars. While she was still too befuddled to resist, Cissy manhandled her around, scrabbling to release the fastenings on her pack and yank it off. With a crow of triumph, Cissy pranced with her captured booty.

Lying flopped in the dust like a rag doll, Melissa struggled to regain her breath. So much for self-defense. One kick—she had managed to get in only one kick—and even that had been used against her.

Dimly she heard men laugh at the entertainment she had provided, then she heard Jakes issue more orders. Determined to regain at least a smidgen of self-respect, Melissa started to get up.

Helpless in the men's grip, Rick watched in dismay as Jakes' woman dropped the stolen backpack and turned with a pounding run, crashing down on Melissa like a linebacker with a grudge.

Melissa went flat, eyes closed. Rick strained toward her. How seriously was she hurt? A thumping blow across the kidneys staggered him. He went to his knees.

As he struggled to right himself, the boy streaked forward and snatched Rick's fallen machete from the dust. Uttering a wild sound, he spun, swinging the blade at Rick's check as if cutting down corn. Still in the grip of the men, Rick yelped and reared back, unable to escape a slash in his shirt. He felt blood welling on his chest.

Crazy, Rick thought, his stomach churning as coarse laughter exploded all around. Every one of this maniac crew, including the kid, should be locked up in a loony bin. He took another look at Melissa and caught his breath. She was looking back. *She winked.* Hot damn. His heart leaped.

He glanced back to the others and realized that the boy's father must have called the child to him. The boy strutted over and delivered the machete. Eyes glinting wickedly, the man examined it, then without warning, gave it a hard backhanded swing that thwacked the flat of the blade soundly across the boy's left ear. Howling, the child dropped to the ground, his hands wrapped protectively about his head.

One of the women ran to comfort him, but from everyone else more laughter exploded, raucous and cruel.

Rick was still on the ground but no longer being held. He saw his chance. All of them had their attention fixed on the boy. Rick's gaze zipped to Melissa. She was poised to rise. Her nod told him she was thinking the same as he: n*ow or never*. Rick gave another glance around, then dashed toward her as she sprang to her feet. Her hand met his and they streaked toward the trees.

Behind them were outcries, then the explosion of the gun. Shot peppered to one side, but Rick wasn't hit and neither was Melissa.

Despite his bum ankle, Rick felt he raced like the wind. Ahead was a growth of low brush and beyond that, the jungle. He felt a thrill. The gods had smiled. They were going to make it. His hand squeezed tight on Melissa's as they dashed into the brush.

It was as if they flew. Invincible. Unstoppable. Unbeatable. Even if the native caught up, it would make no difference. A karate chop here, smash two heads together there, snatch up the heroine and leap into the trees.

One of his boot heels landed on something that moved. His ankle turned and he heard a blood-curdling squeal, like metal caught in moving gears. More squeals that made no sense. Fat brown and white blobs the size of sandbags rolled, scattering left and right. Melissa screamed and her hand was gone from his. Rick fought for balance and lost. So much for the smiling gods. Going down, he saw a nightmare face, all broad snout and beady eyes. *A pig.*

Rick hit the ground and one of the men smashed down on top of him. Too late, Rick realized that he and Melissa had run into a dust wallow filled with swine. The great escape was over as quickly as it had begun.

CHAPTER NINETEEN

MELISSA WINCED AS CISSY gave her leash a nasty tug, still trying to come to terms with the fact that she and Rick had been turned into slaves. *Slaves.* This just didn't happen to people anymore! Yet when the gang had hauled them back to the village, one of the women brought nooses already made to loop about their necks, a fate apparently planned for outsiders who'd been caught. What had happened to any former ones? She decided not to think about it. Their ankles were hobbled so they could walk but not run. They were put to work, Rick cleaning up the compound and Melissa gathering firewood.

Shuffling along wearily, she toted yet another load of wood into the settlement, her back groaning and her arms about ready to fall off. After dropping the load to the growing pile, she stood up slowly. Too slowly. Cissy, her overseer, said sharp words in Mayan and gave the rope another vicious yank.

Choking, but not as much as she pretended, Melissa let her legs double up under her. Can't get much work out of a dead slave, she thought, sinking to the ground. Then again, that might suit Cissy just fine. The woman had hated her from the start and the reason had become clear when Jakes, stumbling over the pigs, had been the first to reach her. He had rolled her to the ground under him, his hands busy with mischief. Then Cissy caught up, screeching and clawing and pummeling his back with her fists.

Well, you can have him, honey, Melissa thought, her flesh still crawling from Jakes' touch. Glaring at Cissy, she pantomimed wanting a drink. Glaring back, Cissy pantomimed delivering a kick. Melissa decided that maybe she wasn't so thirsty after all. Cissy had kicked her before. The toughened skin of the woman's bare feet looked like leather and felt like concrete.

As Melissa dragged herself upright, another woman—she looked like the woman who had the baby, appeared with a cup of water. Cissy complained but allowed Melissa to accept it. Melissa closed her eyes blissfully as the water trickled down her throat, stale and lukewarm and tasting absolutely wonderful. Before she could offer her thanks to the baby's mother, Cissy knocked the cup from her hand. A hint that rest time was over.

On her way back to the forest, Melissa passed by Rick, who limped as he worked. They exchanged glances and he managed a thumbs-up sign before turning back to his labors.

His bad ankle blazed and the scratches on his arm annoyed and if that claw-fingered, hawk-nosed watch stealer who held the end of his leash gave him one more poke in the ribs with her stick, he was going to grab it and break it over her head. If the bozo with the shotgun wanted to blow holes in him for it, that's how it would have to be. He had cleaned up plenty of stables in his time and none was as crummy as this dump of a compound. Whatever landed on the ground stayed there unless the roaming pigs and chickens took an interest, yet his supervisor, Miss Neat, kept jabbing with her stick and pointing: *pick up this, sweep up that.* All the while the toddler—he didn't know who the kid belonged to—threw corn cobs at the dog, making a new mess.

Rick had come to the conclusion that their captors were most likely criminals hiding from the law. He hoped there was a bounty on their heads because he was eager for Benito Carranza to take an interest. When he paid the man for keeping George on ice, he would tip him off to this jungle hideaway. He liked thinking of Carranza, who seemed no better than he had to be, storming in with his brand of justice. Rick liked thinking of anything that took his mind from his true concern, what might happen to Melissa when the sun went down and Jakes started thinking it would be nice to have another woman around the hut.

The thought filled Rick with rage. The only thing that made him feel better was imagining what he'd eventually do if that scum touched her.

The hot and humid afternoon wore on. A brief thunderstorm left the air hotter and more humid than before. Evening arrived, still and sultry, and with it the dinner hour. To ward off the dark and the mosquitoes, Melissa's hard-earned firewood was made into a smoky fire, around which the settlement residents feasted on food from the confiscated packs while their two slaves sat tethered by the end hut and supped on yesterday's stew.

The boy was apparently their guard but he was more involved in eating a pack of chocolate drink mix, sticking a wet finger into the dry power and transferring it to his mouth. The knotted bruise on his left ear had turned purple. Rick hoped the kid's business with the chocolate wouldn't win him more punishment. Then again, if junior hadn't learned his daddy's rules by now, that was his problem.

Melissa looked up from her half-finished stew. "I think this restaurant's run down since your magazine's last rating."

"Yeah." Rick was glad she could still joke. "See if the food gets five stars *this* time. The ambiance isn't so hot, either." They sat on the damp ground with their leashes tied to trees and their feet still hobbled. To add to the fun, their wrists had been tied together, although in the front so they could use their hands to eat.

Melissa showed a tired smile. "Don't forget to mention that the waitress was nice." It was the baby's mother who had brought them the food, placing the bowls carefully.

As darkness settled, the fire became an orange glow against the night but all was in shadow where Rick and Melissa sat. He glanced to the boy, whose face was no more than a dusky oval in the poor light. Finished with the drink mix, he seemed on the verge of nodding off.

Rick's gaze returned to the campfire where a crock of what looked like home brew was being passed around.

Lowering his voice, he said, "My hands aren't tied very tight. Once the crew gets good and drunk, it should be no trick to work free and clear out of here."

"I was thinking the same," Melissa whispered back.

Rick wondered why he had ever felt hopeless. This crew of derelicts didn't know who they were up against.

Melissa's smile widened. "Before we take off, I'll steal our stuff back. I'm a light-fingered expert."

He smiled back. "Don't forget to grab my watch."

All too soon their smiles faded as the three men got up from the campfire and headed purposefully toward them.

"Oh-oh," Rick muttered, his dinner souring in his stomach as his fears for Melissa resurrected.

What happened was nothing he'd been prepared for. Moving quickly and efficiently, the men took care of him first, tightening the noose about his throat so he was too busy gasping to protest when staked his hobbled legs to the ground. His bound hands were pulled to one side and also staked. By the time the blue had left his face and he was breathing again, Melissa was staked down for the night as firmly as he.

"Lissa . . ." His voice was hoarse. "Are you okay?" His hands had been staked so he was turned away from her. He had to crane his neck to see her.

"So much for plan A," she muttered.

She was trying to sound brave, but she also sounded close to tears. Rick cursed under his breath. "That creep Jakes try anything?"

"Not with his woman so close. She's got a possessive streak, thank God."

Rick chuckled in relief and rolled his head back to a more comfortable position. The skin on his neck was raw and his ankle was tender. The re-injury disgusted him. For anyone who had played football, a pigskin injury should mean something a lot more heroic than a trip over a real pig. He wished some of the smoke from the fire would blow their way and drive off the mosquitoes.

Despising his helplessness, he looked back toward Melissa again.

"Something I've got to say. If Jakes ever—" He could hardly force the words past his throat. "If he ever steps really out of line, you've got to remember it's not the end of the world. I'll get him. You've got to know that." Fury seized him even as he spoke. "Believe me, I'll get him."

"You won't have to." Melissa's voice showed an edge like tempered steel. "It won't be the end of my world, it will be the end of his. *I'll* be the one to make him pay."

"We're in this together," Rick said. "We'll *both* get him."

Together, Melissa thought, not sure if it meant anything for the long haul, but cheered nonetheless.

Cheered as well, Rick was thinking of his ancestral history—the family jinx, landing in the bad part of town. But Don Miguel and Richard had eventually gotten out of their scrapes and somehow, he and Melissa would too.

RICK OPENED HIS EYES. How long had he slept? Stiff from lying on the damp ground, he shifted experimentally. He saw no one around and the fire was down to embers. They all must be tucked in for the night. The dog whimpered in its sleep and a chicken roosting in a nearby tree gave a drowsy cluck. Rick figured the animal noises had disturbed him, then he heard furtive movements from the place where Melissa lay.

Jakes. His blood at an instant boil, Rick was ready to yell bloody murder. He might be tied hand and foot, but he sure in hell could bring Jakes' woman on the run with fire in her eye.

He heard Melissa's cautioning hiss.

"Shhh! One of the women's here." Even in her whisper, Melissa's excitement came through. "She's letting me loose."

Melissa knew it had to be the baby's mother. So happy she could weep, her heart spilled over in gratitude to the woman, so much kinder than any of the others. The woman had a knife. She held the blade to Melissa's throat to warn her to keep quiet when first awakening her, only instead of cutting the ropes, she was untying them. Melissa understood. Punishment would be harsh to anyone who helped the prisoners. It had to look as if they had gotten themselves untied.

Melissa's feet were suddenly free. She longed to share the news with Rick but was afraid of whispering to him again. She lay only a scant yard from the end hut, which she knew was occupied. Silence was imperative.

It was so dark she could barely see an outline of her savior as the woman pulled the peg that held down her hands. Once undone from the peg Melissa was able to work them loose by herself.

Free. The wonderful words sang silently in her head. *Free.*

The woman stood. Now they could both untie Rick, Melissa thought. Still sitting, she lifted her hands to loosen the noose so she could pull it off over her head.

The rope snapped tight and jerked upwards.

Trying not to cough aloud, Melissa struggled to her feet, her stiff muscles making her clumsy. What was the woman doing? She was now behind her, holding her close. Why weren't they untying Rick?

A hard nudge against her spine forced her to take a stumbling step. She came up against the side of the hut. Her toe nudged warm softness. *The dog.* Please God, please don't let it bark, don't let anyone hear them now. The animal stirred but mercifully remained silent.

Melissa felt another hard nudge and then the knife blade once again touched her throat. She felt it slide. Felt it cut. Melissa gasped, her legs going weak. Into her ear came the harsh command she had been hearing all afternoon and then she knew. It wasn't the baby's gentle mother who had untied her, it was Cissy.

She didn't stop to process the how's and why's. In that instant, she only knew that if she went anywhere with Jakes' woman, she would never come back alive.

"Fire!" she screamed. Better to be in a nasty crowd than alone with vengeful Cissy. "Fire! Fire!" And never mind that nobody but Rick knew English. Grabbing the arm that held the knife, she threw herself backward, her head knocking hard against Cissy's, her foot inadvertently hitting the dog, rousing it to bark.

Rick, confused as to what was going on, only knew that instead of being rescued, Melissa had run into trouble. He heard her outcry, then the screams of another woman. Then the voices of the men. He angled his head in the direction where he had last heard Melissa. A light arced. Squinting, he saw only the Maya faces.

No Melissa. Somehow she had gotten away.

Smiling in the darkness, Rick didn't once think of himself still tied and lying on the hard damp ground. Melissa had escaped. Thank God, thank God. Go, Melissa, go!

HER EARS STILL RINGING from the head blow she had delivered to Cissy, Melissa twisted away from the path she was on and dove. The ground rose up to greet her. She rolled, got up and scrambled behind a tree. All too aware of the yelling and commotion behind her, she tore the noose from her neck, her fingers touching blood from the shallow knife cut. She turned away from the village. Her treks back and forth carrying firewood had taught her that the surrounding growth held widely spaced trees and abundant concealing brush. She took off.

From the corner of an eye, she caught a flash of light. She dropped to her hands and knees and crawled. Just when she was about to congratulate herself for her speed, her hand slid forward on nothing. Her body followed. She landed in a shallow gully, jarred but unharmed. Hearing voices and running footsteps, she bellied down and closed her eyes like a terrified child. *If I can't see them, they can't see me.* The ground vibrated as footsteps pounded on by.

When she dared lift her head, she saw a line of lights moving deeper into the jungle, the pace rapid and smooth. Were they on the path that had led into the camp or a different one?

Rising to her knees, she dared look back toward the camp. It was about thirty feet away. She couldn't locate Rick, but she saw the three women and the boy silhouetted against the fire, which had been stirred into life. The dog yapped, sounding as if it ran in useless circles, with no notion of chasing after quarry. *Good dog.*

She bellied down when she heard the men coming back. Again they thundered on by. When she dared take another peek, their lights had moved to the other side of the clearing. Another trail, she guessed. Apparently, it hadn't occurred to them that she'd braved the jungle instead of fleeing on an established path.

Sinking into her burrow, she rested her head on her arms. For the moment she was safe. Eventually, the village would settle down again. Then she would creep back and free Rick. If luck held out, they could be gone long before their captors awoke and discovered they had been outsmarted.

She didn't lift her head again until all sounds from the direction of the camp had ceased. Clouds covered whatever light there was in the sky. The fire must have died down completely. When she got up on her knees and looked, there was nothing she could distinguish.

Standing, she edged cautiously toward the place where she knew the huts must be. She thought she had arrived when she came to a space with neither trees nor bushes. All too soon, however, she realized she had come to the trail instead. A rude shock—she thought she had been traveling parallel to it. Okay, she wasn't lost, only turned around. She would take the trail. Only in which direction should she go?

She decided to walk forty steps. If that didn't bring her to the camp, she would return to the starting place and go the other way.

Forty steps brought her to nothing. Keep calm, she counseled herself: we've got a plan here. She retraced her steps, or so she thought, only somehow the pathway seemed changed. Had the trail branched off? Was she only getting increasingly lost?

Better stop right now.

Snuffing sounds and rustling bushes brought her to stiff attention. *A pig*, she told herself. If she was near the pigs she was practically on top of the village. Except the sounds seems to come from something bigger. As far as she knew, pigs were not nocturnal. Jungle cats were.

Terror billowed up from deep inside of her, shoving her heart up into her throat, squeezing the air from her lungs. She panicked, all rational thought gone. Without consciously giving the order, her booted feet started moving, taking her away from the place of the snuffling sounds, the big-thing-moving-that-could-be-a-jungle-cat sounds.

She found it impossible to make time on a jungle trail at night. Too many twists and turns, too many roots and stumps and vines arching crosswise and dangling down, still she churned through as fast as she could, stumbling and falling only to get up and go on, each step increasing her panic. Was she still on the trail? She had no idea. She only knew that her heart slammed and that the air she breathed seemed as thick as library paste. Each slapping leaf, each snaring vine became a part of the pursuing beast she knew had her name on its menu,

She floundered in brush, fell again, and was too weak to rise. Panting, face in the dirt, she braced for the cruel rip of claws, for the snarl as the teeth found her throat.

She waited.

Nothing pounced. Except for her labored breathing, the only sound was that of the branches she'd disturbed easing back into place.

Sagging limp in the moldering dirt, she felt she would never move again. Her head spun, she felt half sick. After a time of nothingness, she gradually became aware of a change in the light. With an effort she lifted her head, seeing past overhanging trees to the moon, almost full, shining through what had been cloud cover, illuminating a clearing up ahead.

The camp? Had she run in a circle? Dizzy, her legs rubbery, she staggered to her feet. Moving with stiff, halting steps, she made her way through the trees. She had left the trail, she could see that now, but the growth was thin enough to allow her to approach the edge of the clearing. There she paused and stared.

There was no sign of the camp. She had come to a place she had never seen before, one with silvery-looking bare patches and scrubby bushes, the flat ground stretching out as lonely and mysterious as a phantom playground. She took another tottering step. The silvery patches, so eerie in the moonlight, turned out to be outcroppings of white limestone.

Something about the place held a ceremonial air that repelled her, yet drew her at the same time. Light-headed, she let her imagination soar, envisioning sacrificial maidens brought up from their watery graves to this dry place, their bones glowing pale through flesh made transparent from their long immersion.

With a start, she reeled in her wild thoughts. Sacrificial maiden, my aunt Susie. She was exhausted, on the verge of hallucination. Time to shape up.

It was then that she heard it. A sound from behind.

She froze. The animal had caught up with her after all.

A hand landed on her shoulder.

Not an animal, a man. One of the gang. She screamed soundlessly, her throat closed tight. Somehow she managed to turn.

A giant loomed before her. Taller and wider than any mortal man. Moonlight glinted on a golden tooth as he spoke. "I've been waiting for the two of you here."

CHAPTER TWENTY

MELISSA DRIFTED IN A SOFT, hazy dream world. It made no sense, but that's how dreams were. In it, she had been talking with Xavier, and now she dreamed that Xavier and Rick were discussing the cave.

"As a kid, I imagined the cave as a tunnel going through a mountain," Rick said. "Super illogical, but I didn't know back then that there're no Yucatán mountains."

Xavier nodded "The cave leads to a cavern. Trusting the map, I thought there must be a way through and all underground."

Melissa smiled to herself. Next, she supposed she would dream about the cave itself. Aladdin's magic lamp would probably be in it. *Poof!* Xavier would show up again as the genie. "Three wishes," he would say. "At your command."

Amused by the nonsense of it, she relaxed into a deeper sleep and didn't know anything more until Rick softly called her name.

"Lissa," he murmured. "Lissa, honey." Gently he half lifted her and turned her toward him. "The sun's up and we'll need all the daylight we can get. How are you feeling?"

"Fine, I'm fine," she murmured in a blurry voice as she burrowed into the warmth of his shoulder. So much talk when all she wanted to do was to go back to sleep.

He nuzzled her temple, hugged her close and kissed her cheek. "I must have aged a hundred years in those hours after you left, not knowing what had happened to you. Hell, I aged a thousand."

Her face still hidden, Melissa tried to fight off the disturbing pictures that intruded. A scar-faced man with an ugly look in his eye. A woman screaming orders. She saw herself as if on film, running through the jungle, alone and frightened. She shook her head in silent protest and told herself that the images must be from another part of her dream, but memories kept coming back. Slowly at first, like water seeping in through cracks, then like a flood.

Jakes. Cissy. She whimpered in protest as reality overcame her. She remembered everything: how she and Rick had been captured, her hairbreadth escape. But she'd had to leave Rick behind . . . .

Her eyes snapped open and she stared up at him in disbelief.

"Rick?" Her voice was hoarse as she spoke his name. She saw weary smudges under his eyes and one cheek was scraped and bruised, but he was smiling. Confused, she looked around. They were in a sheltered spot, a snug space enclosed by bushes and vine-draped trees. It was just past dawn and there were no huts in view, no Jakes, no Cissy, no hawk-nosed woman who'd been bossing Rick around.

For the moment, she didn't question what seemed a miracle. She sobbed, her emotions spilling over. "Oh God, you're here, you got loose." She pressed her cheek against his shirt, wetting it with her tears. "I got lost. I thought I would never see you again."

He rocked her as if she were a child. "Don't you remember that Xavier found you? You told him we had been captured. He came to the village and rescued me."

"Good morning," spoke a deep rumbling voice.

Melissa turned. Xavier stepped into the camp enclosure, his massive frame garbed in sturdy khakis, the trouser legs stuffed into camouflage boots that to her blurry eyes looked as big and broad as flying carpets.

She gasped. "I didn't dream you after all!" But even as she spoke, it was all coming back to her. She had collapsed in Xavier's arms—

fainting like a pathetic Victorian lady. They'd talked, and when he'd left her to get Rick she'd been determined to stay awake, only exhaustion must have overcome her, then dreams and reality had gotten mixed up.

"I am very real." He chuckled, the early morning light winking on his gold tooth. "I promised to bring Rick back to you and so I did."

Rick explained. Frustrated over Melissa's escape, the gang had knocked him around, then had drunk themselves unconscious. "They didn't hear when Xavier sneaked in to cut me loose. Then the dog started barking."

Melissa made a sound of alarm. She wasn't sure just where the camp lay, but it couldn't be too distant. "We should start moving. It's daylight. They might be after us already."

"No, no." Rick laughed. "Did you ever hear of a good old Irish brawl? This one was Cuban-Irish." He sent Xavier a look of camaraderie. "Believe me, they're in no shape to be coming after anybody."

"But the women! Two of them are as vicious as the men."

"They've traded in their nasty hats for nursing caps," Rick said with another laugh.

His confident tone and Xavier's satisfied nod had Melissa relaxing and it wasn't only because she had belatedly noticed the gun strapped to Xavier's side. If he and Rick agreed that the gang was no longer a threat, she could trust that it was true.

Xavier handed her a steaming mug of tea, then wandered off. As soon as they were alone, Rick said, "There's something I want to talk about."

"Okay," she said, "but first I've got a question. How in the world did Xavier get here?" Maybe there really was a magic lamp.

Rick looked grim. "The old man sent him."

"Your grandfather?" Startled, Melissa almost spilled her tea.

"Yeah." Rick gave a hollow laugh. "He got concerned about our welfare."

Confused, Melissa said, "But how did Xavier find us?"

"Actually, *you* found him. You stumbled into the clearing near the cave. Xavier had made camp here. He expected us to come from another direction, the way we would have come if we hadn't been hijacked by that gang." He grimaced. "You were right; we should have doubled back. We were on the wrong trail."

"Did Xavier go through the jungle too?"

"No. It turns out my grandfather knew a hell of a lot more about the map than he ever let on. Instead of wandering all over the Yucatan chasing clues, we could have come directly here."

"Oh my God." Melissa's initial shock was swiftly replaced by anger. "I can't believe this. He knew? Think of all that happened to us! Pedro, George, Jakes and the rest of his horrid crew and lord knows what was stalking me in the jungle!"

Rick's face contorted. "You think I haven't gone over it a hundred times? I told myself I understood him, that no matter how his high-handedness infuriated me, I knew he cared and it's just his way. But he went too far with this one." He cursed violently. "When he put you in danger, he went too far."

Melissa's emotions paled before Rick's. The strength of his fury alarmed her. Not sure how to respond, she finally said, "At least we weren't seriously hurt."

"No thanks to him."

Melissa suddenly wanted to lighten the mood. "He did send a giant with a gun."

Not amused, Rick spoke on, his voice hard. "I was so glad to see Xavier that I didn't have questions at first. Even this morning when I knew the truth, I kept telling myself to keep calm. But when we were laughing and talking and I looked at you and thought of what could have happened. You could have been raped, killed." He slammed a fist into his palm. "And all because things have to be done *his* way."

Melissa saw the pain behind Rick's anger. He loved his grandfather. Whether he knew it or not, he needed to feel good about him.

"He didn't know we would be in so much danger," she said. "No one could have anticipated it."

Rick laughed harshly. "Right, no one could anticipate, but that's his problem. He thinks he can control everything. He convinced himself he could keep tabs on us. Xavier says that he sent our photos to the airport in Merida and had people there on the alert—"

"*Our* photos?" she interrupted. "How did he get a photo of me?"

"I asked Xavier the same thing. He took a picture of the portrait and sent a photo of that. Some irony, huh? Besides the airport, he also had people on the lookout in other locations. As soon as he learned we had checked into a hotel at Carrillo Puerto, he had Xavier fly on ahead to intercept us here. Some protection, huh?"

She nodded. "It left us to go through the jungle on our own."

"Exactly. A journey we never needed to make."

Something struck Melissa as funny. "What was Xavier supposed to do if we never turned up? Start showing our photos to wild animals? 'Excuse me, Mr. Jaguar, but have you seen this man, this woman? Had them for lunch, perhaps?'"

Rick glared, his brows drawn together in a single black line. "It's not a joke."

Her expression went soft. "It hasn't all been bad, has it?"

He knew she was thinking of their night in Carrillo Puerto. Despite his attempts to hold on to outrage, the memory warmed him. He gave her a puzzled look. "How come you're making excuses for him?"

"Because he's your grandfather. You keep calling him an old man and it's true. His time is past, yet he still believes he can control every aspect, even from a distance. He can't, but—" She struggled for a moment with a renewed surge of anger over what had happened, then she made herself relax. "What he did was wrong, but he really does care. The last thing he would have wanted was for us to be hurt." She looked into Rick's eyes. "Don't hold this against him. Let it go. Please."

Rick ran a hand through his hair. "I don't know." Her attitude amazed him, yet he was grateful for it in a way he couldn't quite identify. All at once, he saw her stiffen.

"He doesn't know where the temple is too, does he?" Her eyes narrowed. "That we could have gone directly to it? That *would* be too much. Can you be sure?"

Rick blew out his breath in a noisy gust. "Yeah, I can be sure. If he had ever reached the temple, he would have never turned back,"

He glanced to the side as Xavier reappeared. Beckoning the man to him, he said, "Tell Melissa about my grandfather's visit here."

"Not exactly a visit," Xavier said, sitting on the ground cross-legged. "All he knew for sure was that there was a limestone area near the cave entrance."

Melissa frowned. "If he knew that much, why didn't he find the temple?"

"Because he only saw it from the air. He said he was never on the ground because there was no place for his plane to land. He flew on and searched for the temple from his airplane, but all he saw were treetops. He had to go home unsatisfied."

"And that stung him badly," Rick said with a faint smile. "He likes telling stories filled with drama. Talking about the time he came home with his tail between his legs didn't make the cut."

Melissa frowned and said to Xavier, "If a plane can't land, how did you get here if you didn't go through the jungle?"

"By helicopter. Arrangements had been made ahead of time for the pilot to be waiting for me with whatever I would need when I arrived, including firearms and equipment for going through the cave. The helicopter then brought me here. From the air, I searched for signs of the temple, but it was as Rick's grandfather said. There is nothing to see except trees."

Melissa pursed her lips. "So we have to do what the map says, go through the cave." She turned to Rick. "I heard you and Xavier talking while I was still half asleep. Is it really all underground?"

"Yeah. That's why I want an early start. I would like to get on through and find the temple while there's still daylight left."

Melissa looked wary. "Will we be in the cave all day?"

"I'm not sure. When Xavier got here yesterday, he took a look and saw no end to it."

"No end? When you told me about Richard hiding inside it, I imagined a tunnel, like on a highway, only rugged, with him crouched behind rocks while natives with torches ran from one opening to the other. Now you're saying we're going to be in it for hours."

"*Might*," he corrected. "What's the trouble?"

"The cave made sense to me with what I thought before, but why aren't we just going overland to the temple?"

"Because we don't know where the temple is. The cave is an underground trail. There may be a long way around above ground, but all I know is that when we emerge from the cave, we will be at the temple."

Melissa frowned. "On our way back, will we have to go through the cave again?"

"No. Once we find the diamond, he'll signal for the helicopter. The pilot will radio my grandfather to let him know of our progress. The old man thinks he's thought of everything." A horrid thought struck him. He took a breath. "Is this when you tell me you've got claustrophobia?"

"No. You *know* what the problem is."

"Bats?" he asked hopefully.

She couldn't help laughing at his expression. "Yes, bats. It's not the idea of the cave that bothers me, it's what might be inside it. Bats especially, but also lizards and beetles and spiders and all the other horrid things that like to hide in the dark."

Relief lit Rick's face like sunshine. Not claustrophobia. Thank you, God. "Come on. Xavier brought along lights that will cut straight through the cave gloom. The trip will be interesting. Even fun."

"I bet," she said sourly, not making a big rush out of getting to her feet. "The Seven Dwarfs could be down there singing *Hi-ho* and I still wouldn't think it was fun."

Xavier cleared his throat. "Rick, before we make further plans to go on, there is something I must say."

Rick gave the man a sharp look. "What? Something else my grandfather *forgot* to tell me?"

Xavier smiled faintly. "Regardless of what you think about your grandfather, he would not have sent me if he wasn't having second thoughts about this journey. Now that you have been in danger—" The big man's shrug was eloquent. "Who knows what lies ahead of us in the cave? It is you he cares about Rick, not the diamond. I think he would want me to call for the helicopter now. I think he would want you to come home."

CHAPTER TWENTY-ONE

RICK COULDN'T BELIEVE IT. Now that they were almost there, Xavier was saying to give up? "He *told* you that?"

"No, but I know the strength of his feelings for you. Now that you have been in such danger—"

"Danger be damned," Rick interrupted, emotion roughening his voice. "How bad off is he? Worse than when we left?"

"He continues to recover but the attack has taken its toll. His doctor fears the next one will be the end."

Rick looked at the big man. For all his size, Xavier, first a surgeon, now a cook, nurtured the physical person. It was different for his grandfather. Whatever else the old man might feel for him, Rick knew he had no use for quitters.

"Instead of making me want to run home, what you've told me makes me feel it's even more important to go on."

"I agree," Melissa said with quiet strength.

Rick viewed her with surprise. With all her concerns about the cave, this was the last thing he expected her to say.

"Hey," she said, "Don't you remember how mad I got when I thought you might leave me behind?" A smile softened her words. "Bring on the cave Malone, I'm in."

Despite her assurances, he searched her eyes. "If it's only because of the money, you don't have to worry. I'll make it up to you."

She looked insulted. "It's not the money. It's because . . ." She flashed Xavier an apologetic look. "I'm afraid I don't agree with Xavier. No matter how concerned your grandfather might be, I think he would want you to go on."

"You do?" The fact that she understood his unspoken conviction pleased him in a way he couldn't explain.

"I do," she said firmly. "All your disagreements with him have been about respect, haven't they? You struggling to show him that despite your differences, you're worthy? You are of course, but so far he hasn't been able to admit it. At last, you've got something you and he can both agree on—going after the Honeycomb Fire. I don't know if it actually matters whether you find the diamond or not but you've got to follow this quest to the end."

Rick grinned. "You're right about everything except that the diamond *does* matter. For you, for me and for my grandfather. We're not going home without it." He looked at Xavier. "You're okay with that?"

The man shrugged and smiled. "Where you go Rick, I go too. I can do nothing less."

Rick turned to Melissa. "You're sure?"

"Better believe it."

At her words, he impulsively opened his arms and she flew into them. She *understood*, he thought, thinking how right she felt in his embrace. Xavier, who had known both him and his grandfather for so long, had let his concerns twist his judgment, but Melissa had seen straight through to the heart of it.

Looking up at him, she smiled and gave him a quick kiss. The worst part was surely behind them. And just in case there *was* more trouble, Xavier was with them now, with lights for the cave and even a weapon.

"Onward," she said, not wanting to give herself time for second thoughts. *Onward to the cave, the temple and the diamond,* she thought. *And pray God, not too many bats.*

THE HIGH PRIEST SQUINTED against the dazzling glare of the rising sun and spoke in a strange, faraway voice. "Soon the moon will rule where the sun rules now. Tonight makes the last time I call for the goddess."

Eduardo looked away from the white-haired priest and concentrated on the breakfast that he and the other men of the village were sharing. It was best, he thought, to ignore the old man's senseless prattle. Balam, however, greeted his aged father's announcement with alarm.

"The final time? Father, are you saying you feel ill?"

"I have never felt better, thank you." The High Priest shifted his attention to Eduardo. "Are the plans in readiness for the celebration?"

"As ready as they can be," Eduardo answered, silently thinking, *as ready as they can be when we don't know the date.*

The old priest gave him a beatific smile. "Do not be disturbed," he said gently. "The time draws near."

"Draws near?" echoed Eduardo, disconcerted. It was as if his disgruntled thoughts had been laid bare to the white-haired man. But if he had been startled then, he was even more startled by what the High Priest said next:

"Tonight is the last time I shall stand alone in the temple. When I next lift the crown to the four corners of the earth, the goddess herself will stand before me."

CHAPTER TWENTY-TWO

RICK AND MELISSA FOLLOWED Xavier to the limestone area she had seen the night before as if in a hazy netherworld. By daylight and with the comforting presence of the two men, she simply found it a relief from so much jungle. There had been so many shades of green, vines tangling about her feet, the air filled with the peeps and screeches of birds, plus the ever-present mysterious rustling sounds in the treetops and worse, in nearby bushes. She was glad to be done worrying about that.

Xavier led them to a rise that ended in a rock outcropping with a low opening. They had to crawl to get inside. Once there they could stand. Xavier showed his flashlight around.

"There's nothing here," Rick to Xavier. "You said you went into it, that it's underground. Where? How did you get to it?"

The big man laughed, his gold tooth winking in the poor light. "Despite my doubts, I trusted the map and searched." He led them to an alcove behind a pile of rocks and flashed his light downward.

"Hey," Rick said, puzzled. "A giant hole with what looks like a new-looking rope ladder with a shiny metal hook jammed in a crack between stones?

Xavier laughed, "I brought it with me. If it holds my weight, and it does, it will hold yours. We three will soon be entering the underground tunnel."

"You came well equipped," Rick said admiringly.

I did." He flashed his light to a long duffle bag. "More supplies, including those that are medical. It is good to be prepared."

Melissa moved closer. "And we climb down there?" The opening was roughly circular, no more than four feet across at its widest point and nothing but blackness below. She shuddered. "It looks like a well."

Xavier flashed his light downward. "It's about ten feet deep."

He first lowered his duffle into the bottom of the hole, and then turning to face them he nimbly descended the rope ladder.

A draft blew up from the cave's interior. *Troll's breath*, Melissa thought, wrinkling her nose, expecting a mildew odor. There was only dry air, but she wasn't fooled. The inside of the cave would smell dank and foul, the perfect environment for creatures that shunned the light.

"I'm down," the big man called up.

Melissa, who was to climb down next, faced Rick and got situated on the ladder. It hadn't looked shaky with Xavier but it felt shaky to her. She gripped each side of the contraption, the rope harsh against her palms.

She looked at Rick, gritted her teeth and took her first step into the darkness. *Bride of the mole people* she thought, and then clambered down as fast as she could manage.

Once she was there, Rick descended smoothly. Xavier, using a branch that Xavier had handy, reached up and unhooked the ladder. "We will take this along in case we reach another tough spot and need it again," he said.

Melissa didn't want to think about more tough spots. She concentrated on the pleasant fact that the air around them felt dry and odorless.

Their plan was, once they had the diamond, they would find their way outside and then use the radio to contact Rick's grandfather, who would be waiting in a nearby town for the message to send a helicopter for them.

Xavier coiled and stowed the ladder in his big duffle, then took out helmets. Soon he had the headlamps, which had been stored separately, attached.

"Terrific!" Melissa said as she fastened on her helmet and switched on her headlamp. Now that she was actually on the last leg of their journey, she'd wondered if she'd have the courage to bravely keep on if they ran into anything truly difficult. Professional gear made her feel prepared. *Don't mess with me*, it said. *I'm experienced, in control.*

"A woman with a new hat," Xavier observed with a smile.

She laughed. Xavier's unexpected jest delighted her.

Staying in the lead, Xavier swung his duffle over his broad back and shoulder and guided them along the route he had previously explored. Melissa was pleased to find that the tunnel floor became smooth as they left the rubble-strewn entry and thanks to her light, she could see where she was stepping.

Rick, bringing up the rear, thought of his ancestor, Richard, who had braved the cave only to come back empty-handed. *This one's for you too, Richard*, he said silently, anticipating his success. By the time the sun went down, the Honeycomb Fire would be in his hands.

As they wound their way deeper into the earth, he was glad to see how well Melissa held up. There were a couple of tricky situations in which Xavier gave her a hand or he gave her a boost, but he felt she could have managed on her own had it been necessary. She was gutsy, he thought, feeling proud.

When the going was easy, he had the chance to tell her some of the other news that Xavier had brought. "My grandfather made good on his vow to poke into George's affairs. Turns out when George is on travel junkets for location shoots, he's also making deals with crooks for stolen treasures to add to his collection."

Melissa pursed her lips in a silent whistle. "And to think he made himself out such a great adventurer, discovering items and of course, without saying, acquiring them legally."

"Seems there's a museum in Turkey that's recently found that a certain ruby-studded chalice had been replaced by a fake, and guess what? The switch was made at the same time George was doing a photo-shoot on the Aegean. Some coincidence, huh?"

"And you think the real chalice is now in his collection?"

"I'm betting on it." Rick had wanted the satisfaction of smashing a fist into George's face, but his grandfather was right, the man should be behind bars. "He's left enough of a paper trail to get the authorities involved and they've gotten a warrant to search. It's going to be interesting when we fetch him from Carranza and he learns his elevated reputation is shot to hell." For the sake of their former friendship, Rick would have almost felt bad about it, but not when George had been willing to order Melissa's death.

Having taken the needs of their journey into consideration, Xavier had brought them backpacks filled with provisions and other items, including a compass, which Rick immediately tucked into his pocket.

"A compass is accurate underground," Xavier said. "The trouble is, cave tunnels follow routes of their own. You're at their mercy."

When they reached the place where Xavier had finished his explorations, they paused for a breakfast of granola bars, oranges and tea from an insulated container. The hot drink was welcome now that they had stopped moving and the wine-cellar coolness of the cave crept through the sweatshirts.

Peeling an orange, Melissa said to Rick, "So far, this hasn't been too bad." She dropped her orange peels in the trash bag Xavier had pulled from his backpack and said to him, "Food, some sort of battery transmitter, ropes, helmets, backpacks, lights, medical equipment, and now, trash bags. Xavier, is there anything you didn't think to bring along?"

The man smiled. "Very little."

"Except a watch," Rick said. "I've lost two watches starting from the first damn day of this trip and here I am, hooked up with a guy who hasn't worn one since he left Cuba."

Xavier shrugged and stowed the trash bag in a pouch on his pack. "Schedules and pressure and wearing two watches . . . that was my old life. I long ago gave up the need for clocks."

Rick winked at Melissa. "Just don't ask him for a three-minute egg."

"Insolent pup," Xavier retorted good-naturedly as he stood. "I make excellent eggs." He gestured as he spoke, his scarred hands moving capably. "It is a gift."

Melissa grinned to herself. The longer she knew Xavier, the better she liked him. He would look terrific in a tux. Maybe she should consider taking *three* escorts to her reunion.

When they started off again, Rick took the lead.

The path wound ever further downward but there was no real difficulty until they came to what rock climbers would call a "chimney"—a vertical chute that dropped down to a path on a lower level. Had they been in the cave for the fun of it, they could have worked their way down on handholds, but since they were only in the cave to get through it, they took a quicker way—the rope ladder.

Once Melissa's feet were on solid ground again she felt revved for more challenges. Xavier was still coming down when she joked and said to Rick, "I thought you said that was going to be easy."

"Fast, not easy," he corrected.

"Excuse me." She cocked her head. "I like it when we take it slow."

He winked. "I'll remember that."

Hearing Xavier coming down, Melissa stepped to one side and cast the beam of her light around. "How would Don Miguel—"

"Hold on, here comes Santa," Rick said as one of Xavier's booted feet became visible in the opening of the chute.

The big man dropped to the floor. He freed the rope ladder and stowed it in his pack again.

"Now, what were you saying about Don Miguel?" Rick asked, returning his attention to Melissa.

"This route goes away from the chute we just came down. You said we're following the same route that Don Miguel followed all those years ago and he came back this way too. How would he have seen this chimney hole above his head? It's high and he didn't have good lights like we do. Maybe he went back and found another way out. We think we're following his route, but maybe we're not."

Rick looked around with a thoughtful frown. "You're right. Don Miguel would have had a devil of a time finding the opening in the ceiling, especially with only a torch. And even if he did find it, how could he get up to it?"

"He could jump up and then climb," Xavier said.

"*You* could do it, and I guess I could too, but weren't people a lot shorter then? I don't see—"

Melissa laughed as an idea struck. "Mrs. Don Miguel."

"What?"

"Mrs. Miguel, Doña Miguel, whatever. He could have lifted her up. She was with him, wasn't she? That's the story I heard from you. The natives kept the diamond and let him and his wife go free."

Rick stared. "I'd forgotten about her."

Melissa rolled her eyes. "History from the male viewpoint. The female is in the story only to illuminate the hero. Let her climb a cave chimney and then take off her skirt or whatever she wore and twist it into a rope and haul the hero up and nobody wants to think about it."

"*You* did."

"Because I'm a woman too."

Rick chuckled and gave Melissa a quick kiss before they continued on their way, but he now wondered. All along he had assumed there was only one passage through the cave and that they were on it. But the discussion opened the possibility of other tunnels.

It was easy going for the next half hour, going deeper all the time. The deeper they went, the damper it became.

If they kept going down, Melissa wondered, wouldn't they eventually come to where the rain had seeped down through porous limestone and collected? So far they'd had no trouble keeping warm, but if they got wet it would be a different story. At the same time, she realized she wasn't as apprehensive as she would have expected. If they found water, they would also find a way past it. The cave was testing her, but she was rising to the challenges. She supposed they would never know exactly which route Rick's ancestors had taken, still, she felt glowing warmth as she thought to herself, *Me and Mrs. Miguel.*

After stopping for a snack break, they were on the move again. They rounded a corner and unexpectedly found themselves in a large, high-roofed chamber.

Melissa wrinkled her nose. "What's that smell?" This was the first time anything in the cave had any particular odor and it was awful, like dirty ammonia.

"Bats," Rick said.

"Bats?" She could hear the sounds then, faint, high-pitched twittering. Despite her helmet and the fact that her hair was braided, she instinctively lifted her hands to protect her head. Cringing, she looked up, her lamp showing the cave roof studded with dark patches—some of them individual bats, others clustered tightly together. A number of them, disturbed by the noise and lights, had separated from the colony to dart in spasmodic, crooked patterns before once again affixing themselves to the ceiling. Melissa let out a high-pitched sound of her own and scurried to the continuation of the tunnel.

"I don't care for this," she said in an awesome understatement. "I'm warning you, if one of them comes at me, I'm going to drop dead on the spot."

"Nothing's going to come at you," Rick said, his eyes fixed on the roof. "These little guys fly up and out." There was litter on the floor as if from a crumbling ceiling. "Turn off your lamps. We should see sunlight where the ceiling has broken through."

When the lamps were turned off, the ceiling was all black. "Weird," Rick said. "They have to get out somewhere."

"If one flies at me," Melissa said, "I'm keeling over and you'll have to drag my body the rest of the way because if you leave me in this place, I'll haunt you forever."

She had said it all in one breath and Rick heard the panic behind her attempt to joke. "Okay," he said, reluctantly starting to move, "but I'd still like to know how they get out."

"There," Xavier said. "Move to your right for a different angle. You will see a glimpse of light that's even higher up."

"*Sunlight*," Rick said in a tone of awe. "It's like this huge area has another roof above it." He gazed at the warm yellow glow, yearning with unexpected sharpness for the world of light outside.

"Lissa—" He beckoned. "Come see."

"Is it a place where we can get out?"

"Not unless you've grown wings."

She didn't laugh. "I want the people exit, okay?"

"Okay," he said. As they left the bat chamber behind, he took Melissa's hand. It was as cold as ice. "I shouldn't have teased."

"Forget it, but the farther we move from that cavern, the better I like it." Unable to resist glancing over her shoulder, she was reassured by Xavier's bulk behind them. She knew it was ridiculous, but she was nevertheless plagued by the notion that a bat might follow them.

As the journey continued the route became steeper, taking them away from any suggestion of dampness. Rick's lack of sleep started to catch up with him but he woke up when they came to a division in the tunnel, both branches looking equally promising.

"To the right," he announced with sudden conviction. Maybe his ancestors were slipping him hints because what he felt was more than a hunch. He *knew* the tunnel to the right was correct.

Xavier questioned his judgment. "Feel the air move through the left passage. That should make it a more superior way, should it not?"

His weariness forgotten, Rick sent the other man a challenging grin. "Bet you five bucks the draft over here is even better."

Xavier produced a candle and matches. "Poor friend, I will be stealing your money."

They tested the respective drafts. Failing to come to a firm conclusion, they upped the wager.

Melissa rolled her eyes. *Men.*

"A suggestion," she said. "Check out both passages. Go a short distance in each one, and *then* decide which one we should take."

Rick's eyes sparkled. "Twenty steps down each one." He shot Xavier a grin. "We'll save time by checking out your tunnel first. Twenty bucks says we'll hit a dead end within twenty feet."

"Not with this strong draft. My fingers already count my new wealth. I'll take half and buy you the best ten-dollar watch I can find."

"Thanks but I'm not holding my breath," Rick said with a laugh, following Xavier into the left tunnel.

The tunnel wasn't straight. It twisted this way and that, but the headroom was good and the floor was smooth.

"A waste of time to contemplate a different path," Xavier said after they had walked half the distance that had been agreed upon. Triumph colored his voice.

Melissa said nothing, but she found this tunnel portion was one of the smoothest they'd traveled through. She heard Rick say, "It's not over till it's over. We've not completed twenty steps."

Xavier rounded a corner. Rick and Melissa caught up and found the man confronted by a wall of stone.

"A dead end." He sounded stunned.

"Too bad, buddy," Rick said.

"I do not understand. How could there be air movement if the tunnel comes to an end?"

Rick directed his light to dark shadows up and around the rough sidewalls. "There must be enough cracks for the air to pass through." And then he said to Melissa, "Come on. Let's head back to the *real* tunnel."

With Xavier still muttering, Rick turned and he and Melissa started back the way they'd come.

"Hold on," she soon cautioned. "We don't want to get too far ahead."

Agreeing, Rick came to a stop. He looked down at the floor and frowned at the pea-sized chunks of limestone scattered on their path. "There wasn't rubble here before."

"The tunnel is wide at this point," Melissa said. "We must have walked along the wall on the other side."

"No, this rubble goes clear across. There's no way we could have avoided it."

Melissa looked up. "The roof must have crumbled since we walked through." Even as she spoke, she realized they would have heard the falling stones, but what other explanation was there? That's all they needed, the roof caving in. Spooked, she grabbed Rick's hand. "Let's get out of here."

"Hold on, Chicken Little." Rick gave her hand a reassuring squeeze and then arced the beam of his light around. His boots on the debris made crunching sounds. "You know what? This isn't how we came in."

"Of course it is. All we did was turn around."

"Sure, turned around and at one of those twisty turns there was a second path and we took it." Although the ease with which they had gotten fooled chilled him, he managed to keep his voice matter-of-fact. He raised his voice. "Hey, Xavier."

"Rick? Where are you?"

"Around the bend. I've found the explanation for the draft. When you turn back, you'll see there's a branch off the tunnel. Melissa and I just took it." *Took the wrong way, just like that*, he thought. Thank God there was a difference in the floor. They could have continued on without knowing it and been thoroughly lost.

Watching the glow of Xavier's approaching light, Rick heard a muffled, groaning sound. The floor suddenly shifted under his feet. To his horror, he realized that something under them had collapsed. He tried to jump to a safe spot, but it was too late. The groaning sounds increased. His feet slipped out from under him. The ground was falling away and there was nothing he could do to save himself. Melissa was caught in it too. He felt her weight slam against his backpack. The sound of her scream rose above what was now a roar of spilling stone. They were on the toboggan run of their lives, sliding with terrifying speed into the dark unknown.

CHAPTER TWENTY-THREE

THE SOUND OF COLLAPSING rock was deafening, There was nothing for Rick to grab onto, no way to stop his descent. He felt Melissa's weight jammed against his pack as if she were his passenger on a ride to hell. They bumped over a rough ridge and shot off to one side, tumbling wildly, which saved them from the main landslide that would have crushed them into blood-soaked dust.

Rick felt the incline beneath him turn slick and cold as it started to level out. He slammed in his heels and skidded to a stop. Ears still ringing from the sound, he felt cold wetness under his hands, feeling it squash and suck around his boot heels.

His backpack had been torn off, with one shoulder strap hanging loose, but he still wore his helmet and the light still worked. Getting his thoughts in order, he called for Melissa. No answer.

Melissa. Where was Melissa?

Fighting panic, he cast his light around and found her.

She lay still. She was breathing, but she didn't answer when he called her name. Her helmet had been torn off. Frantic, he ran his fingers under her hair, around her head and neck. He found no signs of injury, yet she remained unresponsive.

His thoughts raced. *Would she awake? Would she be all right?*

She stirred and hope filled him. Her eyes opened and then closed again and she didn't respond to her name. What did that mean? Xavier would know, but he wasn't there. After sitting beside her a while and worrying uselessly, Rick stood and looked around.

He couldn't figure out what he slid into that had felt wet. Had his canteen smashed? They kept them in their packs—no sense having them slinging around when they walked. He found his intact. Angling his headlamp he was surprised to see a pool of water about ten feet across. Moving to it, he knelt, dipped his fingers into it, and then cupped some up with his hand. It looked clear in his light and it had no scent. He couldn't see where it had come from.

The cavern they'd slid into was rectangular, about the width and length of his Philadelphia apartment living room, maybe twelve by sixteen. The cave ceiling was maybe thirty feet up. One of the walls sloped steeply because of the rock slide, but the other three were craggy and more or less straight. He saw no water dripping down. Maybe an underground stream. Making use of it, he splashed water on his face, washing away the grit that clung to his skin. He moved around to the side of the pool, saw an opening, climbed up and found a narrow tunnel. After wriggling through a short distance, it widened to a passage that looked promising.

He returned to Melissa, finding her unchanged. He took the spare T-shirt that he'd used for himself, re-dampened one end of it in the pool. Gently he patted around her face and eyes with the cool wet cloth, and then, thank God, her eyes opened.

SHE SAW THE HEADLAMP'S glare against the surrounding darkness. *Rick.* Felt his touch. She tried to speak through a throat clogged with dust. She choked. Rick helped her sit and supported her until her coughing fit subsided, then pressed her against his chest. She felt his warmth, heard the beating of his heart.

Getting her breath back, she said, "Are you all right?"

"Yes, but you were out of it for a while."

"*Out of it?*" She didn't like the sound of that, but she guessed it was

Beverly T. Haaf

true if he said so. Her teeth hurt as if she'd clenched them together when they had started falling and her arms felt bruised, but otherwise, she felt okay.

"My helmet's gone!" She peered around for its light.

"It's here," Rick said, thinking with relief that she sounded normal. "The light's broken but it will still protect your head." He placed her helmet in her hands. "And here's one of the flashlights." Her pack had been torn off too, but he had found it and the flashlight inside it.

"Where's Xavier?

"Up where we were a few minutes ago."

When he angled his head, Melissa looked up and by his headlamp saw nothing but a landslide of rocks.

"The whole side of the passage we were in collapsed?"

"And part of the ceiling, too," he said. "I yelled for Xavier but heard nothing from him."

Oh, God!" Her voice reflected horror. "Was he caught in it?" She turned her head to look backward, but without her headlamp, she could see nothing. "Is he somewhere under the rubble?"

"He was off to the side when the floor gave way. He's safe." He spoke with confidence, hoping he was right.

"We should make sure."

"There no way we can do that," he said.

She frowned. "When I was little, my mother said if I got lost, I shouldn't wander around trying to find her. I should go to where I last saw her and she would find me."

"You mean we should just sit and hope Xavier finds us? That's not going to work." He told her about the passage he'd found.

"You think it will lead us outside? If Xavier—"

He cut her off. "Xavier will do what seems best and that's to go back the way we first came in. He would expect me to do what's best from where we are. What I think is best is to take that passage I found."

As he spoke, he vowed to set all concerns about Xavier aside. He could do nothing, so worry was pointless. He needed to concentrate on what he *could* do. His job now was his and Melissa's safety. She still looked worried. He decided to try for a distraction. "Hey," he said, "I've got something to show you."

He took her flashlight and showed her the pool, the surface gleaming under his light like black glass. "I washed the grit off of me and, here—" He handed over his T-shirt. "Use it like a washcloth and a towel. It's not fancy but it's better than nothing."

"Fancy enough for an underground Bellevue-Stratford," she said, thinking she'd never had the money to stay in the famed Philadelphia landmark hotel. "Where's my backpack?"

"Here," he said. He figured her Bellevue-Stratford remark was a joke—if she could joke, that was good. Damned good. He handed over her backpack. "Mine got a strap broken but yours is okay."

She nodded. Taking Rick's T-shirt and her backpack, she moved to the pool, stopping at a flat rock on the edge of the water.

She pulled off her sweatshirt, shook it out and set it aside. Kneeling, she pushed her hair back and bent over the water, rinsing off the grit and grime and sweat. She wished she knew if the water was safe to drink, wished it wasn't so cold, wished she was in a real hotel. The cheapest one would do as long as it had a hot shower.

After patting herself dry, she put her sweatshirt back on and then rummaged in her pack to see if Xavier had included a toothbrush, toothpaste and a comb. Yes! As she worked the tangles out of her hair and then re-braided it, she made a silent prayer for the big man's safety. Returning items to her pack, she felt around for her comb, which she had placed on the rock in front of her.

"Hmm," she murmured when she found it. She dried it off and returned it to its place in her pack and returned to Rick.

"I think we should head for that passage you found."

"Good," he said. "Let's get going."

"Yes," she said. "Especially since the water is rising."

"*What!*"

He didn't believe her, not even when she told him how she'd set her comb down in front of her knees and when she picked it up, it was in the water.

"Your comb probably slid down the rock," he said.

Following along behind him, she saw by the light of her flashlight that he had reached the place where she had washed. Moving closer, she said, "There's the flat stone."

"That can't be where you knelt. It's almost all under the water."

"Right. Now keep watching." Bending, she placed a small stone on the edge of the dry part of the rock still exposed.

"I'll be damned," he said as his headlamp showed water creeping toward the stone.

"I think one wall here is the side of a cenote. The rock slide broke something and it's sprung a leak. A big one. Water's coming fast enough for us to see the pool rising,"

Still dumbfounded by what he was seeing, Rick could now hear faint sounds as the water crept up on the loose debris from the rock slide—soft clicks, taps and tiny shifting noises as the water moved higher. He cast his light around, seeing that the damp area he'd slid into earlier had become a puddle."

"Should have believed you," he said to Melissa.

She grinned. "Nobody's perfect. And now, either we call the manager of this hotel and say somebody left the water running, or we go to that passage you found and move to a better place."

"Yeah, let's grab our packs and your helmet and get moving."

A few moments later, pushing their packs ahead of them, they squirmed through the narrow tunnel that opened to a passage where they could stand and walk. They moved quickly, eager to put distance between themselves and thoughts of the rapidly rising water behind them. Fortunately, the path went upward.

"I can't believe there are people who do this for sport," she said as she clambered over sharp-edged boulders that lay tumbled like a giant's set of toy blocks.

"Takes all kinds," he said, boosting her over a high place.

On level ground again, she paused, jamming her flashlight into her waistband and slipping off her helmet. If only the dratted lamp still worked. It had been so nice not having to depend on holding her flashlight. Rick, who had also paused, stood just behind her, one hand lightly touching her hip. She felt the warmth emanating from his body. For a second, the truth that she had been struggling with settled like a stone in her stomach: if this trail led nowhere, they were truly stuck. To keep on going she had to cling to hope. She shined her flashlight ahead. Like an encouragement, she saw a smooth, lighter-colored wall that didn't gobble up every speck of light and she felt a faint breeze.

Rick felt it too. "A draft. We're getting somewhere."

"Of course," she said, turning to kiss him.

They held each other for a moment, then they continued following the passage in an upwards direction.

"It seems we're climbing up more than we climbed down before," she said, all too aware of her aching muscles and sore knees.

"Yeah, rough going," he said. "Time for a break."

They dined on cold, meat-stuffed tortillas washed down with water from their canteens. Melissa flashed her light on her hands. "My kingdom for a manicure." An unexpected thrill came as she remembered overcoming rough moments during their journey. They would soon find the temple, she knew it.

On their way again, still climbing up, they were now in an area of dark walls that absorbed the light. Rick had no idea of the time. *My kingdom for a watch*, he thought. How long had they been in the cave? They couldn't keep going forever. He would have felt like a rat trapped in a maze if not for the beckoning pull of air. He had to trust that the tunnel was taking them somewhere.

All at once, they glimpsed a misty light filtering in through the passageway ahead. Their weariness forgotten, they stumbled forward.

Melissa gave a cry. "Our way out!" Excitedly she raced past Rick and darted around a corner. Before Rick caught up, he heard her wail of dismay— "It's too high. We'll never reach it!"

He rounded the corner and saw the light, bright and scarlet, shining through a jagged opening in the cave roof twenty feet above their heads. Melissa sat slumped on a ridge about as high as a small wall, her helmet on the ground beside her.

She turned to him, her face clearly visible in the natural light.

"It's sunset," she said, sounding close to tears.

"Sunset," Rick echoed, blinking against the light and then staring as if hypnotized by the brilliance of the sky.

Getting up, Melissa moved up a steep incline to the area where the light struck the floor. "It's warm," she said, placing one hand on the sun-struck spot. "Come up here and feel it. It's so warm!"

Not moving, standing several yards from her, Rick thought she looked ethereal in the light surrounding her as if she was in some other world. With a shiver, he wondered if she realized that this scrap of sky might be their last view of the world outside.

He dropped his gaze to where she stood. With horror, he knew where they were. That glimpse of outside light was what they'd seen hours before with Xavier—seen it through the broken roof of an evil-smelling cavern filled with bats. The passage they'd been following had led them in a circle, only on a much higher level. What they had earlier seen as a decaying ceiling, was now the floor on which Melissa stood, with jagged openings on either side of her. Why the bat dirt smell hadn't yet reached her, he didn't know, but now that he *did* know, he smelled it.

Because of the slope, she was higher than he. Stepping over the ridge and closer, he said urgently, "Melissa! Don't move!"

Startled, she looked down at him. "What's wrong?"

"You're standing on a narrow bridge of stone. There is no floor to your left or to your right."

She glanced down, seeing that the sun-bright rock under her feet had nothing but impenetrable blackness on either side. Her heart thumped. She remembered hurrying toward the light, eyes heavenward. If not for luck, she could have placed her feet on nothing but air.

Seeing her stunned expression and fearing for her, Rick stepped over the ridge Melissa had been sitting on before she'd gone forward again. "It's okay," he said, reaching out his hands. "Come toward me."

Without hesitation, she stepped toward him.

He stepped toward her.

They had almost touched hands when their combined weight shifted the stone beneath their feet.

Melissa cried out and instinctively jumped back. Rick did the same.

The section that had been under their feet groaned, see-sawed, broke loose and dropped away. The cave shook with the impact of broken rock thundering into the chamber below.

For a moment, rising stone dust obscured everything. When Rick could see again, there was only open space between him and Melissa.

She cried out as a shape sailed past her face. Then another and another, soft, furry missiles boiling up on both sides of her, zooming past her hips, her arms, a wing briefly brushing her hair. *Bats*.

Disturbed by the rock fall, the entire colony poured forth from the lower chamber, pin-wheeling past Melissa in their mad flight to escape through the hole in the roof above her head.

"*Bats!*" she cried, thinking of nothing else. "*Bats all over me!*"

Helpless, Rick saw that any second she might fall. Stepping back behind the ridge for a more secure position, he thanked God that she was above him and still fairly close. He did the only thing he could think of, yelling, "Forget the damn bats! Jump to me. I'll catch you!"

But she only knew panic. Her worst nightmare had become a reality. She was covered in bats, smothered in bats. Mindless of her precarious situation, she let her flashlight drop and crouched with her arms about her head, her hysterical cries mingling with the shrieks of the bats as they swirled past her in frantic clusters, their musky scent filling her nostrils.

"Jump to me! I'll catch you!" Rick repeated. Helpless, he saw her twisting in a macabre dance, her arms around her head. One misstep and she would be forever lost, disappearing into darkness below. And now he saw pieces falling from the stone bridge on which she stood.

Any second, the whole thing could go, taking her with it.

As the last of the bats skittered past her face, Melissa saw Rick reaching toward her, saw the desperation in his face, saw him leaning toward her and heard him shout, "The rock under you is going! I'll catch you! Jump!"

She felt the shifting under her feet. She gave a single glance at the horrid emptiness between them and cried, "I'm coming!"

She leaped out and toward him as the shelf behind her collapsed, roaring down.

Her flying approach blocked Rick's light and in that instant he knew he had falsely imagined her coming toward him after a running jump, soaring and landing in his waiting arms, her momentum carrying them both back safely from the precipice. But she'd had no time for a running jump. She wasn't coming down close enough to him!

Sinking to his knees and stretching out as far as possible he grabbed her one arm and by some miracle managed to sling his other arm about her waist, his fingers grasping the back of her belt and managing to hold on despite the jolt of her full weight, her legs dangling over nothingness. For a heart-stopping moment he thought they would both go down, and then with a desperate strength he hadn't known he possessed, he reared back and jerked to his feet, levering her up, her legs dragging over the ridge where he'd braced himself. With his arms wrapped around her, he slammed back against the solid wall behind him.

With the background clamor of the falling rock and the rise of dust, he held her painfully tight as he kept repeating, almost sobbing in grateful relief, "I caught you . . . I caught you . . . ."

And she was sobbing, "You caught me . . . you caught me . . . ."

Exhausted, their legs folded under them. They sagged to the stone floor, holding one another, their breathing labored, pulses still racing.

Finally, after what seemed an eon, he drew a long, deep breath and said, "Next time, no running ahead."

Next time? She wondered how she could summon a smile but she did. "So now it's my fault?"

"Right. And another thing. Use the brains God gave you. I'm leading and you're following and no shoving to be first."

"I didn't shove."

"Same thing. Your flashlight is lost somewhere in that pit and that's where your rushing ahead stunt could have landed you."

"*Stunt*!" It felt terrific to have a nonsensical spat after what had almost happened. "I was safe. It was only when we stepped toward each other that the rock gave away."

"So? You're lucky to be alive."

"Ha! If you'd gone ahead and I'd been on your tail like you just said, we would both have stepped on the weak place at the same time, and we'd both gone down, right?'

"Wrong," he said.

The sunset was fading, but there was still enough light for her to see his face. Was he fighting a smile?

"What do you mean, I'm wrong?" she challenged.

"I look ahead. I would have seen the broken gaps to either side of where you walked, known we were on top of that bat cave with the rotten ceiling and I would have turned both of us back. Okay?"

"Monday morning quarterback," she said, but maybe he was right. "Okay, I'll do what you said."

"And don't forget it," he said.

"Always have to have the last word."

"Damned right, and don't forget *that*, either!" Grinning, he tapped her nose. "Let's get moving. You do know where we're going, don't you?"

"Going back to find another passage, right?"

"Head of the class, Teach," he said.

They finally found another passage, telling each other it would be a way out, but Rick, remembering what Clem, the old wrangler, once told him: "There's no such thing as a sure thing."

After what must have been another hour, Rick said, "It's night by now and we've had a hell of a day. We need to rest and recharge."

And, from the way his bad ankle ached, stopping wouldn't come a minute too soon. He drew his flashlight from his pack. "I'll look around and do a ceiling check."

"For bats?" She laughed. "I'm cured, but don't Mexican bats use radar? I didn't know they could be so dimwitted."

"They were as scared as you were." Complaints about bat

intelligence seemed a sign of complete recovery. "They didn't expect to find you between them and their exit." For an instant, a memory of the dungeon from his nightmare winked in his mind. Had the bat chamber resembled a dungeon?

"Rick, I want to say something. I could have gotten both of us killed."

"Yeah, but you didn't. Enough said."

She knew he meant it—she'd come to understand that's how he was. If something was done and over, he didn't want to hear more about it.

"Look—" He aimed his light, showing they were in a section that held a small chamber to one side, a niche in the wall, a snug alcove set a trifle higher than the rest of the floor.

"We couldn't have found a better place for the night if we had planned it," he said.

"We sleep here?"

"Sure. And when we wake, we start moving again but for now, this is good."

There were so many things he didn't want to think about. Like how lost they were. Soon they would be blindly following the trail— really blind, because batteries for helmet lamps and flashlights don't last forever. With their lights gone they would be in darkness and their food and water would soon be gone. Lights out, curtain down, the end. As for his grandfather, Rick figured his failure to return would also be the end of the old man.

Too much to think about He just wouldn't think.

He took out his rolled blanket and shook it. "Get your blanket too. Cave temperature won't go lower, but it's too cold for sleeping without a cover." Bending, he spread his blanket in the alcove, which had plenty of space for two—a cozy hideaway.

"Come here," he said, sitting down, taking Melissa's hand and bringing her to sit beside him. He removed her helmet and placed it on the floor by his feet, then did the same with his own, regretfully seeing that its lamp was fading. Suppressing a shudder, he kept it on for a second more and then determinedly switched it off.

In the darkness, Melissa sighed and rested her head against his shoulder. "That miserable bat back home didn't use his radar either."

"The one that flew into your hair?" He loosened her hair from its braid as he spoke. It cascaded softly over his hands like silken rain.

She settled herself against him more comfortably. "I'm a wimp."

"If something I was scared of flew at me, I'd have wimped out too."

"Wimped out," she said distastefully. "I hate it."

"Shhh," he whispered, slipping a hand under the back of her shirt. "Think about something else." Caressing her was a definite distraction for him and he hoped it was the same for her. "Shhh," he repeated, resting his forehead against hers.

She lifted her face so that their lips brushed.

"I was so scared."

Not as scared as I was for you, he thought, but didn't say it, didn't want to think about it.

He pulled her close, his mouth blending with hers. Rolling to his back, he took her with him, her body sprawling luxuriously across his.

All the good things Melissa had known with him seemed to be combined, the trust, the laughter, the feeling of being treasured and protected, all of it melding together and enhanced by the dreamy sweet arousal of desire.

"So beautiful," he said, kissing her tenderly and then with passion. Clothing was loosened, pushed aside. She sat astride him as his touch skimmed lightly across her skin. "So beautiful," he repeated, taking her wrists in his hands, kissing her palms, then extending her arms and lifting them, raising his body as he did so until her arms were high above her head. When he unlaced his fingers and stroked his hands downward, she kept her arms as he had placed them, as if her wrists were invisibly bound to a canopy over their heads. His willing captive. She shivered and gasped as his touch found her once more.

"What are you doing?" she asked, barely able to frame the words.

"Anything, everything . . ."

And so he did, sending blinding, writhing pleasure shattering through her until she could endure no more. With a moan of surrender, she lowered her arms and sank forward, her hair spilling in a curtain about their faces. He lifted her, lowered her gently until, with a shuddering, thrilling sigh she became one with him. Hands clasped about her hips, he moved slowly, then urged on by her response, more forcefully until they were both caught up in sweet violence, answering need for need.

"Lissa," he chanted, "Lissa, Lissa," as if his lips knew no other name as a blaze of ecstasy consumed them both.

Later she roused to find him tucking the other blanket around them, her body still half pillowed on his.

"Keeping each other warm," he murmured, content and not wanting to think beyond that point, easing back into slumber as he snuggled her close.

She relaxed and drifted, the events of the past day floating dreamily through her mind. She knew he had said *enough said*, but she couldn't stop herself from saying, "I would have fallen."

Her words roused him. "Yeah, well I would have been embarrassed to go home alone. Explanations are awkward. I would have had to jump down too."

"And catch me in mid-air."

"And go down with you."

"Save you from the awful embarrassment."

"Yeah," he said, but she sensed desperation in his kiss as his lips found hers.

"Let's make magic," he whispered.

Let's make love, she thought, wondering if the words could be as true for him as she realized they were for her.

CHAPTER TWENTY-FOUR

"**LISSA, HONEY, TIME TO** wake up." Rick's lips were close to her ear.

Her eyes opened. He came into focus. She blinked. "Is it morning?"

He gave a glance at the flashlight working on the last of their batteries. "Who the devil knows, but there are dragons to conquer and walls to storm."

"Better than yesterday's adventures," she said, working the stiffness out of her muscles.

"If we keep climbing at least we know we must be closer to the surface."

Or near the top of another bat cave, she thought but didn't say it. She knew he felt responsible not only for himself but for her—a double load. The least she could do was be encouraging.

He told her he'd played around with the compass and they were roughly on track with the map.

"That's wonderful." She put enthusiasm into her voice.

He responded with a grin, the roughness of his unshaven beard making unfamiliar shadows in the hollows of his cheeks. "Onward, Lissa. Onward, and *pray*."

Dear lord, she did love this man. More than ever now, when he could summon a smile even though he must be as worried as she was.

She lost track of how long they kept walking. She knew it must have been hours and she was hungry again, but she didn't want to stop going forward. Finally, they stopped long enough to sip water, careful not to spill a drop, and then started on again, still uphill.

She didn't know how much longer it was when she caught a faint glimmer from the corner of one eye. She told herself it was wishful thinking. A visual trick, a mirage. She was afraid to hope, but still . . . .

"Rick . . ." Her voice cracked with tension. When he turned, she indicated a small passage that took off to one side. "Turn off your light."

Not asking why, he did so "My God," he breathed as he saw the faint glow. "A passageway. And I went past without a second glance."

"Let me peek in," she said. "Not going ahead like before, but it's so narrow and I'm smaller. Just to look."

He saw her point. "A peek, but if you start pulling your feet in, I'm pulling you back."

"A promise," She took off her pack and stuck her head and shoulders in. "The sides look more like dirt than rock," she called back. "I think it goes up. I see light coming directly down in front of me."

She gave a gasp.

"What?" he said. She felt his hands tighten on her ankles.

"I see roots!" she called back. "Tree roots." She wasn't going to admit her first horrified thought had been *snakes*.

She started wriggling backward and he helped her out. She showed him what she'd brought out.

"Dirt," he said in wonder. "Honest to goodness dirt."

The next ten minutes were spent widening the entrance to make room for the breadth of his shoulders.

And this time he was going in first.

"Not fair," she said.

"You saw, now I get to see." He took off his backpack.

"I found it. I've got the right," she said.

"Going to cry next?"

"If it works."

He laughed. "I'll go in far enough to see what you saw."

They were both feeling good, wanting to laugh and kid around. They were almost out and safe. And please God, no more disappointments.

"I'll yank you back if you keep going on," she said.

"Can't. I'm too big,"

"I'll bite your ankles."

"Through my boots?'

"I'll yank them off first. Now go on and watch out for the snakes."

He turned his head and his lamp in her direction.

"*Snakes*?"

She kept her face straight. "Didn't believe me about the rising water, did you? You'll see."

"Ha!" he said and started in.

His feet moved further in. She was about to grab one of his boots when he called back, his voice muffled, "I see the snakes. Pretty ones with black and red stripes. Cute little things. I can't believe you were afraid."

"You're making that up!" Yet her guidebook had related that deadly coral snakes lived in the Yucatán. "Don't touch them!" she said. "Red and black with yellow stripes?"

"And purple plaid."

"What?'

She heard him laughing as he called back to her. "The tree roots do look like snakes. Is that what you thought at first?"

"Of course not," she lied.

"Sure," he said, and then, "Ok, I'm going up. No more fooling around. Come on behind me. Let's get out of here!"

After widening openings around the roots, they popped up like rabbits from a hole, emerging in a strip of clearing surrounded by jungle—a place of rocky soil and rough grass and white flowers buzzing with bees. Dusting themselves off, they thankfully greeted the sun. From its height, it looked to be around three o'clock in the afternoon.

Intoxicated with freedom, Melissa relished the warm light and soft wind, the hum of the insects and the perfume of the blossoms. Tossing her helmet to the ground, she spun in a circle, then flung herself into Rick's arms. "We're out of the cave. We're out!" She kissed him hard on the mouth, then yanked off his helmet and threw it to the ground beside her own. "Don't anybody ever say the word *cave* to me again."

Laughing, he returned her kiss, rubbed a smudge of dirt from her cheek—a useless exercise since they both resembled chimney sweeps —and then he hugged her tight. Only now could he admit to himself how worried he had been. But they were okay now, and as he gazed into Melissa's uplifted face and saw her sparkling eyes, he knew exactly what he wanted to do when this was all over and the sooner they got moving, the sooner they could celebrate.

After giving her another hug, he released her and looked around. The clearing was limestone, similar to what had been about the cavern entrance. The only thing growing in it was their friend, the tree.

Closing her eyes, she thrust her face up into the sun. So warm, so bright. No wonder people worshiped it. Hearing sounds, she opened her eyes. Above her was the sole of Rick's boot.

He was climbing the tree! "What are you doing?" she called.

"This tree helped us once. It might help again."

"How?"

"We don't know where we've come out, right? Suppose we're near the temple? From up here I can look around."

The temple. She couldn't believe she'd forgotten about it. That was crazy—the temple had been their goal all along.

Rick reached a perch that allowed him to gaze out over a sea of treetops. Everything appeared the same at first, then off to one side, he noticed something different. His eyes focused in.

"Lissa!" His voice rose in amazement. He would have never believed it could be so easy. "I think I've found it."

"The temple?"

"I don't know what else it could be. It—"

"No, wait." She started up the tree. "Let me see for myself."

Joining him, she asked where to look and before he could answer, she said, "You mean that gray spot?" To the southwest, a smudge of gray showed up against the green.

"Sure, what else? It's probably about a mile away. I can't make out carvings at this distance, but what else could it be except the temple?"

"A big rock?"

"Nah. This isn't the kind of country with rocks like that. Anything that size would be man-made."

"If it's the temple, how come Xavier didn't see it from the air?"

"Because the tree tops hid it. We're in a position to glimpse it, but taller trees shelter it."

"He was in a helicopter, probably zooming up and down hunting for it. If we can see it, how come he couldn't?"

"The angle?"

"Sure," she said. She was sorry she had mentioned Xavier. It made her feel bad and surely made Rick feel worse. Had he gotten out of the cave? Was he safe? Would they ever know what had happened to him?

Rick had taken out the compass and fiddled around with it—at least that's how it looked to Melissa. Put her in a boat with a compass and oars and she would row herself off the edge. Melissa Magellan, proving the Earth was flat.

"It's the only thing I see that could be right," Rick said.

She still thought the gray blob was probably a big rock, but if it was in the right direction, at least they would be going somewhere. She was confused, however. She had thought going through the cave would take them directly to the temple. Then again, there's been a lot of time since the stories had been told and the map had been made. And they sure took unexpected routes. They were lucky to emerge and see something that *could* be the temple.

Before they walked further, they had breakfast sitting under the tree, neither of them ever remembering feeling so hungry. They drained Rick's canteen. Melissa still had some water left for later.

They started off again in high spirits but soon were tiring. After crossing the clearing, they were in the jungle again

A mile as the crow flies and a mile trudging through a jungle are entirely different units of measurement. Rick cursed because he had forgotten how miserable it was to hack through the brush. Especially since his pack had a bush knife and not his big machete. Melissa was so hot and sweaty that the coolness of the cave started looking good. The cave hadn't had any spiders either. Only moments before one had dropped down on her, a big one with fur on its legs, and she had screamed loud enough to break its eardrums—if spiders *had* eardrums.

Rick flicked the creature away and brushed web fragments from Melissa's hair. "Probably a lady out hunting for food so she could nourish her eggs. I would have imagined another female would show more understanding."

Melissa had not been amused. *Spiders* . . . What had God been thinking?

Ten minutes later, Rick sank down on a fallen log and wiped sweat off his face, then promptly jumped up again as a cloud of mosquitoes swarmed up around him.

Melissa laughed. "All pregnant ladies, I'm sure. What a gentleman to stand."

Rick muttered something she was glad she didn't understand and swatted the mosquitoes away. They had come to an area where a storm had swept through, leaving snapped trees and flattened vegetation, the debris offering more places than usual for rain to collect and insects to incubate. He glanced up.

"Ah-ha!"

"Ah-ha, what?" Melissa jerked her head up to see where he looked and then they were both seeing an opening left when a tree had fallen, no doubt the victim of a recent storm. They peered through the space and saw a tall, narrow wall and realized they had reached their goal.

"That explains it," Rick said, feeling vindicated. "When Xavier flew by, the temple must have been hidden by that tree that's now gone."

"And I was afraid we were chasing after a big rock." Melissa laughed, delighted. The temple at last. Now that they had arrived, the trip didn't seem so bad after all.

But as they drew closer, her eagerness faded. "It's all ruins except for this one section. I don't see zigzag designs. And where's the altar?

"It's been a long time since Don Miguel's visit. The part with the altar must have fallen in."

Melissa groaned. "You're saying it's under all that rubble?" Extending out from one side of the wall was a huge mound of broken stone, as high as their heads at the tallest point and overgrown with vegetation.

"Maybe we've come up on the wrong side," Rick said. "I bet we'll find the altar when we go around to the front."

Hoping he was right, Melissa moved to follow him, touching a lichen-covered section of the wall for support as she stepped over a fallen stone.

Pausing, she took a closer look at the wall. "Under this green stuff, there might be a design after all. Oh, boy, I think I see the outline of a face."

"We'll look at it later." Having decided that climbing over the rubble pile would be easier than going around it, Rick grabbed a vine to help hoist himself over a rough spot. "Are you coming?"

"Just give me a minute."

She glanced and saw he was almost to the top. Shrugging, she knelt and scraped at the wall with a shard of stone only to discover that what had appeared to be the forehead and nose of a face in profile was only a squiggly crack.

"Damn and double-damn," she muttered under her breath as she shifted her attention to the rubble pile. That's where the altar was, she just knew it. The altar and the diamond were buried under tons of rock. Why was there never a forklift around when you needed one?

"Rick," she said, getting to her feet. She heard him returning.

He appeared, standing above her on the vine-covered rubble. There was an odd expression on his face.

"Don't tell me," she said with a sigh. "Let me guess. The other side is as blank as this one."

"Not . . . exactly." His voice sounded funny and he looked dazed. Then his eyes rolled up and his knees sagged. He collapsed, falling face down on the rubble.

CHAPTER TWENTY-FIVE

"RICK!" SHE STARTED TO RUSH to him, then froze as a swarthy man stepped out and stood where Rick had been standing only seconds before. In one hand he carried a shotgun, and in the other hand he gripped a club. In a sickening parody of a big game hunter, he grinned and planted his foot on the center of Rick's back.

Melissa gasped. *Rick*! This stranger must have clubbed him down. How hurt was he?

"Do not think of escape," the stranger warned with a snarl that showed broken teeth. His accent was Spanish, his words altogether too clear. "I wish to make no move I might later regret."

Melissa stared at him. He was garbed in a khaki cap and a sweat-stained army uniform, the fabric stretched to fit over his meaty shoulders and bowling-ball stomach. Stunned, she realized he was one of the men she had seen at the airfield in Piste.

She opened her mouth to ask what was going on, then watched in horror as he drew back his foot and gave Rick's limp body a kick that sent it tumbling the rest of the distance to the ground. The stranger clambered down to crouch beside the unconscious man. Looking up at Melissa, who stood as if paralyzed, he said gruffly, "Is this man your husband?"

Thoughts flying, Melissa moistened her dry lips. "No." She wondered if it made any difference what she said.

"A good friend then," the man said with a nasty chuckle. "I see how you look at him." He rocked back on his heels, and despite his smile, the eyes he pinned on her were as cold as death. "Listen woman, and listen well. Your life is nothing to me. The only reason you still breathe is because I allow it. Do you hear me?"

Although rigid with fear, Melissa's mind still worked. What did this man want? How had he come to ambush them? How could she and Rick get away? She realized he waited for her answer. "Yes . . . yes, I hear you."

"Then hear this. I will put down my gun and tie his hands. You will wait for me to do the same to yours. Do you know why you will not run?"

What was this, Twenty Questions? Melissa's heart pounded hard enough to shake her chest. She cast a glance at Rick, praying he only pretended to be knocked out, but his pallor and the sag of his jaw told her the prayer was in vain.

She heard the man's question repeated as he gave his shotgun an impatient jog. Wildly she groped for an answer. "Because I won't get away?" Only she would, she thought. While he was chasing her, Rick would have time to wake up and escape. The man would end up with neither of them.

"Sí," he said. "In the jungle, there is no easy place to run. And should you try, you will not go far. Do you know why?"

He was crazy, she decided, and if she didn't come up with the right answers to his loony quiz, she would be sorry. "Because you would catch me?"

"Sí, I will catch you." Unexpectedly he set the shotgun aside. "But do you know what I will do before I chase after you? I will take one of his eyes." He grabbed Rick by the hair, and as if from nowhere, a switchblade appeared in his other hand, seven inches of gleaming steel.

The breath whooshed from Melissa as if she had been sucker-punched. "No, you wouldn't!"

"You doubt me? Then I shall take it now. He needs but one eye for my purposes. Then if you run, I will take his tongue—"

"No, no . . . ." Melissa heard herself scream. She wanted to run forward to Rick but as in a nightmare, her feet stuck like glue. She dropped to her knees. This monster, this fiend straight from hell, she had no doubt he would do as he said. "No, please, no! Don't hurt him, I'll do anything, anything . . . ."

"You will do nothing, except as I tell you." His expression satisfied, he let Rick's head drop. The knife disappeared.

Sobbing, Melissa sagged to the ground. The vision of the knife poised over Rick's face swam before her. The fiend had meant it. He would maim and kill without a second thought.

RICK REGAINED CONSCIOUSNESS WHEN a canteen of water was dumped over his head. Coughing and sputtering, he tried to sit up and found his hands tied behind his back. He caught sight of his captor.

"Carranza." Glaring, he recognized the man he had hired to waylay George and Vince.

Carranza bowed. "Benito Carranza. Again we meet."

Blinking, Rick tried to get his bearings. His head ached as if somebody had tried to split it like a log. The last thing he remembered after climbing the rubble pile was a figure appearing as if from nowhere. Carranza must have been lying in wait. Only how? What was going on? Then he saw Melissa sitting nearby, her hands also tied, hers in front. She looked terrified, her eyes huge in a white, pinched face. On the ground beside her lay their packs, the contents strewn all over the ground. Carranza's voice snapped his attention back.

"Where is the crown?"

Rick stared stupidly.

"The crown." Carranza backhanded him across the face. "The Crown of the Goddess that holds the big diamond. It is not in your bag. Where did you hide it?"

"Don't hit him," Melissa cried. "Please don't. I told you we don't have any crown, didn't even know—"

"Silence!" Carranza roared, but she kept right on, her words running together as she said to Rick, "He's after the Honeycomb Fire himself. He's already tried to get it once and now he's making a second try. He says the stone's been put in some crown and he thinks we took it from the temple—"

"Hold on." Rick's roar was as loud as Carranza's had been. "How could we have the diamond? We haven't had time to look." Tasting blood, he spat on the ground. "Jumping out at us like a damn jack-in-the-box. You must know we just got here."

"Here? Where is *here*?" Carranza demanded, gesturing toward the wall. "What is this place?"

Rick felt as if he had been called into a game without knowing the plays. Carranza seemed to know more about the stone than they did. So why was he asking this question?

The man made a threatening gesture. "This place where we are, tell me the name of it."

Rick spat out more blood and wondered if he was going to get hit again and decided he didn't care. "It's the temple, you bozo, what do you think? It's the temple."

To Rick's surprise, Carranza burst into laughter. "The woman told the truth then. The ruins of an old tower and you thought it was the temple." He found their mistake hilarious. "You come after the treasure and you did not know? The temple is in a chamber deep under the ground."

Confused, Rick played back what Melissa had said. Carranza was after the diamond himself. A sick feeling churned in his gut. The worst possible combination—Carranza and George—both of them after the diamond and he was the one who had put them together. What a blind switch. Hoarsely he asked, "Where's George?"

"Ah, that is another story." Carranza leaned back against a tree. "He and his friend arrived at Piste a few hours after you. They were soon my prisoners. Then I discovered that the story you told me was wrong. George knew nothing about working for a magazine. When I searched him, I found a map. That is when George told me the truth—that you and he were both after the Honeycomb Fire. I saw the cave marked on the map and was happy to recognize it. Although I knew the temple was in a cave, I did not know there was an underground route."

"So you made a deal?"

"With George, not the other one. That one I left in the keeping of a friend."

Rick narrowed his eyes. "You killed him didn't you?"

Carranza's smile was sly. "I tell you the same as I told George. I did not want him to think me a violent man."

"And then you killed George," Rick said flatly, knowing it was true and regretting it. It wasn't the way he had wanted George to pay for his betrayal. He was surprised when Carranza shook his head.

"I did not kill him, although he deserved it. Somehow he drugged me and made off with my supplies. He didn't go far. When I was myself again, I heard him groaning from a deep shaft where he had fallen. There was no way for me to reach him. So sad."

Carranza smiled briefly, and then his expression hardened. "It seems there are many passageways in the cave. Instead of coming up inside the temple, I came out in the forest. I was not sure what to do, but I knew from George that you were coming, so I stayed in the area. This morning I heard voices. When I saw you here, I could only think that you had already captured the diamond. What I could not understand is how you escaped the traps."

"Traps?" Rick said. The map had no information about traps.

"The Traps of the Stings." Carranza observed Rick with contempt. "You and your enemy George chase for the treasure, yet know nothing. He knew nothing of the traps. I did not tell him, but when I saw you, I thought you must be smarter. It was to learn how you escaped the traps that I keep you alive. How many are there where should one walk? Such information would interest me. But now?" Carranza shrugged.

Rick tensed. The talk about George had momentarily distracted Carranza, but he had clearly concluded he had no use for them.

"Tell me about the traps," Rick said, making his voice eager as if he didn't realize the tight spot they were in. "Sounds like a lot of trouble to protect one diamond. Maybe there's more than one treasure."

Carranza showed his bad teeth. "I like the way you think."

"I like the idea of enough treasure to share."

"Share?" Carranza laughed openly.

Rick shrugged. "If we help you, sure. Sounds like there must be plenty to go around."

"And how could you help me?" As if finding the conversation interesting, Carranza slid down the tree he'd been leaning against and took a comfortable seat on the ground. "Tell me, please, the help you would be to me?"

Rick knew damned well that Carranza only toyed with him, but as long as the conversation stayed alive, so did he and Melissa. Speaking earnestly, he said, "If one person falls into a trap, they're stuck, right? But if there are others around to help him out, it's a different story."

Carranza grimaced. "I am to trust you and a woman to pull me out?" His expression turned thoughtful. "You have given me an idea. It would be good to have someone to go ahead and find the traps."

"Whoa, wait just a damn minute," Rick said indignantly. He hadn't expected this angle, but he could work with it. "How dumb do you think I am?" Plenty, he hoped. The mistake about the tower had already convinced Carranza that they didn't know which end was up. Best to keep him thinking exactly that. "If you won't trust us to pull you out of a hole, why should we trust you— Oh, I get it!" He spoke as if a light bulb had just flashed on in his head. "You don't know how many traps there are. You would have to have to pull us out to keep on going."

Carranza nodded. "I will save you because I will need you."

And as soon as you don't, we're dead, Rick thought, seeing the smile Carranza had tried to hide. He wished he dared glance at Melissa but he didn't want to risk anything that might shift Carranza's attention to her.

Aloud he said, "If we're going to work together, what are we waiting for?" If there was to be any chance of outsmarting Carranza, it seemed it would be easier on a jungle trail instead of the way it was now, with the man sitting with his back against a tree, his shotgun by his hand. "Come on, let's go."

But instead of getting up, Carranza settled himself more comfortably. "How ignorant you are. Because of the traps, there is no guard outside the temple; but to get there, we must cross the fields where villagers work. Does some magic make us invisible?"

Rick frowned. "You mean the temple is still being used?"

"For as long as anyone can remember." Carranza took off his cap and ran his fingers through his greasy curls. "The Indians worship a goddess who gave the diamond to their ancestors." He jeered at the tale. "The Honeycomb Fire now rests in a golden crown. The priests teach that when the goddess returns and the crown sits on her head then all in the village will become rich and happy." He spat to show his disdain for such superstition.

Rick's jaw sagged. "You mean the diamond *belongs* to somebody?"

"To the People of the Goddess. A village of fools. So certain they could keep the crown safe from thieves."

Rick shook his head, confounded. He had always assumed the diamond lay forgotten, that the only people aware of it were people like his grandfather, and of course him, and dammit, George. He still wasn't sure he had it straight. "Did these villagers make the traps to protect the stone?"

"Their ancestors did." He laughed and puffed his chest. "To protect the crown and the diamond from terrible thieves like me."

Ignoring Carranza's posturing, Rick figured how the story must fit together. After Don Miguel left the diamond at the temple altar, a cult must have grown up around the stone. He was awed by his conclusion. The gem his forbears had brought into the jungle had become an object of worship.

The thought boggled his mind. His grandfather hadn't had a clue. Not even Richard had gotten close enough to learn the whole story. Hell, if the diamond belonged to some village, he wasn't going to take it. He wasn't a thief. Not that Carranza would believe it, and it sure wasn't to their advantage to admit it.

"You're right, I am ignorant," he said to Carranza. "How did you learn all of this?"

Responding to the respectful tone in Rick's voice, Carranza preened. "For many months I flew supplies into the village. I heard many interesting things." He pulled a cigarette from his pocket and carefully lit it, all the time keeping his gun at the ready. "When the moon changes the priests hold ceremonies but it is dangerous to try and follow, for the path is marked by hidden traps. My men attacked the natives to try and force someone to take us to the temple but our plan failed. I alone escaped and returned to the place where we had hidden my plane."

Carranza's voice dropped to a growl as he touched his upper arm. "I was wounded. Although it was not serious, the intent was to kill me. I vowed I would not only come back to take the stone, I would also make them pay for my wound. The trouble was, I was out of money. Now thanks to you, I am not only back here sooner than I expected, but I also have a way past the traps."

"You betcha," Rick said, hoping he wasn't pushing his dumb act too far.

Carranza's lips curved in a thin smile as he blew out smoke. "When the farmers return to their village for their evening meal, we will go to the temple and find the crown." His eyes glittered darkly. "This is excellent timing. There is a full moon tonight and the priests will proceed to the temple. When they do, they will find a surprise."

Rick felt a chill, but he forced a laugh. "Yeah, they're going to get there and find the crown has gone bye-bye." But he knew that Carranza planned a far different surprise. The crown would be gone all right, but in its place would be two dead bodies, his and Melissa's.

CHAPTER TWENTY-SIX

CARRANZA SAID THEY WOULD move again when the sun started to sink behind the trees. He enjoyed his evening meal with Rick and Melissa on their sides and tied back-to-back, their bodies forming his comfortable leaning place as he lounged and wolfed down the remaining food from their packs. As he gobbled he talked about what lay ahead.

According to him, the natives made certain there was only one path to the temple entrance that would-be thieves would take.

"The path is kept cleared but there is thick jungle on both sides—" He lowered his voice to sound even more menacing than usual. "A jungle of poisonwood trees. The trees were planted close together ages ago, which was bad enough but now full-grown, they must be like a wall.

"Trying to cut through the trees has poison sap gushing out," Carranza said. "Even without sap touching you, the fumes destroy your lungs. Even rain coming down through the leaves washes down poison. A sure death. Better to risk the traps."

Rick didn't know if the guy knew what he was talking about. Maybe it was a mix of truth and superstition, but he obviously believed it. Rick remembered something from the map about "impenetrable" jungle,

fox

but no mention of poison. He'd been in Belize after the damage from Hurricane Hattie and stayed in the new capital city, Belmopan. He'd been invited by a customer, a racing enthusiast he'd sold a winning horse to. He'd heard about poisonwood trees, but nothing about them being as deadly as Carranza described. Maybe this was a different kind.

After Carranza finished the food and then, still using their bodies as a comfortable bolster, he enjoyed a long siesta, his steady snores allowing Rick and Melissa a few whispered words, mostly giving one another encouragement in the face of a bleak situation.

The man finally got them moving again. It was through a boggy area with trees and swamp water. Melissa was placed first in the line, her hands still tied. A long rope was now tied between one of her ankles and Rick's. It was long enough to drag through the water between them. Rick's hands were still tied behind his back and Carranza held another rope looped around Rick's neck.

Carranza was last in line, carrying his ever-present shotgun, with which he amused himself by giving Rick swiping jabs in the back and claiming to be crushing mosquitoes.

"Another one! Another one!" he would cry as they continued sloshing through the muck. "How lucky you are to have such a good friend in me."

Wincing from the jabs, Rick cheered himself by thinking what he'd do to his "good friend" the first chance he got: spin the guy around and shove the shotgun up where the sun didn't shine.

They arrived at the place where the jungle had been cleared. A long slope planted with beans and corn stretched out before them. At the foot of the slope was an expanse of bare limestone and thin soil that supported only scrubby bushes and stunted trees, as barren as the clearing Rick and Melissa had found when emerging from the cave earlier that day. The only sound was that of the wind moving through the corn, a soft sighing, like lovers whispering their final good-byes.

"It is as I thought," Carranza murmured with satisfaction. "The farmers have gone home." He pointed to the clearing. "That space must be crossed before we come to the opening to the temple."

Rick scowled. "And that's where the traps are." He was still coming to terms with the fact that the temple was still being used. That the diamond belonged to somebody.

"*Sí,* the traps." Carranza looked around in the place where they stood and uttered a vengeful growl. "After the map led me to the crown, my plan was to destroy the temple, but my explosives were lost in the cave with your friend George. Now I must find some other way to punish those who tried to take my life."

"Speaking of punishment," Rick grumbled, "how come I'm still tied up? We're on the same side, aren't we? Why do I have to have my hands knotted behind my back?"

Carranza shrugged. "Tied up as you are, you will not even think of running away. And do not look to the woman for help. There is nothing she could do that would distract me long enough for her to loosen your rope."

"I thought you and I were partners."

"You have not yet proved your worth."

"How can I prove anything tied up?"

"You will surprise yourself." Carranza shifted his gaze to Melissa. "I have remembered more of the legend. The goddess is said to have hair the color of honey. Like you, woman, eh? Try not to get stung too badly by the traps." He chuckled, his face shiny from the exertion of walking through the swamp. "After the crown is mine, I might like to see how it would look on your head."

"Hold it, buddy." Rick's bristling tone hid his fear for Melissa. "Let's not forget, she belongs to me."

"I forget nothing," Carranza responded slyly. He gave Melissa one last look, then turned to Rick. "As you say, for the temple to be so protected it must hold much treasure. There will be plenty for all of us."

Pretending to be placated, Rick, filled with dark foreboding, followed Melissa across a bean field as Carranza had directed. Unless he could get his hands loose—and he was working on it—they were the walking dead. And what would Carranza do to Melissa first? He twisted his hands against his ropes, welcoming the distraction of physical pain.

Having reached the end of the fields, they surveyed the limestone area ahead. Close up, it was even wilder than it had looked from a distance. It was, however, bordered by thick tree growth on either side. Poison trees if Carranza knew what he'd been talking about.

The man directed Melissa's attention to a vine-draped tree that lay about two hundred yards away and on the other side of a line of bushes.

"It was by that spot I watched the priests disappear and reappear as if by magic. The entrance to the temple must be there. We head that way but with caution. I believe the traps are openings that drop into the caverns below."

"I'll go first," Rick said.

Carranza's chuckle was a wet sound deep in his throat. "The woman goes first. If she falls we may be able to lift her out. With you, it would be too much trouble."

Not waiting to be prodded, Melissa took her first cautious step. Although expressionless, she seethed with hatred. The memory of Carranza brandishing his knife over Rick's unconscious face burned like acid in her brain. This man must not be allowed to win. Somehow, in some way, she would find a way to best him. If worse came to worse, even dying by the traps would be a victory if it kept him from reaching his goal, but for now, she could only pray that a better solution would come to her. Her knees quaked and sweat coated her palms as she moved ahead. Where were the traps? How could they be avoided?

Every once in a while Carranza did or said something that caused Rick to slow to the extent that the rope around her leg pulled tight. This happened as she attempted to step over a vine that had grown across her path. A tendril caught on her boot heel.

This is it, she thought as she lost the fight to keep her balance, positive she had triggered a trap. Why didn't she and Rick have any jungle animal friends rushing to their rescue like in that Jungle Book cartoon she'd seen when she was still in school?

To her grateful relief, she landed on firm ground.

Carranza roared in anger. "Clumsy woman. From now on take more care."

Having landed on one knee, she twisted her face in a parody of pain. So they didn't have cartoon friends. She at least had a brain.

"I hit my knee," she moaned. "It really hurts." It wasn't true but he wouldn't know. She might be able to use a supposed weakness to her advantage.

"Limp then." Carranza spat angrily. "Remember my promise about the man's eye."

Silently damning him, Melissa prepared to get up. A whiff of something unpleasant drifted past her nose.

"Wait," she said, sensing that Carranza was about to holler again. "I smell something bad."

"It is your future if you do not move."

"No," she said. "It smells awful. Like bats." It smelled even worse, but bats were the only way she could think of to describe it. If the traps opened to the cave below, could she be smelling bats that were down inside?

Carranza's face reddened with anger. "There are no bats, you try my patience. Get up, now. Get up!"

"Wait . . . ." Kneeling, she had just spied a crack in the ground that had a suspiciously straight edge. She turned to tell Carranza what she had found and she saw him coming angrily toward her.

"Get up," he roared, "I told you—"

Still on her hands and knees, she scrambled to do his bidding. Carranza halted as a grating sound came from below. Before Melissa could even think of what the sound might be, the ground beneath her hands disappeared. Her upper body pitched forward. If it hadn't been for the rope pulling tight about her leg, she would have plunged head-first into the pit that suddenly opened below her.

With Rick and Carranza working together, she was pulled up and backward but not before she saw the horror that lay below. Unmindful of the raw scrape on one palm, she got to her feet and rushed the few steps to Rick and pointed.

"Down there!" She cried. "Down in the pit, a man . . . ."

Even though the sun was lower, she had been able to see bones showing through rotting flesh and patches of long, dark hair still clinging to the remains of a skull. She couldn't stop shaking. "Scorpions . . . there's scorpions crawling all over."

"It is Diaz," Carranza said, peering into the pit. Chuckling with amusement, he spoke to the corpse. "So Diaz, you did not die with the others as I believed."

There came another grating sound. From the stricken expression on Carranza's face, it was obvious he thought he had tripped another trap, and then he laughed. "The door has lifted back into place. See, it waits for its next victim."

Melissa stared. The opening to the pitfall had disappeared. From where she stood, she couldn't even see the straight line in the dirt. There was nothing to indicate that the trap existed.

Carranza turned and saw his prisoners pressed close together. His smile fading, he stepped forward waving his shotgun and tore Melissa from Rick.

"That man you saw down there tried to double-cross me." He gave her a shake. "I hope you have no such ideas. Do you wish to look at him again?"

"Ah, give us a break," Rick said with disgust, although the look he gave Melissa was anxious. She was so pale. "All we want is a piece of the treasure. When she almost fell in, I almost got dragged in with her. You might have lost both of us. What would you have done then? Let her untie me." He had succeeded in loosening the ropes, but he still had a ways to go before he was free. "Maybe you don't trust me, but you've got the gun. What am I going to do against that, huh? A little cooperation will work out better for all of us."

Carranza scowled. "We stay as we are."

Melissa pulled away from Carranza's grip. The scorpion trap had been a lot more sophisticated than the brush-covered hole she had expected and a lot more grotesque. Not waiting for the man to shove her ahead, she carefully stepped around the area of the pit and moved on. She had to stop shaking, she thought, taking deep breaths in an attempt to calm herself. She knew that if she and Rick were to have any chance at all, she had to keep her wits about her. The poisonwood trees still kept them on a path. Her eyes darted this way and that, alert to any possible hint of another trap as she went step by careful step, alert also for any scheme that might help her outwit their captor.

Nearing the line of bushes, she paused and looked over her shoulder at Carranza.

"It looks like a line of bushes up ahead." She had learned to make it clear she was addressing him, not Rick. Any time it appeared that the two of them might be having a conversation, Rick got the gun barrel jabbed painfully into his back.

Carranza's response was a growl and an impatient gesture for her to continue walking. She came to a place where she saw that the bushes seemed to line the far side of what looked like a ditch. She moved closer. The ditch was about four and a half feet wide and maybe eight feet deep. Thorn bushes grew thick on the bottom and there were more thorn bushes on the opposite side. She paused at the edge as Rick and Carranza came up behind her.

"I can't jump this, not with my hurt knee. It's probably too wide for any of us. If we do get across, we'll be in the middle of thorns."

She was thinking that she could persuade Carranza to retrace their steps and try for a different route. If she could get him to once again pass by the scorpion pit, maybe she could trigger the opening and send him to join his dead companion.

Carranza cursed. "Use your eyes. There are safe places to land on the other side. See those gaps between the bushes?"

Rick spoke "Those gaps are only wide enough for one foot here, one foot there. She'll be cut to ribbons." His hands were almost free. All he needed was a bit more time.

"Let's go back and try to find a different way," Melissa said, hoping he would fall for it. "This ditch may be another trap."

Carranza scoffed. "It is no trap; it is a natural thing."

As he examined the ditch, his eyes narrowed thoughtfully. "I now understand what I saw that night I spied on the priests. There must know a safe way through the poisonwood trees to reach this place.

When they visit the temple, they lay a plank across this space and go toward that tree." He pointed again at a lone tree, with vines falling to the ground all around it. "That is what I saw them headed after they traveled over this ditch. Then they disappeared. That tree must hide the entrance to the temple."

"A bridge of some kind, that's what she needs," Rick said.

"She needs nothing but courage." With a stroke of his knife, Carranza cut the rope between Melissa and Rick. "Go now. Jump! Enough wasting time."

Rick started to argue further, but Melissa quickly said, "It's okay. I think I can make it after all." Carranza's determination to forge on had given her a new idea. Trusting that Rick would understand she had a plan, she forced a smile in Carranza's direction. "We're so close to the temple, I can hardly wait. I keep thinking of what you said, about how the crown would look on my head."

"Ah, you think of that, eh?" He chuckled, pleased.

"Yes I think of that," she said, and then quickly, before she could lose her nerve, she stepped back to give herself a running start. Rushing forward, she zeroed in on a bare patch between two of the bushes on the other side and leaped.

She had been confident she could successfully span the gap and she almost did. Her toe touched solid ground and if she could have thrown herself forward, she would have been all right; but at the last second, the idea of flinging herself face-first into the thorns caused her to flinch. Her toe slipped and she slid down the inside wall of the ditch, grabbing a hand-hold at the last possible minute. She found her boot toes braced against the wall, her right hand clutching the stem of a bush, a stem that was blessedly free of thorns.

With no energy to respond to either Carranza's insults or Rick's call of concern, Melissa concentrated on climbing back up to level ground. Belatedly, she realized that her slip had been fortunate. From her present vantage point, she could see that the bushes were shaped like umbrellas, with two-foot-high bare stems, the foliage crowned with wicked-looking thorns spreading out across the tops. Instead of trying to wend her way through them, she could crawl under the branches, squirming on her belly until she was clear of the entire patch.

Laboriously lifting herself to level ground, she wiggled in under the spreading bushes, using the sturdy stems to help her worm her way along.

It was hot, sweaty work, but she eventually reached the end of the thorn patch. Out of breath, she clambered to her feet and stood dusting off her clothing. Furtively, she sent a glance toward the tree roughly thirty paces away. The thick vines twining over its branches made a tent shape that reached to the dust. Was that really where the temple was located? If her plan worked, Carranza would be in no condition to ever find out.

"Walk around," he ordered from the far side of the ditch. "Show me there are no traps on the ground beyond the bushes."

She saw no sign of traps but she pretended to search, while at the same time, she found a route back to the edge where the arrangement of bushes formed a narrow walkway. The lowering sun was still bright enough for her shadow to stretch long on the stony ground as she walked to the edge and stood looking across the ditch at Carranza.

"Everything looks good," she called. "Jump and safely land here."

"Move back," he ordered.

Obediently she stepped back until she was positioned roughly six feet from the place where he would land.

"What about me?" Rick called as Carranza made ready for the leap. "How am I supposed to get across if I'm still tied up?"

Carranza only laughed. Clutching the shotgun in his meaty fist, he took a running start and threw himself across the ditch.

He was still in midair when Melissa rushed forward.

CHAPTER TWENTY-SEVEN

MELISSA REACHED CARRANZA JUST as his feet touched the ground, her arms outstretched to push him backward and into the ditch. His eyes went wide as she slammed into him. He had expected no attack from her.

All at once, everything went wrong. Carranza was toppling backward all right, but she was falling too, coming down on top of him in the ditch.

"The gun!" Rick shouted. "Grab his gun."

There was a confused moment before Melissa saw that the wind had been knocked out of Carranza. Scrambling to her feet amidst the thorn bushes, she saw the gun barrel poking up. She grabbed it and passed it up to Rick, only then realizing that he was untied and that he had leaped over the ditch. Setting the gun aside, he reached down and pulled her up. Clutching her close, he set her carefully on the path.

"You okay?" he asked. There had been a few moments when he feared neither of them would ever be okay again.

"A couple of scratches, that's all." Landing on Carranza had protected her, but she still had blood on one arm from the bushes and gouges on her lower legs where thorns had snagged through her pants. "They sting," she said, but it was worth it and more to have gotten Carranza. "Did you get stuck, too?"

He shook his head. "My boots are higher and I landed in the best place on the path. Unlike our friend." Eyes hard, he watched Carranza struggling to get up. The back of the man's shirt and his neck showed blood from numerous punctures. With each cursing, groaning move, he jabbed himself more.

Feeling satisfaction as she watched Carranza, Melissa tried to ignore the irritation from the thorns. She had suffered only a few punctures compared with the dozens Carranza had gotten. "Shoot him," she said, remembering his threat to take one of Rick's eyes. "He probably planned to turn around and shoot you across the ditch."

"Yeah, only he didn't know I had already worked my hands loose. Shooting him is too easy on him. Let the people he wanted to steal from take care of him. We'll haul him out and tie him up." He raised his eyebrows. "Is there any chance you can shoot a gun?"

She nodded grimly, as she took the gun from Rick. "Enough to know to pull the trigger if I need to."

Rick wondered if they could find the village Carranza spoke of. The people had trouble with Carranza. Handing him over might earn him and Melissa some racing points. If the villagers knew Spanish, he could explain who they were and why they had come, not knowing the diamond belonged to anyone after all these years.

He had expected resistance from Carranza, but the man obediently threw his pack up to him on command. When Rick found a rope inside and threw it down, Carranza docilely allowed himself to be pulled up. Once on level ground, he appeared dazed. He stumbled to a cleared space and sank to a huddled position. Alert for some trick, Rick prepared to tie the man. Carranza groaned and touched the back of his neck. His hand came away smeared with blood.

"Hot," he mumbled. His face was flushed and he labored for air.

Rick flashed a glance at Melissa, who stood holding the shotgun. She looked equally puzzled by the man's behavior. Still expecting some trick, Rick backed a step away.

"Fire," Carranza muttered, and then he gasped and stiffened. "Fire," he screamed, this time in Spanish. Eyes widening, he clawed at his shirt as if suddenly desperate to tear it off, all the while babbling about fire. Writhing, his cries increased. He screeched that he was burning. Continuing to shriek, he clawed at his neck and shoulders, his fingernails tearing through his shirt, tearing bloody ribbons in his skin. His body jerked spasmodically, his congested face going from red to blue. He clutched his throat and was wracked by another spasm and then went limp.

Rick stood still for a shocked moment and then cautiously knelt at the stricken man's side. He heard Melissa say something. At the same time, he saw that Carranza's half-opened eyes had started to glaze.

My God, Rick thought. The man was dead!

"Such a tiny scratch," Melissa said, "but it feels so hot."

The truth chilled Rick to his marrow. The thorns that had poisoned Carranza had poisoned Melissa, too. He leaped to his feet. Even as rushed to her, an unnatural redness blossomed across her face.

"Oh God . . . ." Rick hugged her close against his body. She fought him, shuddering and struggling for breath, but at least she wasn't going into the spasms that had wracked Carranza. At least not yet. Rick had no idea how to help her. What could he do? What *should* he do?

He heard his name being called. With disbelief, Rick recognized the voice. Almost afraid to hope, he looked toward the sound.

Xavier stood on the far side of the thorn ditch, backlit by the lurid, sunset sky. With him were six robed Maya, one of them, elderly and white-haired, had a gold pendant swinging from his neck. Another member of their company carried a wide board and placed it over the ditch.

Repeating Rick's name, Xavier rushed over the bridge made by the board. "Rick, what has happened?"

"Melissa's been poisoned," Rick answered hoarsely. She had gone heavy in his arms, her breathing strained. "Poison thorns. They killed that guy over there. They stuck her too."

Xavier knelt beside her limp form as Rick placed her gently on the ground. The Maya men who had followed Xavier at a slower pace, gathered close. Muttering unintelligibly, the white-haired man sank stiffly to his knees at Melissa's side.

A much younger man, one with a hunched shoulder, spoke to Rick in Spanish. "She suffers from the Fire Sting."

Rick looked at him with desperate eyes. "You know what it is? What can you do about it?"

The man pursed his lips. He seemed to debate with himself and then he touched the bag he carried about his waist. "There is an antidote—"

"No . . . ." A thin Maya with an authoritative voice stepped forward, blocking the other man's move. "Nothing will be done."

Rick had no trouble understanding either the man's words or the guns he suddenly saw two of the other men produce, one pointing at Xavier and one pointing at him.

"But she can't breathe," Rick cried desperately. Couldn't these guys see what was happening? "If she doesn't get help she could die."

The old man lifted his hands. Rocking his knees, he uttered a strange chant. The thin man glared angrily at Rick. "If what the old one says is right, the Fire Sting will not harm her. We will do nothing."

Rick went berserk. Melissa was dying before his eyes and no way was anybody withholding the cure. With one hand he grabbed the shotgun from the ground, and with the other hand, he grabbed the shoulder of the old man's robe and pulled him close. He hated manhandling the old guy, but he was the easiest to reach and from the look of his jewelry, he was somebody important. Rick pressed the twin barrels of the shotgun against his captive's withered neck.

"She gets help or your pal gets blown into the middle of next week. Xavier, look in that guy's bag for the antidote."

The natives stood frozen as Xavier took the bag and removed a bottle. Frowning, he unstopped the container and sniffed. He looked at the man with the hunched shoulder. "Eduardo, is this it? How much should I give her?"

"I would give her—" The man broke off, his eyes widening. "Wait, look. She is recovering. See, her breathing is easier."

Apparently stunned, he glanced toward the old man, who despite the discomfort he must have felt in Rick's grip, nodded complacently as if Melissa's recovery was only to be expected

"He is right," Xavier said. "She is breathing more normally."

"Are you sure?" All Rick saw was that she was still unconscious.

"I am sure." Xavier touched the back of his hand to her cheek, and then put his fingers to her pulse. "I thought she might be going into shock, but her skin is no longer clammy and her pulse is steadier."

The man Xavier had addressed as Eduardo spoke to Rick. "Release the High Priest. The woman's recovery is in the hands of fate."

"He's got a point, Rick," Xavier said. "Relax. Let the old man go. You might as well put down that shotgun, too."

Doing as he was told, Rick focused all his attention on Melissa. Her natural color had returned and her breathing was easier, no question.

"Thank God." He sagged weakly. If he had lost her, he didn't know what he would have done. He couldn't even imagine it. Sitting, he gathered her into his arms.

The old man touched his shoulder. Rick looked up into the aged, brown face of the High Priest.

Smiling, the old man spoke. Eduardo translated. "He says he forgives you for the harsh way you touched him. He says it is only right that you should protect her."

Rick turned to Xavier. "What's going on? You know this one guy's name, you seem to be in with them, yet there's a gun on you too."

"They are suspicious, Rick, and with reason. After the collapse in the cave that cut me off from you and Melissa, I kept hunting for a way to find you. Your grandfather trusted me and I had failed."

"What? To protect me? You didn't fail. Scratch that thought right now. That damn collapsing tunnel had all of us wondering if we'd ever get out." For a moment, he realized it had been worse for Xavier. He not only believed he'd failed, he'd been alone. Not wanting to think of that, Rick said, "When we got out we came up under tree roots to sunshine. How did you get out?"

"I backtracked, or so I thought, but I soon realized I was in a different tunnel. I just kept walking, trying to conserve my water. The tunnel opened into a larger space. The air was fresher so I know there was a draft and once again I found two openings.'"

"Two tunnels, two choices," Rick said, not wanting to think about how Xavier must have felt. "Don't forget, you owe me a new watch."

"You never proved your tunnel would have been better."

Rick grinned. "Your tunnel led Melissa and me to a landslide."

"Only because you went off into a different tunnel."

"Cheapskate. Go on with your story."

"Very well. It was good that I had spare batteries. The cave darkness allowed no reflections. All I could follow was the beam of light. I found one opening that seemed to be going down, which was where I didn't want to go. I chose another one that had an upward slant. Toward the end, I admit I had doubts. My water was almost gone yet I was encouraged because I could still feel the movement of air."

"Sounds good," Rick said. Just hearing about the man's trials was making him sweat, which was stupid because Xavier was standing before him, perfectly okay.

As if reading Rick's mind, Xavier grinned. "Not quite good yet. As I kept walking, the ceiling became so low I had to bend forward. Plus, it was getting narrower. I finally had to crawl, dragging my pack behind me tied to one boot by shoelaces. A smaller man could have kept crawling, but I finally had to squirm on my belly like a worm. The only thing that made it easier was that the route was going downhill, although it was in the opposite direction from the one I wanted. And, if the passage got smaller, I was stuck in all meanings of the word."

Rick shuddered. "Walls closing in. Like one of those Edgar Allen Poe horror stories I thought were so cool when I was a kid."

"Yes and by then my headlamp was gone and I was in darkness. The only thing that gave me hope was I could still feel the movement of air. I struggled on. I saw a dim glow ahead and heard voices. I thought I was hallucinating. My downward route eventually opened into a small cavern. I was on a ledge near the cavern roof.

I dropped to the floor, groped for my canteen and drank. They heard me—" he pointed at the robed priests "Where I'd landed was adjacent to the temple where they were preparing for a celebration. They used the cavern for storage. The opening I came through was near the ceiling above a natural formation that kept it in darkness. They had no idea. They believed they'd closed off any connection to the cave."

"Probably closed it after Richard got through," Rick said.

"Probably, yes. And, of course, they were sure I'd come to steal the diamond. They came at me with guns. After they bound and blindfolded me they led me to their village. It was good that Eduardo could speak Spanish. They had a recent bad experience with that man, Carranza." He gestured to the dead body. "They thought he and I worked together."

Xavier's gold tooth flashed as he smiled. "Once in their village, I was able to put some medical knowledge to good use. They decided I wasn't such a bad fellow after all, but since they were on guard against Carranza, I feared they might make the mistake of thinking you and Melissa worked with him. I explained that you were a descendant of the pair who first brought the diamond to them."

Rick grimaced. "Bet that impressed them a whole lot."

Xavier's eyes sparkled. "It did. They remembered well the story of Don Miguel and they especially remembered—"

The white-haired man's joyful exclamation cut off Xavier's words. Pointing at Melissa, he spoke excitedly.

Eyes fluttering open, she blinked and looked around in confusion.

"Lissa," Rick's voice was rough with emotion as he turned to her. "God, lady." He gathered her close and pressed his rough face against her smooth cheek. "If you only knew how you scared me."

The old priest spoke again, his words spilling out in an enthusiastic rush. Hearing him, the thin man burst out in an angry tirade, his fist waving. Paying no attention, the old priest spoke again.

Eduardo listened, then shrugged, as if he were no longer sure what to believe. Looking at Rick, he translated: "The High Priest says that the goddess has awakened."

Rick stared. "Goddess?"

"They remember Don Miguel's blonde-haired, blue-eyed wife," Xavier said quietly in English. "In their village, I learned that over the many years, a religion formed around her expected return."

"They think this goddess is Melissa?"

Xavier nodded. "I described the two of you and the old priest immediately recognized her from their legends. Melissa's appearance has confirmed his expectations. It is different with the younger ones."

"Yeah, like with the thin guy."

"He is the old priest's son. He is trying to guard his people, Rick. Despite their guns, they are good men. This is their home. It is we who are the invaders."

"So what are you saying?" Rick asked impatiently. "I can see that nobody's rolling out the red carpet. What's it going to take to convince them we're good guys too?"

Eduardo interrupted. "The goddess must prove herself. It is a wonder indeed that she has gotten through the first two stings, the pit of Many Stings, and the Fire Stings. If she is truly the goddess, she will pass safely through the Great Sting. If she fails, it will be the end for all of you."

CHAPTER TWENTY-EIGHT

WHILE WAITING FOR MELISSA to fully recover, the Maya men set up camp a short distance from the vine-covered tree and lit a fire. Rick learned from Xavier that the old man was their High Priest. When he called other men to a ceremony in the temple, as he had done for that night, they served as priests as well.

Rick argued with Eduardo, who he considered the most reasonable one of the bunch, which wasn't saying much. "It's like Xavier told you, we're not thieves." To think he had innocently planned on walking in on this block-headed crew. There was no other light except that of the campfire. The trees overhead hid the stars and the moon. The blackness fit his mood. "You wouldn't even have the diamond if it wasn't for my ancestors," Rick said. "Doesn't that count for anything?"

"Nothing that's in your favor," Eduardo responded, the firelight dancing across his smooth, golden-tan complexion. He was a small-boned man with the classic Maya profile. "Balam, the son of the High Priest, has correctly observed that you have the hairy face of a conquistador. The Maya have not yet forgotten the wickedness of the Spanish. It would have been better for you to have taken after your female ancestor."

Rick laughed bitterly. "Sure, and when Melissa comes along and fits her description, you guys can't wait to see her dead."

"Hold on," Melissa complained. Rick had lapsed back into Spanish because it was easier for Eduardo. "You can't use my name and not translate."

"Don't act so lively," Rick murmured, tightening the arm he held about her waist. The High Priest had insisted that they couldn't enter the temple until the "goddess" was feeling strong, so it was to their benefit for Melissa to keep pretending to be woozy.

"That's not liveliness," she answered, trying to sound brash instead of terrified. "It's twanging nerves and nobody's fooling anybody. They can see how awake I am."

With Carranza dead she had thought things would start going their way, only then she'd passed out and awakened to find that their troubles were worse.

She thought the High Priest and Eduardo didn't seem so bad. The old priest was a darling. He had ordered water brought and allowed her privacy so she could wash and then they had offered her refreshments. With the coming of darkness, he had slipped into a doze, but every once in a while he would blink himself awake and send her a sleepy smile across the campfire. Definitely a darling. If she ever got out of this mess alive, maybe she could add him to her list of reunion escorts.

The remaining men, however, were cut from a different cloth. Two of them, a round-faced pair with identical haircuts—imagine a sinister Tweedledum and Tweedledee—had dragged Carranza's body away as if it was all in a day's work, then returned to take up their rifles and resume their impassive guard over their prisoners. A third priest, Luis, now had Carranza's shotgun and seemed itching for an excuse to use it.

Worst of all was the High Priest's son, Balam, an old name that Eduardo said meant jaguar. Although he let Eduardo do the talking, Balam clearly had superior command and his murderous glare told Melissa he considered her a fraud and couldn't wait to see her sliced and diced or whatever horror the next trap had in store.

She gave Rick an anxious glance.

"It's okay," he said in a comforting tone. "We can make a deal."

To Xavier, he said, "You were in their village. What do these people need and what do they want?

"I saw medical needs."

"You would."

Xavier smiled. "They need no help with cooking so I go to the next thing. They need more modern medicine and a way to store it. This man, Eduardo, has gotten an old refrigerator, but when the generator runs out of fuel, which is often, medicine can spoil.

"Their need gives us bargaining points," Rick said. "How do they connect with the outside world? A radio? My grandfather's prepared for radio contact, right?"

"Yes. I tried to tell them we could give them help, but except for Eduardo, they did not want to listen."

"They'll listen to me," Rick said, determined. He had noticed that Eduardo had twice hushed the grumbling of the others, keeping an ear cocked to what he and Xavier discussed—a good sign. Encouraged by this, he said to the man, "In exchange for our safe passage out of here, we'll arrange for fuel and medical supplies to be brought in. All it will take is a few messages by radio." If the situation weren't so dicey, he thought he might get a charge out of helping the village where Don Miguel had visited so many centuries ago.

As Xavier had suggested, however, Eduardo alone seemed interested, and after a discussion with his disapproving companions, he regretfully shook his head. "In matters concerning the goddess, we must see it through as our ancestors would."

Rick sensed that his bargaining time was running dry. "Let's forget old legends, okay? They've got nothing to do with our deal."

Eduardo's eyes twinkled. "You doubt our legend? Perhaps I would too, yet here are my people, forgotten Maya in a forgotten jungle in a forgotten place in the world. What are the chances that a blond-haired blue-eyed woman would ever come to us? Now, it has happened for the second time. This is clearly a miracle. Who else could this woman be except the goddess, the Giver of Gifts?"

He tossed a stick into the fire. "The legend says she will go safely through all the Stings, so that she must do. Once she wears the crown, all good things will follow."

"But if she fails, you end up with nothing," Rick said in frustration. He had to make this man see reason. "What I'm offering is a sure thing. I will—"

"Your friend has explained," Eduardo interrupted. "You have money and your rich grandfather has more. There is one problem."

"Like what?"

"If you are thieves, your promises mean nothing. If you are not thieves, the goddess will prove it by passing safely through the Great Sting."

Melissa didn't need translation to know that the talk had turned against them. "Please . . ." She reached out to Eduardo. "Isn't there some way you can help us? I never claimed to be a goddess, can't you understand? I only got this far by luck."

For a moment Eduardo seemed torn, then he clamped his jaw. "Pray then that your luck stays with you."

A man who had gone on ahead reappeared from behind the vine-covered tree. He gave a signal to Balam and the High Priest.

Balam stood and clapped his hands. "The procession to the temple will begin."

"Wait," Rick said, "can't we—" He heard the click of a gun being cocked.

"The procession," Eduardo said firmly, repeating Balam's words, "will begin."

Afraid that Rick might try something, Melissa scrambled to her feet. "I'm ready," she said, fighting to pump strength into her quaking knees. There were three guards with guns and they were unarmed. Any heroics and one of them would get hurt for sure—better to take their chances with the trap. Maybe her luck *would* hold out. All the same, she wished she had told Rick that she loved him. She couldn't get over the terrible feeling she wouldn't survive the coming experience.

Eduardo, holding a torch aloft, led the way.

A cold spot settled in the pit of Melissa's stomach as they reached the vine-draped tree. Eduardo pulled the vines apart, revealing a staircase cut into the stone. The High Priest's son descended the first few steps, then paused to assist his aged father.

Signaling for Melissa to come after him, Eduardo then turned and followed the High Priest's son. Hesitating, she glanced back trying to see Rick, but Tweedledum was between them.

This was it, Melissa thought as she started down the steps—Bride of the Mole People, take two. As she moved, she reasoned that since the priests weren't making her go first, this trap had to be different from the ones she had already encountered.

Rick had similar thoughts. What sort of trap was a threat to only one person in a procession? At Luis's signal, he began his own descent, his tread heavy with defeat. With an armed priest behind him, and Luis and the shotgun behind Xavier, there was no use even thinking of a way to escape with Melissa.

The steps gave way to an incline and a maze of twisting paths. As they proceeded, they passed by lighted wall torches that gave off a smell of incense. The High Priest began to chant. The procession passed under a lintel, its zigzag design emphasized with red and blue paint. At that point, the floor changed. Instead of the natural stone floor continuing, it became highly polished red and blue tiles.

"The Temple is ahead," Eduardo said, glancing over his shoulder.

The procession turned another corner and Melissa was lost from view. Rick didn't breathe easy again until he too turned the corner and saw her again, her hair gleaming gold under the light of another torch.

She stood at the bottom of a short flight of steps, waiting to enter a giant-size doorway cut through a wall that was at least three feet thick. The sides of the doorway showed curious carvings and odd projections. Balam had just passed passing through, entering a dark, inner chamber. Next in line, the aged priest moved forward.

Rick narrowed his eyes to pierce the murky, incense-laden air.

The old priest knelt and bent low, his chant thin and eerie. The scent of incense increased, the effect dizzying in low-roofed space. The old man bowed first to the right and then to the left, his white hair brushing the tiles. Still chanting, he struggled to his feet.

Rick had seen him being assisted frequently but he was now managing on his own, using the carved projections as hand-holds to lift himself up. When he finally shuffled into the inner chamber, Eduardo took his place, kneeling and beginning a chant of his own.

Light in the inner chamber drew Rick's eyes. The fire-lit altar jumped from the gloom—a decorated waist-high block of limestone set against the wall. Rick felt a clawing along his spine. Something about the inner chamber seemed oddly familiar. With dark foreboding, he studied the altar. Was this where the Honeycomb Fire was hidden?

He didn't look back at Melissa until Eduardo was passing through to the inner chamber and joined Balam and the High Priest. They all turned and faced Melissa at the doorway.

The High Priest beckoned to her.

Rick's gaze returned to the inner chamber, his tension increasing as chords of memory stirred. For no reason he could explain, the place seemed increasingly familiar. The stone walls, the carvings, the thick doorway . . . . He knew it was crazy, but, he felt as if he had been there before.

MELISSA PAUSED A FEW steps before the opening to the inner chamber and swallowed hard. Where was the trap? Her heart was beating so hard it seemed it would burst.

The old priest sent her an encouraging smile, but Balam's expression was fiendishly expectant. Was she about to do something wrong? Drawing back further, she saw that there were deep carvings of stylized flowers on the outside of the entry, with more carvings on its inner walls, honeybees in combat, four to each side.

The natives had bowed left and right as if paying homage to the bees. Should she do the same? If she were *really* a goddess, it seemed she would expect to be knelt to rather than being the one who knelt.

From the corner of her eye, she thought she saw Eduardo gesture.

He had moved his hands, she was sure of it, yet when she looked, his hands were still. Her gaze lifted to his face, finding it as impassive as stone. She was suddenly convinced he had given her a sign of what to do, only she had missed it. Had his hands gone up or down? Was she to kneel or not kneel? The man behind her made an impatient sound and she knew Eduardo didn't dare risk giving her another sign.

It came to her that this next trap might be more of a test. If she didn't behave like the goddess, then she *wasn't* the goddess. Brilliant deduction, Watson, only how did a goddess behave? Did she kneel or not kneel? In any case, Melissa knew there was no way in God's green earth that she could mimic the chant. She stiffened her spine, her decision made. She had no idea what would happen once she reached the altar, but a goddess bows to no one. She stepped forward.

"LISSA! NO!" RICK'S VOICE.

With one foot ready to step toward the doorway, Melissa heard his cry. She turned to see him rushing down the steps toward her. Tweedledum tried to block his way, but Rick darted nimbly around him, leaving the man grasping air.

Frozen with surprise, Melissa saw Rick diving toward her. Before she could even think, his arms went around her legs. She went over like a ninepin, falling across his back as his momentum on the slick tiles carried them both through the doorway. Clanging sounds reverberated above her head a moment after they slid through the opening and skidded to a stop at the feet of the gaping High Priest. Melissa rolled from Rick's shoulders to the tiles and scrambled to sit up.

Gasping for breath she saw Rick staring back toward the door opening. Her gaze followed his and she gasped.

Eight metal spikes had sprung out from the sides of the passage walls. If Rick's quick action hadn't slid them safely under the lowest bars, she would have been skewered through and through.

For a moment there was nothing but stunned silence, then with an angry stomp of his foot, Balam shouted at Eduardo, who shouted back.

Ignored for the moment, Melissa stared at Rick. "How did you know what to do?"

"I didn't." His face had paled. "This is the dungeon from my nightmare." He spoke in a haunted whisper. "I saw you trapped in an Iron Maiden. I expected the doorway to somehow snap shut; I wanted to get you through to the other side before that happened." He swallowed hard. "It was even more of an Iron Maiden than I thought."

He looked at the opening again only to see that the spikes had withdrawn into the walls, one 'stinger' for each bee. Spellbound, he watched the next priest in the line step forward to kneel and bow. Chanting, he arose and pressed on the projections on either side of the entry as if bestowing a blessing. As the man passed safely through, Rick cursed under his breath. *Levers.* The projections that looked like bee stingers were actually levers. That's how the first three men had gotten safely inside the chamber, by pressing on the levers which disarmed the deadly spikes. As he watched, Xavier, who must have been instructed, and the remaining three priests safely entered the inner chamber.

"Eduardo tried to tell me," Melissa whispered, clutching Rick's hand. "He signaled, but I couldn't understand what he meant." A light touch on her shoulder startled her. She looked up at the High Priest. His wrinkled face aglow, he spoke and extended his hands. Uncertain, she clung tighter to Rick. "What am I supposed to do?"

Eduardo turned from Balam, who had fallen silent. "The High Priest bids you to arise and approach the altar," he instructed."

"And then what?" Close to hysteria, Melissa fought off a giddy laugh. "After the way I got through that doorway, you still think I'm the goddess?"

Eduardo shrugged. "As I have told the son of the High Priest, we should not question the wisdom of Kananholcan, the Warden of Heaven's gate and the King of Bees." A glance at Balam, reveal clearly by the wall torches and flaming braziers, showed that Eduardo had made him reconsider what had happened. Although he still regarded Melissa with suspicion, he no longer seemed so sure she deserved a bath in boiling oil.

"Despite the method used," Eduardo continued, "we only know that Kananholcan has permitted your safe entrance."

Rick squeezed Melissa's hand to urge caution, but Eduardo's reasoning struck her as so preposterous that she couldn't help blurting, "He may have permitted it, but I sure didn't do it without help."

Eduardo nodded. "True, but you will have no help for your next task."

Next task? Shocked, Melissa lost her voice, but Rick had no trouble finding his.

"What?" he shouted, loud enough to have the armed men gripping their guns, not sure what to expect from him next. "You're telling me you blood-hungry bastards have cooked up yet another trap?"

"Not a trap," Eduardo answered, sending a calming glance at the armed men. "A riddle."

Rick glared. "And what happens if she fails to solve this riddle? *Then*, the trap springs?"

Eduardo folded his hands. "There is no need for another trap. If she fails, we will know she is not the long-awaited Giver of Gifts. Let us hope it does not come to that."

CHAPTER TWENTY-NINE

EDUARDO BROUGHT MELISSA TO the altar where she stood hemmed in by him to her right, the High Priest and his narrowed-eyed son to her left. Her mouth was never so dry, her palms never so wet. If Rick had been allowed to approach the altar with her, it would have made all the difference but he had been pulled to stand next to Xavier.

"Look well," Eduardo said, directing Melissa's attention to the ancient murals that circled the room. "Look at these drawings and then hear the riddle: How does Kananholcan, the King of Bees, look upon those who worship him, how does the King of the Honeycomb show his love for his people?"

Time and dampness had damaged the plaster and the murals, but enough flaking paint remained to show trees, fruits, flowers, vegetables and grains. It also showed tiny human figures bowing to a golden deity who had the enlarged eyes of an insect. Belatedly, Melissa realized it must be this bug-eyed King of the Bees, not the bees themselves that the priests had paid homage to.

"Is that the riddle? How he shows his love to his people?" she asked. It seemed almost too easy. The mural clearly showed that the King and the bees he ruled were given credit for every green thing that sprang from the earth. The King gave the people food and he sustained their lives.

"That is the riddle, yes," Eduardo answered, "but it is not solved by words."

"Oh." A catch, she should have guessed.

Looking like a lecturer preparing students for a test, Eduardo explained. "From the beginning of time, the temple has stood within the honeycomb passages of the cave. After the goddess made a gift of the yellow stone to Kananholcan, our forefathers placed the stone in a crown of gold. The crown is kept here, in the Riddle Place." He pointed to the front of the altar, which had decorated panels. The ones to the left and right were illustrated with bees. The central panel was an incomprehensible design composed of red, yellow and blue ceramic tiles set inside a wooden frame.

Eduardo pushed against one of the tiles and Melissa was surprised to see it slide. "The sacred symbol is pictured here," he explained, "but it has become confused. When you solve the riddle, you will know how to arrange the tiles to reveal the sacred symbol. When that is done, the door to the hiding place of the crown will be revealed."

She frowned. "Then the riddle is actually a puzzle?"

"You could call it that, yes."

All too aware of the watchful attention of the natives, she knelt to examine the central panel, seeing that what she had first thought was a missing tile was a deliberate omission that allowed the remaining tiles to be moved. Despite the feeling that lightning might strike, she summoned her nerve, leaned forward and experimentally pushed one of the tiles. It shifted into a new position with a faint click that seemed very loud in the hush of the chamber. She realized the puzzle was similar to a childhood game she remembered. Only that game had been plastic and small enough to fit into the palm of a hand. The object had been to slide the tiles around in the frame to form a picture. She had been good at it. The difference was, back then, she had known how the finished picture was supposed to look.

She sent Eduardo a glance. He'd tried to tell her about the levers. Would he give her another clue? But he was immersed in ancient history, first speaking to their priests, in a tone that sounded to her like an oft-repeated speech, first in Mayan and then repeated in English so she could understand. It told how a hiding place for the crown had been devised and how the sacred symbol had been painted on the tiles, creating the Riddle Place.

Staring at the panel, she squeezed her eyes shut and opened them again, hoping a sensible pattern would jump out at her but none did. A glance in Rick's direction showed him as baffled by the tiles as she.

She cast another glance at the murals. No help there. As Eduardo droned on, she once again heard the word "honeycomb." Was he sending her a hint after all? She looked at him, but his attention was on the High Priest. Discouraged, she returned her attention to the altar.

The carved honeybees on the left and right showed the pollen baskets on their legs filled to overflowing. Where did bees take pollen? To the hive of course. But she saw no way to arrange the tiles to form a beehive and that didn't seem the proper answer to the riddle. As Eduardo continued speaking, the High Priest started chanting, perhaps to encourage her but the noise only further jangled her nerves.

Watching Melissa's obvious perplexity, Rick wished he could speak with Xavier. Maybe they could plan something if worse came to worse, but two round-faces priests with haircuts that made them look alike stood between them,

Glancing back toward Melissa, he tensed. She was still before the altar but her body attitude had changed. Watching her suddenly rapt expression, he wondered if she was faking to buy time or if she was really on to something.

For the first time since confronting the riddle place, Melissa felt a spurt of hope. Eduardo had kept repeating the word "honeycomb." She suddenly thought she understood. *Honey*. That was it! Bless you, Eduardo. But the job wasn't done yet. Now she had to guess the sacred symbol.

She slid a sideways look toward Eduardo, but his attention remained on the High Priest, who stood with a reverent hand on his chest. The design on his pendant caught the light.

Melissa's attention snapped back to the puzzle. This time, she knew she had the answer. When properly placed, the designs on the tiles would form a hexagon, like a six-sided honeycomb cell. The sacred symbol was a honeycomb, which was what Eduardo had been trying to tell her all along. It was also, she realized, the shape of the pendant worn by the High Priest.

Excited, she began to work. The High Priest uttered a murmur of approval that told her she was on the right track.

Slide a tile here, slide one there . . . She saw the pattern take form, although she was puzzled when several yellow tiles seemed locked in the middle. Then seeing it didn't matter, she worked faster. A tile here, no, not that way, *here*. And then, here, and then, this way. Yes. And now this one, then that . . . no . . . yes . . . . *Yes!*

It was done.

Before her was a perfect hexagon that formed a honeycomb cell. In the middle was a yellow circle—a comb filled with honey. She couldn't see why it had taken her so long to figure it out.

Expecting approval at her accomplishment, at least from the High Priest, she looked up. Balam's suspicion had been replaced with an expression of breathless anticipation. A similar expression marked the faces of the others. The High Priest's eyes were bright and filled with expectation. Confusion swept through her. She had solved the riddle. The sacred symbol was a honeycomb and that was exactly what the middle design now showed. So what were they waiting for?

"The crown," Eduardo murmured.

That's when she remembered the whole point of the riddle was to reveal the hiding place of the crown. Had she done the puzzle wrong? Then she remembered she'd found that the yellow tiles in the middle wouldn't move. Suppose the entire panel rotated around the center? Something would unlock then, wouldn't it?

She put her hands on the wooden frame and then froze. Her reading had told her more than she wanted to know about primitive cultures that planted their goddesses along with the crops to ensure a good harvest. Heart in her throat, she cast an anxious look toward Eduardo, who did not meet her gaze.

She realized he couldn't. If he gave her help now, it would re-awaken the doubts of Balam, who was the most suspicious. She then heard Eduardo speaking in his native tongue. He wore an expression of awe as he gestured toward Rick and Xavier.

Was he emphasizing the miracle that had come to his people? That after so many years, a fair-haired, blue-eyed woman had come, bringing along two men who promised medical and financial help?

Yes, she thought as she saw the other priests nodding. Eduardo was clever. He wanted the diamond gone in exchange for what had been promised. And she was the key to make it happen.

The last time she tried to figure out how a goddess should behave, it had been a near disaster. But now, she was sure what to do. But, she thought, let's add a little drama.

She raised her arms and gazed up and around at the murals in a worshipful manner. Eduardo stopped speaking. From the corner of an eye, she saw that the priests had all turned to watch her as if spellbound.

She put her hands again to the wooden frame, gave it a turn and felt something give. She drew back as the entire panel sprang forward, revealing a carved box. She lifted the lids.

Balam's announcement was made in ringing tones. "Behold," Eduardo translated. "The goddess has revealed her crown."

Melissa stared into the box.

"All the old stories were true," said Rick, who had at last been allowed to move close to Melissa. Together they gazed at the crown, spellbound. Voice husky, he finally said, "Everything we were told about the Honeycomb Fire was true, all true and more."

There, on a cloth of midnight black, lay the Crown of the Goddess. Torchlight blazed on the crown's most precious ornament. It was shaped like a giant honeybee, its body a magnificent yellow diamond the size of an infant's fist. The gem, the Honeycomb Fire, was encased in gold filigree with spreading gold lace wings, the eyes twin clusters of tiny rubies and black jade.

Cheers broke out as the natives surged forward. Glad tears ran down the withered cheeks of the High Priest. Melissa needed no words to receive the message, their faces made it clear: the Giver of Gifts had returned. The time of prosperity was at hand.

"Arise," Eduardo said with a joyous smile.

Rick assisted Melissa to her feet. One of the priests produced an elaborately decorated cape which Balam draped reverently around her shoulders, a close-woven fabric decorated with the brilliantly colored feathers of countless hummingbirds.

The priests began a hymn of joy. Eduardo joined in, the glow in his eyes revealing that even a most practical man could dismiss all other concerns as the legend of the past was reclaimed and embraced.

Rick gripped Melissa's hand as the High Priest lifted the crown. Much taller than he, Melissa bent her knees and bowed her head. With her eyes closed, she felt the crown placed upon her head.

Baaaam!

The sound of gunfire in the enclosed space was momentarily deafening. With a scream of pain, one guard fell back, his dropped rifle skittering off behind him as he grasped his bleeding arm.

There was a moment of stunned confusion as the others stared at the wounded man. A second shot crashed into the wall, spattering chunks of limestone and just missing Luis's legs. He scrambled to one side and lifted his shotgun, only to hesitate as he saw his assailant held one of the priests as a shield.

"Drop the weapons," came the order.

"George!" Rick gasped the name in disbelief.

George's response was to fire his pistol a third time. Spattered by more flaking stone and unwilling to risk a shot that might harm a fellow priest, Luis dropped the shotgun to the floor.

"Excellent," George said, shoving his prisoner aside. "Now, all move from the weapons." He signaled to the right of the altar.

Speaking in his native language, Eduardo conveyed the order.

As they moved, George used his foot to shove the dropped weapons in the direction from which he had come. Satisfied, he stood with the pistol in the other and his other hand on a pouch that was slung from a cord around his neck.

His well-groomed appearance was a thing of the past; his hair was wild and the flesh of his chunky face sagged behind a scraggly beard. His eyes were reddened and swollen with dark circles underneath and his forehead showed bruises. The elbows of his shirt had been worn through and the trousers he had once worn with tailored assurance were now filthy with sweat and embedded grime, the pants legs torn at both knees, the cuffs dragging.

"Keep together," George snapped, gesturing, clustering his prisoners to the far right of Melissa and far from the weapons he'd shoved aside with his foot. His gaze fell hungrily on the crown on Melissa's head, the great yellow diamond casting off sparks from its internal fire.

"Perfection," he said. "I show up in time to snatch the prize after everyone else has done the work."

Rick narrowed his eyes. "I doubt it's been easy. You look like hell."

"That's what two days wandering underground does to a man!" George spoke in a shrill voice. "You think you're so smart Ricky, but you made a bad mistake when you hired Carranza. After I learned what I needed from him, I drugged him with my new antihistamines and left him to die."

Rick decided that George's emotional shape wasn't much better than his physical one. He remembered Carranza saying that George had fallen into a hole. Maybe it had been part of a tunnel that led him to the temple in much the same way as Xavier had been led.

Deciding he wanted to keep George talking so he wouldn't start shooting, Rick said in a taunting voice, "Carranza's had his last breath, old buddy, but it was in the outside air."

"Sounds as if you had something to do with it. Ricky on the spot, as always. Again, perfect for me. Every loose end tied up by someone else."

"All the loose ends tied up except one," Rick said, imperceptibly shifting his feet, preparing for action and sensing the same gathering readiness in Xavier. "How do you expect to get away with the crown? You can't kill all of us."

"I can try." A high-pitched giggle confirmed Rick's suspicions about George's precarious state of mind. "Carranza planned to dynamite the temple. When I made off with his supplies, I found I also had his sticks of dynamite. When I leave," George said, "The flaming braziers on either side of the door are where I'll place the dynamite." He laughed at he looked at the room's occupants. "You will have thirty seconds to decide what to do. My suggestion is, run to the storeroom, the way I came in."

Rick stared in disbelief. "Dynamite in a cave? You can't be serious."

"We need have no concern," Eduardo said, speaking up unexpectedly. Although he addressed no one in particular, his words were English. "Kananholcan will protect the crown."

Wondering at such wishful thinking, Rick's gaze flickered over the company of priests. They stood silent and impassive. Even Balam, the hothead of the group if there ever was one, seemed strangely calm. Did they understand that George intended to make off with the crown they had treasured for so long? Did Eduardo understand about the dynamite? Whatever, it was clear there was no use counting on the Maya natives for help.

"Come on George," he said in a persuasive tone, changing tactics now that he knew just how crazy and desperate the man was. "We can work something out." He thanked his lucky stars that George didn't know about the investigation back home. "Finding the crown is the real thrill, isn't it George? Remember how we talked about it when we were kids? You don't have to try to make it your own."

"You understand nothing," George said with a screech that told Rick his soothing words had backfired. "Making the Honeycomb Fire my own is exactly what this is about. What does a peasant like you know about the love of beautiful things? You with a grandfather who would have given you the world, yet you asked for nothing, appreciate nothing."

Sputtering and stammering, his face boiled-lobster red, George abruptly shifted his attention to Melissa. Making a supreme effort to calm himself, he bared his teeth in a parody of a smile. "How like a medieval princess, my dear." The collar of the cape had fallen open, revealing a rich blue lining, an ideal background for the honey-gold curls that tumbled softly about her shoulders. The crown on her head gleamed. "I wish I could record the sight of you on film, but there's never enough time for everything, is there? I regret interrupting your coronation, but I believe the crown is now mine. Bring it to me, please. Do it!" he screeched when she didn't move immediately, showing just how thin the veneer of his control was.

"Go ahead," Rick murmured, having gotten an inspiration. Through the thickness of the hummingbird cloak, he gave her a hug, and then said, "Do as he says. Go right up to him."

She gave him a startled look.

"It will be all right," he promised, thinking his idea damned well better work because it was probably the last one he would get. "He doesn't want to harm you; all he wants is the crown."

Melissa wondered if Rick was as nutsy as George. The man had a gun and explosives and she was supposed to walk to him?

"Go ahead," Rick encouraged, giving her a gentle push. "Fly to him."

Fly to him? She remembered something Rick had once told her and suddenly she got it. Taking a deep breath, she said to George. "Is what he says true? That you only want the crown?"

"Of course, of course," George said impatiently, but her timid manner seemed to take the edge from his anger. "Just get over here."

Taking another breath, she did as he asked.

Managing to keep one eye on her and the other on his prisoners, George stopped Melissa when she was about three feet from him. "That's far enough."

Wanting to move closer, but afraid of alarming him, Melissa asked, "Should I hand the crown to you or what?"

He chuckled. "So I would have to release my hold on my gun or the dynamite to take it?"

That hadn't been her thought. Not wanting to increase his suspicions, she said, "Then . . . then what should I do?"

"Put your back to me. Together we will move toward the doorway."

Obediently she turned, moving back a step as she did so, feeling the feathered cape brush against him. Looking over her shoulder, she said, "You really do care about the diamond and the crown, don't you? I mean, it's not just that it's valuable, it's because it's beautiful."

"I do appreciate it, my dear, but I hope you're not trying to distract me." He sniffed, wrinkling his nose. "If you have any clever moves in mind, rest assured that the person I will shoot first is Rick."

Melissa had no doubt that's what he would do. Looking over her shoulder again, she fluttered her arms in a seemingly helpless gesture. "Please, I don't want anybody hurt. Just tell me what to do."

"Just move along with me," he said, snuffling. "We will—" He drew in a sharp breath. "What I want is—" Drawing in a gasping breath, he pressed the back of his hand to his nose, which pointed the pistol away from his prisoners. Realizing his error, he tried to correct to move, but before he could reposition the gun, he sneezed.

Losing no time, Rick rushed forward but George, fighting a second sneeze, tossed the dynamite toward one of the braziers and grabbed the crown from Melissa's head. Seeing Rick coming, he shoved Melissa towards him and then whirled to make his getaway.

"No!" Rick shouted, seeing all at once that this side of the doorway also had projections. "George, don't . . ." With no more time for warnings, he leaped, grabbing the seat of George's trousers and pulling him back just as he started his dash through the doorway.

With a frightful clang, the spikes sprang across the door opening, one of them catching George's sleeve, pinning the arm that held the gun. Caught, George screamed, "The dynamite!"

"Harmless on the floor," Rick said as he grabbed the gun, knowing that dynamite wasn't an impact explosive.

The spikes withdrew and George, dragging his torn sleeve, sank sobbing to the floor, the crown still clutched in one hand.

"Well done my friend," Eduardo said to Rick as he stepped forward and wrenched the crown from George's grasp. "But as you see, Kananholcan has ways to protect what is his."

"Just as long as he leaves George to me," came Rick's grim reply.

"You saved me," George said hoarsely, staring at Rick through bloodshot eyes.

"Yeah, but only because seeing you turned into shish kabob is too good for you. I want you back in Philadelphia, watching your stolen collection being taken apart. I want you paying for your crimes."

George's anguished pleas for mercy were interrupted as one of the feathers that had come loose from the hummingbird cape floated down and tickled his nose. He screwed up his face and drew a breath.

The moment had come for Rick to do what he had been wanting to do for a long, long time. He cocked his fist just as George sneezed again.

"Gesundheit," Rick said and socked him in the jaw.

CHAPTER THIRTY

OUTSIDE THE TEMPLE, THE STARS wheeled in the sky, the night birds sang and the answer to questions that had not even been thought of an hour ago were decided upon.

"All I want to do is go home," Melissa said from the security of Rick's arms after the men who had served as priests had bound George securely and dragged him away. Her voice was hoarse and she swayed weakly. "I know it's impossible, I know home is too far away, but that's what I wish we could do."

Eduardo spoke, announcing that despite the late hour, Balam would send a man ahead to the village to announce that the miracle foretold by the legend had come to pass—the Giver of Gifts had returned.

Despite his pagan robes, Eduardo's grin made him very much the modern man as he added to Melissa, "It is not every day that a goddess comes to town. By the time we reach the village, a place will have been made for you for the night, and women will be waiting to attend you." He shifted his attention to Rick and Xavier. "A place also will be made for you two as well, our honored guests. There will be—"

"Wait a minute," Rick said. "I'm going with her. Whatever you call her, she's not going anywhere without me."

Eduardo frowned. "You cannot share the same hammock for the night."

"Why the hell not?" Rick said, wondering what was going on.

Turning people into shish-kabobs was fine, but now they were as straight-laced as Victorian chaperones. "Wherever she's going, we're going together."

Clearly troubled, Eduardo turned to Balam. The High Priest's son listened to what Eduardo had to say, then spoke emphatically.

Eduardo translated. "She is the goddess. To share the same hut, the same hammock? No, it cannot be done."

"What do you mean it can't be done?" Rick asked in frustration. "If she's the goddess, she ought to be able to do any damn thing she pleases."

"I want to be with him," Melissa said. Wouldn't you know, she thought. Just when things had started looking good . . . .

Eduardo frowned. "If she were an ordinary woman, it would be different. But the goddess belongs to Kananholcan until she goes to her husband and you are not her husband."

"Says who?" Rick blustered.

Xavier spoke up. "I am sorry Rick. I was afraid they would think you were partners with Carranza, so I tried to make things clear. When I explained that Don Miguel was your ancestor, I also said that Melissa was a friend who was making the journey with us."

Rick cursed under his breath. He knew Melissa reeled from exhaustion. After all that they had been through in the past few hours, no way was he letting her out of his sight.

"Okay," he said, taking a deep breath. "Okay, so we're not married, yet," he said to Eduardo. "We were planning on it okay?" He felt Melissa tense with surprise, but heedless, he spoke on. "We're engaged. No ring, but we're engaged. Is that good enough for your Kananholcan?"

Lips pursed, Eduardo studied them as they clung together. He was still confounded by the High Priest's mysterious foreknowledge. It didn't matter that this woman was clearly mortal; it was that the old priest had *known* she was coming. He had known this with such confidence that he had ordered the celebration *before* she had arrived. He did not understand such a mystery and he probably never would.

What he did know was that however it had happened, the fates had conspired in a most agreeable fashion. With a thoughtful expression, he turned to Balam. After a short discussion, he faced Rick and Melissa again, his smile bright.

"The problem has been solved. There is to be a celebration and its purpose will now be twofold. Tomorrow there will be the public coronation of the goddess, then will come her wedding, the time when she becomes the bride to the man she has chosen."

"Bride?" Melissa echoed, staring at Rick.

"Wedding?" Rick echoed, staring at Melissa.

AND SO IT WAS that after the hastily made agreement, Rick and Melissa spent the night in the same hut, although not in the same hammock and not alone. One of the older women, Ynez, had taken Melissa's stained travel garments, bathed her feet, applied soothing ointment to the thorn scratches and dressed her in a fresh huipil. Rick was then brought in. Ynez was a woman with a stern set to her mouth. She watched as Melissa settled into her hammock and Rick made his bed on a pallet on the floor beside it. She kept watch as they fell into an exhausted sleep and the hands they held tightly clasped finally loosened and slipped away. Only then did a twinkle come into Ynez's eyes as she allowed herself to sleep.

IN THE MORNING. RICK spoke on the radio with his grandfather. Xavier had talked with him first. By the time Rick got on, Stanton already knew they were all alive and well, knew also that the keepers of the altar had not died out but were still in business. Surprised but fascinated by Xavier's report, he had expressed an interest in the idea of funding a clinic and began immediately to make plans. He told Xavier he wanted him to stay on for a while as an overseer. Even better, he would visit the village.

"Yes," he said with an inspired chuckle. "A retreat in the jungle would work out quite nicely. Now let me speak with my grandson."

A smiling Xavier turned the radio over to Rick.

"Grandson?" Despite the static, the old man's voice came through strong and clear. "So you have found the Honeycomb Fire. And before your birthday. Congratulations. A success at last."

The imperious praise rekindled all of Rick's suppressed anger. He didn't care if his grandfather was old and sick. Without his game playing, they could have flown directly to the cave and managed to get through to the other side while George was still bumbling around in Merida. As he said it, he realized going through the cave would still have been a trial but that wasn't the point.

"We found the diamond," he snapped, "only it was never lost. It belongs to the people here. Their high priest says that the crown, plus small gems that decorated the stone are theirs because their ancestors made it, but the diamond must be returned to their legendary goddess who brought it to them. One guy, Eduardo, says the diamond makes the village a target for thieves. True, because Melissa and I ran into one of them and almost got killed. The trouble is, they got next to nothing here. It's only right to leave it."

Rick wasn't sure what kind of reaction he expected this news to win from his grandfather, but what he heard was calm acceptance. "When I arrive, and if this man still feels the same way, I may bargain to take the diamond in exchange for things more meaningful to the people who lived there. In any case, the diamond means little to me. What's important, Grandson, is that you succeeded in finding it."

Clenching his jaw, Rick said nothing. There was a whole lot more the old man didn't know, a lot he was going to hear about whether he wanted to or not but that would wait until they were face to face.

Weaving its way through the static, his grandfather's voice came again. "I'm curious as to how you and Miss Lind got along during the course of your journey. If I recall, the two of you didn't start off on the best of terms. How are things between you now?"

Rick gave a narrow, satisfied smile. "Far better than you could have imagined." His grandfather was about to learn his manipulations could only go so far. "The wedding is this afternoon."

"What?"

Hearing the old man's gasp, Rick's smile broadened. "You heard me. A native thing, but a wedding all the same. Too bad there wasn't time to send out the invitations."

"Splendid!"

Splendid? Rick drew back from the radio as if it had suddenly begun transmitting in Swahili.

"I saw it from the start." The old man's chuckle was rich and satisfied. "I may give your bride the diamond as a wedding gift. You were made for one another. I was positive that your long journey would give the two of you time enough to discover this truth for yourselves."

Rick went rigid. "You *wanted* me and Melissa wandering around together? That's what this was *really* all about?"

Another satisfied chuckle. "Like children in the wilderness, discovering truths along the way. I provided the time for you to get to know one another."

Unparalleled fury swept through Rick. "Time that could have gotten Melissa killed, not once, but a half dozen times. Grandfather, we've come to a reckoning point."

Suddenly hearing the echo of his words, Rick unexpectedly stopped. After all that had happened, was he back to trying to straighten out his grandfather? How dumb could he be? Didn't he know when a job was hopeless? The old man had been wrong. He knew he was wrong, he *had* to know it, but he still found a way to justify himself. And in a way he had been right, hadn't he? Who else could possibly be a better match for him than Melissa?

But Rick had his pride, too. He was his grandfather's grandson, after all. Besides, wouldn't the old man expect a fight? He wouldn't understand it otherwise.

Rick took a breath and spoke, his tone low and deadly serious. "From now on, Grandfather, you will know better than to ever try to manipulate me again."

There was a silence, then Stanton Malone said the words that Rick had never expected to hear.

"You're right, Grandson," he said quietly. "You're a mature man and I've been blind not to see it. I should have acknowledged it in the past. I do so now. You're absolutely right."

Rick nodded in satisfaction, but the older man still managed to have the last word.

"I also admit it was wrong of me to tell Xavier to exaggerate my illness when he wrote to you, or for me to pretend I was ignorant of his letter." He chuckled. "After all that had been between us, I couldn't just ask you to come could I? The last thing I admit is that not even I could have guessed it would work out so well."

WHEN MELISSA AWOKE, THE sun was high. She realized she might have slept the clock around if left on her own, but as it was, a trio of dark-eyed maidens, eager for the honor of attending the goddess, had finally roused her, bringing food and drink.

In response to her anxious inquiries about Rick, she was made to understand he was getting himself ready for her coronation, and the wedding. One of the young women, a pretty girl with jade earrings, pantomimed scraping her cheeks, a performance that caused her companions to dissolve in mirth.

Knowing that most Maya men had much lighter beards or almost none at all. Melissa tried to smile at the joke, but she was feeling confused. It was broad daylight and she still was considered a goddess, which was unreal enough, but the idea of the wedding was preposterous.

Although it was nothing she and Rick had discussed, she could only imagine that he felt the same way. During the trek from the temple, she remembered only that Rick had insisted he didn't want George executed, a task the priests would have been more than willing to perform. Eduardo had agreed to radio the authorities to come and take George away.

Eduardo also said that according to the legend, the diamond belongs to the goddess. Melissa didn't know how Rick felt about it, but she understood why Eduardo wanted it gone. Nothing more was said about it and the wedding hadn't rated a mention.

Her thoughts were interrupted by the arrival of Ynez, their chaperone during the night. Clapping her hands, she gave instructions to the attendants that sent them scurrying, to lead Melissa out into the hazy, sunlit afternoon. It was the first time she realized that the village, which lay under the cover of dense, tropical hardwoods, had its thatch-roofed huts set amidst the stone walls of an ancient city filled with crumbling walls and statuary and stairways that led nowhere. How wonderful if this heritage of these village people could be restored for their use. Perhaps Rick's grandfather . . . .

She stopped the thought as she was led into an enclosed courtyard. She had hoped they would take her to Rick, but instead, she found that a bath in a stone tub had been prepared for her, the water brought from the village cistern and heated over a fire in a hearth that sat at one end of the enclosure.

Despite her disappointment at not seeing Rick, she gratefully sank into the tub. The water, sprinkled with the petals of sweetly scented flowers, was deep enough to reach her shoulders, the soothing warmth melting away her aches and bruises. The hands that washed her hair were gentle. Thoughts drifting, she hoped that Rick was being treated to a similar kind of luxury—without the women, of course. She couldn't wait to be with him again, couldn't wait to be in his arms.

Her relaxed mood gradually changed as she began to consider what the future held for them. In the cave, they spoke of their respective dreams as if they could be fitted together on the ranch—his horse business conducted from there, her preschool established nearby. So many plans, but that had been just talk to fill the time, hadn't it? There had been no commitment.

A deep, longing ache filled her as she realized the only time she could be sure of him was the time they had left together at the village. Her throat tightened. In the temple when she feared she was about to die, she remembered wishing she had told Rick she loved him. Now she was glad she hadn't. They had been through so much together, but she'd known the score from the start. It wasn't up to her to try to tie strings. She couldn't help hoping that things had changed for him. If they had, it was up to him to tell her. She swallowed against the lump in her throat. If things hadn't changed for him, she would have to be strong and accept it.

By the time she was dressed and her hair had been arranged, parade sounds came from a distance. Clucking like a mother hen, Ynez hastily smoothed Melissa's gown, a long flowing white *huipil* embroidered in blue. The music became louder as it moved closer, the flutes thin and piping, the drums pounding. The music increased until it seemed as if the parade must be almost on top of them.

Abruptly all sound ceased.

The long, stretching silence was broken only by a nervous giggle from one of the girls. Melissa found she was holding her breath. All at once, a voice rang out in greeting from the other side of the wall. It was Rick, but the words were Mayan. Thrown by the foreign words, Melissa's thoughts tumbled in confusion. Uncertain of what to expect, she hesitantly allowed Ynez to lead her from the courtyard.

Rick stood outside, garbed in a native costume, white shirt and trousers, a red striped vest worn over the shirt. He looked tall and splendid, yet somehow as foreign as the greeting he had called. The slanting afternoon sun shadowed his eyes and the line of his freshly shaven jaw looked tense. There was no way for Melissa to tell what he was thinking. What *was* he thinking?

He looked her up and down and then smiled, his words a soft echo of the first words he had ever spoken to her, "Hello, Melissa . . . ."

His familiar smile, his voice speaking her name steadied her. Relieved, she stepped toward him, but before they could touch, Balam, who stood nearby, startled her by giving a strange, whistling call. The parade sounds once again exploded into life. The villagers, plus those of neighboring communities as well, came pouring forth.

The next few hours went by with such hubbub and merry confusion that Melissa barely had time to think. Carried at the head of the clamoring procession, she was delivered to an ancient stone platform where the white-haired High Priest led the coronation, a repeat of what had been performed in the temple.

Then, with the crowd still cheering, Rick was brought forward and the wedding began.

Melissa found everything about the ceremony unfamiliar, from the sharp-sweet incense and tuneless flute music, to the words spoken in an unfathomable language. It made it all too easy to remember that none of what was happening held meaning outside of the hidden green world of the village, yet when it came time for them to exchange their vows and Rick clasped her hands, the crowd seemed to fade away.

He looked deeply into her eyes and repeated the soft, sibilant Mayan vowels with such confidence that it suddenly seemed to Melissa that the ceremony might hold meaning for him after all. When it was her turn, her lips echoed the exotic phrases she was given to say, but it was her eyes that sent the message from her heart. For a brief span of time, she felt they were transported; that they were standing alone beneath the ageless Maya sun. Before she could even begin to come to terms with these impressions, the crowd burst into jubilation and the ceremony was at an end.

What followed was a celebration with much eating and drinking and the singing of songs; extremely long songs that went on and on as sunset came, then twilight, then darkness. Rick and Melissa were never left alone for a minute. He was pulled off to play guitar with some of the other men and people kept coming up to Melissa to touch her hair, to offer treats, to show off their children. The crown grew heavy and her face felt numb from smiling. Her head swam from beverages pressed upon them, including a bitter chocolate drink and another, with a heady anise flavor.

The moon was out full when the High Priest was brought forth to bestow the final blessing upon the goddess and her royal consort, and to remove the crown for safe-keeping.

That done, the crowd surged forward. Laughing and jostling, they hustled the newlyweds along a narrow jungle trail to an isolated hut. The door curtain was swept aside and they were gently pushed inside a single small room that held only a double-wide hammock and a low table upon which an oil lamp burned.

The curtain drifted back into place.

At last, they were alone.

As the sounds of the crowd withdrew, Rick opened his arms and Melissa stepped inside them.

Closing her eyes, she pressed her cheek against his shoulder. "Just us," she murmured. It felt so wonderful to be with him. "I thought the celebration would go on forever."

"They never left us alone for a minute." His breath was warm against her hair. "Someone was always coming up to you."

"Or dragging you off somewhere." She smiled against his shoulder. The cotton of his shirt held the faint scent of the campfire and a warm, good smell that was simply him. "Now I know you can play any kind of guitar anywhere, even in a jungle."

He chuckled. She felt the vibrations in his chest. "I think the music was just one more excuse." He caressed her, running his hands from her shoulders to her hips as he molded her body against his. "Did you see the mischief in their eyes? I think it was another one of their customs, keeping the bride and groom apart as much as possible for as long as possible, making them burn . . . ."

His voice broke on the words. His lips caressed hers. "I can taste the honey." Before the old priest took the crown away, he had placed honey on their lips as a blessing.

"Honey to seal our vows," Rick said.

"I wish I understood what we said," she whispered. "I know it wasn't real, but . . . ."

"It was real for me." Gently he cupped her face in his hands. "It was real for me from the moment I told Eduardo that we planned to share our lives."

Starting to tremble, she stared up at him. "You wanted it to be true?"

"For me it is true. I love you, Lissa, you know that don't you?" His grandfather had been wrong on some things, but damn it, he'd been on target with this. "There's no way I can imagine my life without you." He thought of that moment in the wedding ceremony when she had smiled, that wonderful smile that had always knocked him for a loop. He had suddenly known that he would never see her any differently than he did at that moment. Regardless of whatever changes the years might bring, her smile would always be the same to him. Her eyes would be as blue, her hair would be as gold. She would always be soft and slender in his arms, and her touch would never fail to fill him with strength and pride.

"I love you," he whispered. "For now and forever, I love you."

Her eyes misted. "I wanted to go home," she said softly, "but I didn't realize that when I'm with you, I'm already there." She reached up, tenderly smoothing back a lock of his hair that had dipped down on his forehead. "So much has happened to us. For all the time we were together, it seemed we never had much time to talk. When I didn't know what the next moment would bring, if we would live or if we would die, my only regret was that I hadn't said how I felt, hadn't told you how much I loved you."

"So how about telling me now."

"I thought men didn't care about the words."

"This one does."

"I love you." It felt so good to say it. "I love you with all my heart."

With a shuddering sigh, he pressed her close. He thought briefly of his ancestor who had unknowingly begun the cult of the goddess, and now so many years later, he had shown up with a woman who brought it all full circle. It was as if it had been written in the stars. Perhaps there was more to the story than had even been known by the priests.

"For now and forever," he whispered, and then there was no more time for words.

From the Author

Hello Readers,

Honeycomb Fire was a change of pace in my long writing career. I didn't know it could be so much fun to write a romantic adventure.

Eons ago I had six novels published. After that, my job editing a monthly news publication took up much of my time and still does. When not editing, I wrote short stories that appeared in various anthologies and other short fiction publications.

Beverly T. Haaf

Ever take a look at something you've done and say, "I can do better?" When Jersey Pines Ink re-published my novel, *The Chanting*, I had jumped at the chance to make it better. I sure hope I did.

The reworking and the publishing of the new version of *The Chanting* kick started me into wanting to write longer works again.

Will I do another romantic-adventure like *Honeycomb Fire*, or will I do something different?

We shall see.

Bev

Want to know more? Go to my website: Beverlythaaf.com

Or write to me at HaafBeverly@gmail.com

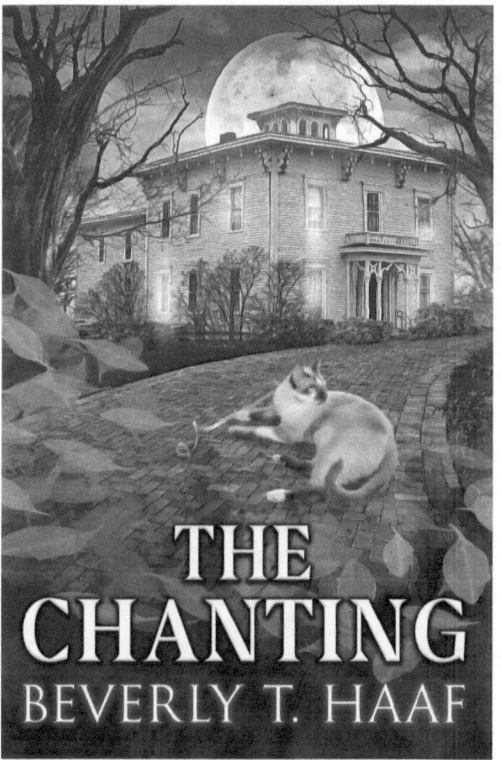

JPI

We Are Horror, Fantasy and Speculative Fiction

TREES

An Anthology Edited by
Dina Leacock

Who Knows What Lurks in the Woods?

Forests! Swamps! Stumpy trees! Throw in some
moss, mushrooms and a ghost or two.
Take a walk in the woods — if you dare.

JERSEY PINES INK

https://www.jerseypinesink.com

JPI

We Are Horror, Fantasy and Speculative Fiction

A collection of 42 entertaining mystery and speculative fiction short stories

JERSEY PINES INK
https://www.jerseypinesink.com

JPI

We Are Mysteries

WHODUNIT

EDITED BY
DINA A. LEACOCK

An anthology of WhoDunits and HowDunits.

JERSEY PINES INK